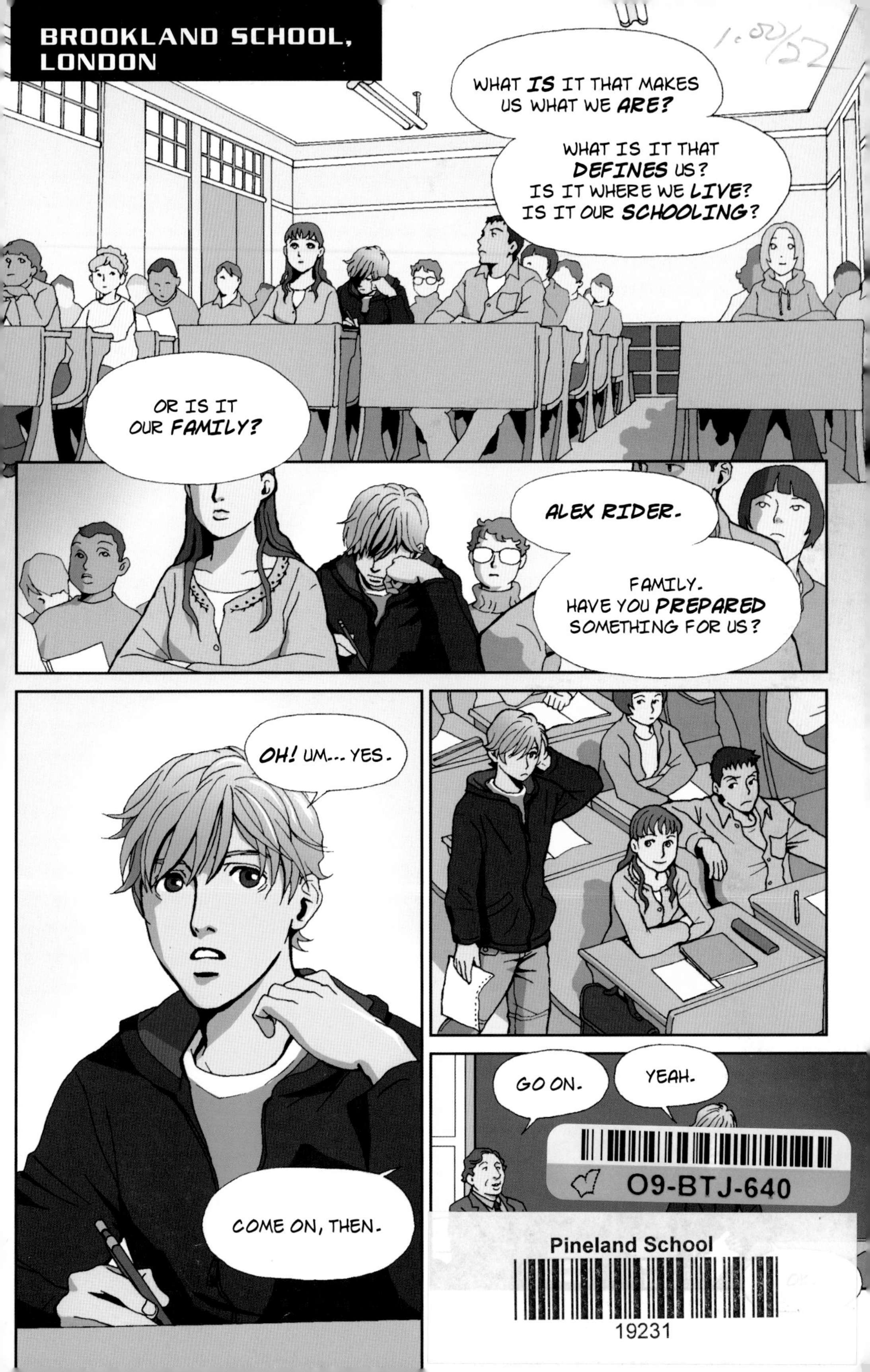
BROOKLAND SCHOOL, LONDON
WHAT IS IT THAT MAKES US WHAT WE ARE?
WHAT IS IT THAT DEFINES US? IS IT WHERE WE LIVE? IS IT OUR SCHOOLING?
OR IS IT OUR FAMILY?
ALEX RIDER.
FAMILY. HAVE YOU PREPARED SOMETHING FOR US?
OH! UM... YES.
COME ON, THEN.
GO ON.
YEAH.

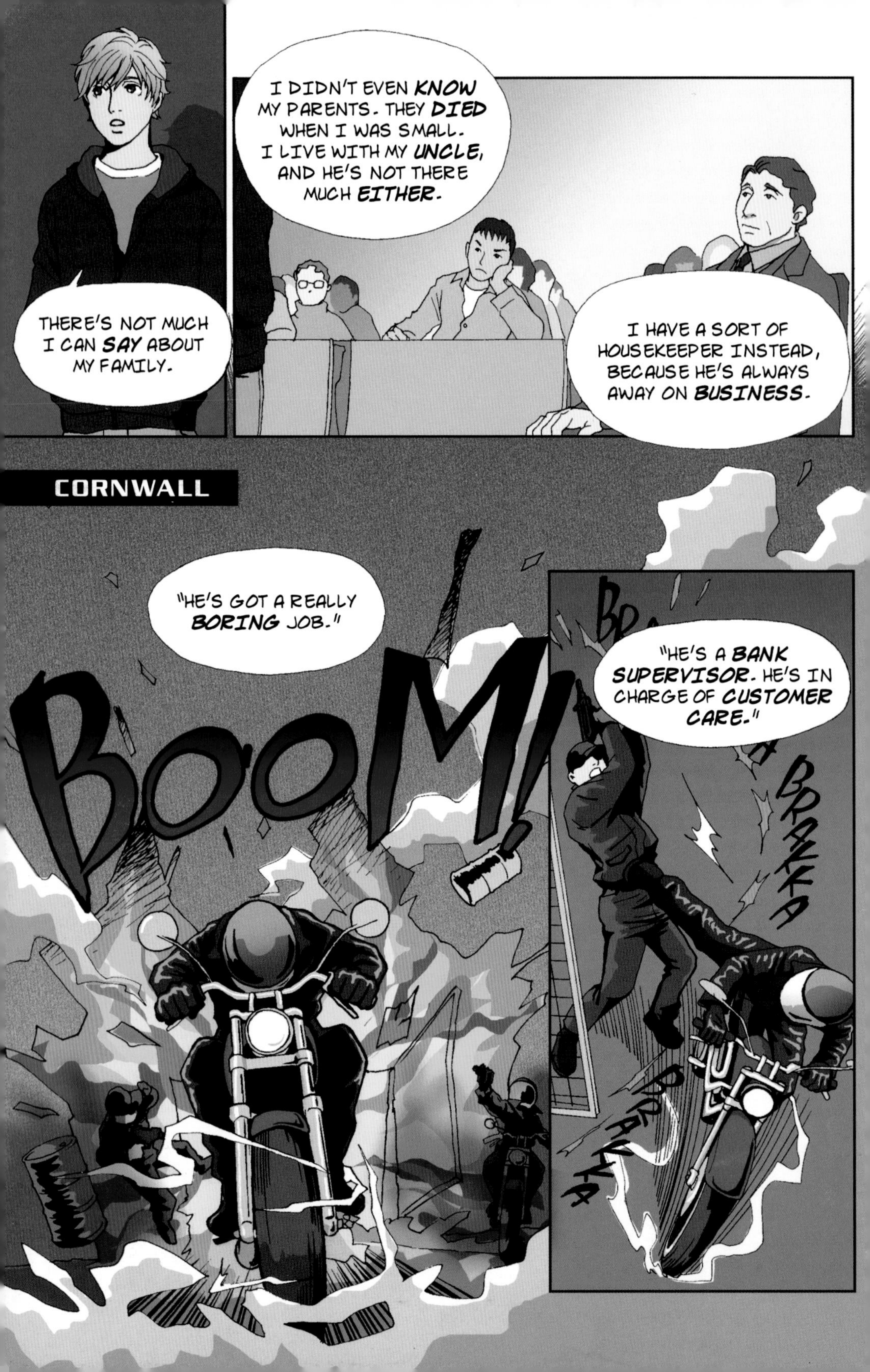
THERE'S NOT MUCH I CAN SAY ABOUT MY FAMILY.
I DIDN'T EVEN KNOW MY PARENTS. THEY DIED WHEN I WAS SMALL. I LIVE WITH MY UNCLE, AND HE'S NOT THERE MUCH EITHER.
I HAVE A SORT OF HOUSEKEEPER INSTEAD, BECAUSE HE'S ALWAYS AWAY ON BUSINESS.
CORNWALL
"HE'S GOT A REALLY BORING JOB."
BOOM!
"HE'S A BANK SUPERVISOR. HE'S IN CHARGE OF CUSTOMER CARE."
BRAKKA
BRAKKA

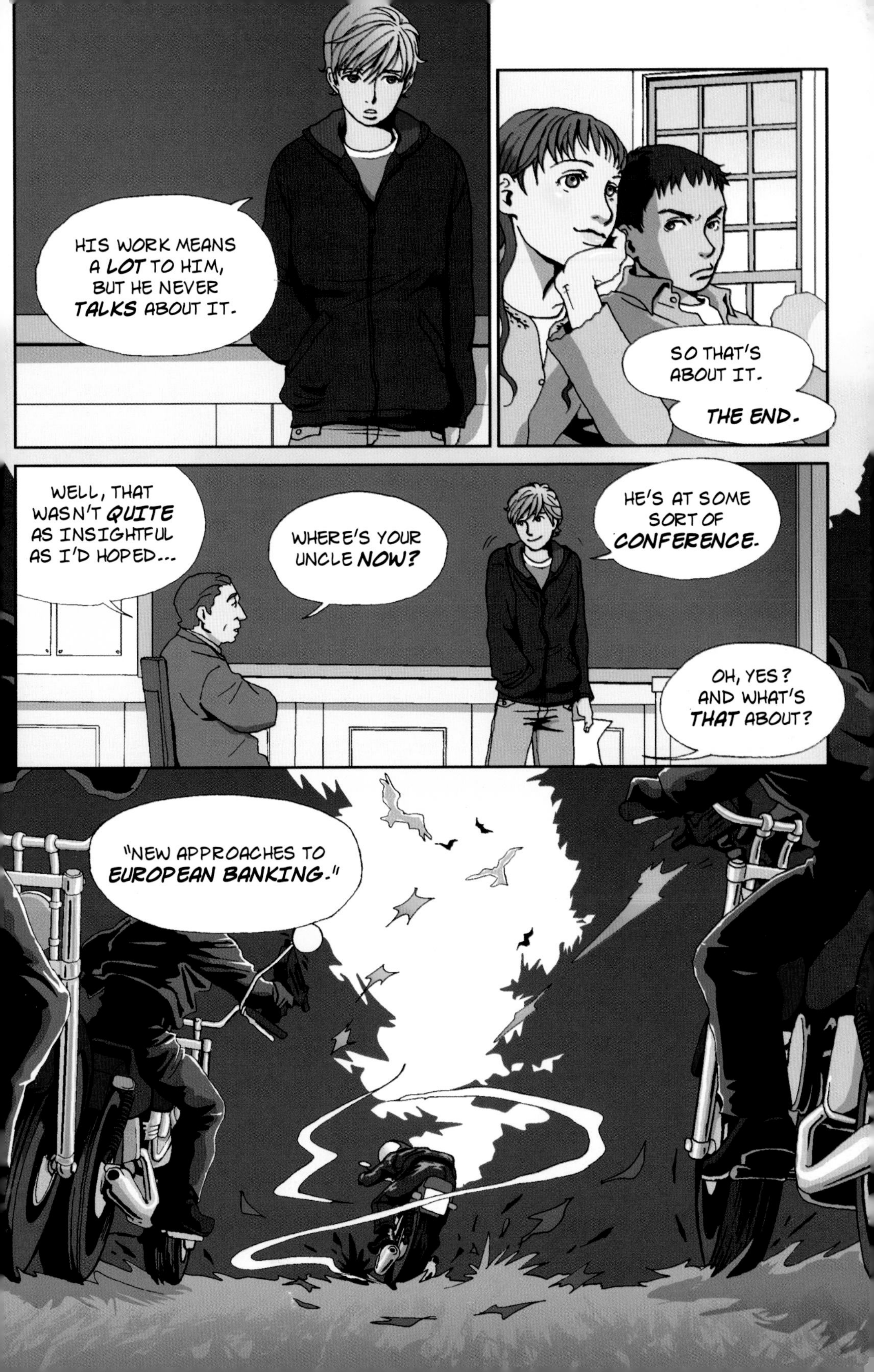
HIS WORK MEANS A LOT TO HIM, BUT HE NEVER TALKS ABOUT IT.
SO THAT'S ABOUT IT.
THE END.
WELL, THAT WASN'T QUITE AS INSIGHTFUL AS I'D HOPED...
WHERE'S YOUR UNCLE NOW?
HE'S AT SOME SORT OF CONFERENCE.
OH, YES? AND WHAT'S THAT ABOUT?
"NEW APPROACHES TO EUROPEAN BANKING."

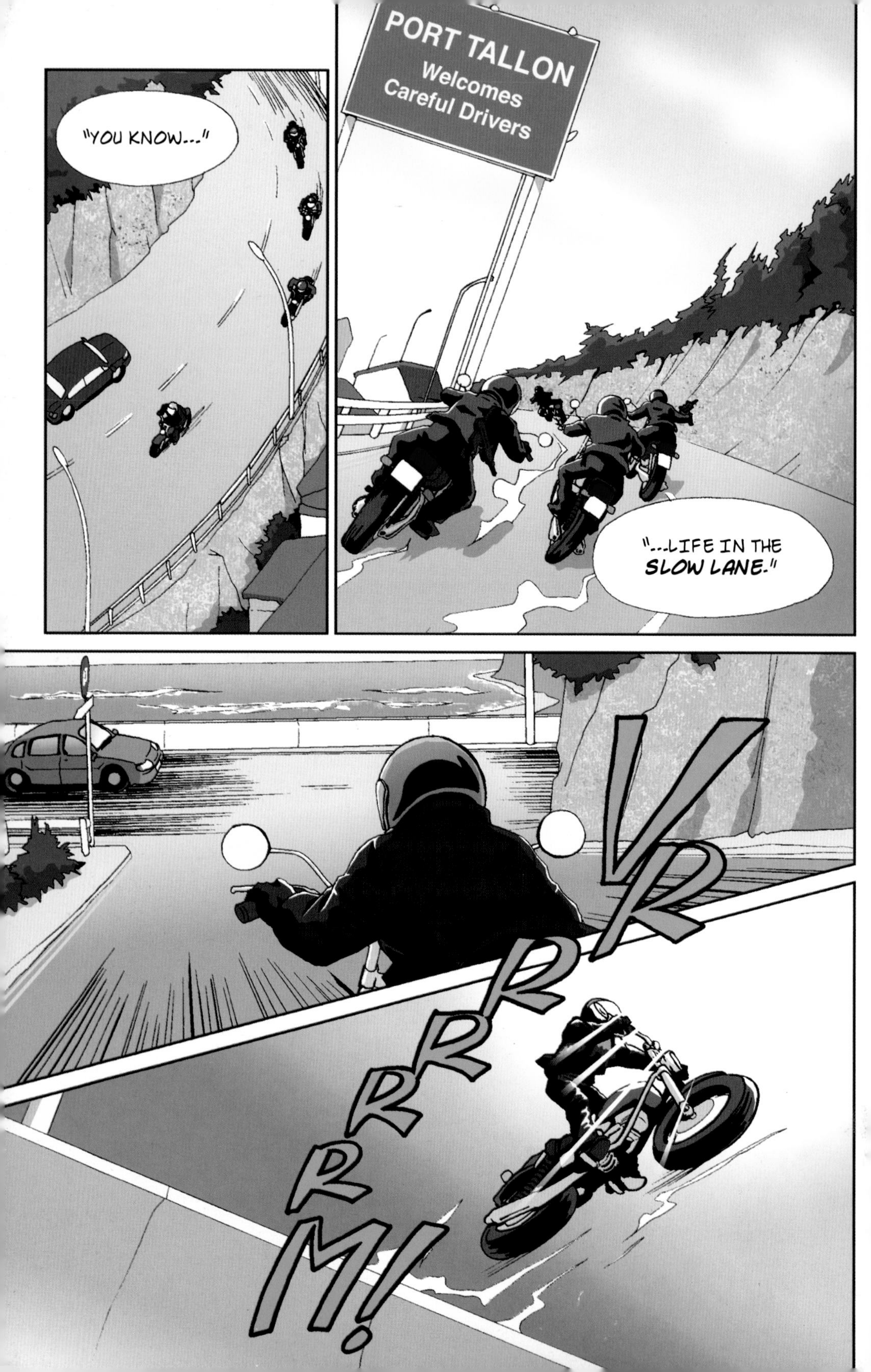
"YOU KNOW..."
PORT TALLON
Welcomes
Careful Drivers
"...LIFE IN THE SLOW LANE."
VRRRRRRM!

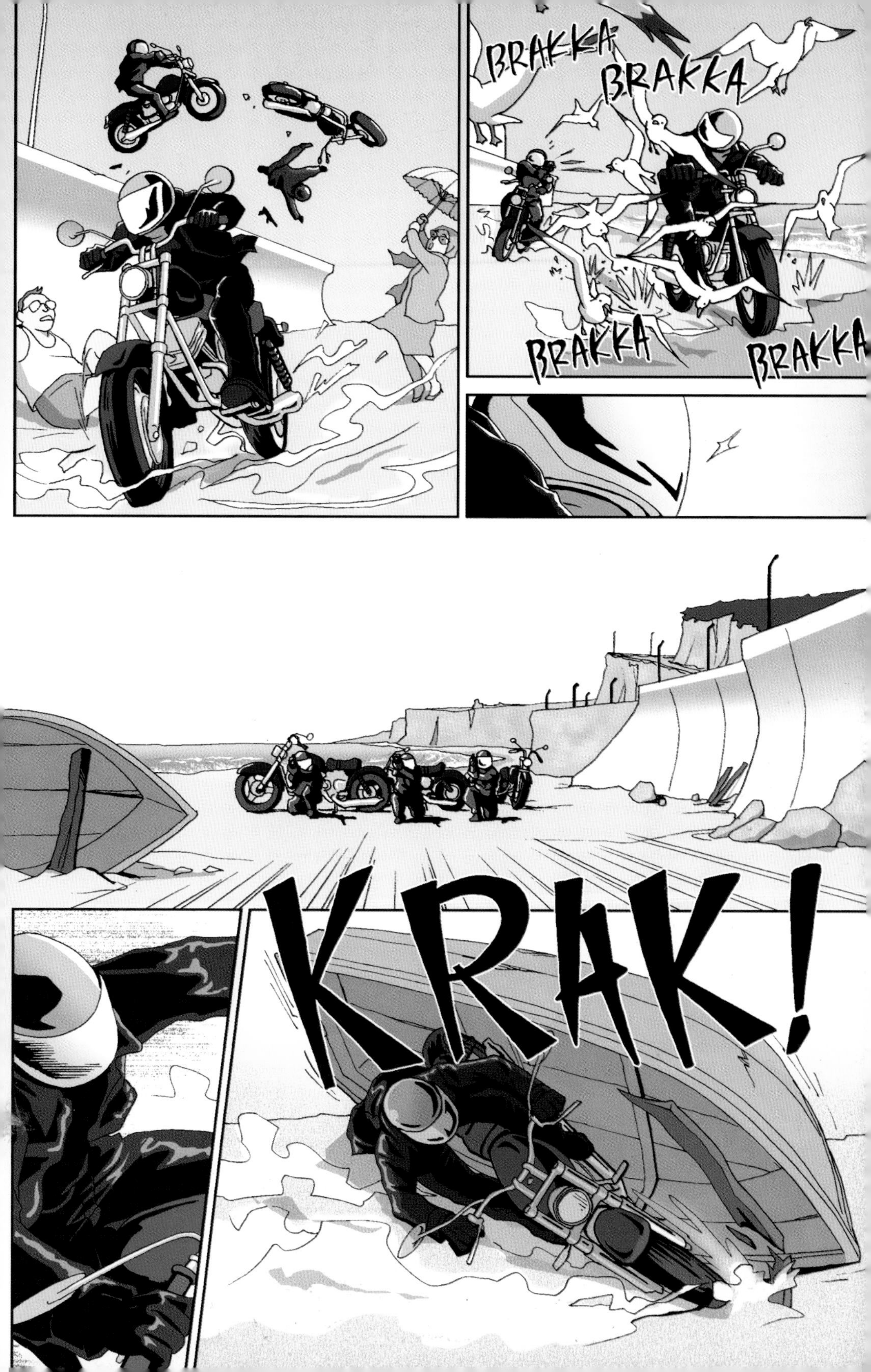
BRAKKA
BRAKKA
BRAKKA
BRAKKA
KRAK!

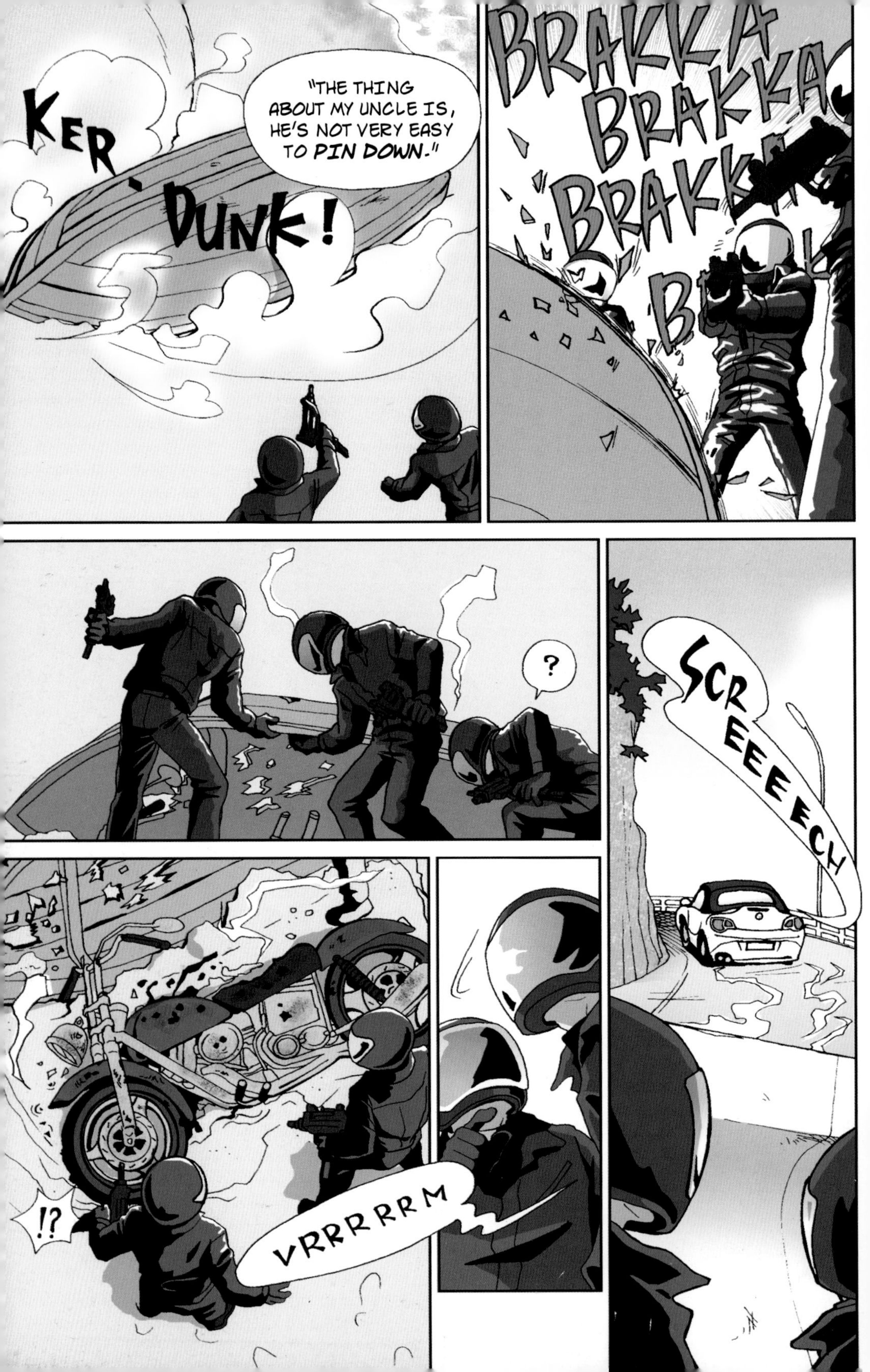
KER-DUNK!
"THE THING ABOUT MY UNCLE IS, HE'S NOT VERY EASY TO PIN DOWN."
BRAKKA BRAKKA BRAKKA
?
SCREEEEECH
!?
VRRRRRM

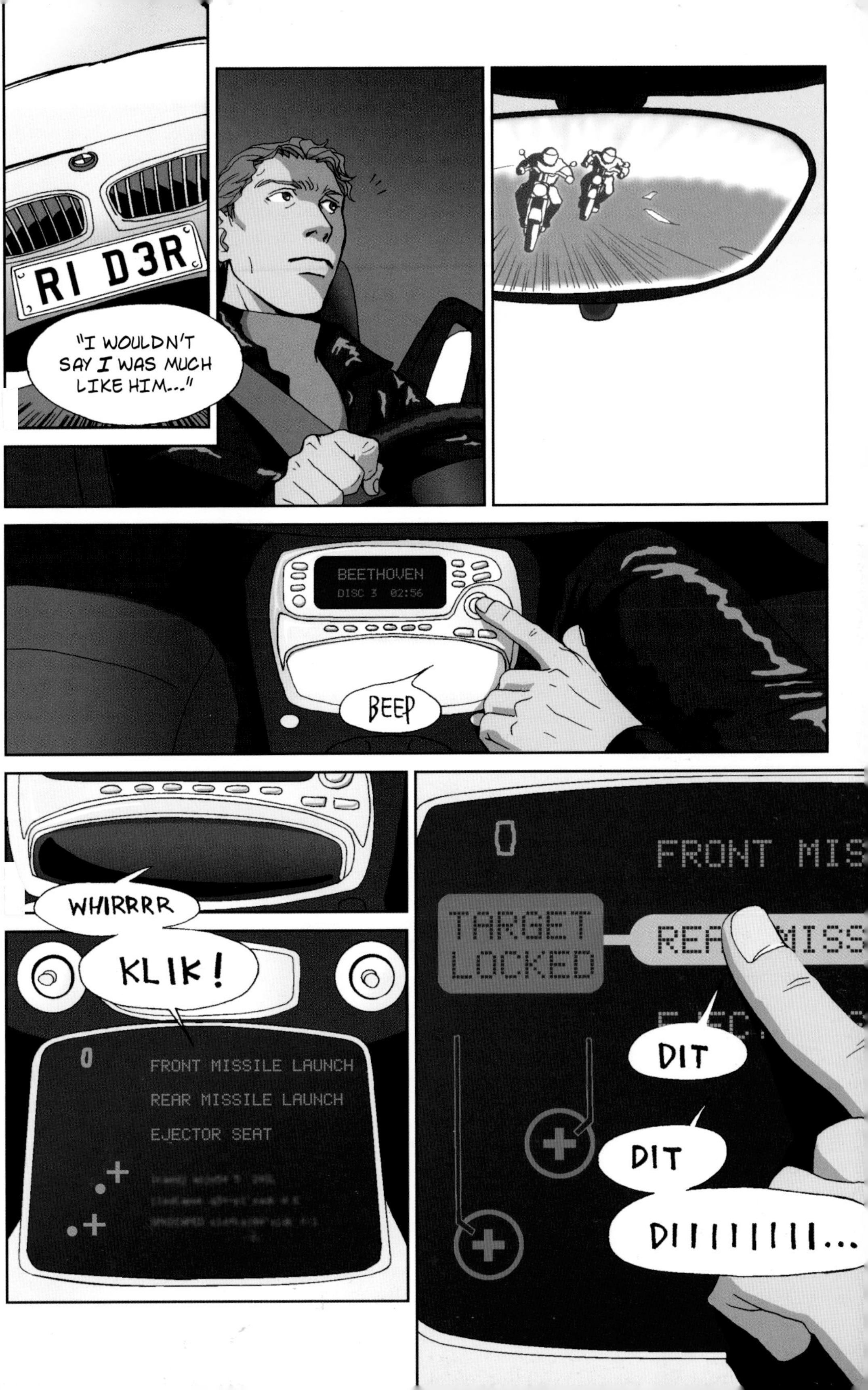
RI D3R
"I WOULDN'T SAY I WAS MUCH LIKE HIM..."
BEETHOVEN
DISC 3 02:56
BEEP
WHIRRRR
KLIK!
FRONT MISSILE LAUNCH
REAR MISSILE LAUNCH
EJECTOR SEAT
FRONT MIS
TARGET LOCKED
DIT
DIT
DIIIIIIII...

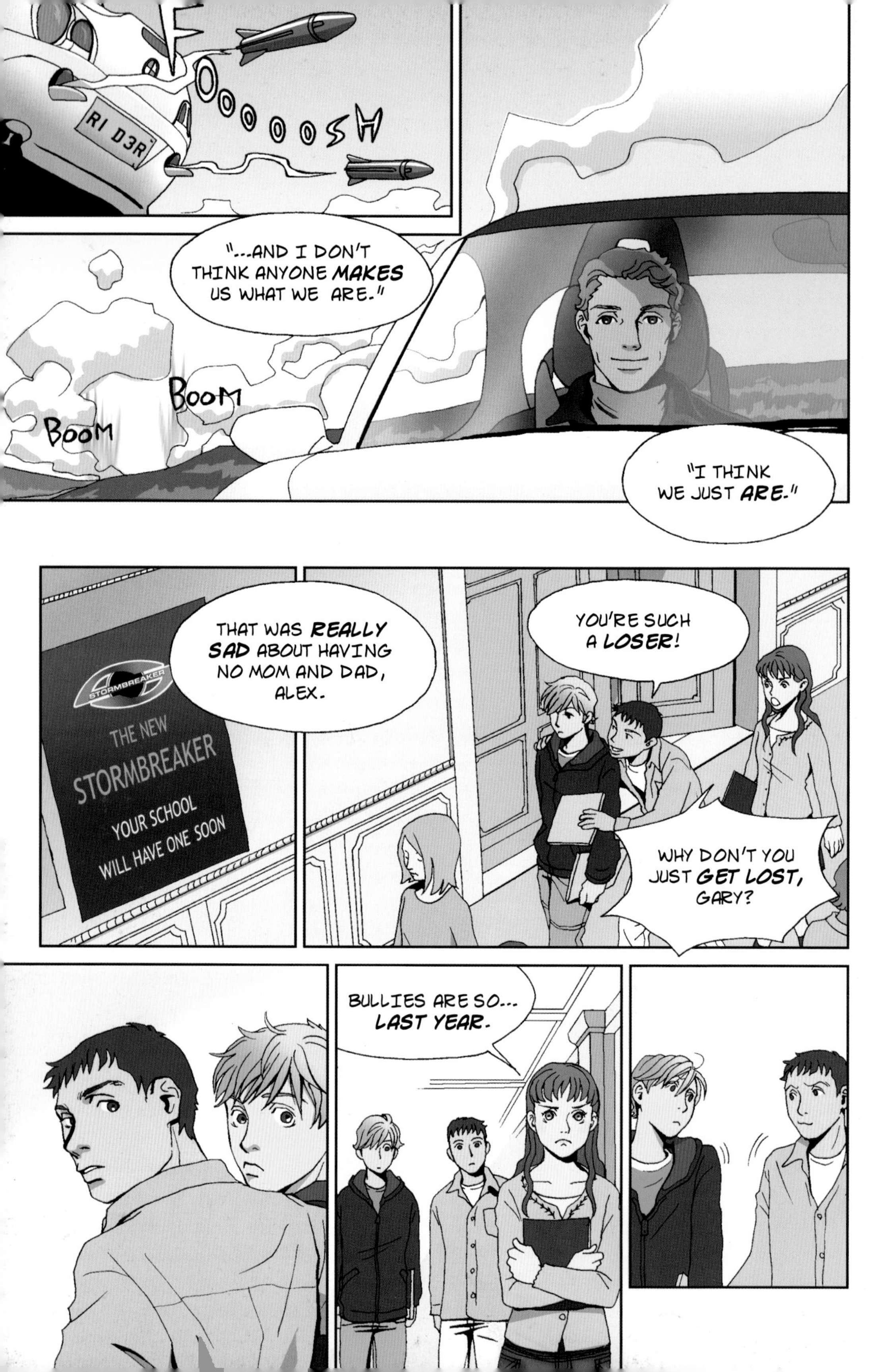

FOOOOOOSH
RI D3R
"...AND I DON'T THINK ANYONE MAKES US WHAT WE ARE."
BOOM
BOOM
"I THINK WE JUST ARE."
STORMBREAKER
THE NEW STORMBREAKER
YOUR SCHOOL WILL HAVE ONE SOON
THAT WAS REALLY SAD ABOUT HAVING NO MOM AND DAD, ALEX.
YOU'RE SUCH A LOSER!
WHY DON'T YOU JUST GET LOST, GARY?
BULLIES ARE SO... LAST YEAR.

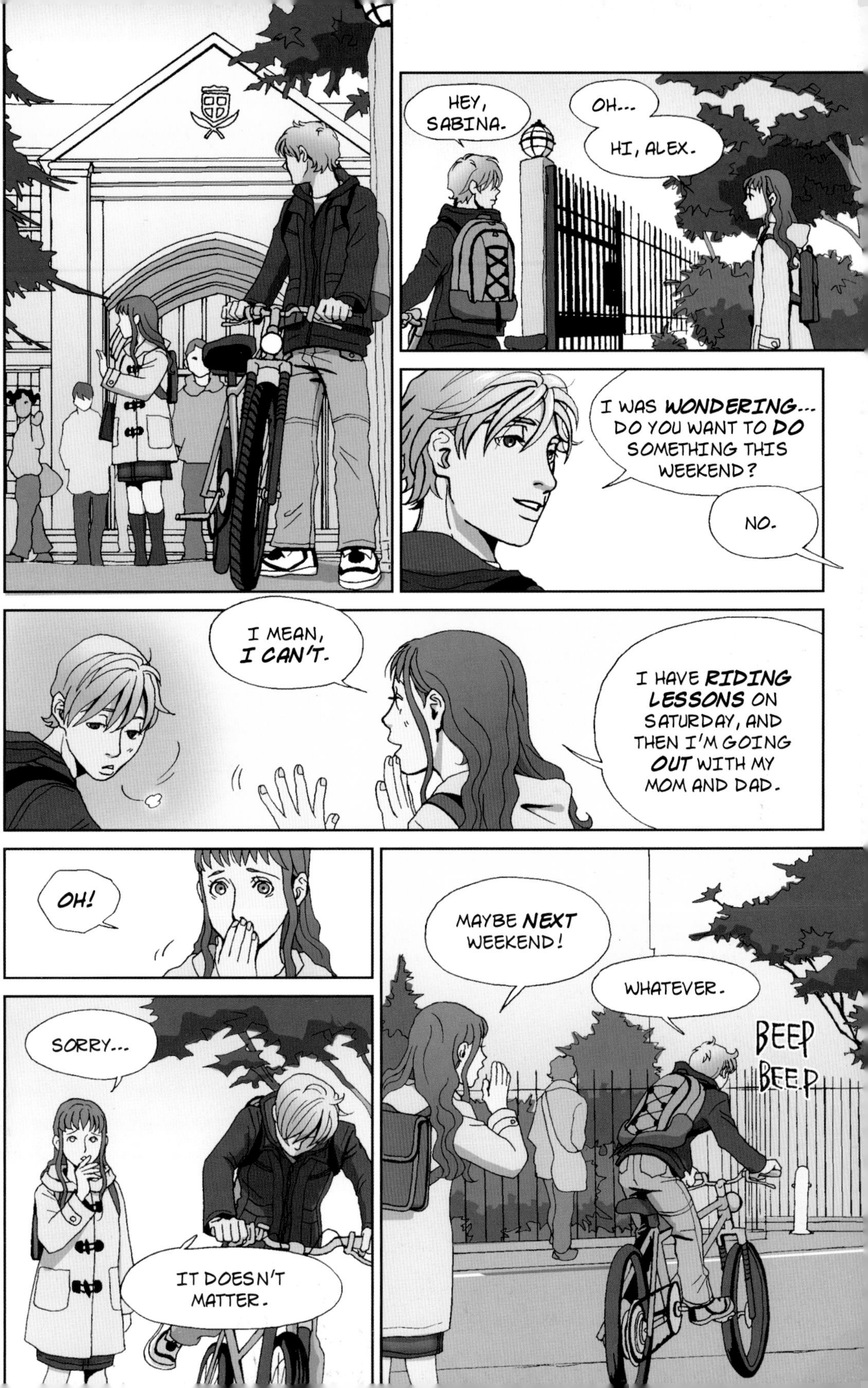
HEY, SABINA.
OH...
HI, ALEX.
I WAS WONDERING... DO YOU WANT TO DO SOMETHING THIS WEEKEND?
NO.
I MEAN, I CAN'T.
I HAVE RIDING LESSONS ON SATURDAY, AND THEN I'M GOING OUT WITH MY MOM AND DAD.
OH!
SORRY...
IT DOESN'T MATTER.
MAYBE NEXT WEEKEND!
WHATEVER.
BEEP
BEEP

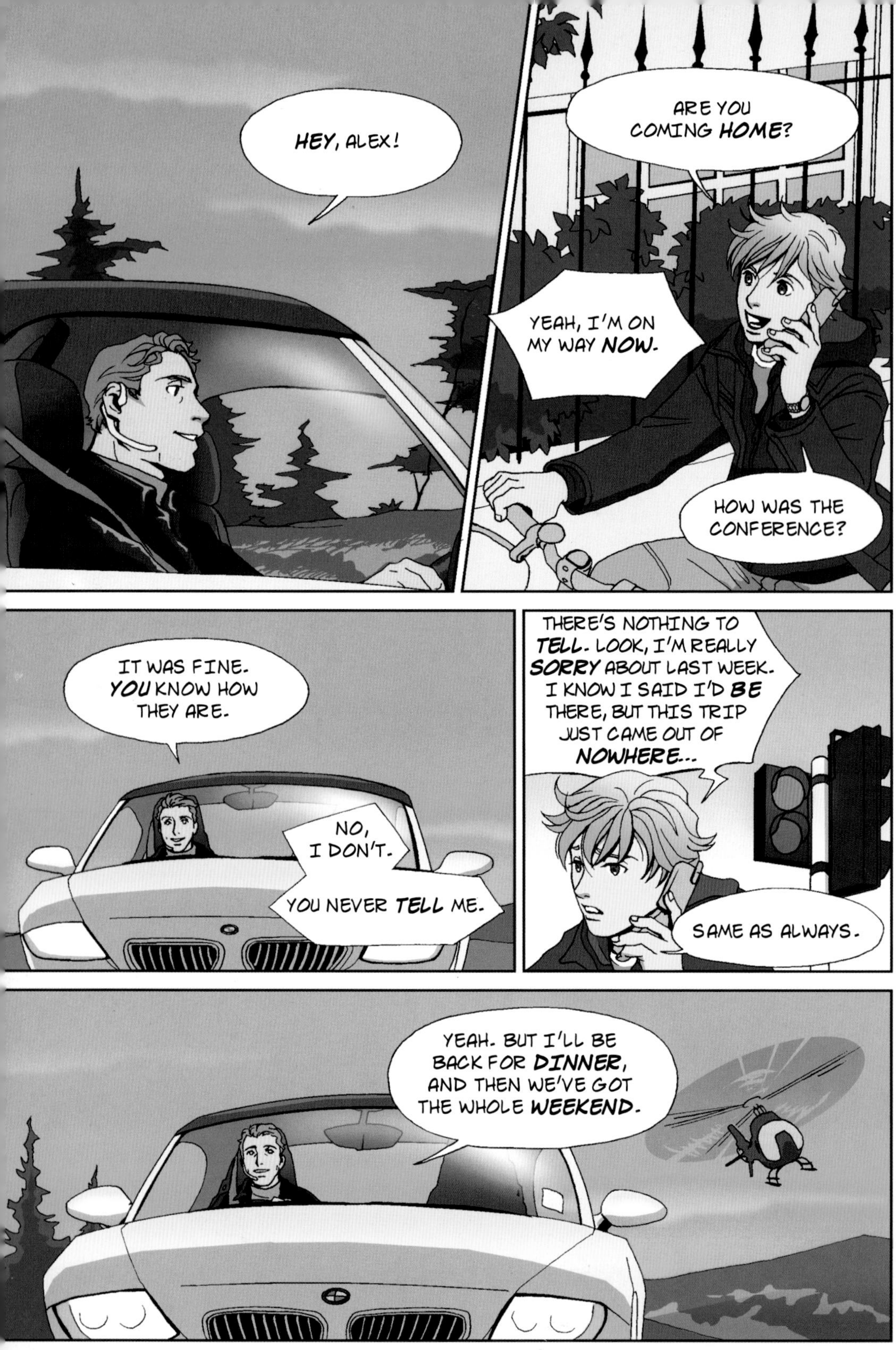
HEY, ALEX!
ARE YOU COMING HOME?
YEAH, I'M ON MY WAY NOW.
HOW WAS THE CONFERENCE?
IT WAS FINE. YOU KNOW HOW THEY ARE.
NO, I DON'T.
YOU NEVER TELL ME.
THERE'S NOTHING TO TELL. LOOK, I'M REALLY SORRY ABOUT LAST WEEK. I KNOW I SAID I'D BE THERE, BUT THIS TRIP JUST CAME OUT OF NOWHERE...
SAME AS ALWAYS.
YEAH. BUT I'LL BE BACK FOR DINNER, AND THEN WE'VE GOT THE WHOLE WEEKEND.

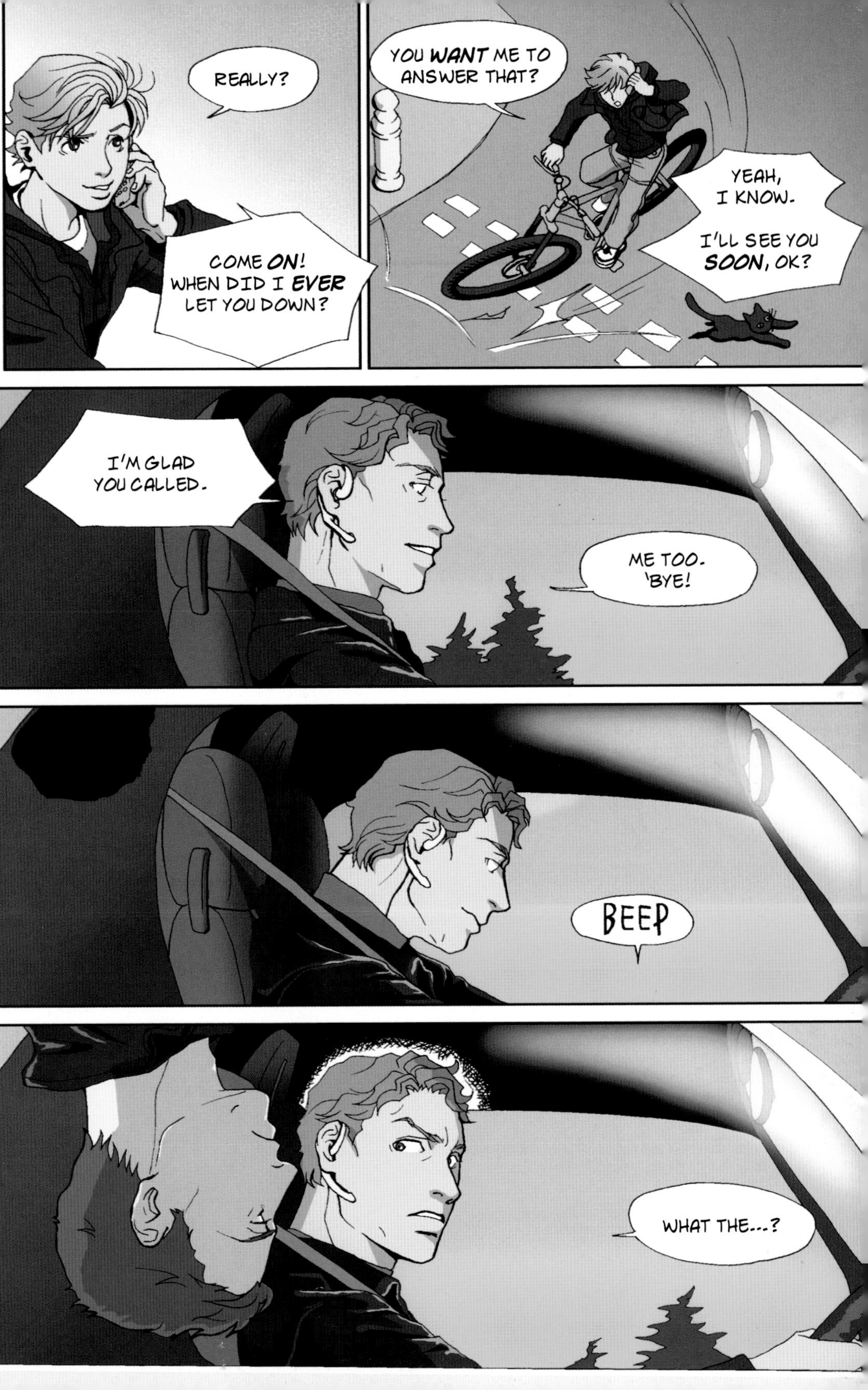
REALLY?
COME ON! WHEN DID I EVER LET YOU DOWN?
YOU WANT ME TO ANSWER THAT?
YEAH, I KNOW.
I'LL SEE YOU SOON, OK?
I'M GLAD YOU CALLED.
ME TOO. 'BYE!
BEEP
WHAT THE...?

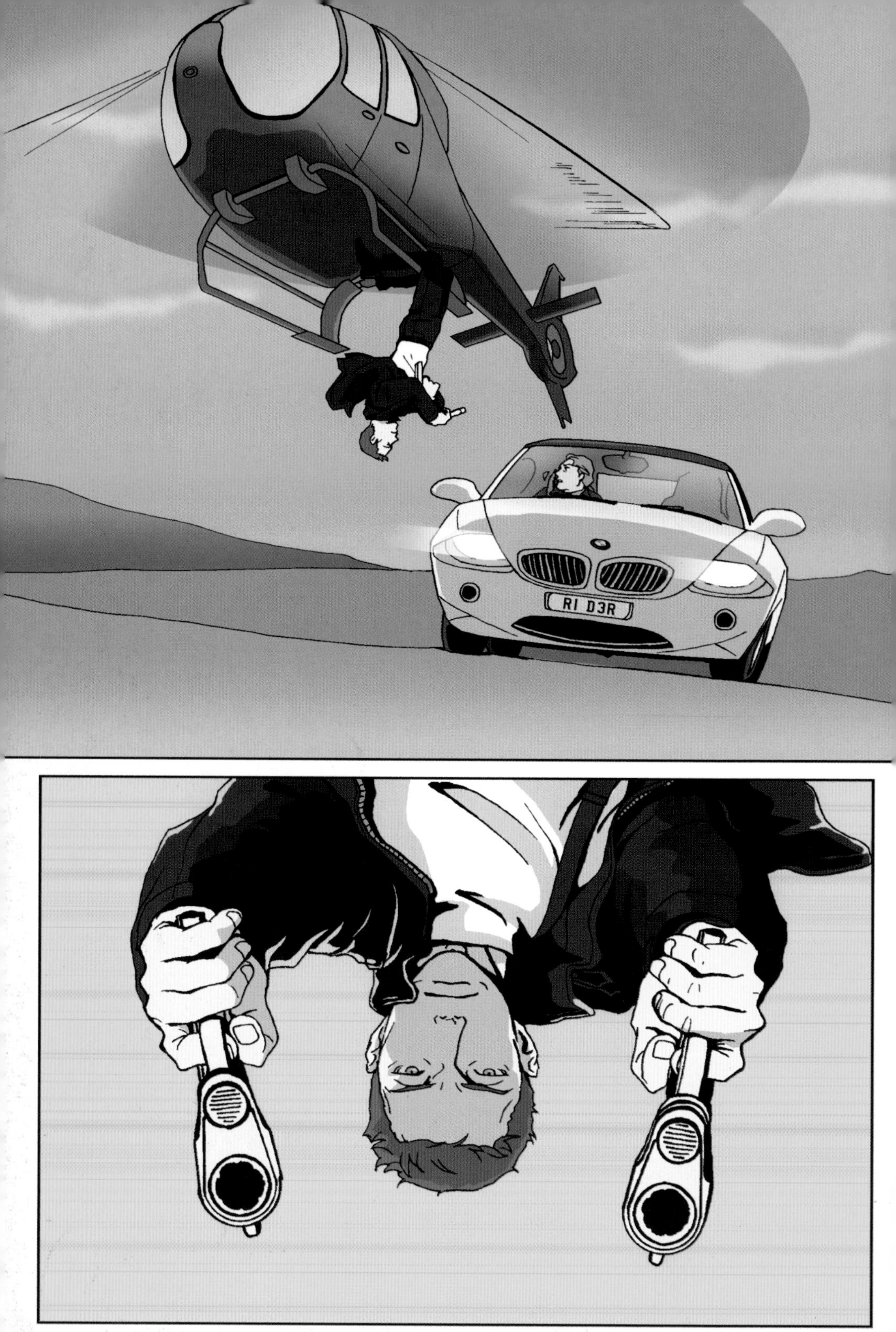
RI D3R

BANG

BANG

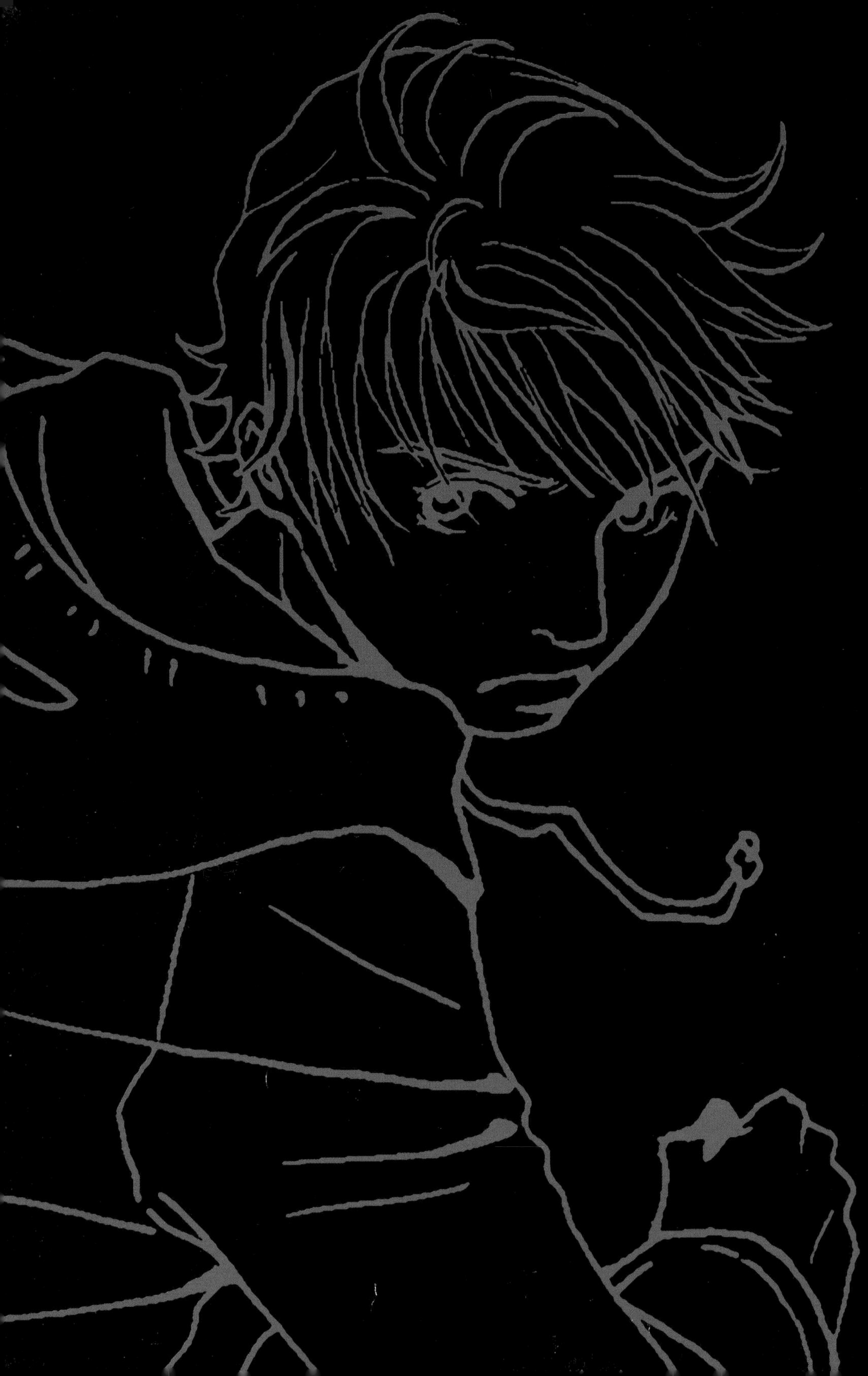

STORMBREAKER™

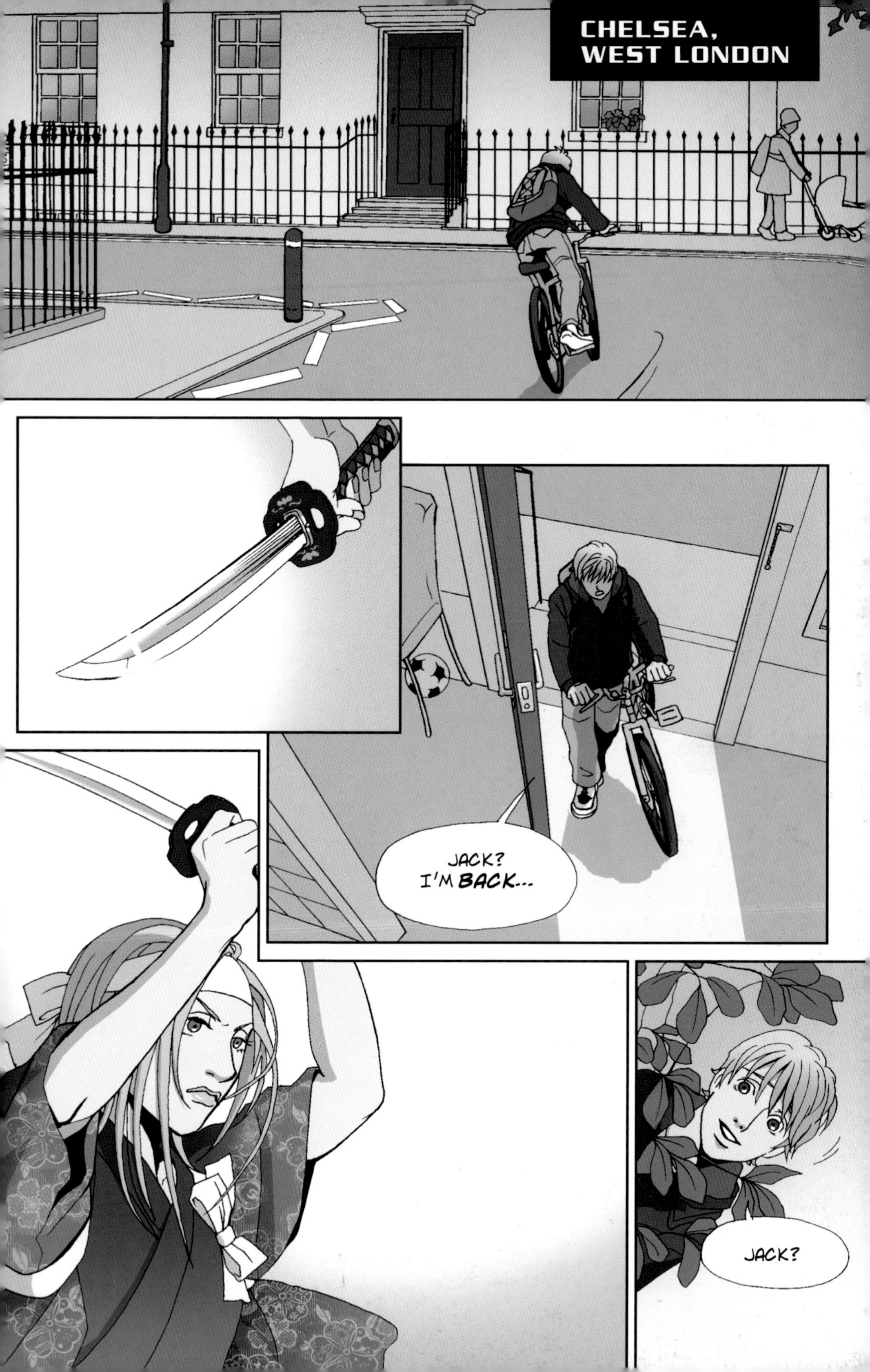
CHELSEA,
WEST LONDON
JACK?
I'M BACK...
JACK?

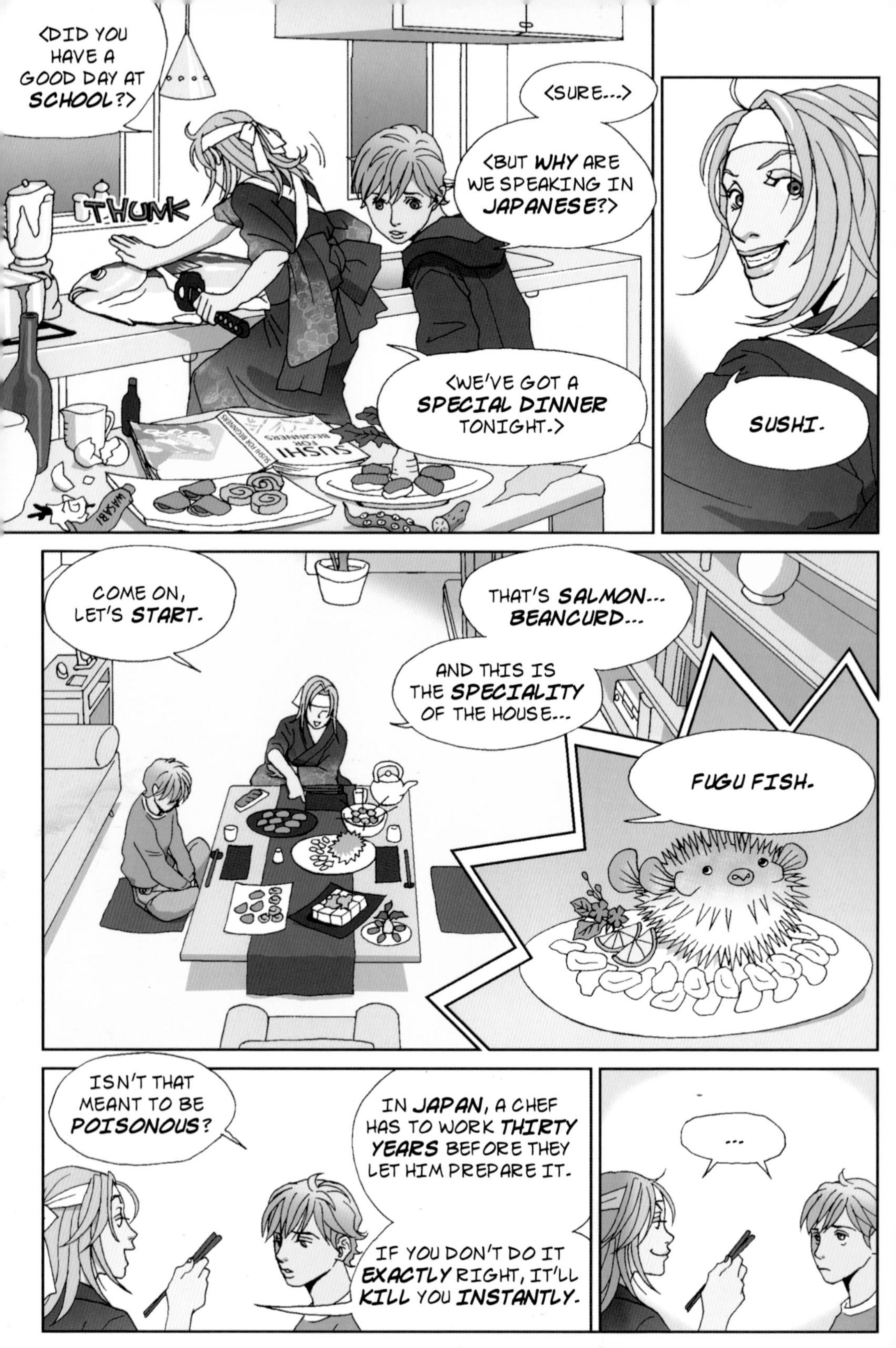
<DID YOU HAVE A GOOD DAY AT SCHOOL?>
THUMK
<SURE...>
<BUT WHY ARE WE SPEAKING IN JAPANESE?>
<WE'VE GOT A SPECIAL DINNER TONIGHT.>
SUSHI FOR BEGINNERS
WASABI
SUSHI.
COME ON, LET'S START.
THAT'S SALMON... BEANCURD...
AND THIS IS THE SPECIALITY OF THE HOUSE...
FUGU FISH.
ISN'T THAT MEANT TO BE POISONOUS?
IN JAPAN, A CHEF HAS TO WORK THIRTY YEARS BEFORE THEY LET HIM PREPARE IT.
IF YOU DON'T DO IT EXACTLY RIGHT, IT'LL KILL YOU INSTANTLY.
...

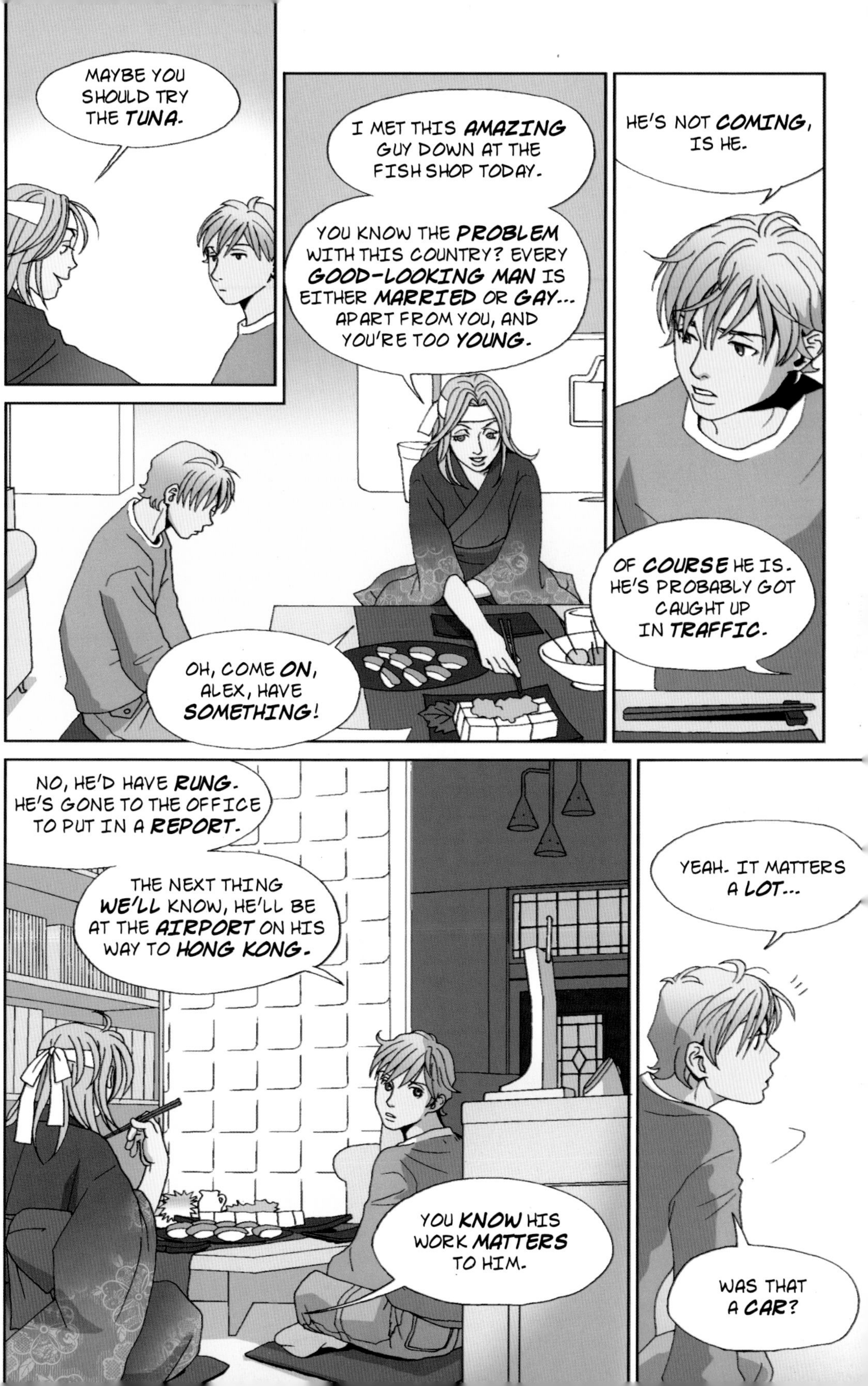
MAYBE YOU SHOULD TRY THE TUNA.
I MET THIS AMAZING GUY DOWN AT THE FISH SHOP TODAY.
YOU KNOW THE PROBLEM WITH THIS COUNTRY? EVERY GOOD-LOOKING MAN IS EITHER MARRIED OR GAY... APART FROM YOU, AND YOU'RE TOO YOUNG.
OH, COME ON, ALEX, HAVE SOMETHING!
HE'S NOT COMING, IS HE.
OF COURSE HE IS. HE'S PROBABLY GOT CAUGHT UP IN TRAFFIC.
NO, HE'D HAVE RUNG. HE'S GONE TO THE OFFICE TO PUT IN A REPORT.
THE NEXT THING WE'LL KNOW, HE'LL BE AT THE AIRPORT ON HIS WAY TO HONG KONG.
YOU KNOW HIS WORK MATTERS TO HIM.
YEAH. IT MATTERS A LOT...
WAS THAT A CAR?

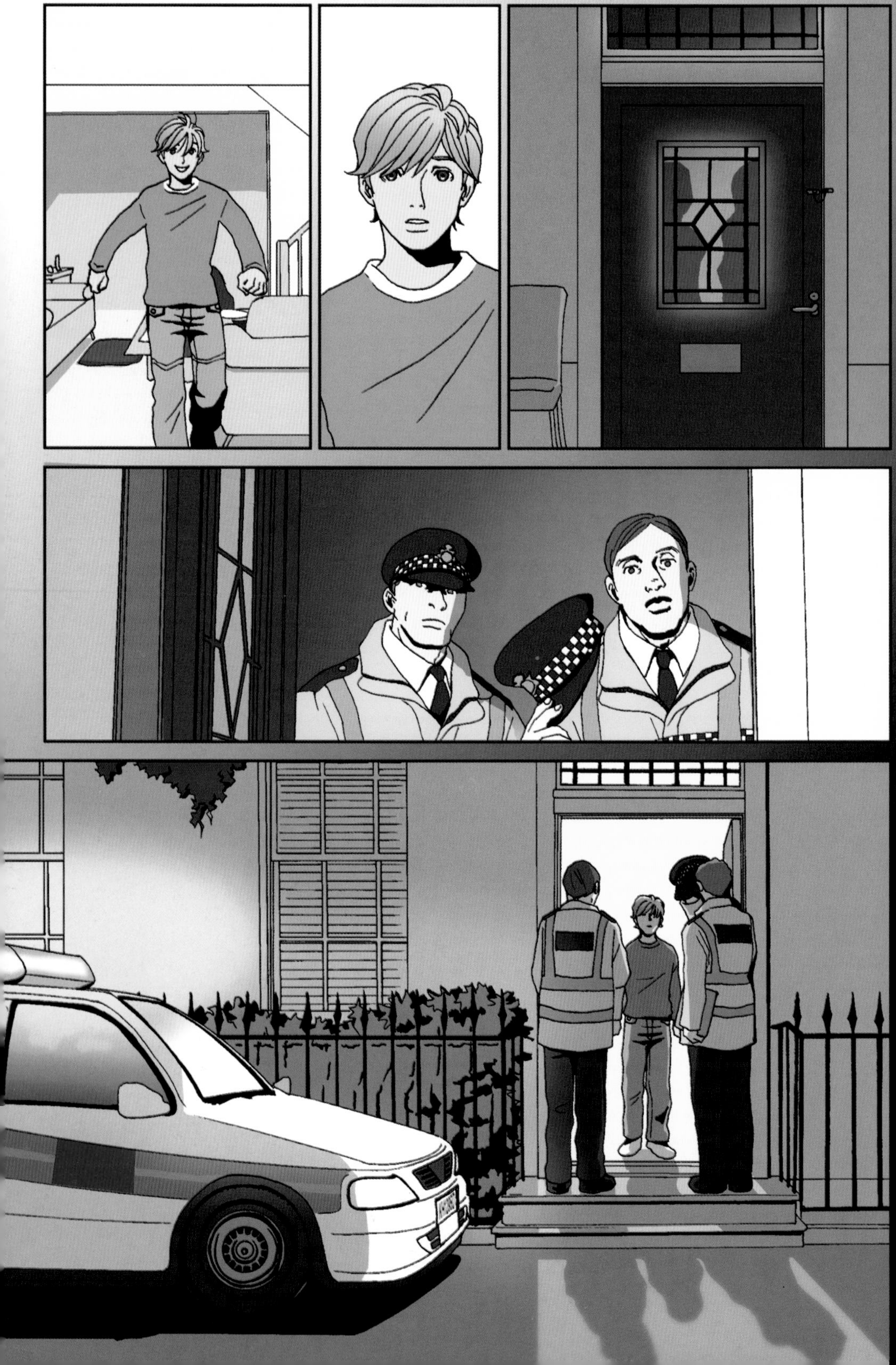

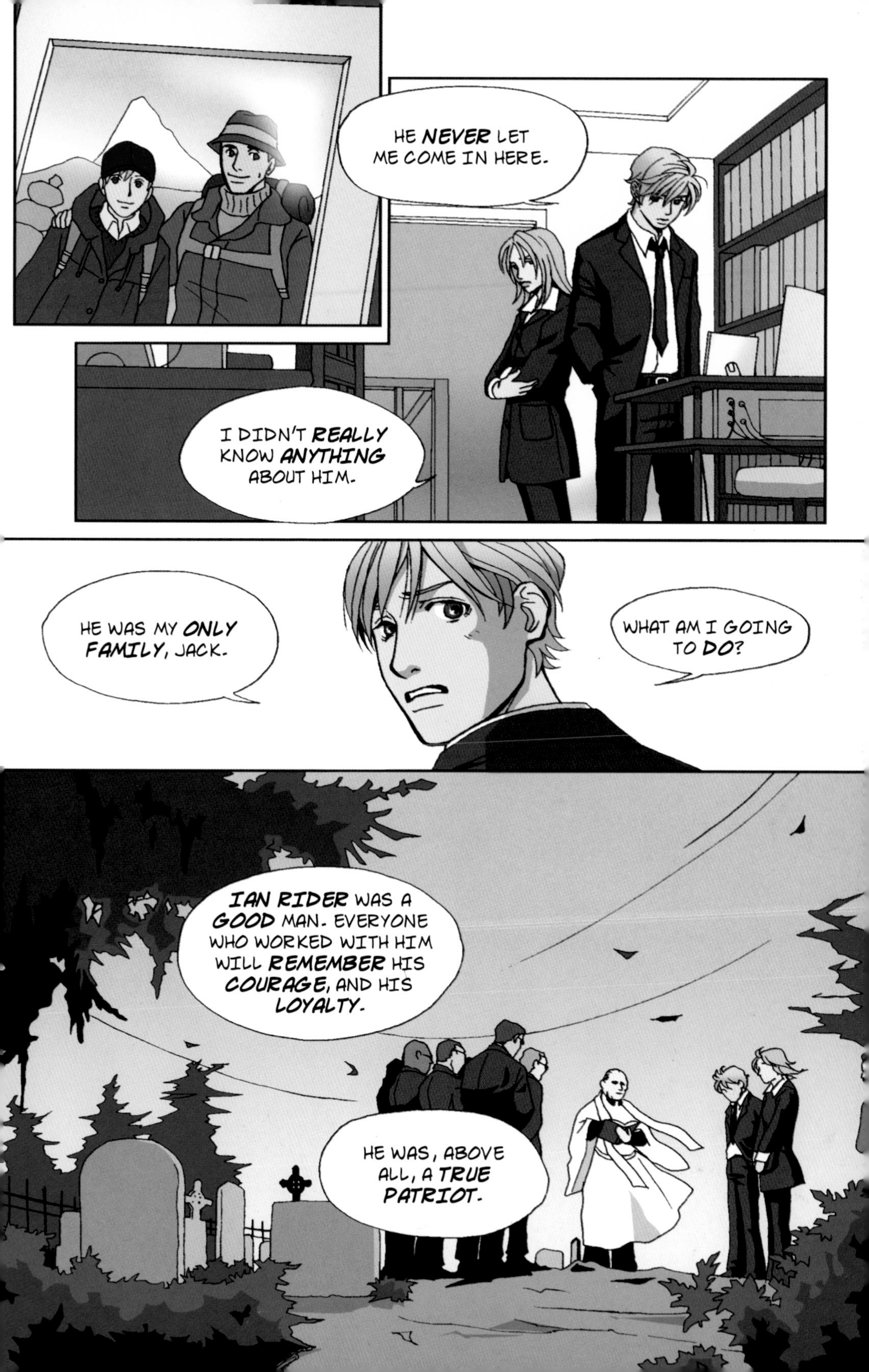
HE NEVER LET ME COME IN HERE.
I DIDN'T REALLY KNOW ANYTHING ABOUT HIM.
HE WAS MY ONLY FAMILY, JACK.
WHAT AM I GOING TO DO?
IAN RIDER WAS A GOOD MAN. EVERYONE WHO WORKED WITH HIM WILL REMEMBER HIS COURAGE, AND HIS LOYALTY.
HE WAS, ABOVE ALL, A TRUE PATRIOT.

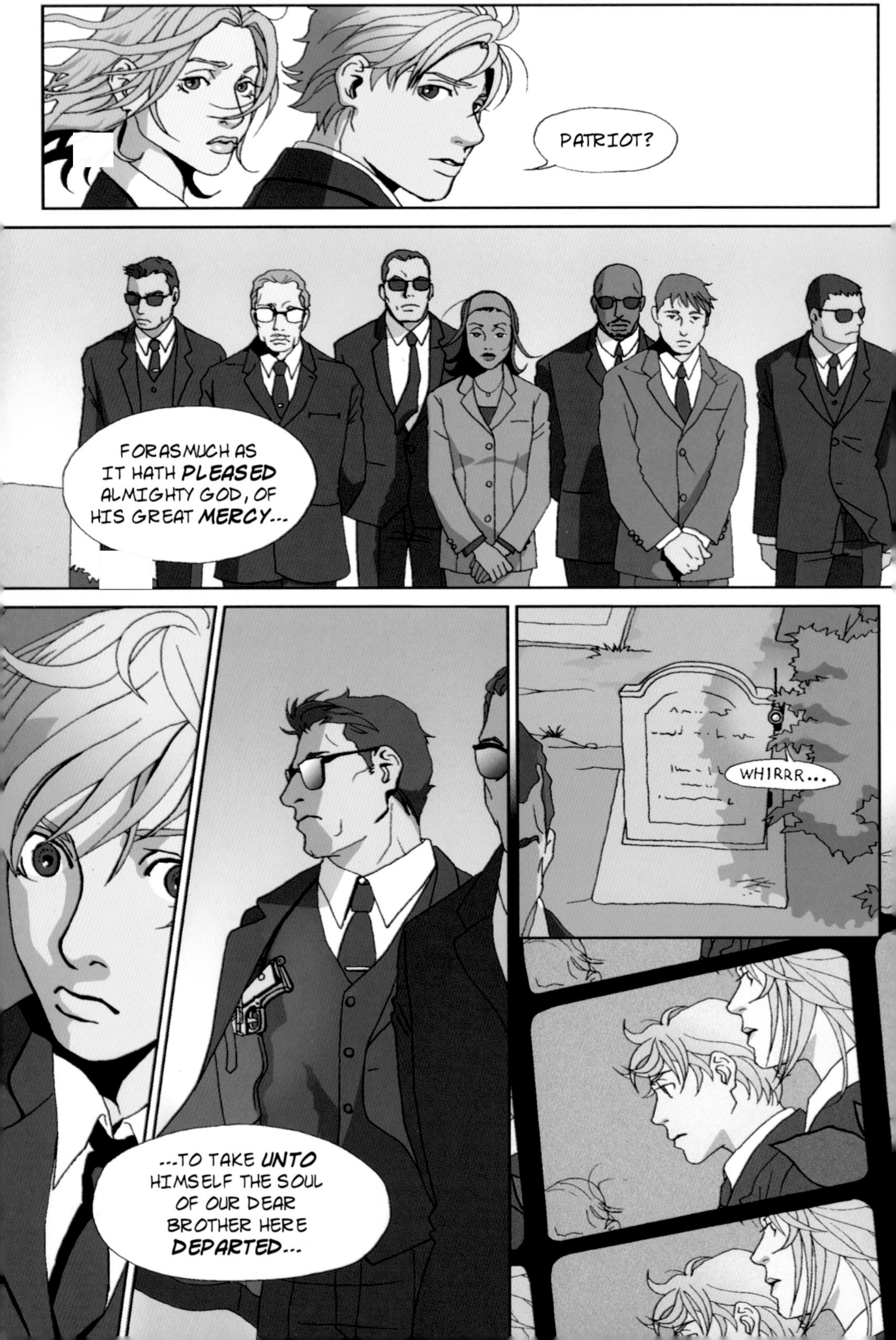
PATRIOT?
FORASMUCH AS IT HATH PLEASED ALMIGHTY GOD, OF HIS GREAT MERCY...
...TO TAKE UNTO HIMSELF THE SOUL OF OUR DEAR BROTHER HERE DEPARTED...
WHIRRR...

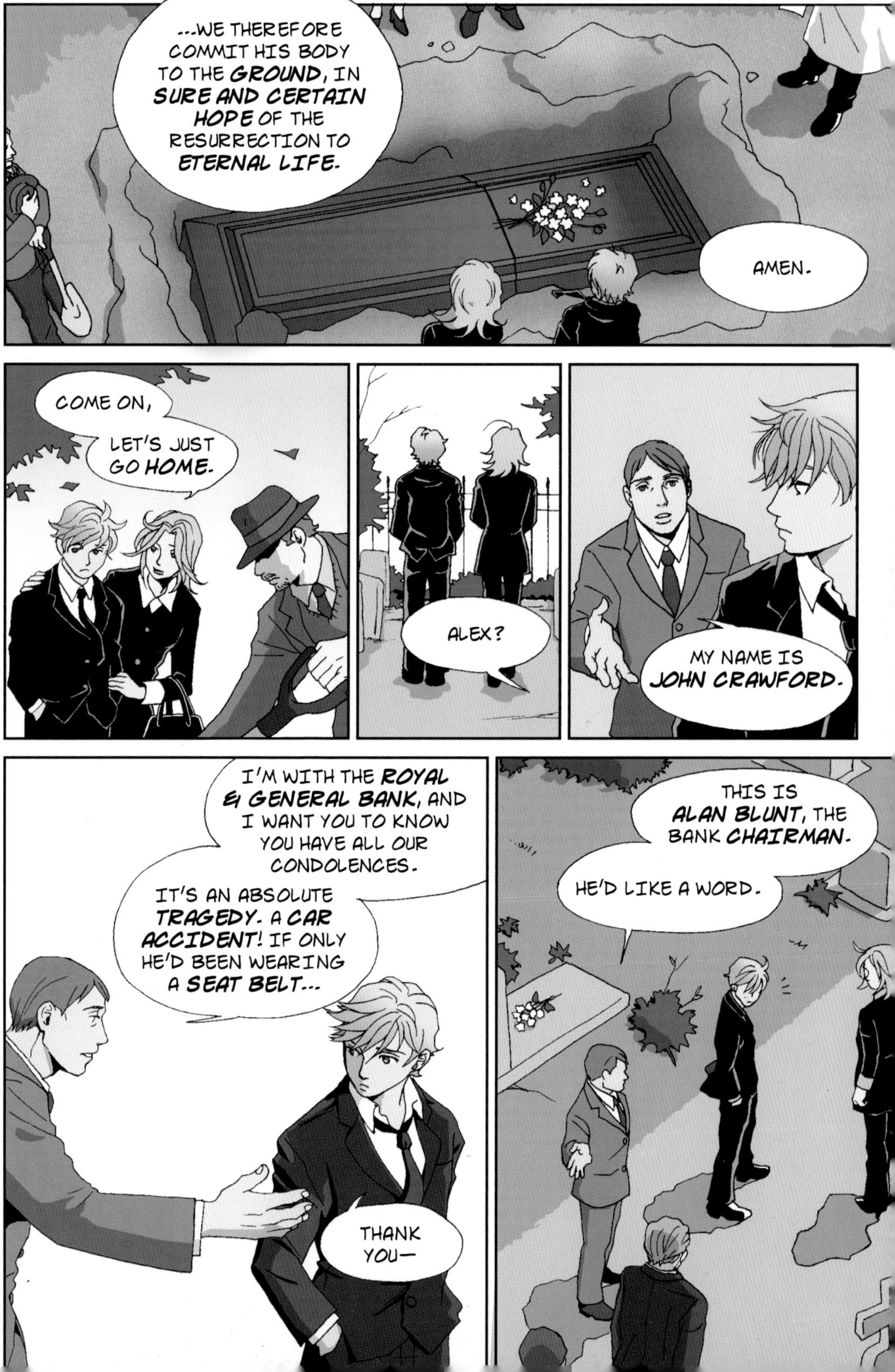
...WE THEREFORE COMMIT HIS BODY TO THE GROUND, IN SURE AND CERTAIN HOPE OF THE RESURRECTION TO ETERNAL LIFE.
AMEN.
COME ON,
LET'S JUST GO HOME.
ALEX?
MY NAME IS JOHN CRAWFORD.
I'M WITH THE ROYAL & GENERAL BANK, AND I WANT YOU TO KNOW YOU HAVE ALL OUR CONDOLENCES.
IT'S AN ABSOLUTE TRAGEDY. A CAR ACCIDENT! IF ONLY HE'D BEEN WEARING A SEAT BELT...
THANK YOU—
THIS IS ALAN BLUNT, THE BANK CHAIRMAN.
HE'D LIKE A WORD.

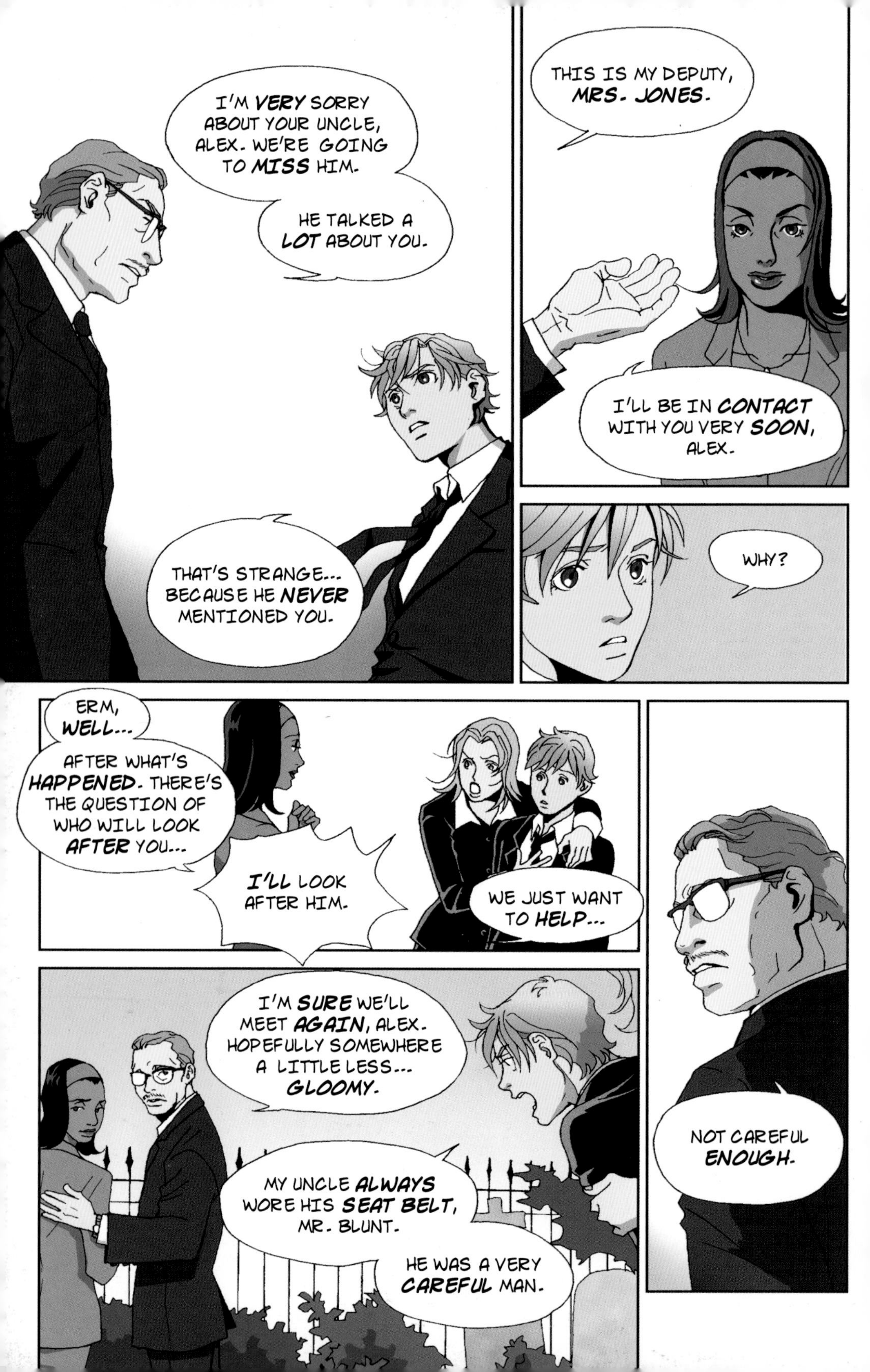
I'M VERY SORRY ABOUT YOUR UNCLE, ALEX. WE'RE GOING TO MISS HIM.
HE TALKED A LOT ABOUT YOU.
THAT'S STRANGE... BECAUSE HE NEVER MENTIONED YOU.
THIS IS MY DEPUTY, MRS. JONES.
I'LL BE IN CONTACT WITH YOU VERY SOON, ALEX.
WHY?
ERM, WELL...
AFTER WHAT'S HAPPENED. THERE'S THE QUESTION OF WHO WILL LOOK AFTER YOU...
I'LL LOOK AFTER HIM.
WE JUST WANT TO HELP...
I'M SURE WE'LL MEET AGAIN, ALEX. HOPEFULLY SOMEWHERE A LITTLE LESS... GLOOMY.
MY UNCLE ALWAYS WORE HIS SEAT BELT, MR. BLUNT.
HE WAS A VERY CAREFUL MAN.
NOT CAREFUL ENOUGH.

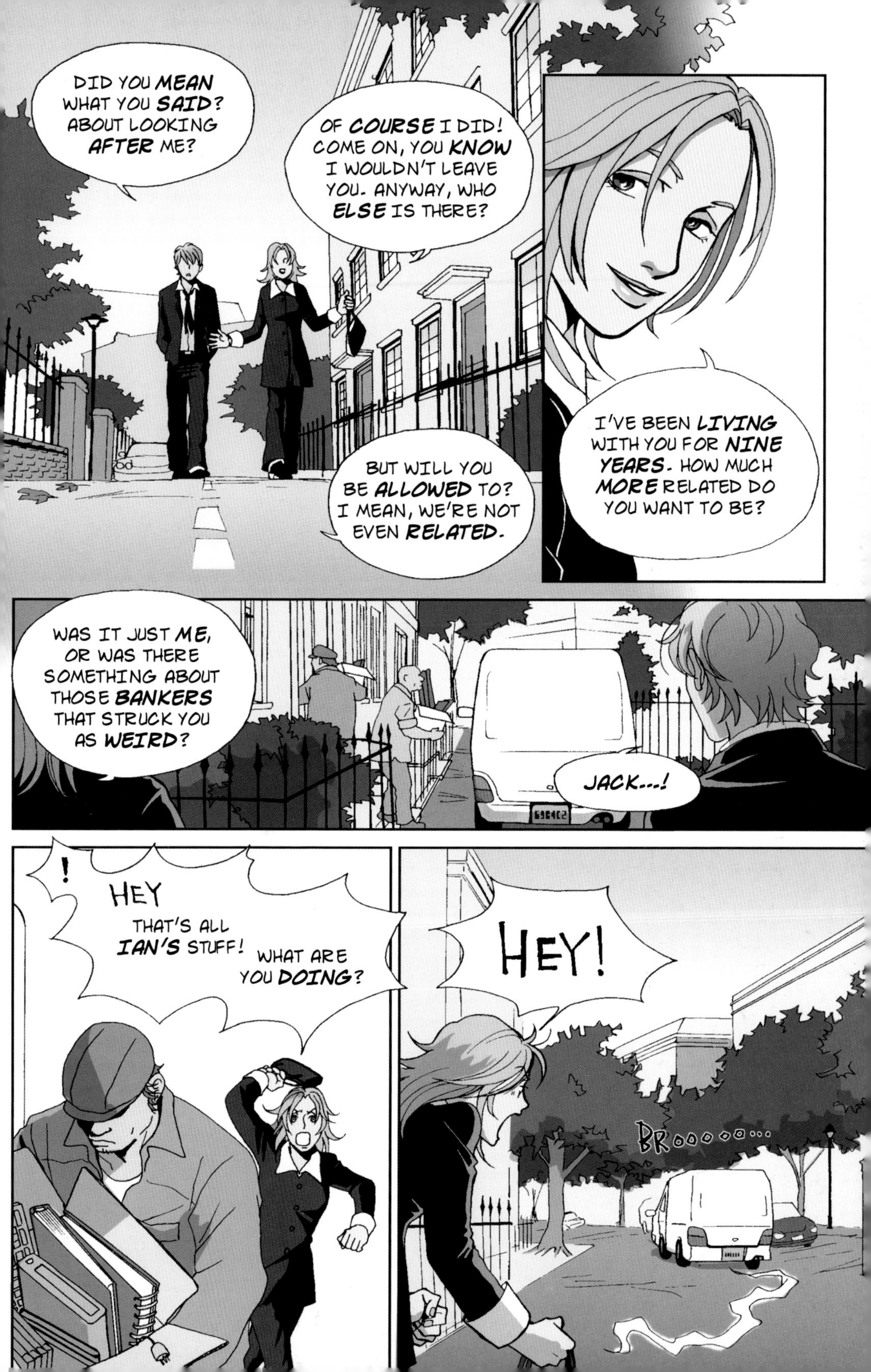
DID YOU MEAN WHAT YOU SAID? ABOUT LOOKING AFTER ME?
OF COURSE I DID! COME ON, YOU KNOW I WOULDN'T LEAVE YOU. ANYWAY, WHO ELSE IS THERE?
BUT WILL YOU BE ALLOWED TO? I MEAN, WE'RE NOT EVEN RELATED.
I'VE BEEN LIVING WITH YOU FOR NINE YEARS. HOW MUCH MORE RELATED DO YOU WANT TO BE?
WAS IT JUST ME, OR WAS THERE SOMETHING ABOUT THOSE BANKERS THAT STRUCK YOU AS WEIRD?
JACK...!
!
HEY
THAT'S ALL IAN'S STUFF!
WHAT ARE YOU DOING?
HEY!
BROOOOOO...

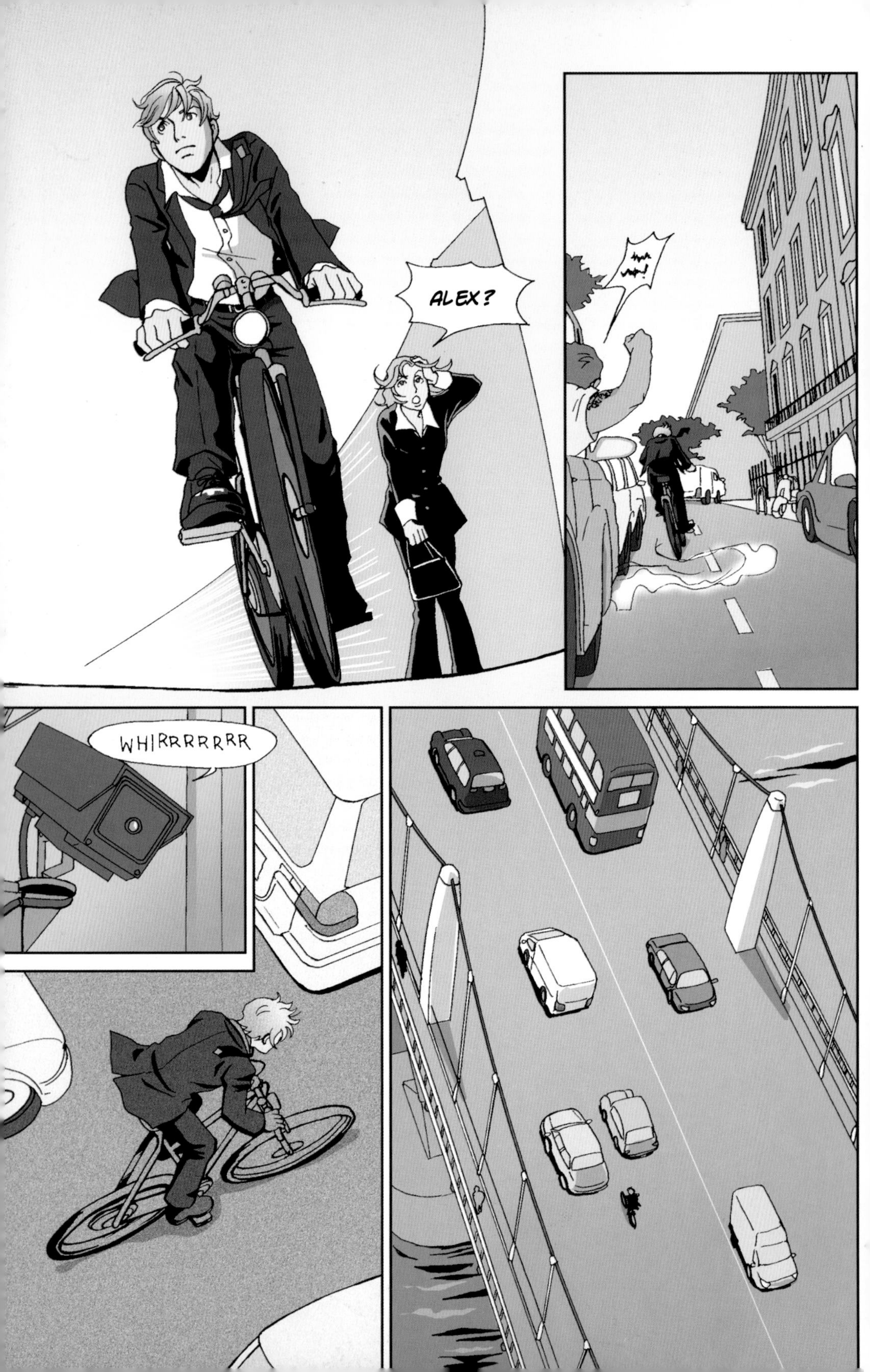
ALEX?
WHIRRRRRRR

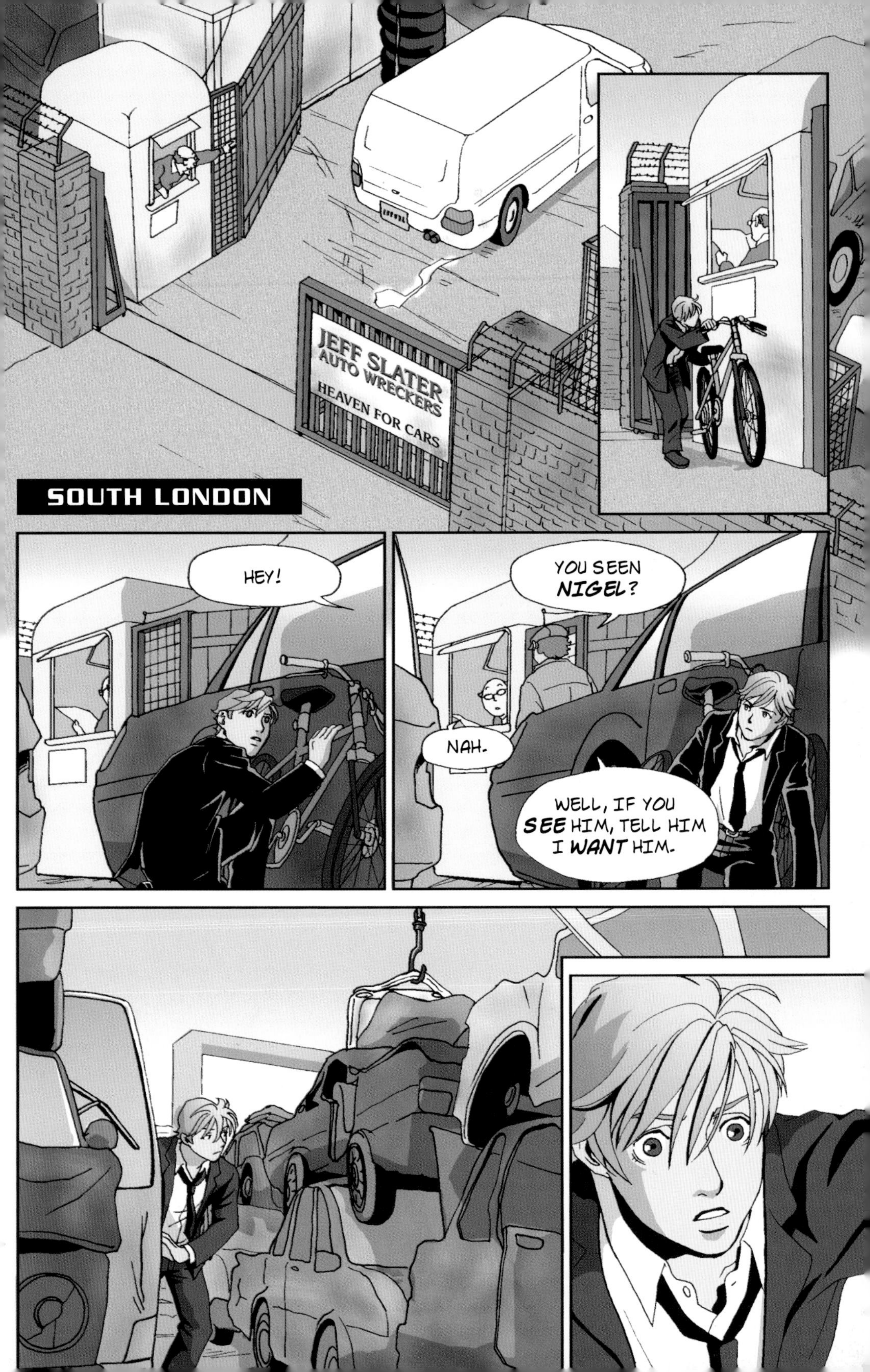
JEFF SLATER AUTO WRECKERS
HEAVEN FOR CARS
SOUTH LONDON
HEY!
YOU SEEN NIGEL?
NAH.
WELL, IF YOU SEE HIM, TELL HIM I WANT HIM.

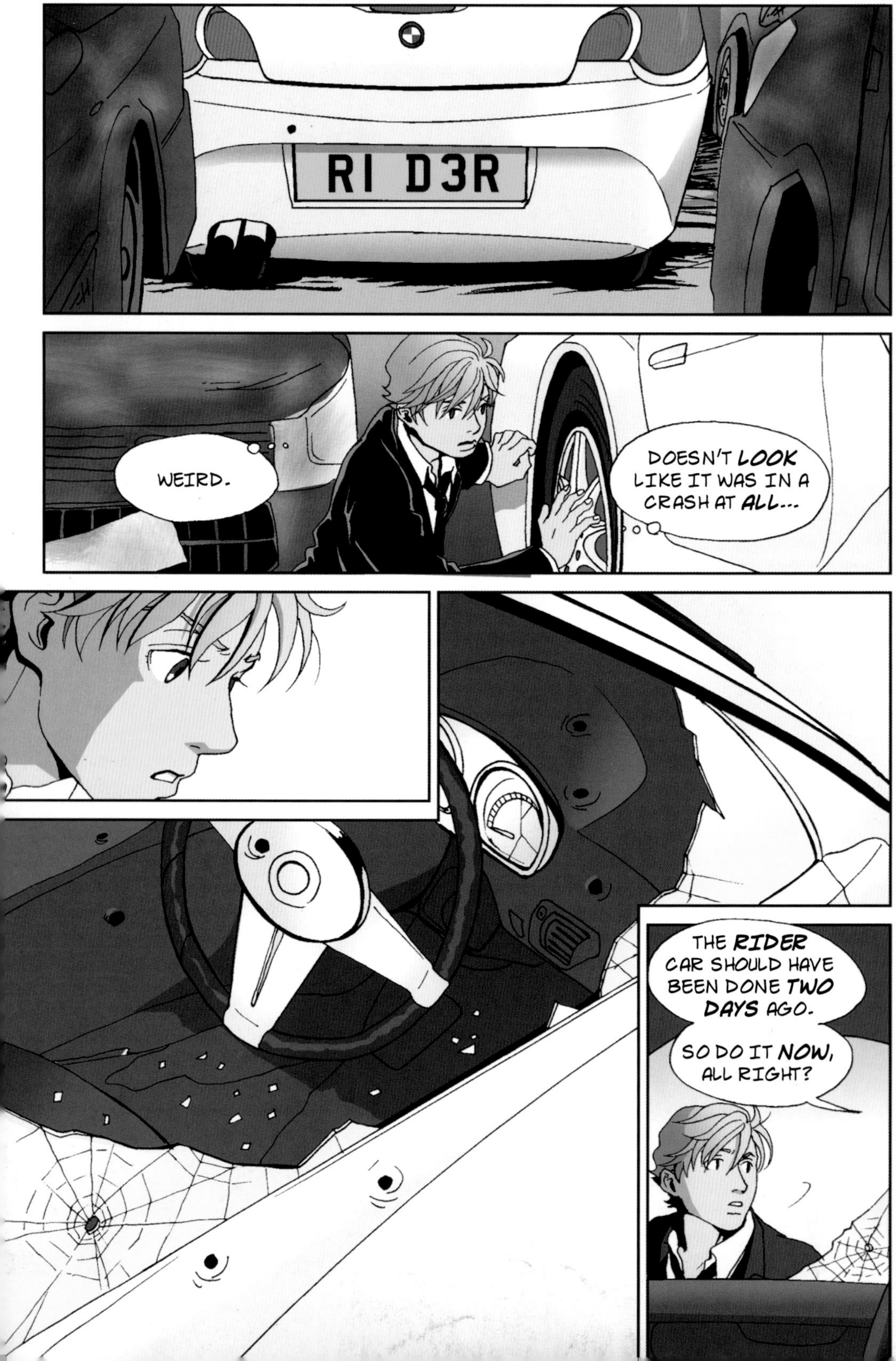
RI D3R
WEIRD.
DOESN'T LOOK LIKE IT WAS IN A CRASH AT ALL...
THE RIDER CAR SHOULD HAVE BEEN DONE TWO DAYS AGO.
SO DO IT NOW, ALL RIGHT?

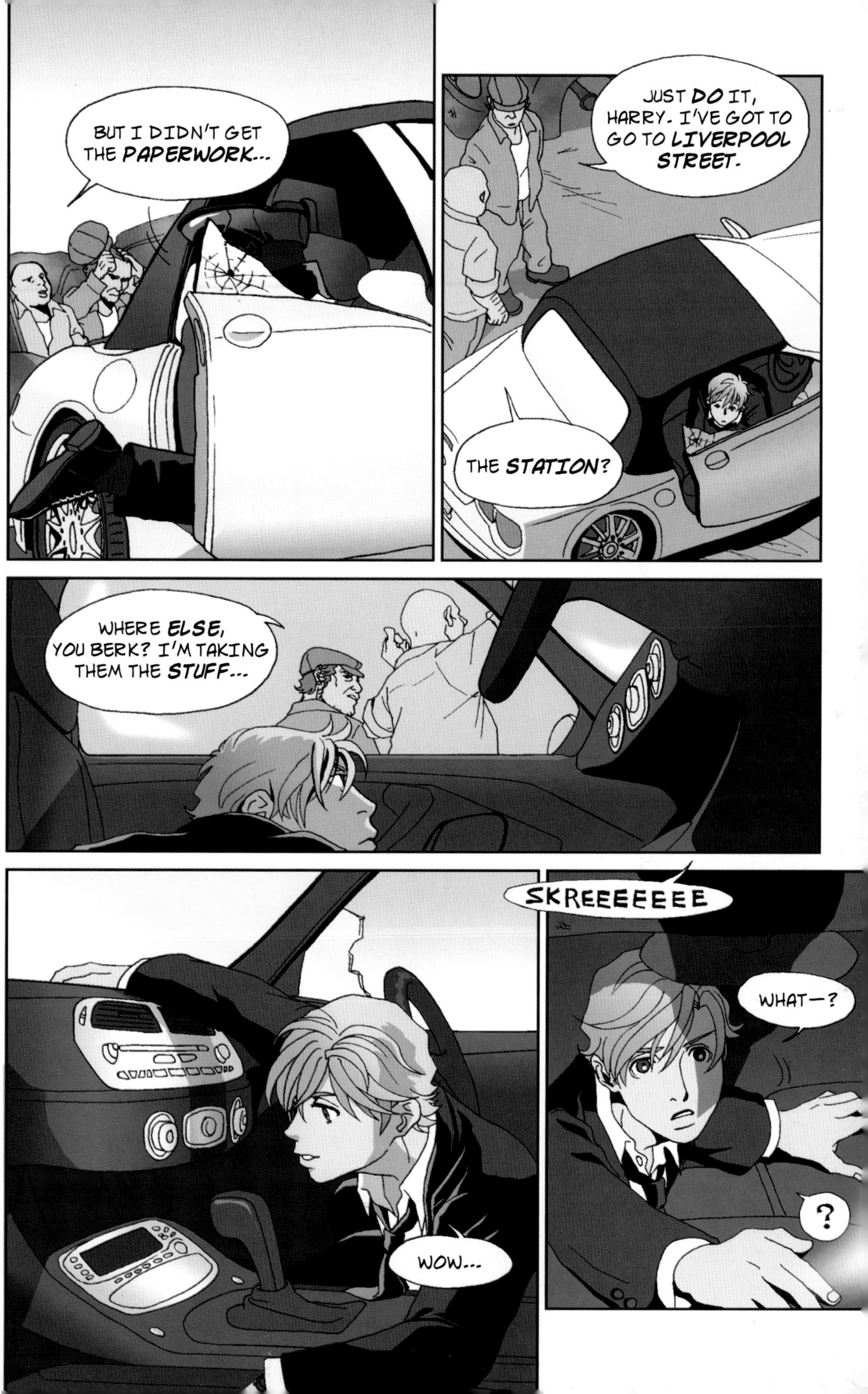
BUT I DIDN'T GET THE PAPERWORK...
JUST DO IT, HARRY. I'VE GOT TO GO TO LIVERPOOL STREET.
THE STATION?
WHERE ELSE, YOU BERK? I'M TAKING THEM THE STUFF...
WOW...
SKREEEEEEEE
WHAT—?
?

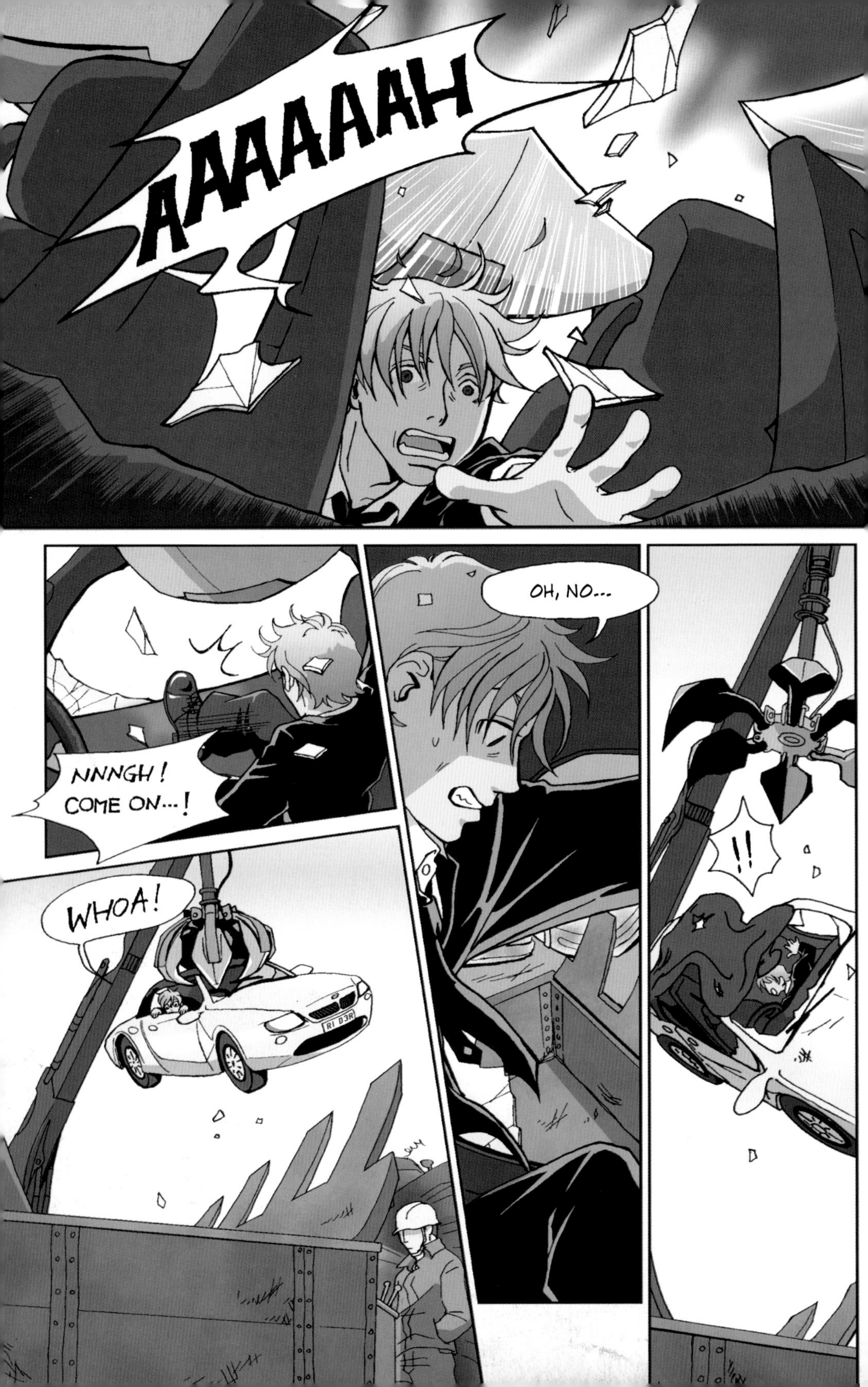
AAAAAAH
NNNGH! COME ON...!
OH, NO...
WHOA!
!!

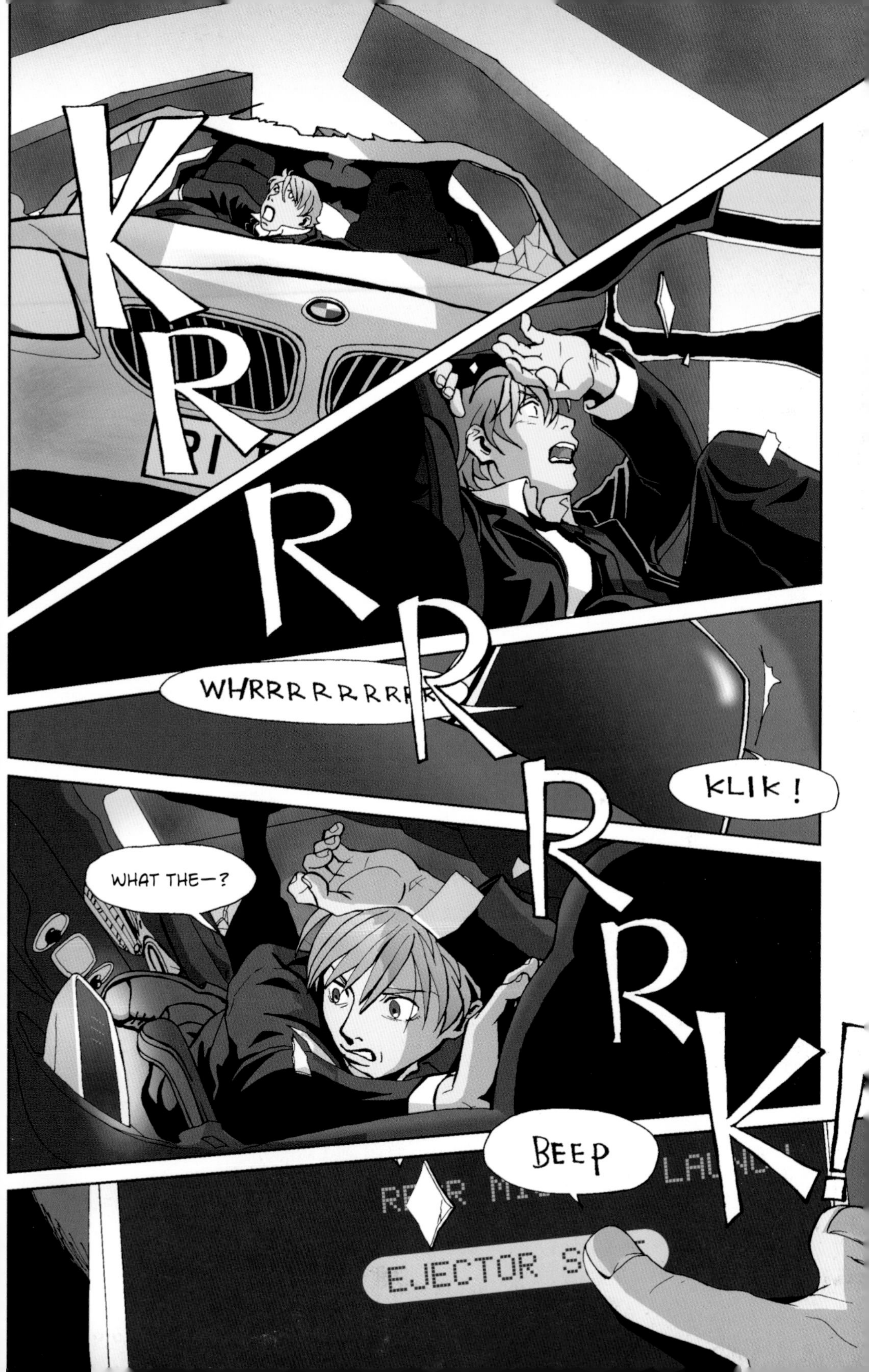
KRRRRRRK!!
WHRRRRRRRRR
KLIK!
WHAT THE—?
BEEP
EJECTOR S

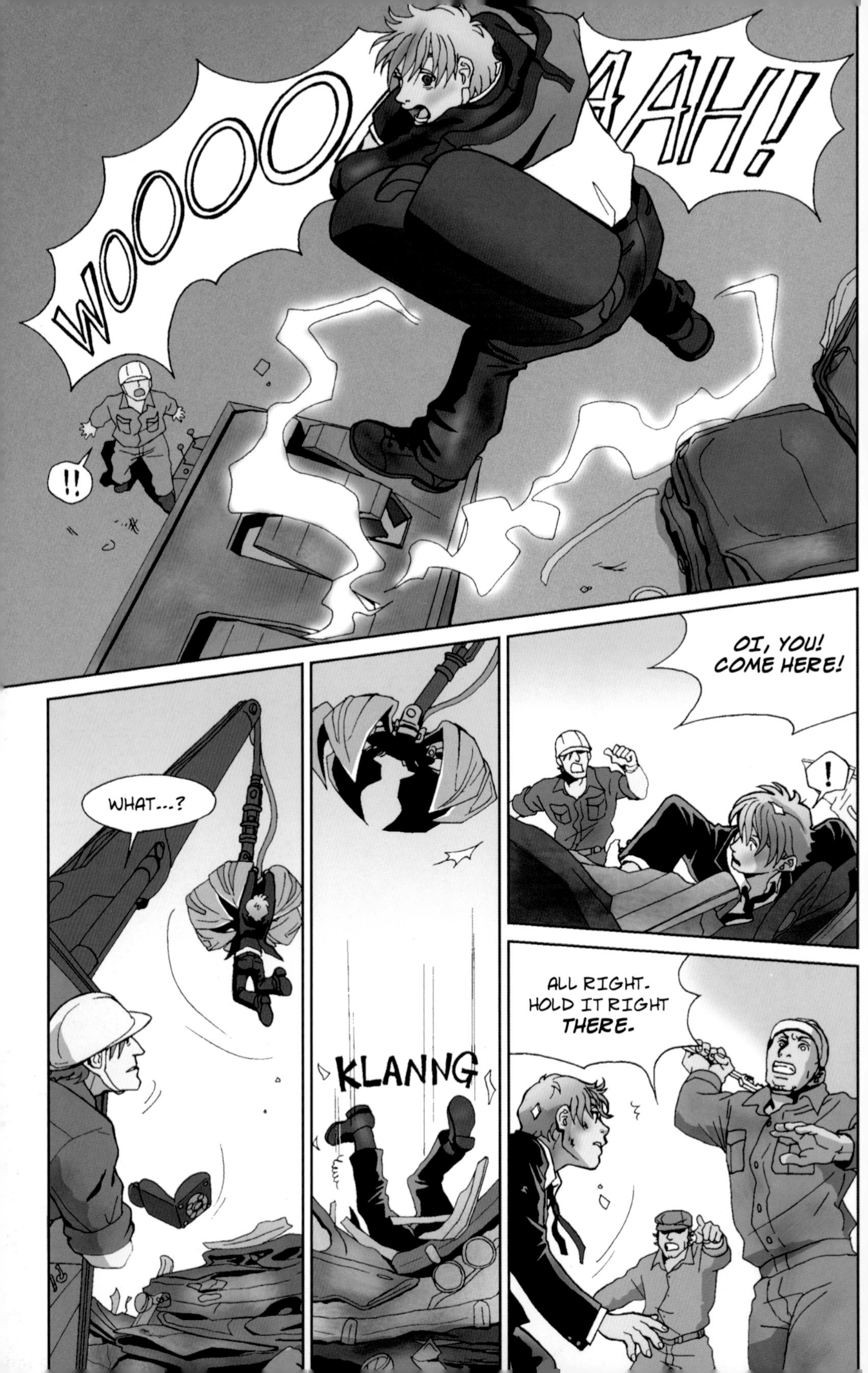
WOOOO AAH!
!!
OI, YOU! COME HERE!
!
WHAT...?
KLANNG
ALL RIGHT. HOLD IT RIGHT THERE.

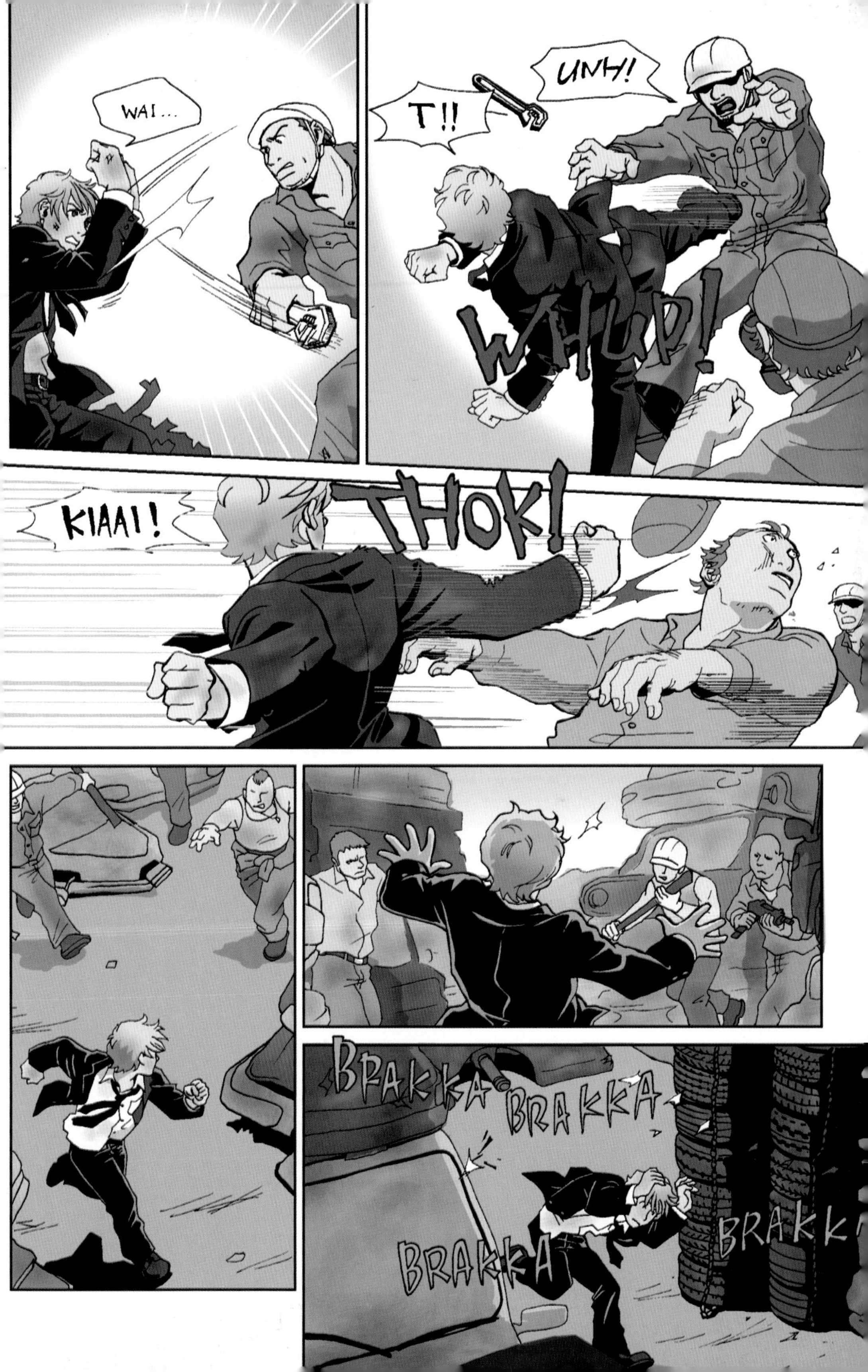
WAI...
T!!
UNH!
WHUP!
KIAAI!
THOK!
BRAKKA
BRAKKA
BRAKKA
BRAKK

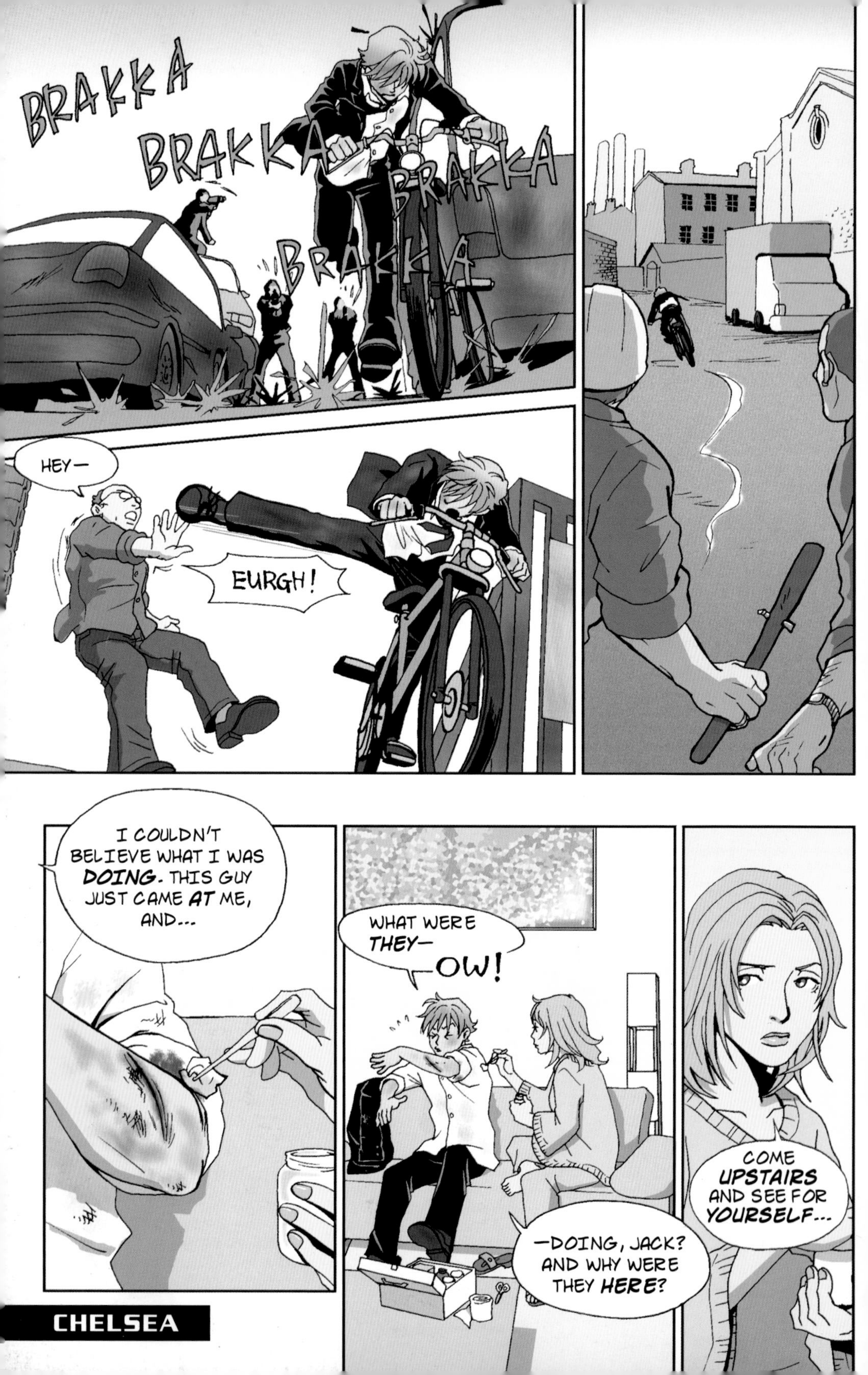
BRAKKA
BRAKKA
BRAKKA
BRAKKA
HEY—
EURGH!
I COULDN'T BELIEVE WHAT I WAS DOING. THIS GUY JUST CAME AT ME, AND...
WHAT WERE THEY—
OW!
—DOING, JACK? AND WHY WERE THEY HERE?
COME UPSTAIRS AND SEE FOR YOURSELF...
CHELSEA

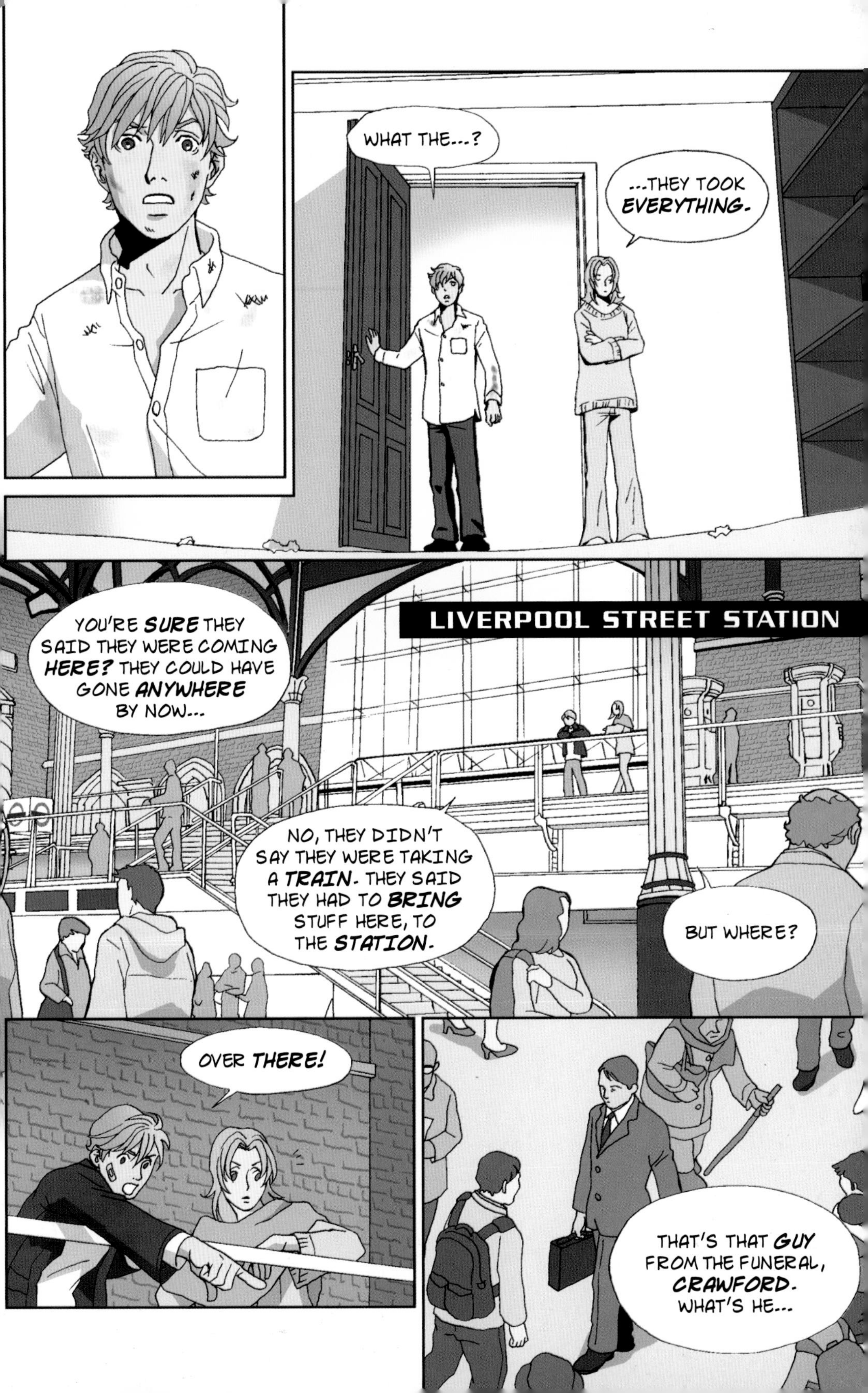
WHAT THE...?
...THEY TOOK EVERYTHING.
LIVERPOOL STREET STATION
YOU'RE SURE THEY SAID THEY WERE COMING HERE? THEY COULD HAVE GONE ANYWHERE BY NOW...
NO, THEY DIDN'T SAY THEY WERE TAKING A TRAIN. THEY SAID THEY HAD TO BRING STUFF HERE, TO THE STATION.
BUT WHERE?
OVER THERE!
THAT'S THAT GUY FROM THE FUNERAL, CRAWFORD. WHAT'S HE...

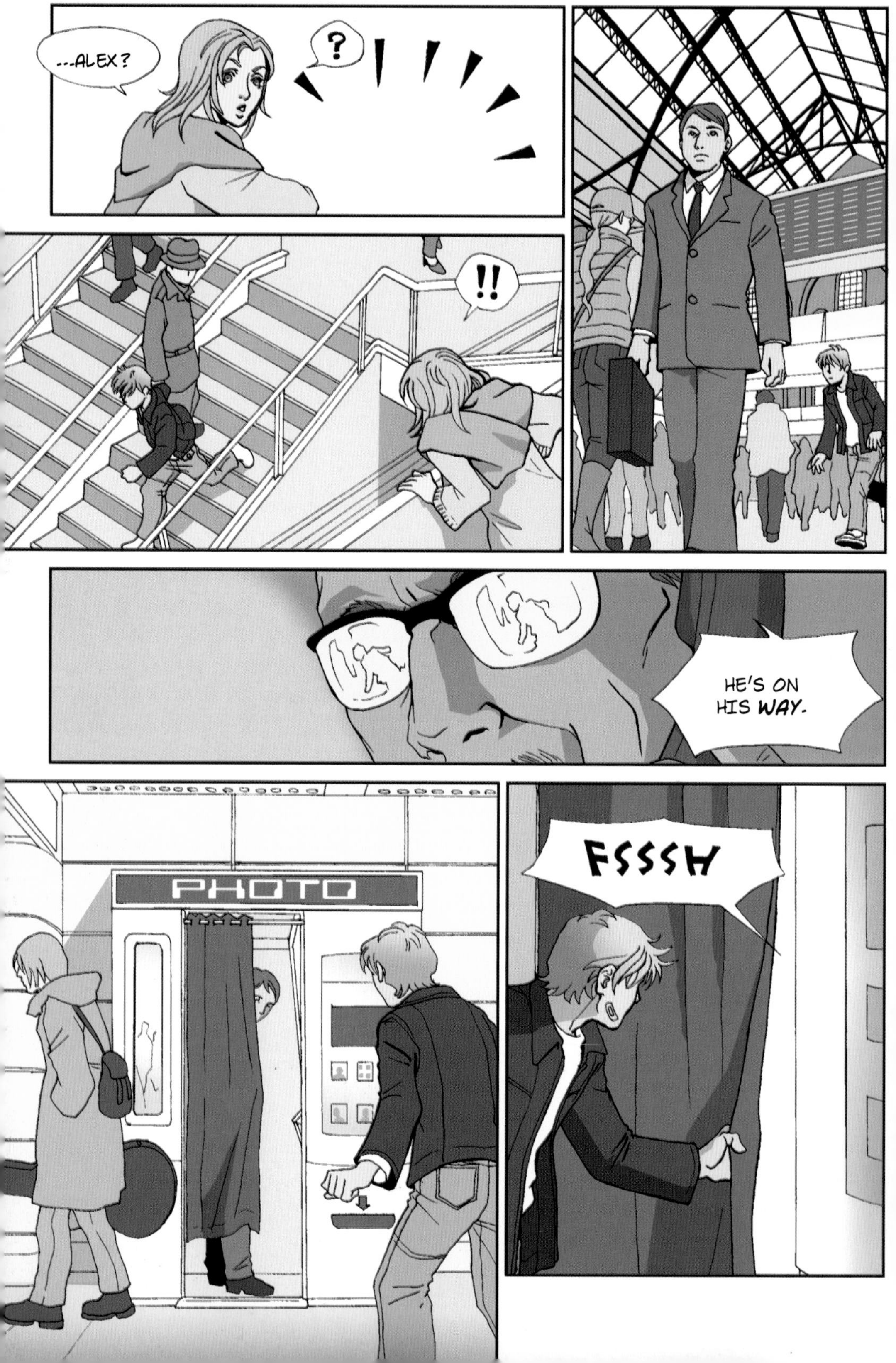
---ALEX?
?
!!
HE'S ON HIS WAY.
PHOTO
FSSSH

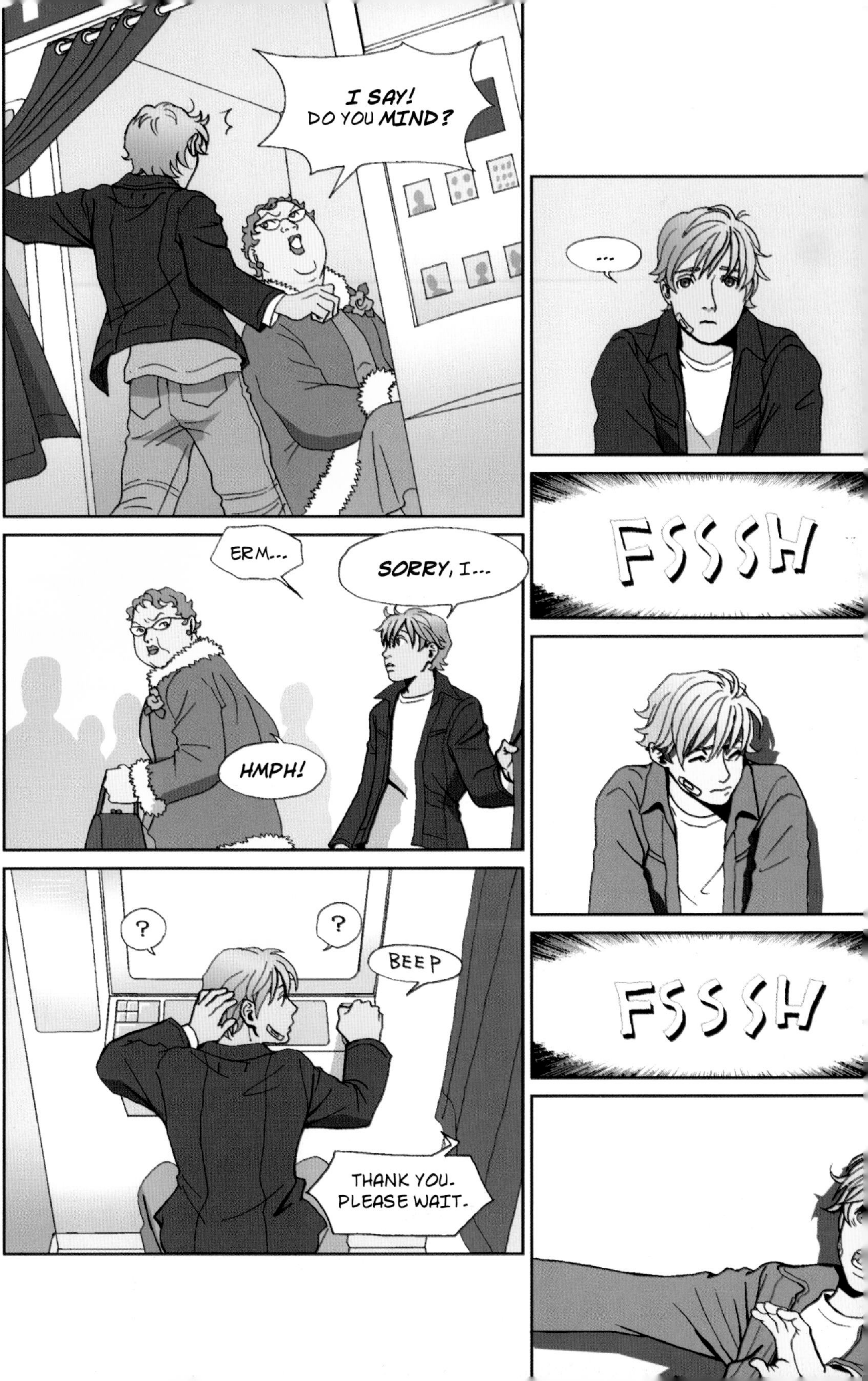
I SAY!
DO YOU MIND?
ERM...
SORRY, I...
HMPH!
?
?
BEEP
THANK YOU.
PLEASE WAIT.
...
FSSSH
FSSSH

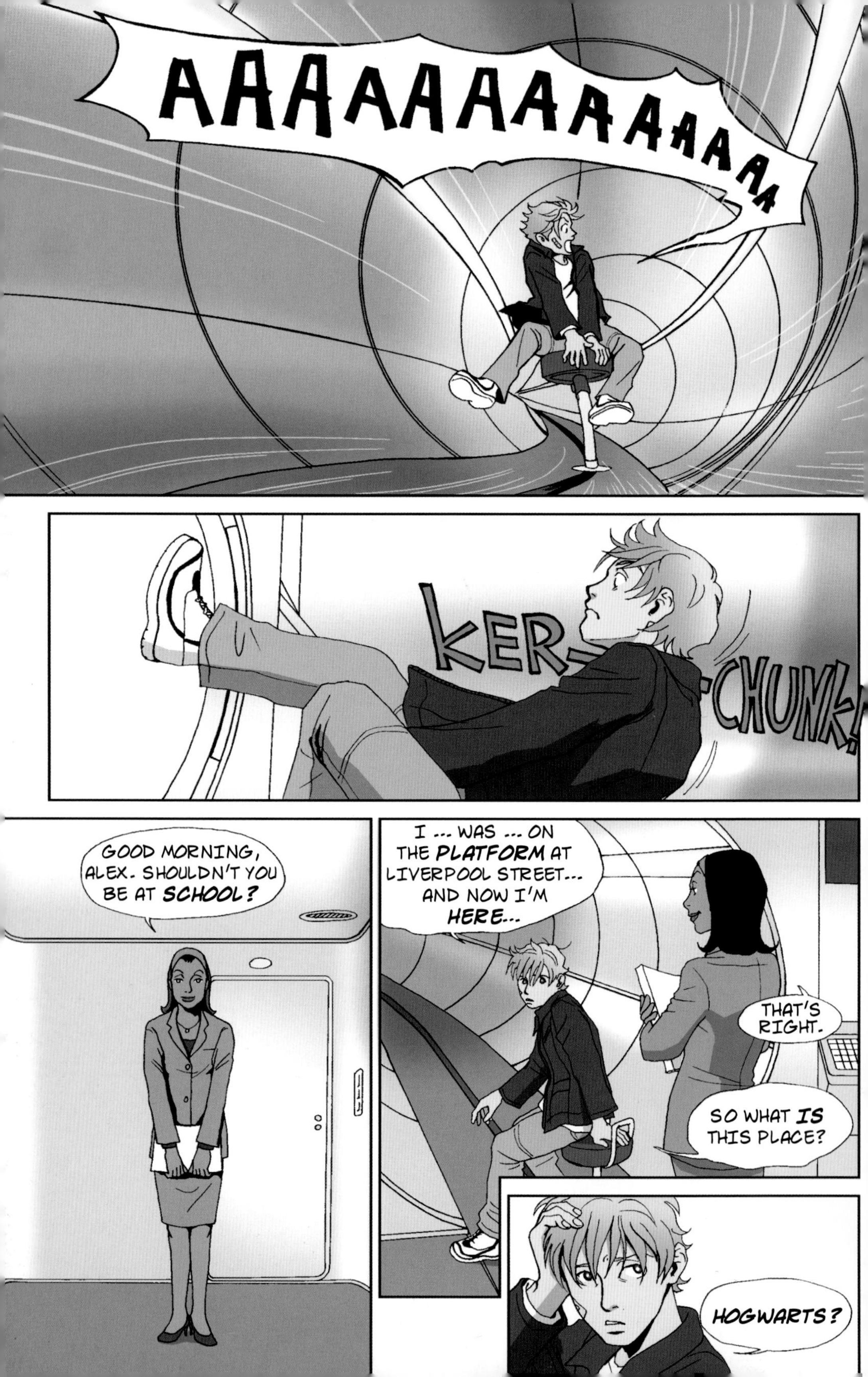
AAAAAAAAAAAAAA
KER-CHUNK!
GOOD MORNING, ALEX. SHOULDN'T YOU BE AT SCHOOL?
I ... WAS ... ON THE PLATFORM AT LIVERPOOL STREET... AND NOW I'M HERE...
THAT'S RIGHT.
SO WHAT IS THIS PLACE?
HOGWARTS?

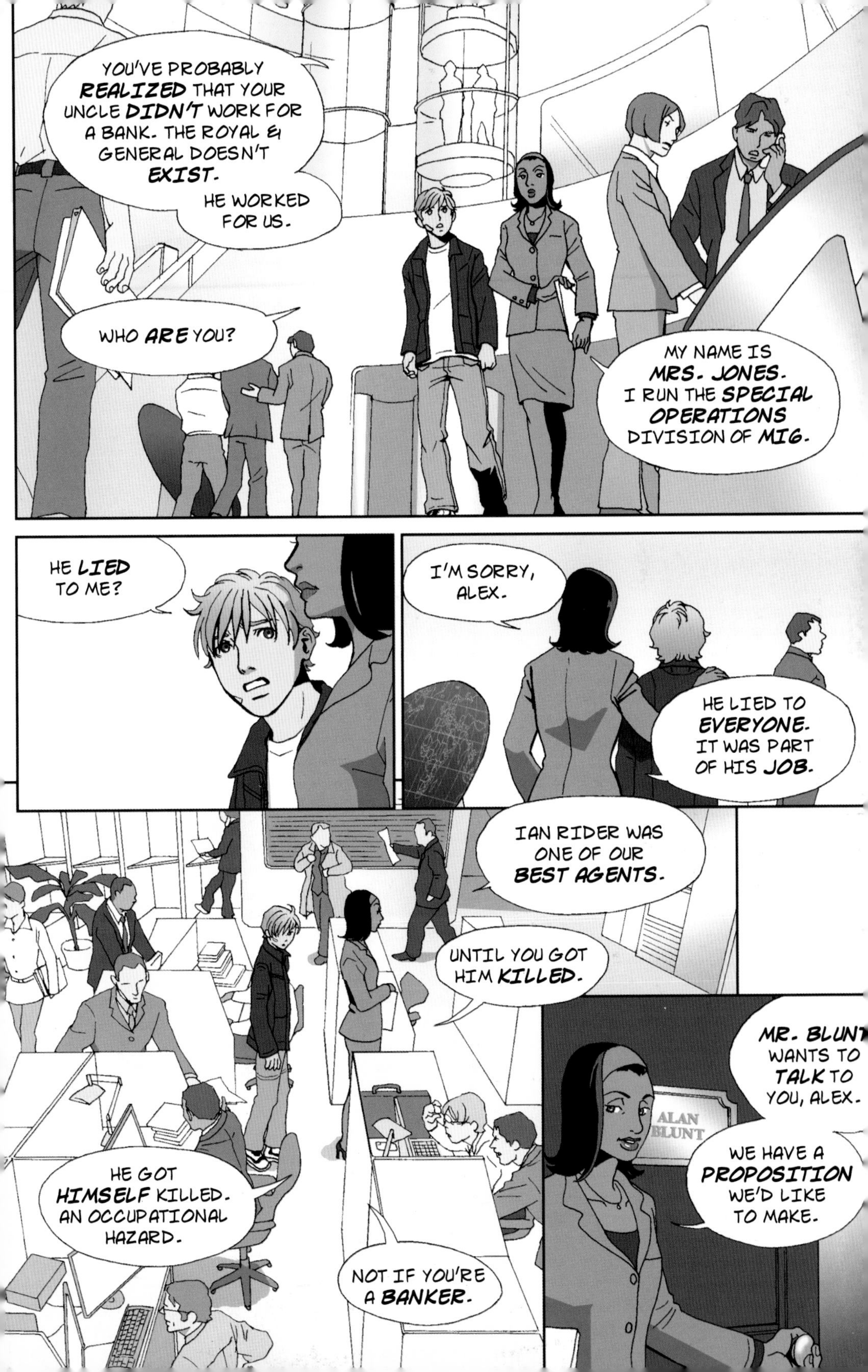
YOU'VE PROBABLY REALIZED THAT YOUR UNCLE DIDN'T WORK FOR A BANK. THE ROYAL & GENERAL DOESN'T EXIST.
HE WORKED FOR US.
WHO ARE YOU?
MY NAME IS MRS. JONES. I RUN THE SPECIAL OPERATIONS DIVISION OF MI6.
HE LIED TO ME?
I'M SORRY, ALEX.
HE LIED TO EVERYONE. IT WAS PART OF HIS JOB.
IAN RIDER WAS ONE OF OUR BEST AGENTS.
UNTIL YOU GOT HIM KILLED.
HE GOT HIMSELF KILLED. AN OCCUPATIONAL HAZARD.
NOT IF YOU'RE A BANKER.
ALAN BLUNT
MR. BLUNT WANTS TO TALK TO YOU, ALEX.
WE HAVE A PROPOSITION WE'D LIKE TO MAKE.

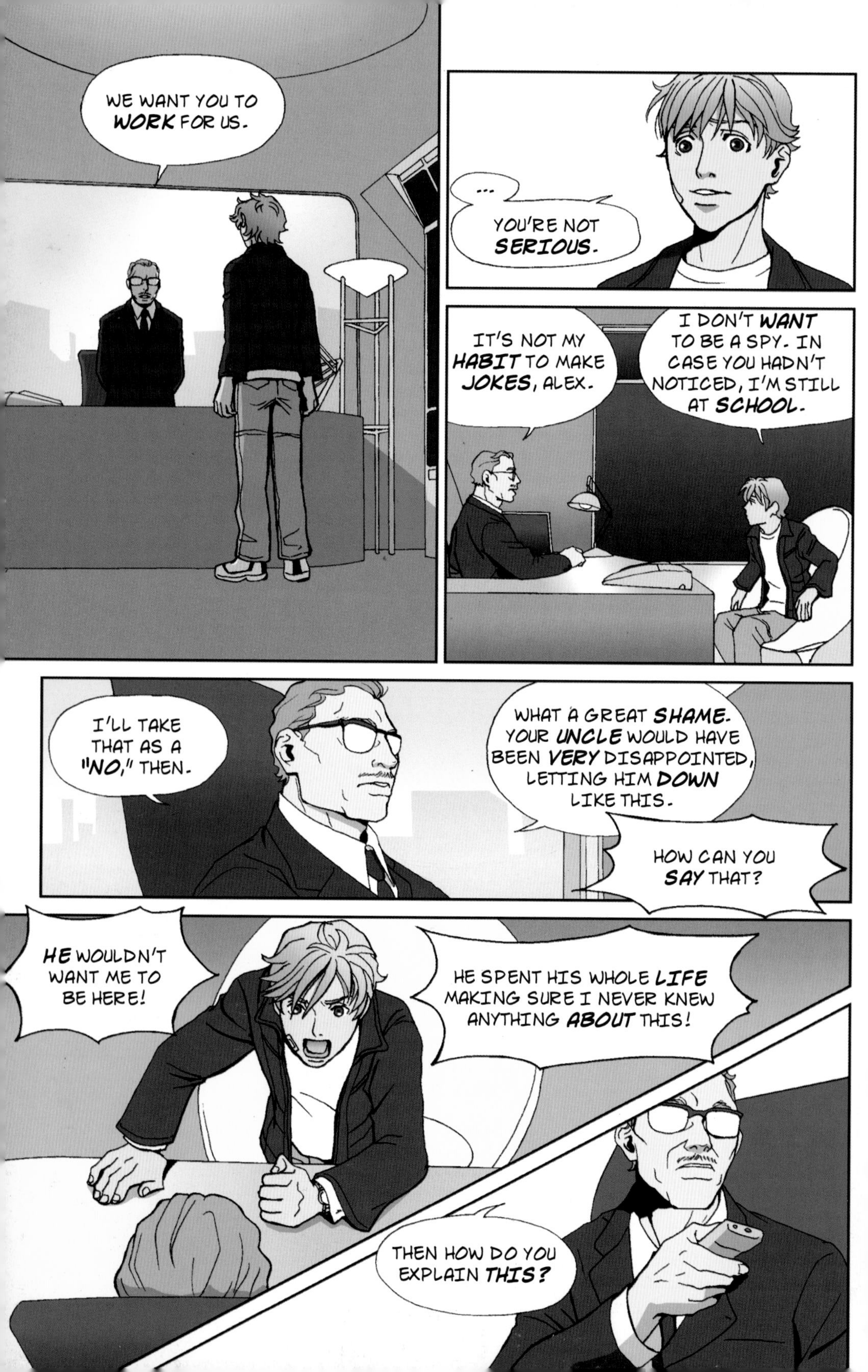
WE WANT YOU TO WORK FOR US.
... YOU'RE NOT SERIOUS.
IT'S NOT MY HABIT TO MAKE JOKES, ALEX.
I DON'T WANT TO BE A SPY. IN CASE YOU HADN'T NOTICED, I'M STILL AT SCHOOL.
I'LL TAKE THAT AS A "NO," THEN.
WHAT A GREAT SHAME. YOUR UNCLE WOULD HAVE BEEN VERY DISAPPOINTED, LETTING HIM DOWN LIKE THIS.
HOW CAN YOU SAY THAT?
HE WOULDN'T WANT ME TO BE HERE!
HE SPENT HIS WHOLE LIFE MAKING SURE I NEVER KNEW ANYTHING ABOUT THIS!
THEN HOW DO YOU EXPLAIN THIS?

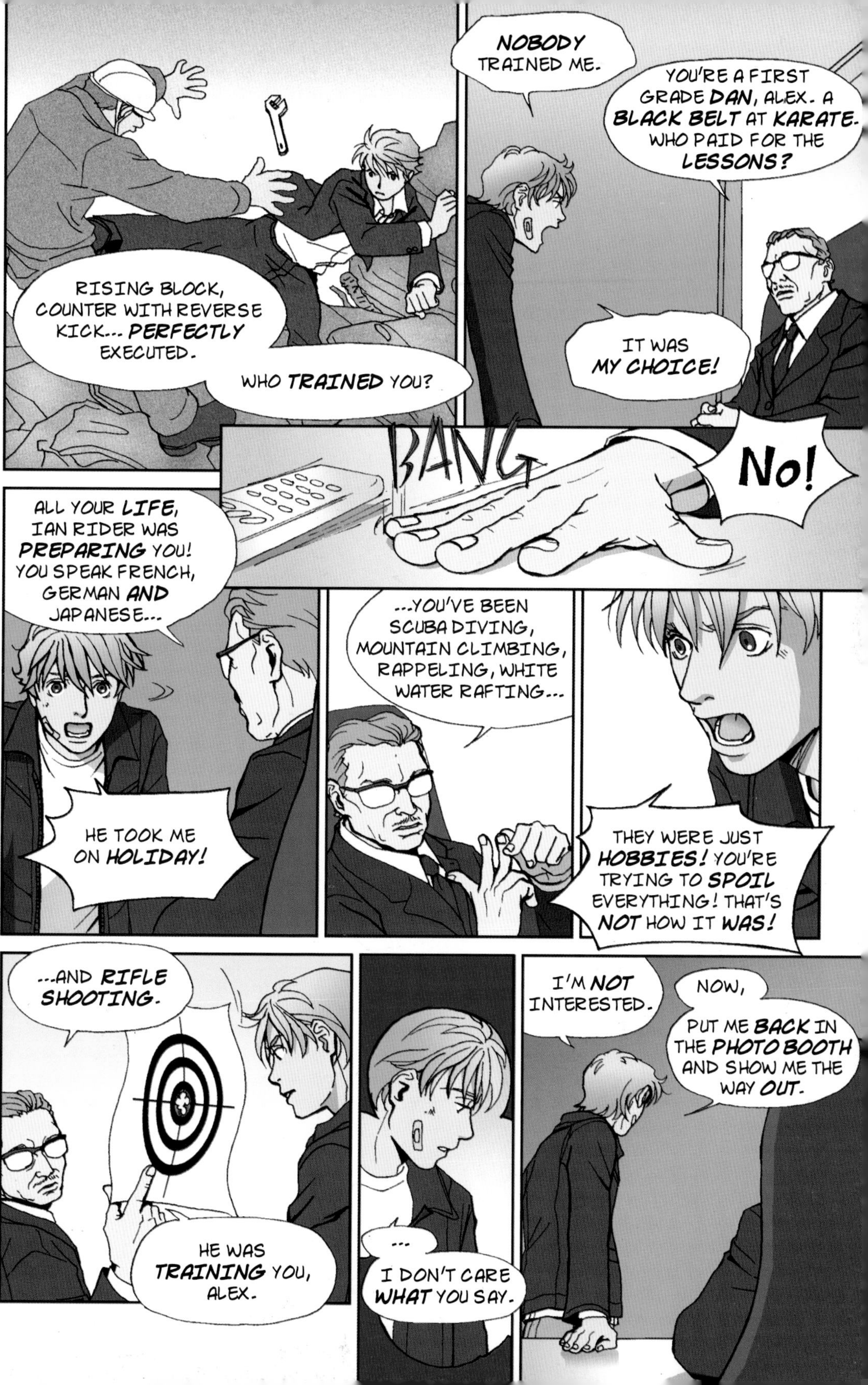
RISING BLOCK, COUNTER WITH REVERSE KICK... PERFECTLY EXECUTED.
WHO TRAINED YOU?
NOBODY TRAINED ME.
YOU'RE A FIRST GRADE DAN, ALEX. A BLACK BELT AT KARATE. WHO PAID FOR THE LESSONS?
IT WAS MY CHOICE!
BANG
No!
ALL YOUR LIFE, IAN RIDER WAS PREPARING YOU! YOU SPEAK FRENCH, GERMAN AND JAPANESE...
HE TOOK ME ON HOLIDAY!
...YOU'VE BEEN SCUBA DIVING, MOUNTAIN CLIMBING, RAPPELING, WHITE WATER RAFTING...
THEY WERE JUST HOBBIES! YOU'RE TRYING TO SPOIL EVERYTHING! THAT'S NOT HOW IT WAS!
...AND RIFLE SHOOTING.
HE WAS TRAINING YOU, ALEX.
...
I DON'T CARE WHAT YOU SAY.
I'M NOT INTERESTED.
NOW,
PUT ME BACK IN THE PHOTO BOOTH AND SHOW ME THE WAY OUT.

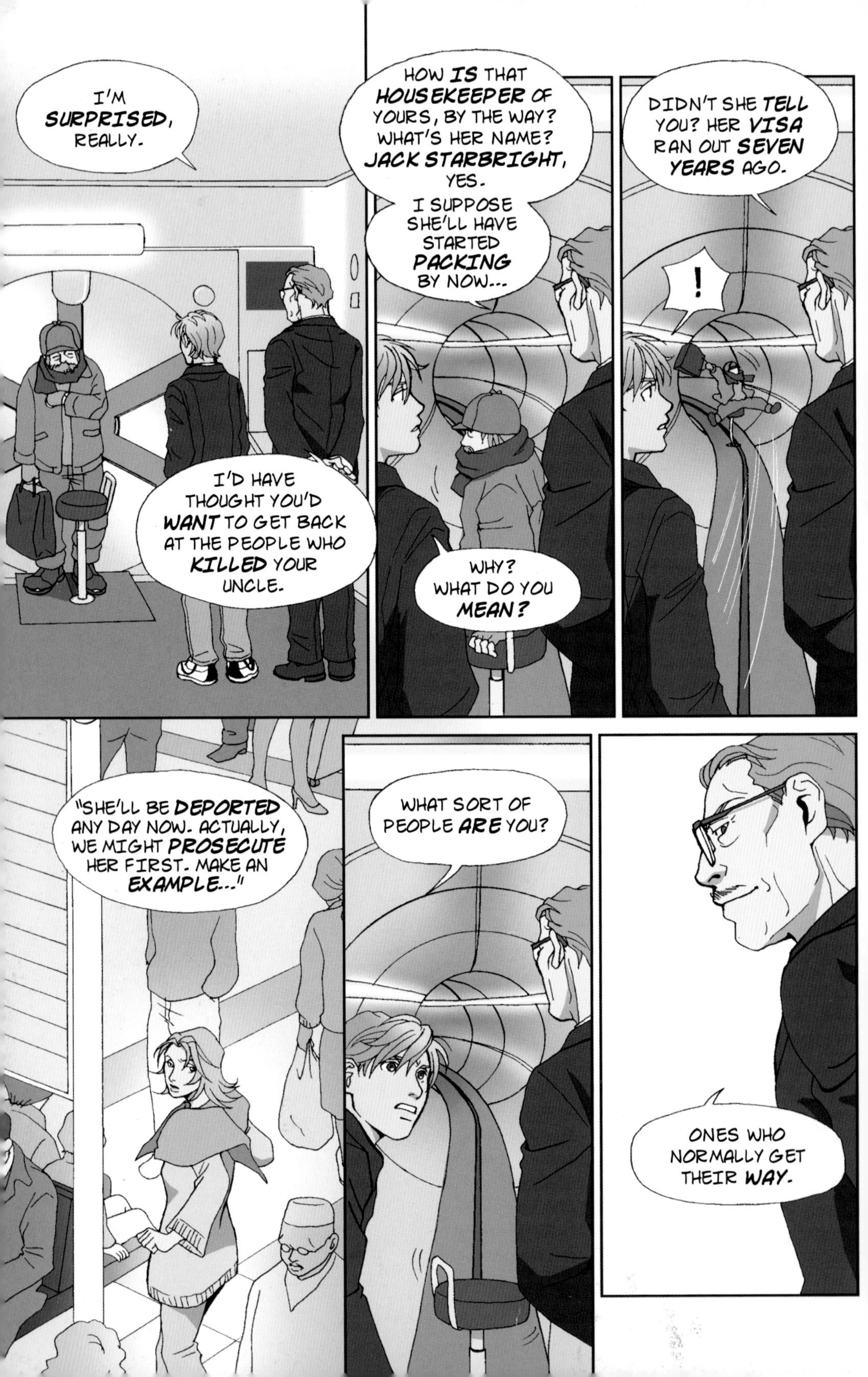
I'M SURPRISED, REALLY.
I'D HAVE THOUGHT YOU'D WANT TO GET BACK AT THE PEOPLE WHO KILLED YOUR UNCLE.
HOW IS THAT HOUSEKEEPER OF YOURS, BY THE WAY? WHAT'S HER NAME? JACK STARBRIGHT, YES.
I SUPPOSE SHE'LL HAVE STARTED PACKING BY NOW...
WHY? WHAT DO YOU MEAN?
DIDN'T SHE TELL YOU? HER VISA RAN OUT SEVEN YEARS AGO.
!
"SHE'LL BE DEPORTED ANY DAY NOW. ACTUALLY, WE MIGHT PROSECUTE HER FIRST. MAKE AN EXAMPLE..."
WHAT SORT OF PEOPLE ARE YOU?
ONES WHO NORMALLY GET THEIR WAY.

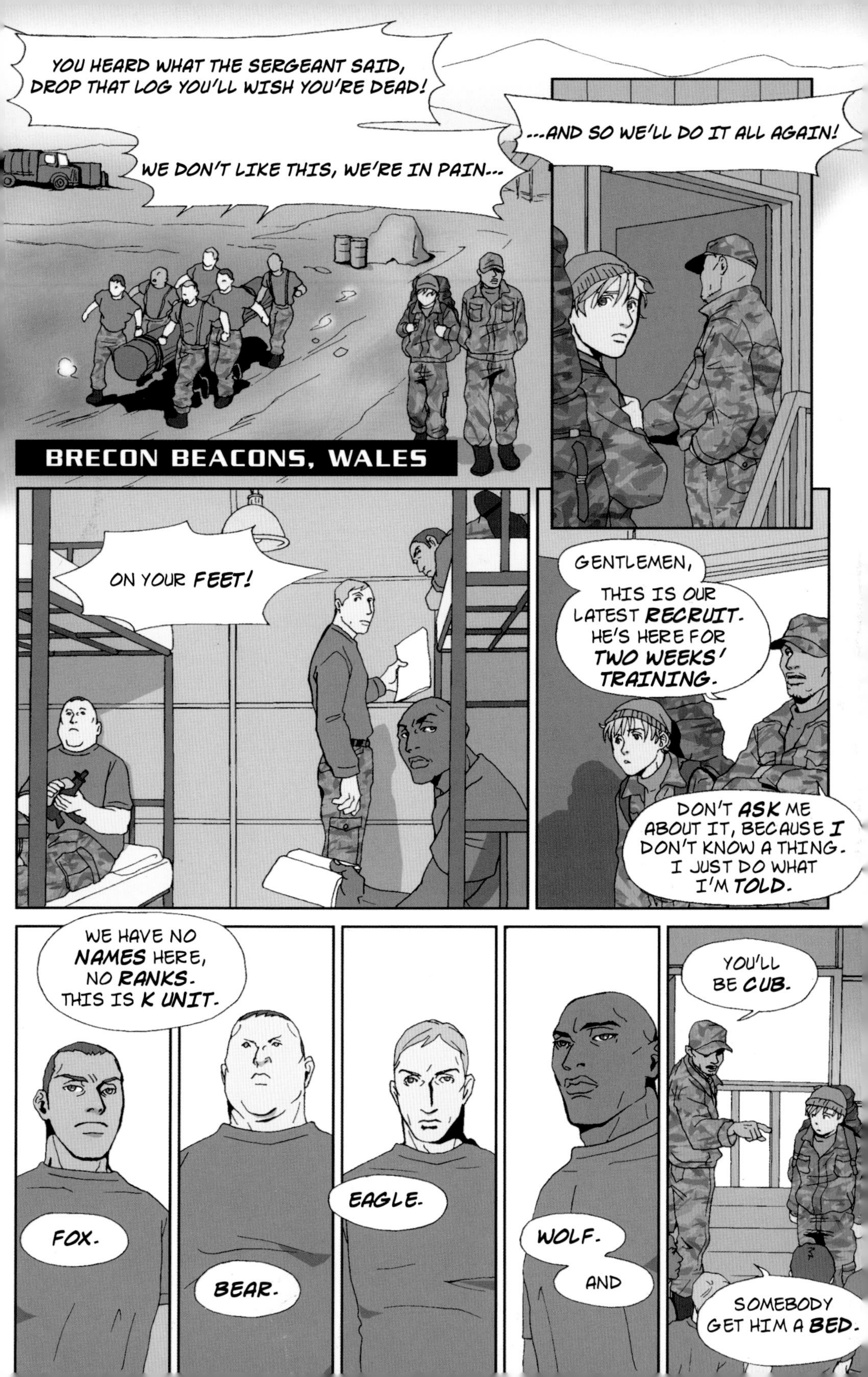
YOU HEARD WHAT THE SERGEANT SAID, DROP THAT LOG YOU'LL WISH YOU'RE DEAD!
WE DON'T LIKE THIS, WE'RE IN PAIN...
...AND SO WE'LL DO IT ALL AGAIN!
BRECON BEACONS, WALES
GENTLEMEN,
THIS IS OUR LATEST RECRUIT. HE'S HERE FOR TWO WEEKS' TRAINING.
DON'T ASK ME ABOUT IT, BECAUSE I DON'T KNOW A THING. I JUST DO WHAT I'M TOLD.
ON YOUR FEET!
WE HAVE NO NAMES HERE, NO RANKS. THIS IS K UNIT.
FOX.
BEAR.
EAGLE.
WOLF.
AND
YOU'LL BE CUB.
SOMEBODY GET HIM A BED.

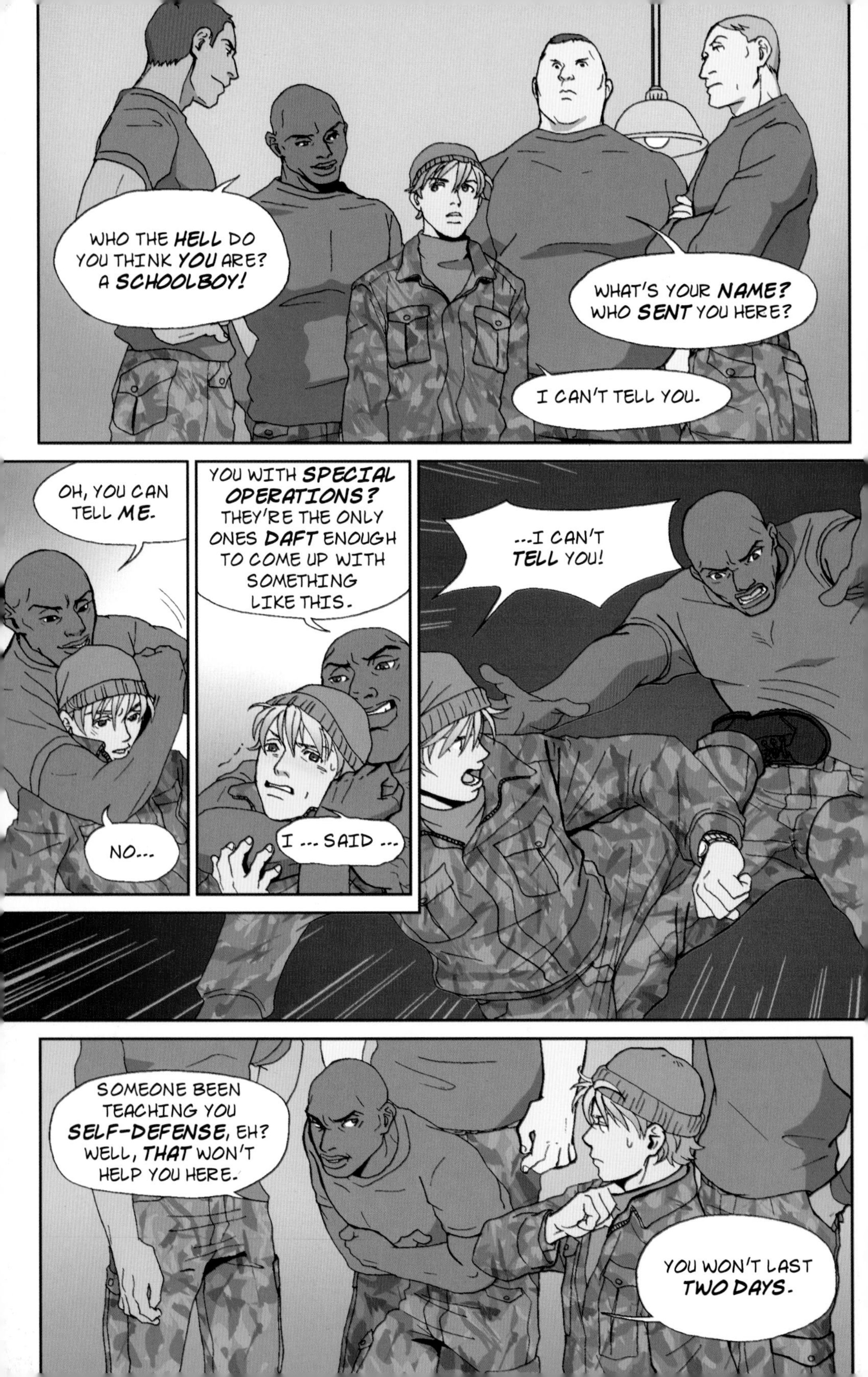
WHO THE HELL DO YOU THINK YOU ARE? A SCHOOLBOY!
WHAT'S YOUR NAME? WHO SENT YOU HERE?
I CAN'T TELL YOU.
OH, YOU CAN TELL ME.
NO...
YOU WITH SPECIAL OPERATIONS? THEY'RE THE ONLY ONES DAFT ENOUGH TO COME UP WITH SOMETHING LIKE THIS.
I ... SAID ...
...I CAN'T TELL YOU!
SOMEONE BEEN TEACHING YOU SELF-DEFENSE, EH? WELL, THAT WON'T HELP YOU HERE.
YOU WON'T LAST TWO DAYS.

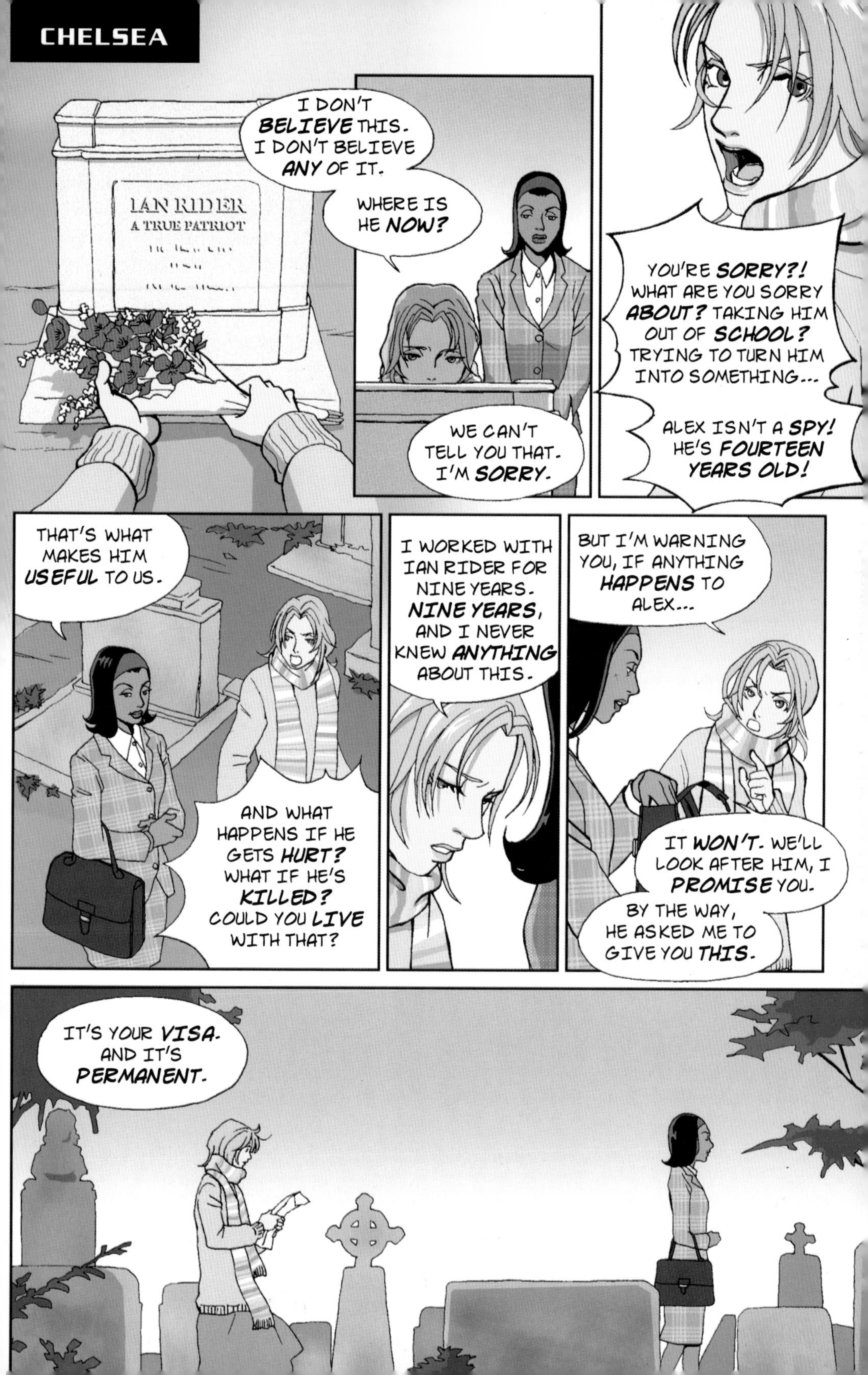
CHELSEA
IAN RIDER
A TRUE PATRIOT
I DON'T BELIEVE THIS. I DON'T BELIEVE ANY OF IT.
WHERE IS HE NOW?
WE CAN'T TELL YOU THAT. I'M SORRY.
YOU'RE SORRY?! WHAT ARE YOU SORRY ABOUT? TAKING HIM OUT OF SCHOOL? TRYING TO TURN HIM INTO SOMETHING...
ALEX ISN'T A SPY! HE'S FOURTEEN YEARS OLD!
THAT'S WHAT MAKES HIM USEFUL TO US.
AND WHAT HAPPENS IF HE GETS HURT? WHAT IF HE'S KILLED? COULD YOU LIVE WITH THAT?
I WORKED WITH IAN RIDER FOR NINE YEARS. NINE YEARS, AND I NEVER KNEW ANYTHING ABOUT THIS.
BUT I'M WARNING YOU, IF ANYTHING HAPPENS TO ALEX...
IT WON'T. WE'LL LOOK AFTER HIM, I PROMISE YOU.
BY THE WAY, HE ASKED ME TO GIVE YOU THIS.
IT'S YOUR VISA. AND IT'S PERMANENT.

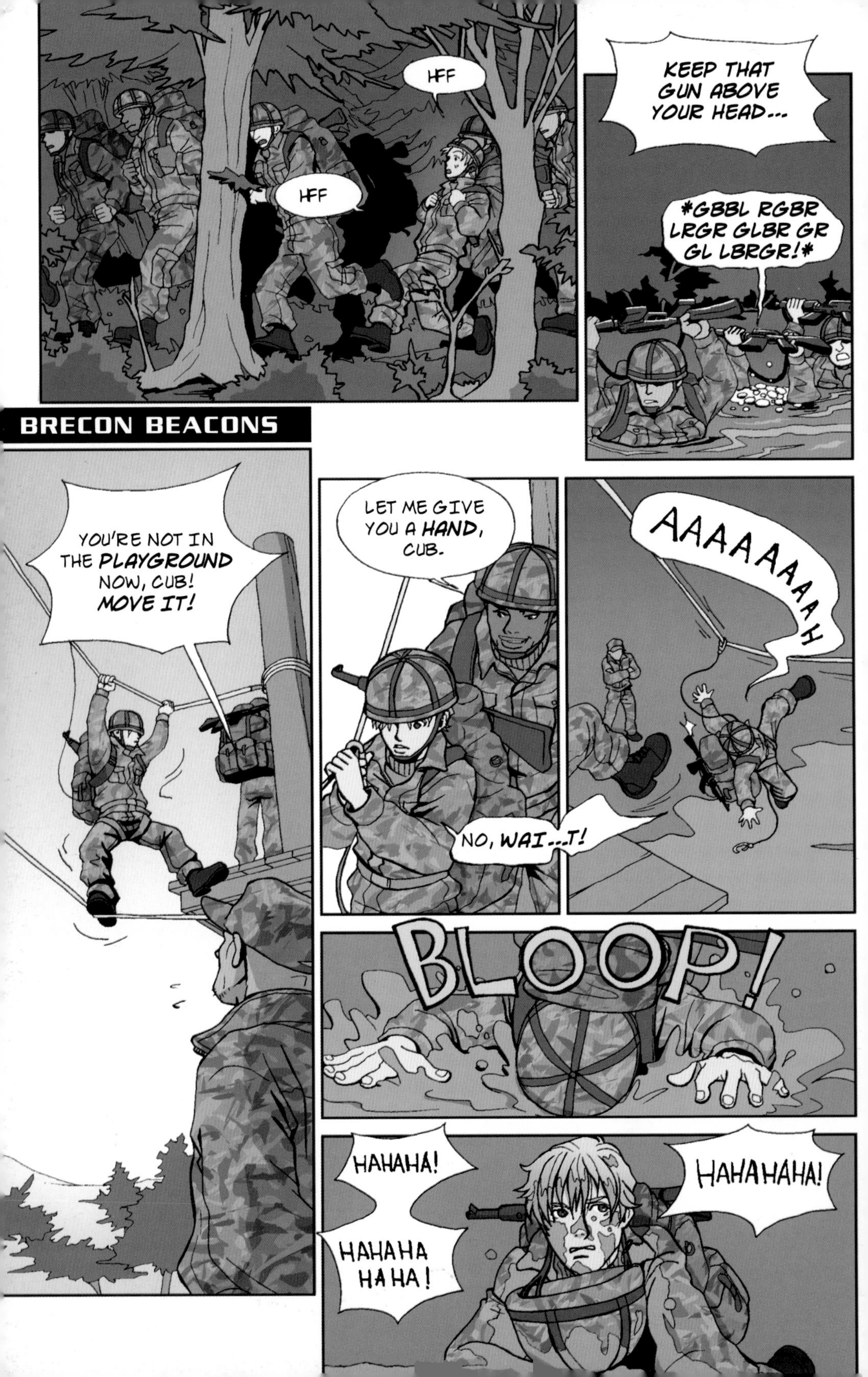
HFF
HFF
KEEP THAT GUN ABOVE YOUR HEAD...
GBBL RGBR LRGR GLBR GR GL LBRGR!
BRECON BEACONS
YOU'RE NOT IN THE PLAYGROUND NOW, CUB! MOVE IT!
LET ME GIVE YOU A HAND, CUB.
NO, WAI...T!
AAAAAAAAAH
BLOOP!
HAHAHA!
HAHAHAHA!
HAHAHA HAHA!

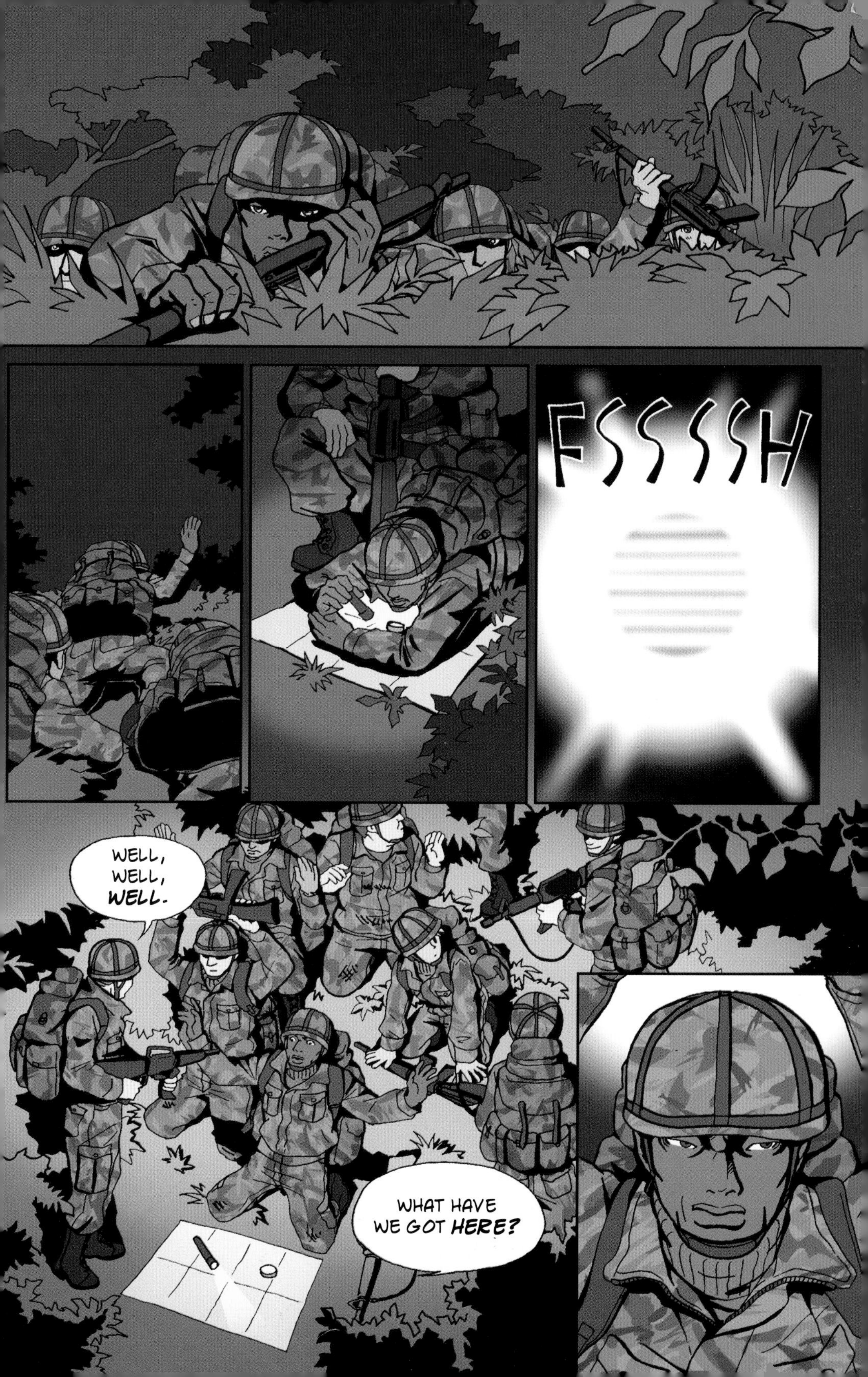
FSSSSH
WELL, WELL, WELL.
WHAT HAVE WE GOT HERE?

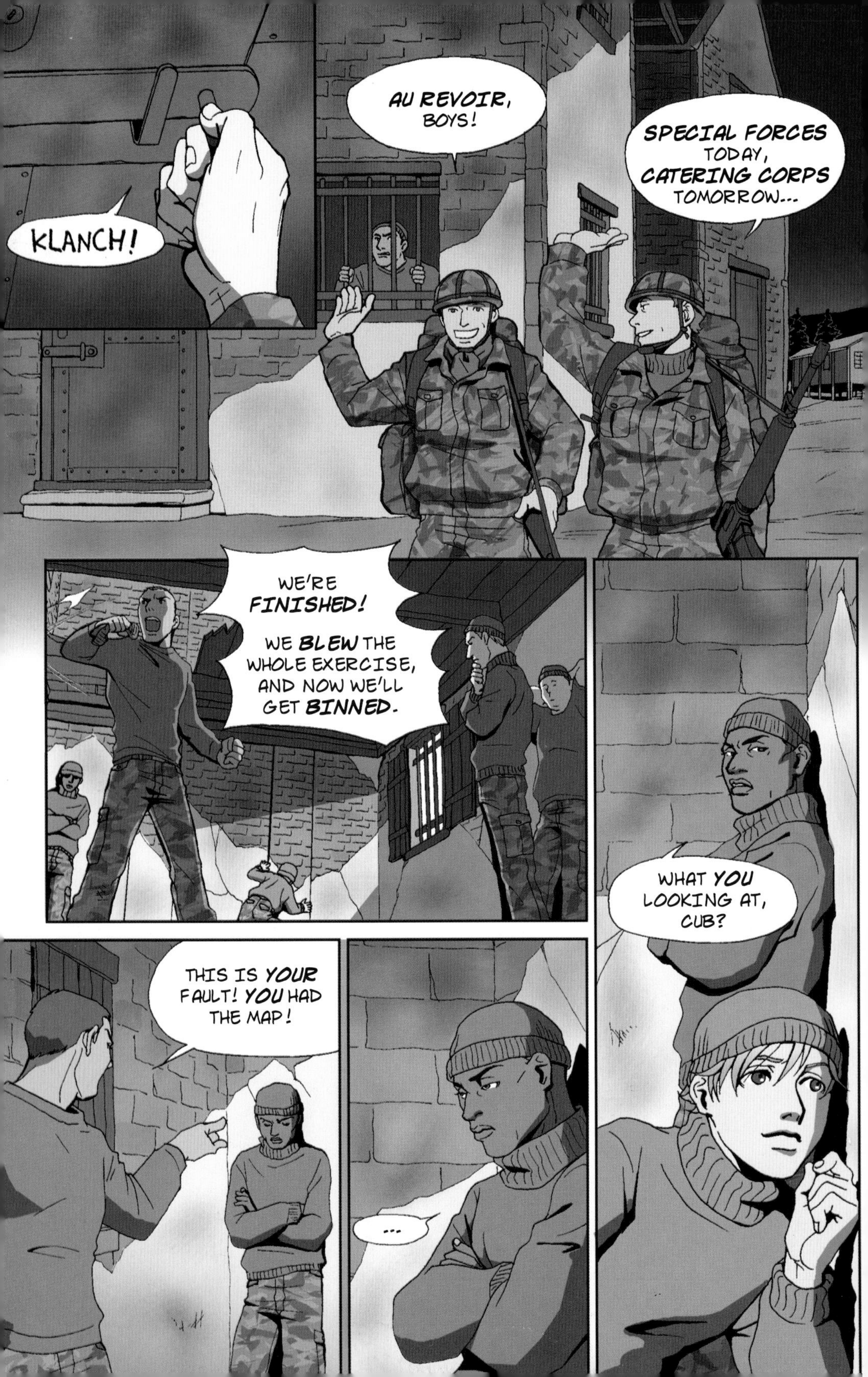
KLANCH!
AU REVOIR, BOYS!
SPECIAL FORCES TODAY, CATERING CORPS TOMORROW...
WE'RE FINISHED!
WE BLEW THE WHOLE EXERCISE, AND NOW WE'LL GET BINNED.
WHAT YOU LOOKING AT, CUB?
THIS IS YOUR FAULT! YOU HAD THE MAP!
...

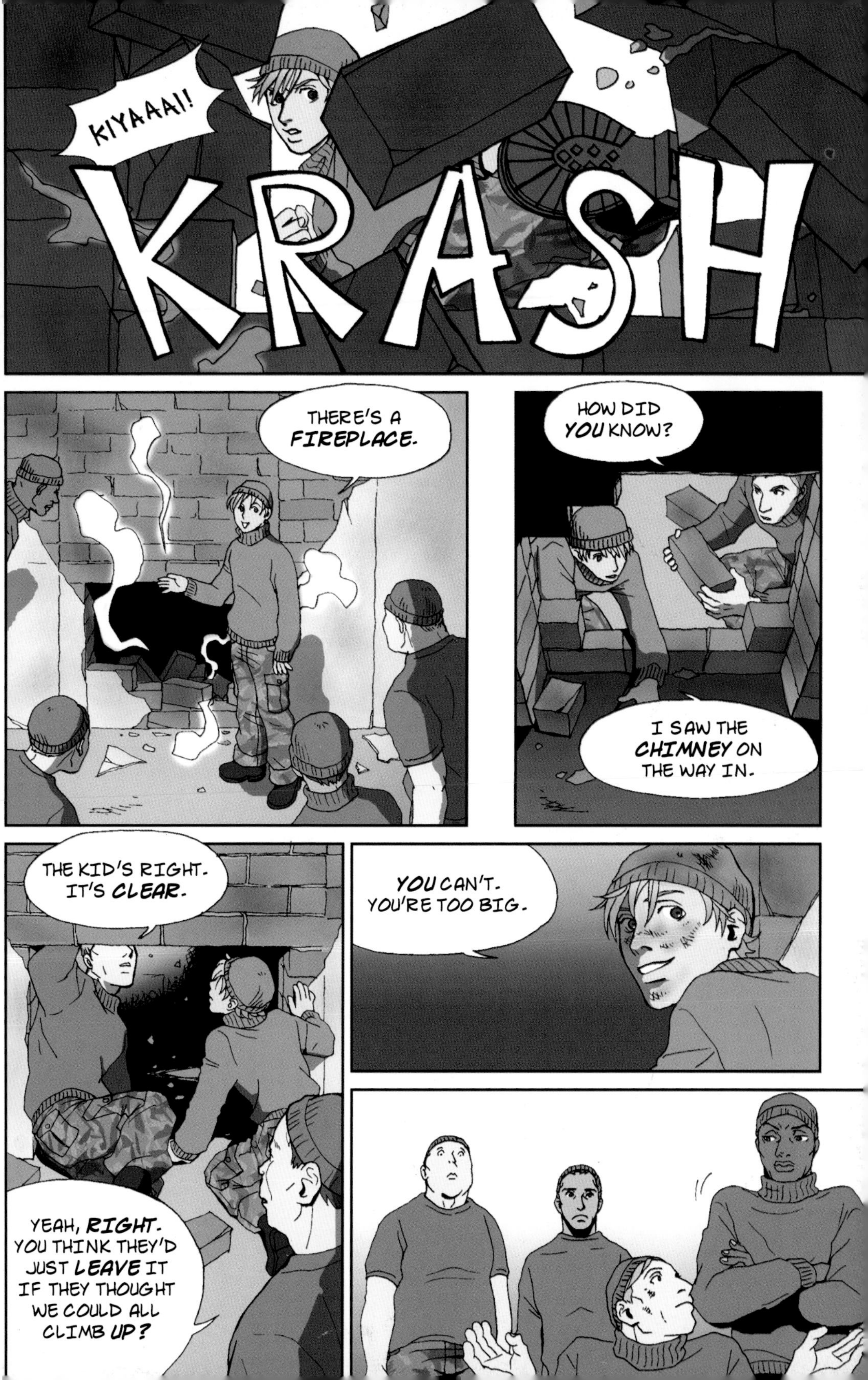
KIYAAAI!
KRASH
THERE'S A FIREPLACE.
HOW DID YOU KNOW?
I SAW THE CHIMNEY ON THE WAY IN.
THE KID'S RIGHT. IT'S CLEAR.
YOU CAN'T. YOU'RE TOO BIG.
YEAH, RIGHT. YOU THINK THEY'D JUST LEAVE IT IF THEY THOUGHT WE COULD ALL CLIMB UP?

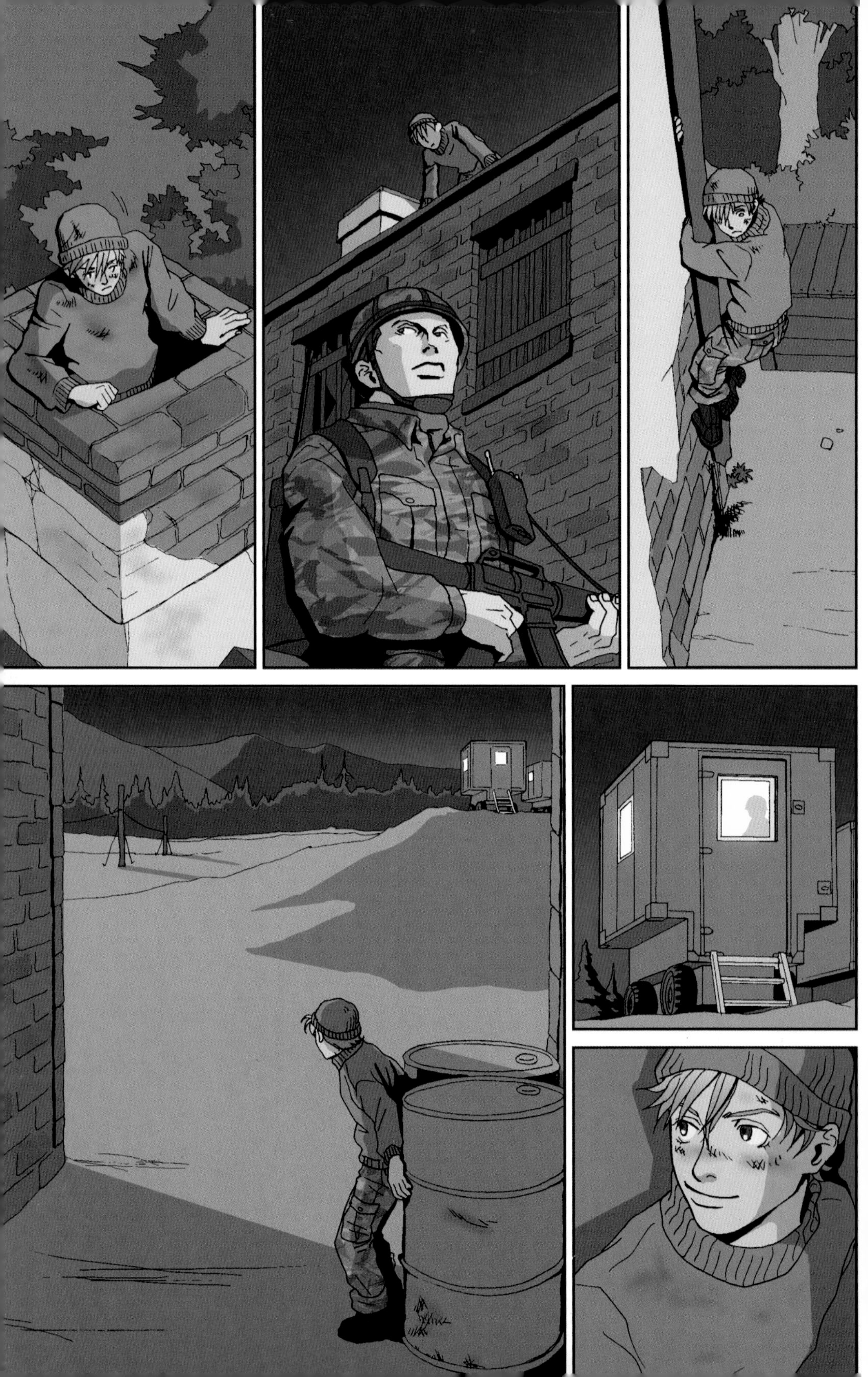

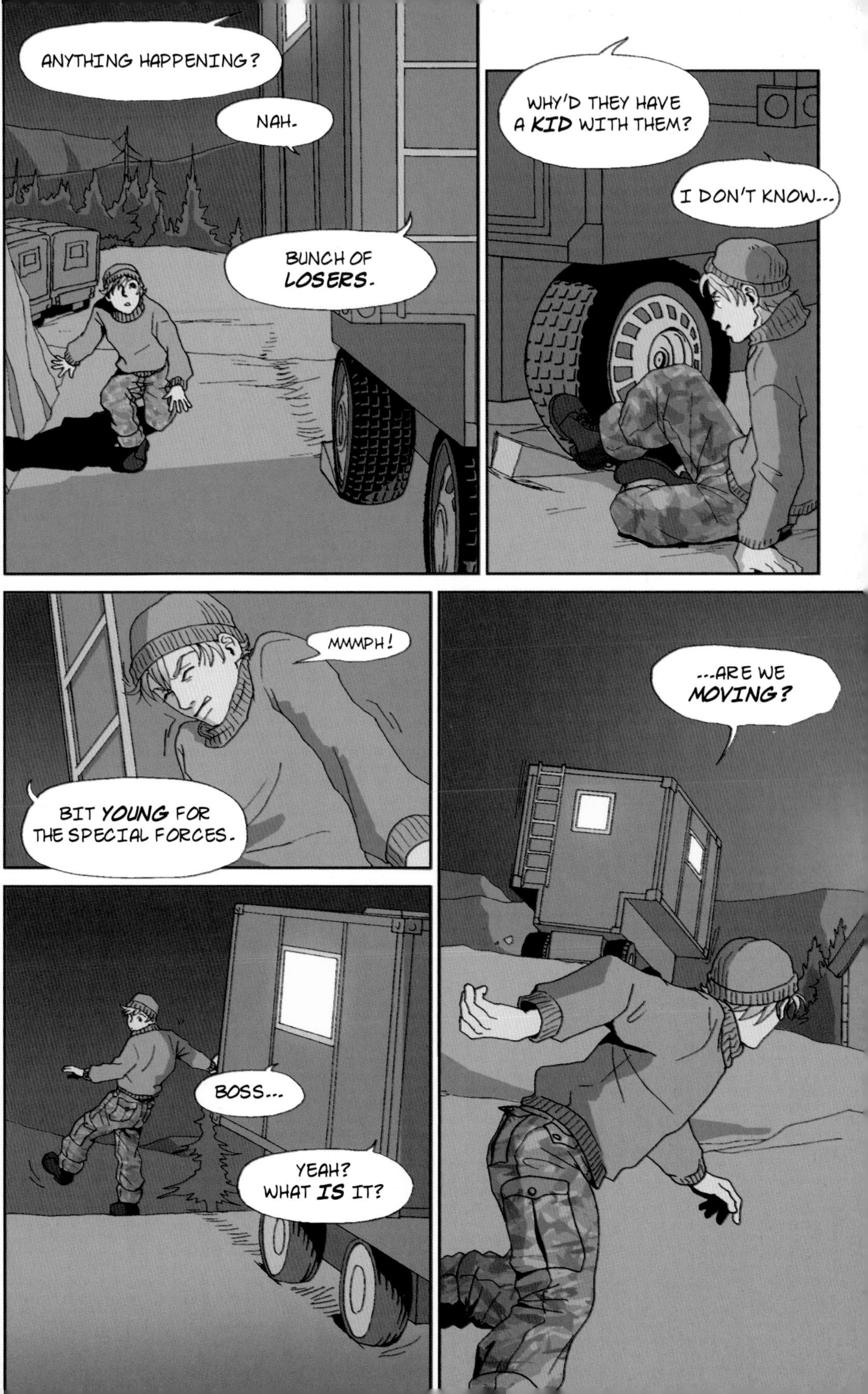
ANYTHING HAPPENING?
NAH.
BUNCH OF LOSERS.
WHY'D THEY HAVE A KID WITH THEM?
I DON'T KNOW...
MMMPH!
BIT YOUNG FOR THE SPECIAL FORCES.
BOSS...
YEAH? WHAT IS IT?
...ARE WE MOVING?

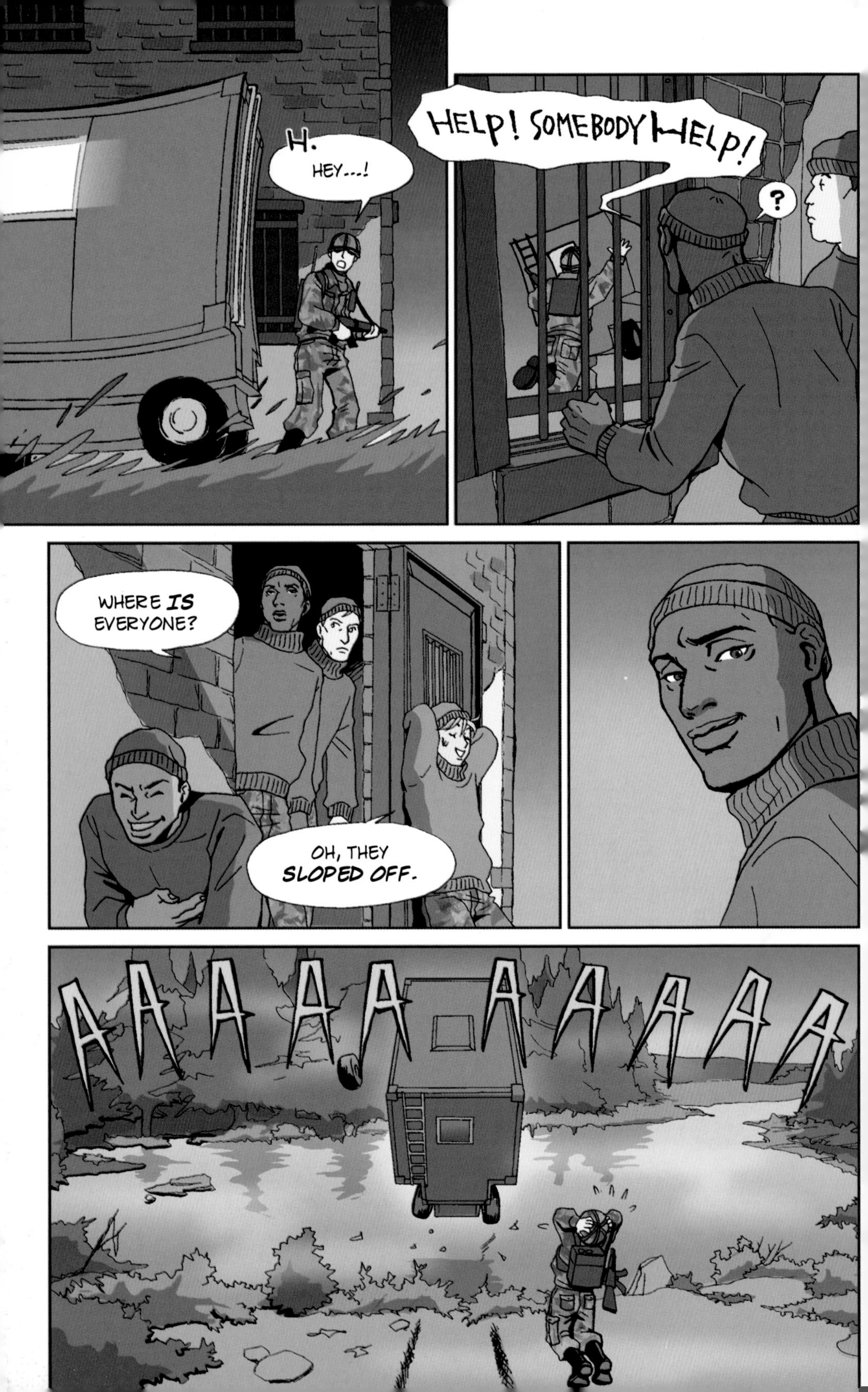
H.
HEY...!
HELP! SOMEBODY HELP!
?
WHERE IS EVERYONE?
OH, THEY SLOPED OFF.
AAAAAAAAAA

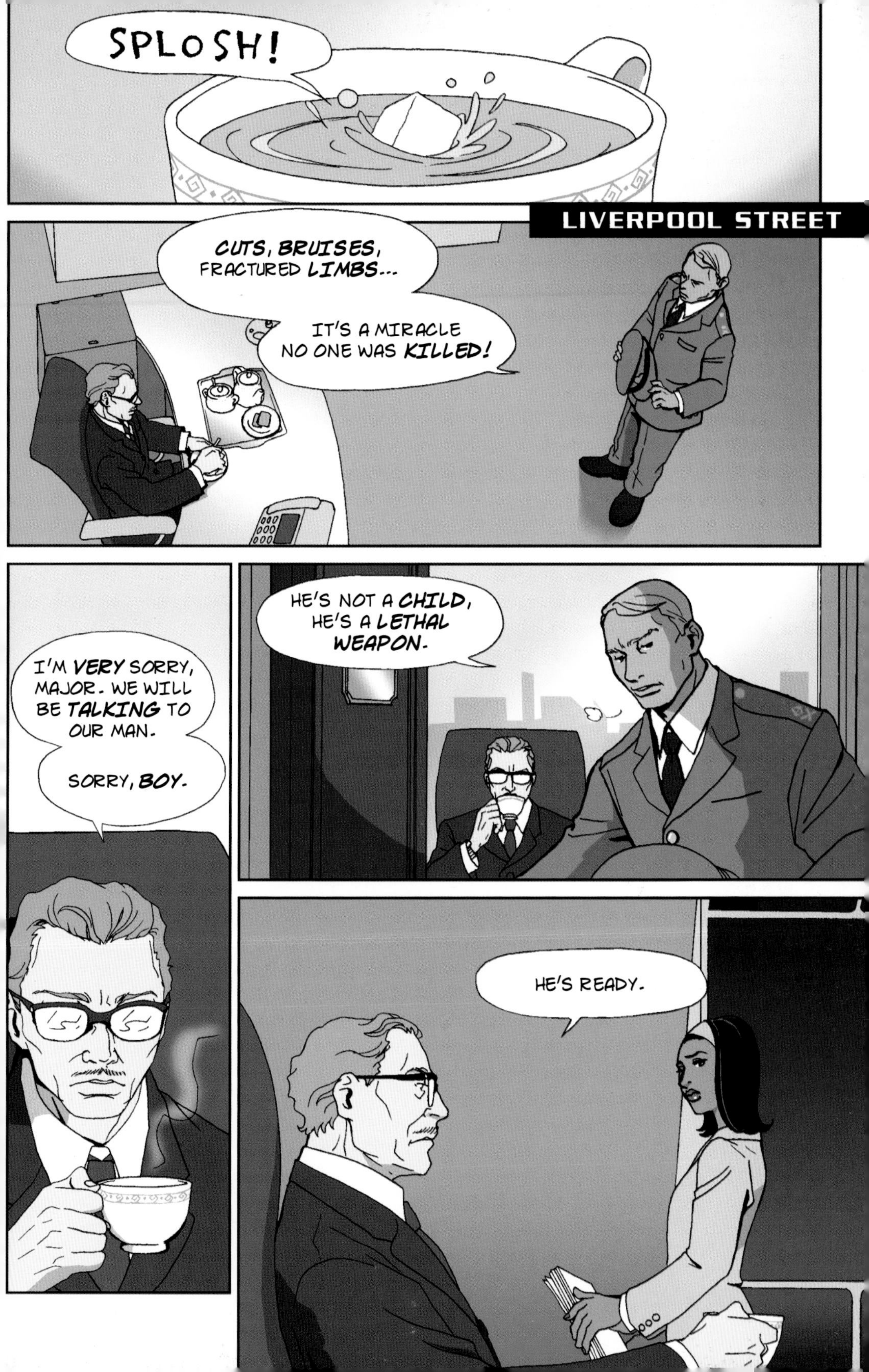
SPLOSH!
LIVERPOOL STREET
CUTS, BRUISES, FRACTURED LIMBS...
IT'S A MIRACLE NO ONE WAS KILLED!
I'M VERY SORRY, MAJOR. WE WILL BE TALKING TO OUR MAN.
SORRY, BOY.
HE'S NOT A CHILD, HE'S A LETHAL WEAPON.
HE'S READY.

FINALLY,

THE MOST **GENEROUS** GIFT **EVER MADE** TO THE BRITISH NATION.

HEADLINES: EVERY SCH... ...HE UR TO BE GI... HE STORMBR...

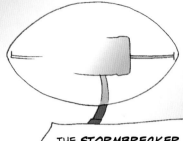

THE **STORMBREAKER** HAS BEEN CALLED THE MOST **SOPHISTICATED** PERSONAL COMPUTER OF THE 21ST CENTURY...

...AND LAST MONTH, ITS MULTIBILLIONAIRE INVENTOR, **DARRIUS SAYLE,** MADE HIS ASTONISHING **ANNOUNCEMENT.**

LIVE

THAT'S **RIGHT,** VIVIEN. I WANT TO GIVE A **FREE STORMBREAKER** TO **EVERY** SCHOOL IN THE COUNTRY.

...HISTICATED PC.

AND WHILE I'M **AT** IT, I WOULDN'T MIND GIVING **YOU** ONE TOO.

LIVE

REALLY, MR. SAYLE!

...PC.   DARRIUS SAYLE S... ...ONTRIBU...

THE **PRIME MINISTER** HAS GIVEN HIS FULL SUPPORT...

THIS IS A **WONDERFUL** OPPORTUNITY FOR BRITISH SCHOOLS, AND I'M **HONORED** THAT MR. SAYLE HAS ASKED **ME** TO PRESS THE BUTTON THAT WILL BRING ALL THE COMPUTERS **ONLINE.**

OOL IN THE UK TO BE GIVEN THE STORMBREAKER.

---JUST AS IT HAS **RECENTLY** COME TO LIGHT THAT HE AND MR. SAYLE WERE AT **SCHOOL** TOGETHER.

FORTUNE

Inside Darrius Sayle
::::::::::::
::::::::::::

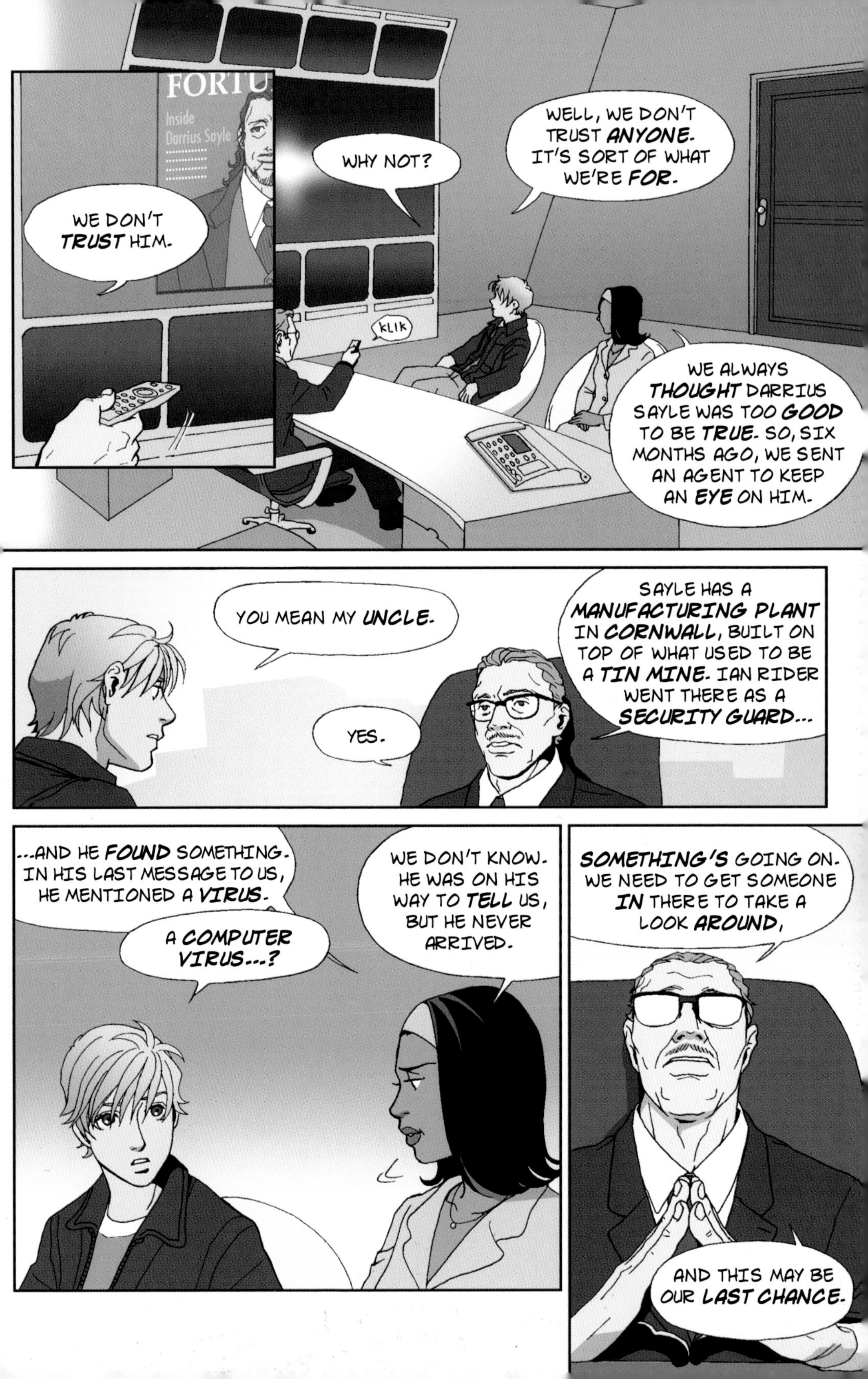
FORTU
Inside Darrius Sayle
WE DON'T TRUST HIM.
WHY NOT?
WELL, WE DON'T TRUST ANYONE. IT'S SORT OF WHAT WE'RE FOR.
KLIK
WE ALWAYS THOUGHT DARRIUS SAYLE WAS TOO GOOD TO BE TRUE. SO, SIX MONTHS AGO, WE SENT AN AGENT TO KEEP AN EYE ON HIM.
YOU MEAN MY UNCLE.
YES.
SAYLE HAS A MANUFACTURING PLANT IN CORNWALL, BUILT ON TOP OF WHAT USED TO BE A TIN MINE. IAN RIDER WENT THERE AS A SECURITY GUARD...
...AND HE FOUND SOMETHING. IN HIS LAST MESSAGE TO US, HE MENTIONED A VIRUS.
A COMPUTER VIRUS...?
WE DON'T KNOW. HE WAS ON HIS WAY TO TELL US, BUT HE NEVER ARRIVED.
SOMETHING'S GOING ON. WE NEED TO GET SOMEONE IN THERE TO TAKE A LOOK AROUND,
AND THIS MAY BE OUR LAST CHANCE.

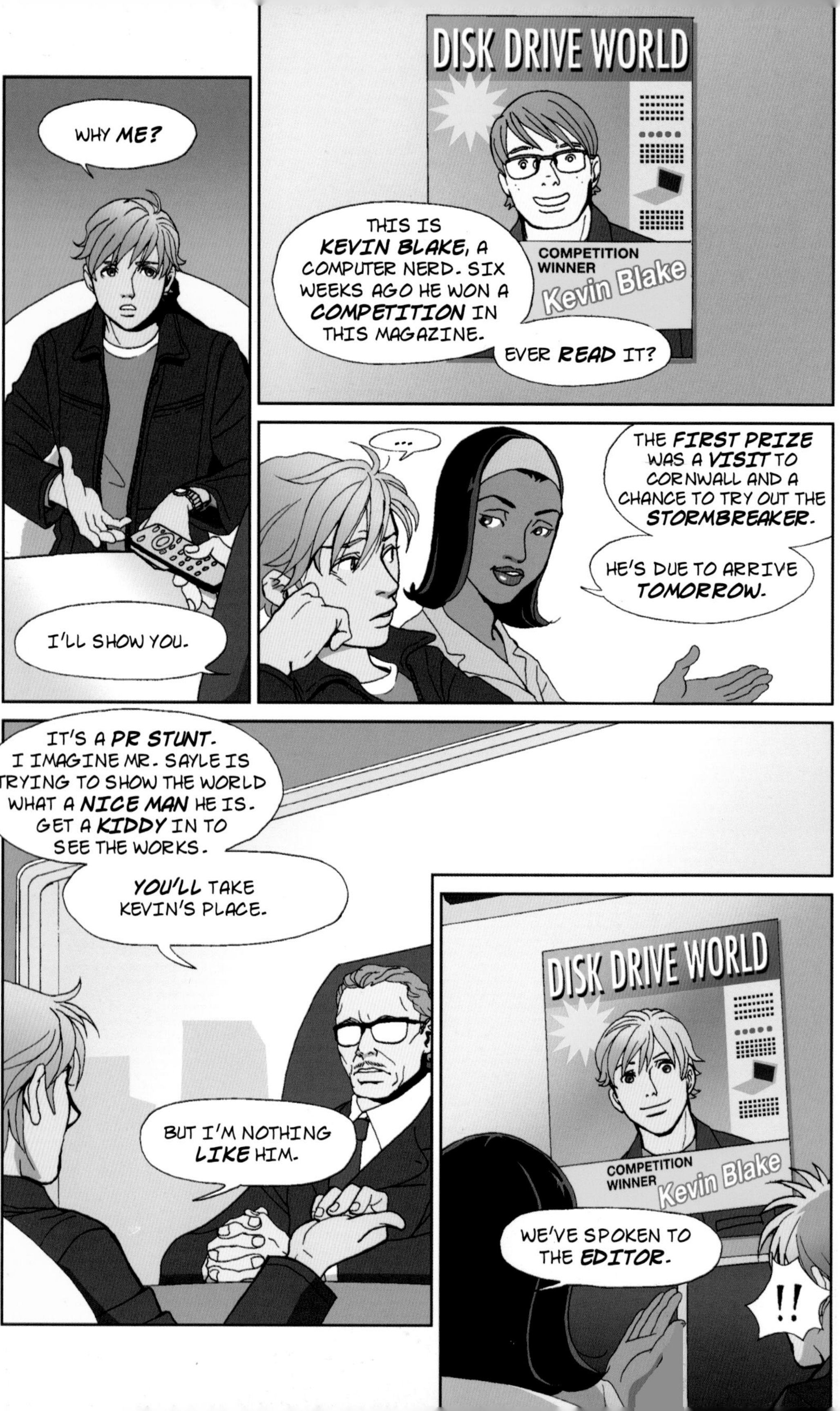
WHY ME?
DISK DRIVE WORLD
THIS IS KEVIN BLAKE, A COMPUTER NERD. SIX WEEKS AGO HE WON A COMPETITION IN THIS MAGAZINE.
COMPETITION WINNER
Kevin Blake
EVER READ IT?
I'LL SHOW YOU.
...
THE FIRST PRIZE WAS A VISIT TO CORNWALL AND A CHANCE TO TRY OUT THE STORMBREAKER.
HE'S DUE TO ARRIVE TOMORROW.
IT'S A PR STUNT. I IMAGINE MR. SAYLE IS TRYING TO SHOW THE WORLD WHAT A NICE MAN HE IS. GET A KIDDY IN TO SEE THE WORKS.
YOU'LL TAKE KEVIN'S PLACE.
BUT I'M NOTHING LIKE HIM.
DISK DRIVE WORLD
COMPETITION WINNER
Kevin Blake
WE'VE SPOKEN TO THE EDITOR.
!!

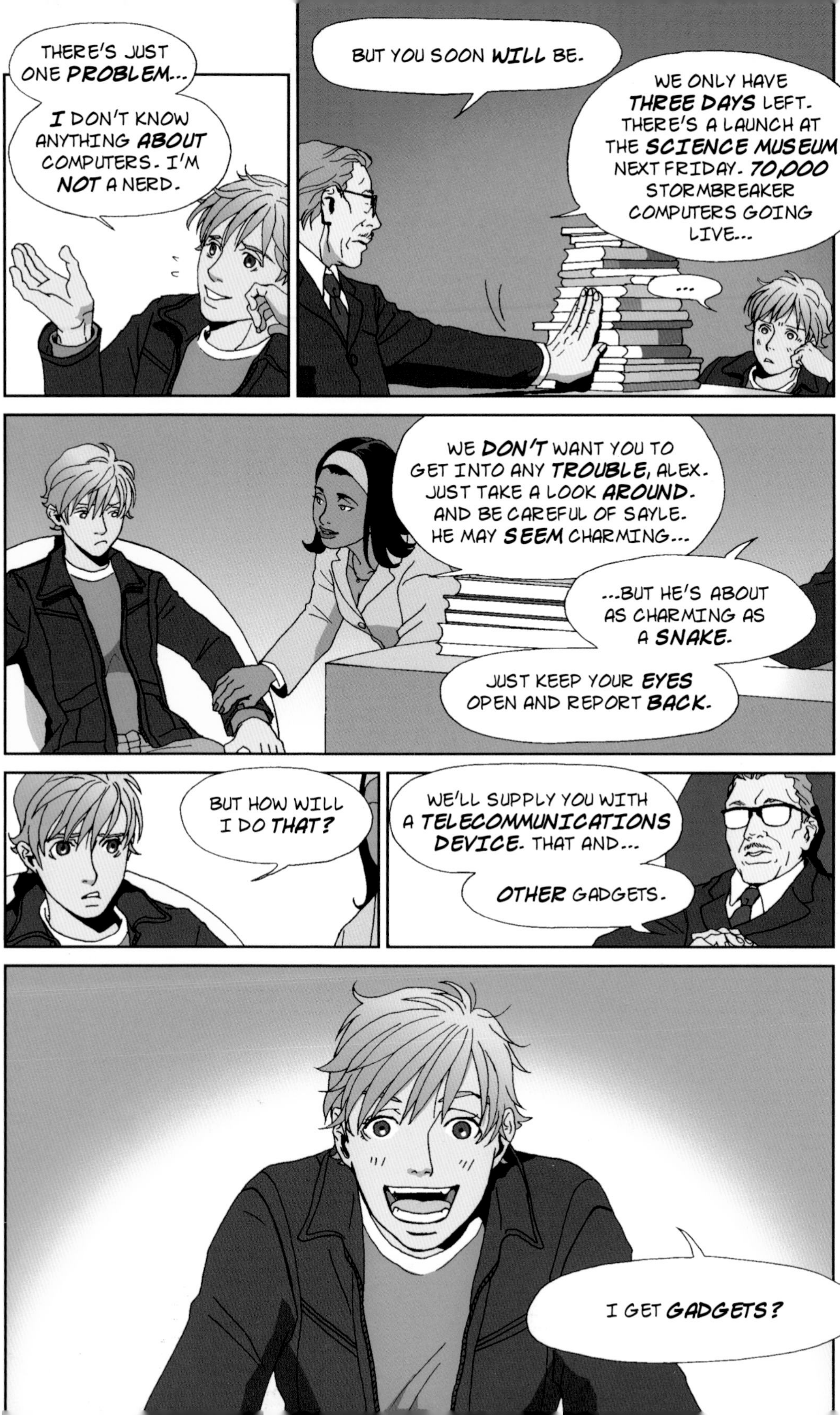
THERE'S JUST ONE PROBLEM...
I DON'T KNOW ANYTHING ABOUT COMPUTERS. I'M NOT A NERD.
BUT YOU SOON WILL BE.
WE ONLY HAVE THREE DAYS LEFT. THERE'S A LAUNCH AT THE SCIENCE MUSEUM NEXT FRIDAY. 70,000 STORMBREAKER COMPUTERS GOING LIVE...
...
WE DON'T WANT YOU TO GET INTO ANY TROUBLE, ALEX. JUST TAKE A LOOK AROUND. AND BE CAREFUL OF SAYLE. HE MAY SEEM CHARMING...
...BUT HE'S ABOUT AS CHARMING AS A SNAKE.
JUST KEEP YOUR EYES OPEN AND REPORT BACK.
BUT HOW WILL I DO THAT?
WE'LL SUPPLY YOU WITH A TELECOMMUNICATIONS DEVICE. THAT AND...
OTHER GADGETS.
I GET GADGETS?

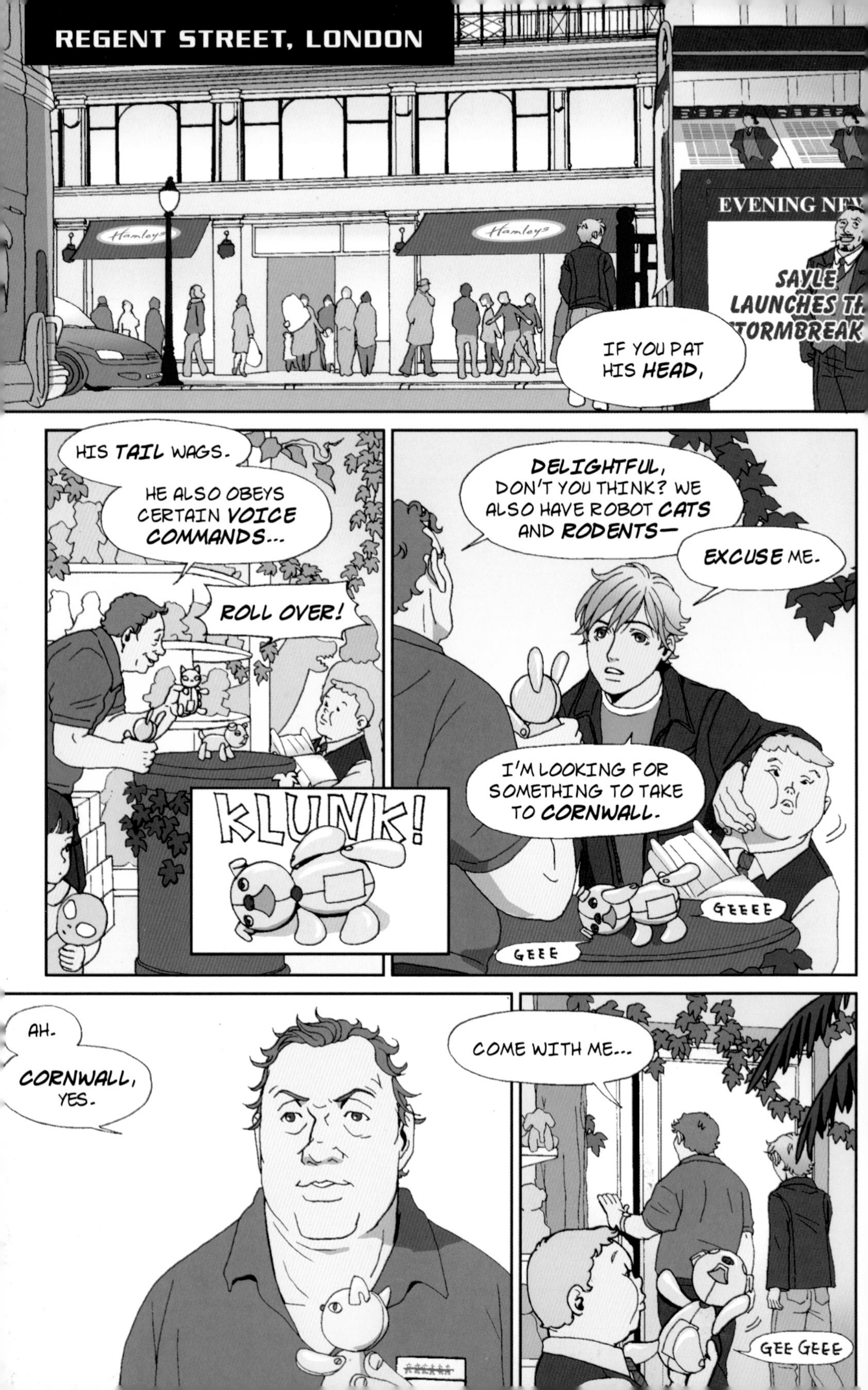
REGENT STREET, LONDON
Hamleys
Hamleys
EVENING NEW
SAYLE LAUNCHES TH
TORMBREAK
IF YOU PAT HIS HEAD,
HIS TAIL WAGS.
HE ALSO OBEYS CERTAIN VOICE COMMANDS...
ROLL OVER!
KLUNK!
DELIGHTFUL, DON'T YOU THINK? WE ALSO HAVE ROBOT CATS AND RODENTS—
EXCUSE ME.
I'M LOOKING FOR SOMETHING TO TAKE TO CORNWALL.
GEEEE
GEEE
AH.
CORNWALL, YES.
COME WITH ME...
GEE GEEE

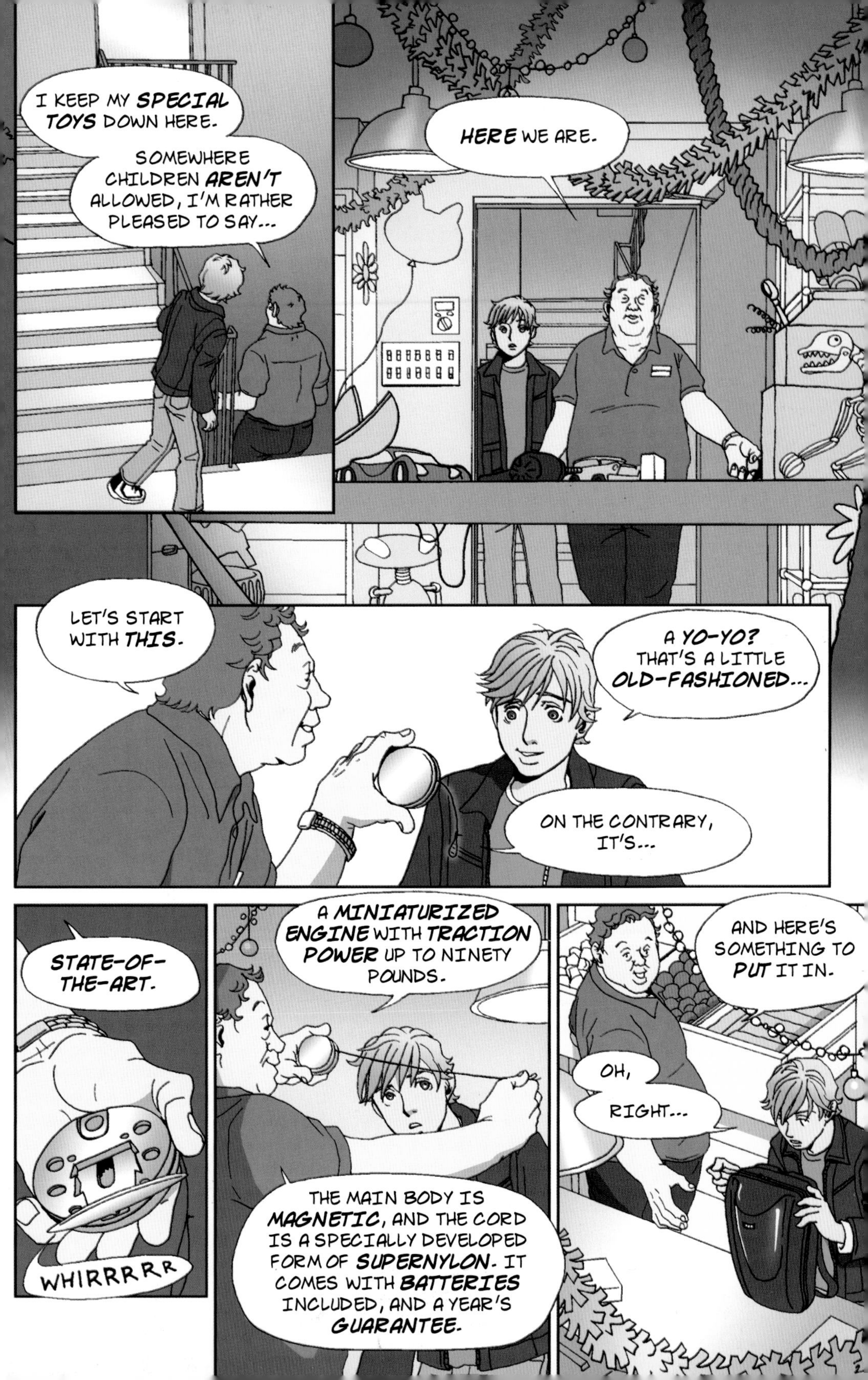

I KEEP MY SPECIAL TOYS DOWN HERE.
SOMEWHERE CHILDREN AREN'T ALLOWED, I'M RATHER PLEASED TO SAY...
HERE WE ARE.
LET'S START WITH THIS.
A YO-YO? THAT'S A LITTLE OLD-FASHIONED...
ON THE CONTRARY, IT'S...
STATE-OF-THE-ART.
WHIRRRRR
A MINIATURIZED ENGINE WITH TRACTION POWER UP TO NINETY POUNDS.
THE MAIN BODY IS MAGNETIC, AND THE CORD IS A SPECIALLY DEVELOPED FORM OF SUPERNYLON. IT COMES WITH BATTERIES INCLUDED, AND A YEAR'S GUARANTEE.
AND HERE'S SOMETHING TO PUT IT IN.
OH,
RIGHT...

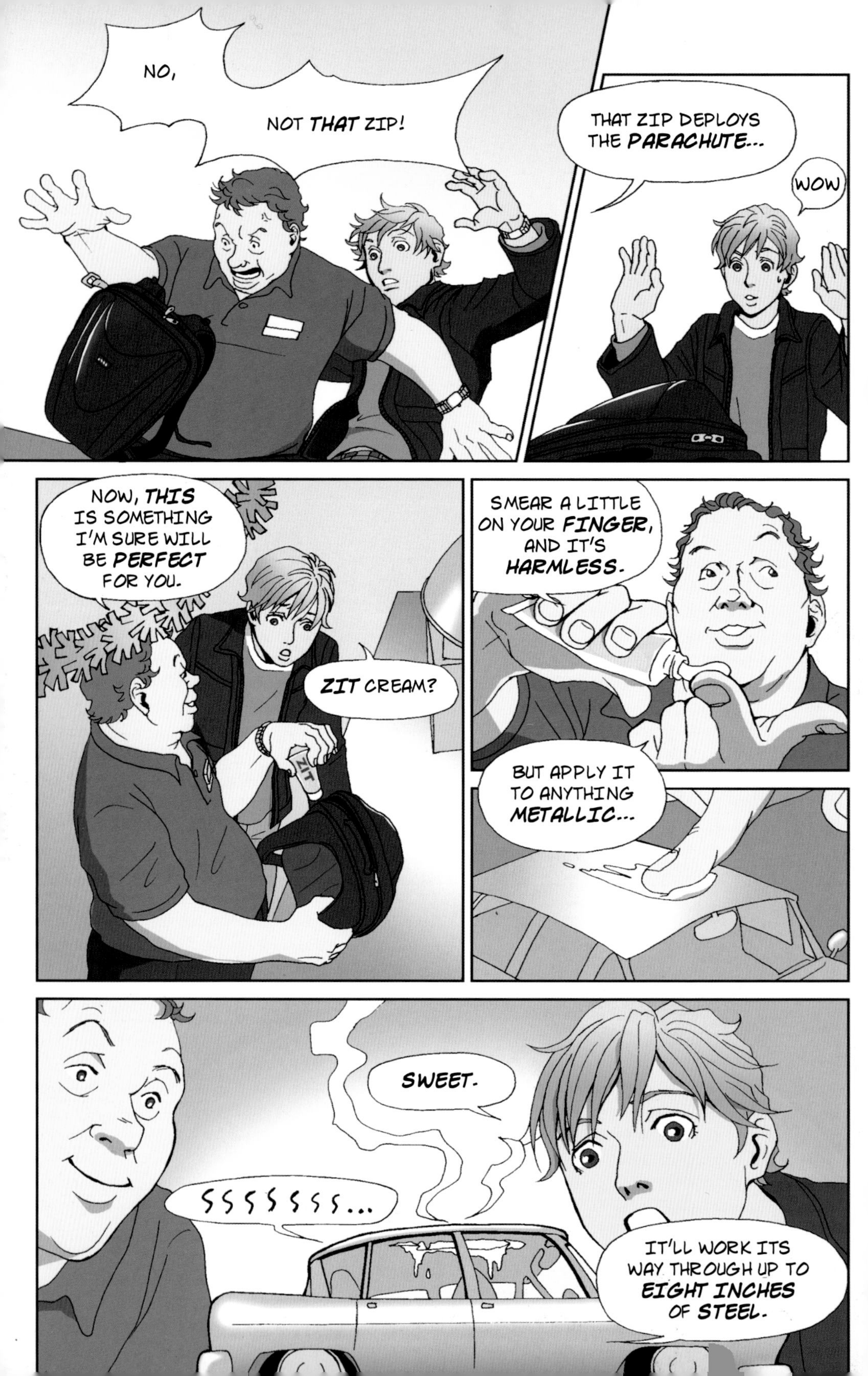
NO,
NOT THAT ZIP!
THAT ZIP DEPLOYS THE PARACHUTE...
WOW
NOW, THIS IS SOMETHING I'M SURE WILL BE PERFECT FOR YOU.
ZIT CREAM?
ZIT
SMEAR A LITTLE ON YOUR FINGER, AND IT'S HARMLESS.
BUT APPLY IT TO ANYTHING METALLIC...
SWEET.
SSSSSSS...
IT'LL WORK ITS WAY THROUGH UP TO EIGHT INCHES OF STEEL.

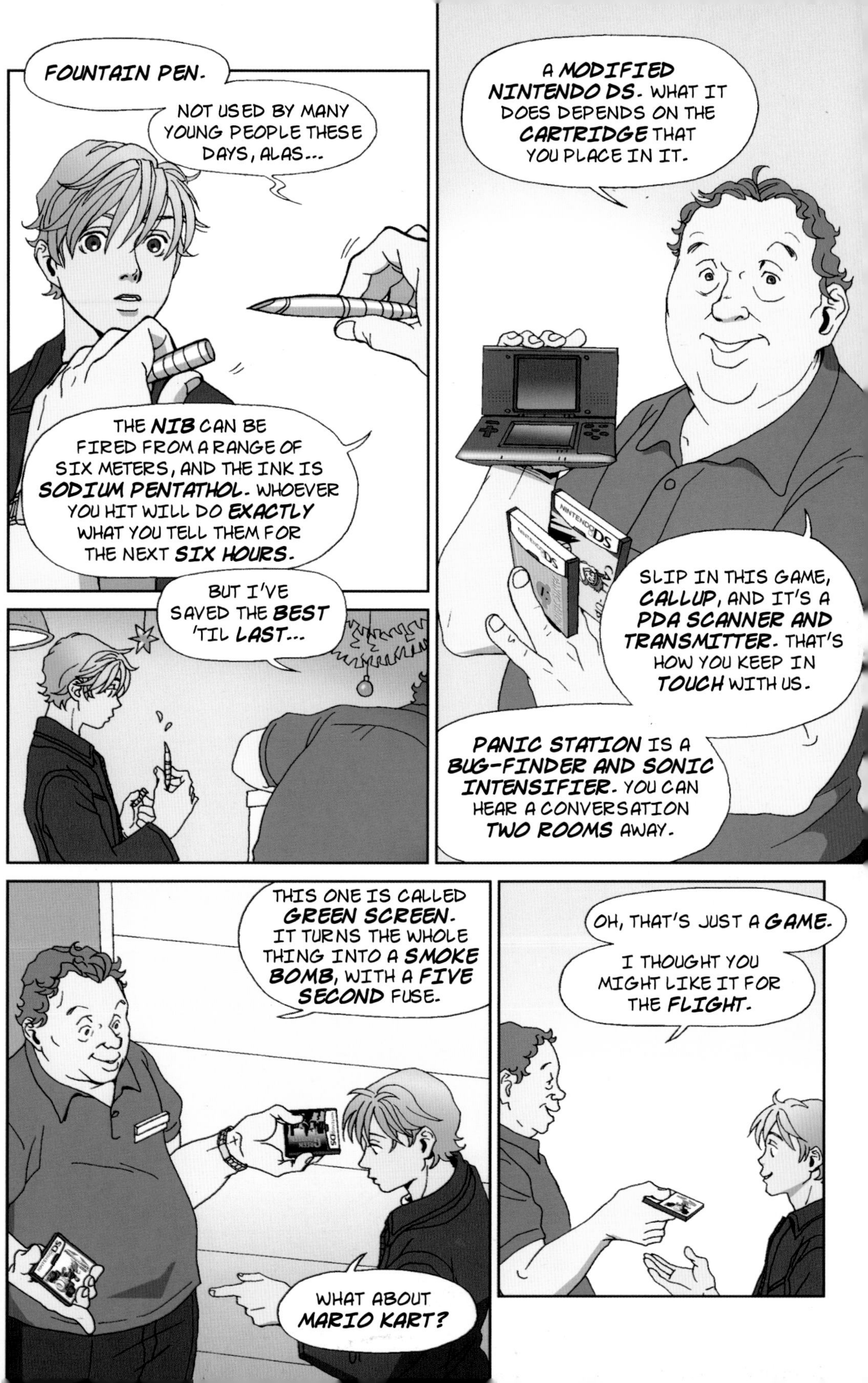
FOUNTAIN PEN.
NOT USED BY MANY YOUNG PEOPLE THESE DAYS, ALAS...
THE NIB CAN BE FIRED FROM A RANGE OF SIX METERS, AND THE INK IS SODIUM PENTATHOL. WHOEVER YOU HIT WILL DO EXACTLY WHAT YOU TELL THEM FOR THE NEXT SIX HOURS.
BUT I'VE SAVED THE BEST 'TIL LAST...
A MODIFIED NINTENDO DS. WHAT IT DOES DEPENDS ON THE CARTRIDGE THAT YOU PLACE IN IT.
SLIP IN THIS GAME, CALLUP, AND IT'S A PDA SCANNER AND TRANSMITTER. THAT'S HOW YOU KEEP IN TOUCH WITH US.
PANIC STATION IS A BUG-FINDER AND SONIC INTENSIFIER. YOU CAN HEAR A CONVERSATION TWO ROOMS AWAY.
THIS ONE IS CALLED GREEN SCREEN. IT TURNS THE WHOLE THING INTO A SMOKE BOMB, WITH A FIVE SECOND FUSE.
WHAT ABOUT MARIO KART?
OH, THAT'S JUST A GAME.
I THOUGHT YOU MIGHT LIKE IT FOR THE FLIGHT.

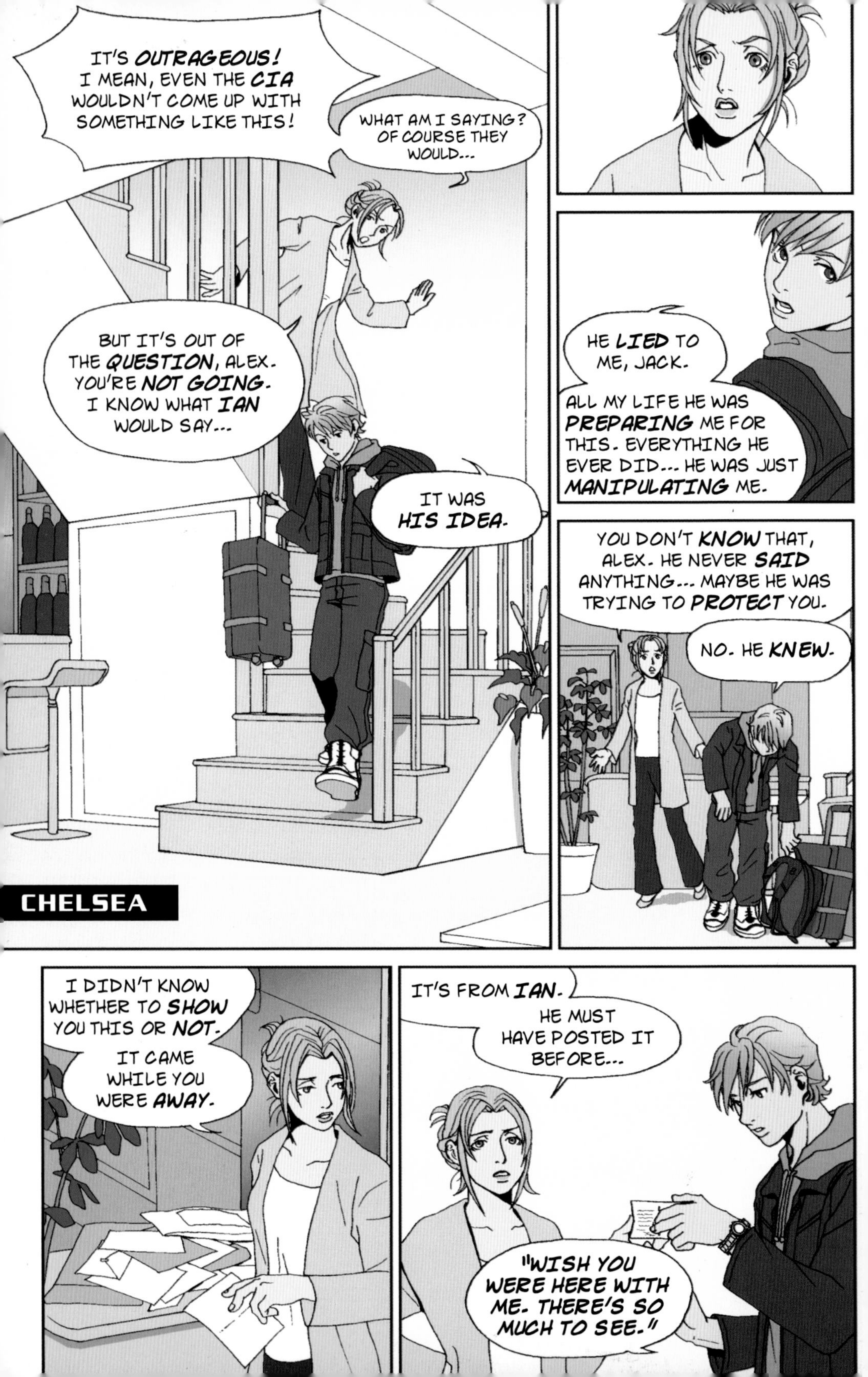

IT'S OUTRAGEOUS! I MEAN, EVEN THE CIA WOULDN'T COME UP WITH SOMETHING LIKE THIS!
WHAT AM I SAYING? OF COURSE THEY WOULD...
BUT IT'S OUT OF THE QUESTION, ALEX. YOU'RE NOT GOING. I KNOW WHAT IAN WOULD SAY...
IT WAS HIS IDEA.
CHELSEA
HE LIED TO ME, JACK.
ALL MY LIFE HE WAS PREPARING ME FOR THIS. EVERYTHING HE EVER DID... HE WAS JUST MANIPULATING ME.
YOU DON'T KNOW THAT, ALEX. HE NEVER SAID ANYTHING... MAYBE HE WAS TRYING TO PROTECT YOU.
NO. HE KNEW.
I DIDN'T KNOW WHETHER TO SHOW YOU THIS OR NOT.
IT CAME WHILE YOU WERE AWAY.
IT'S FROM IAN.
HE MUST HAVE POSTED IT BEFORE...
"WISH YOU WERE HERE WITH ME. THERE'S SO MUCH TO SEE."

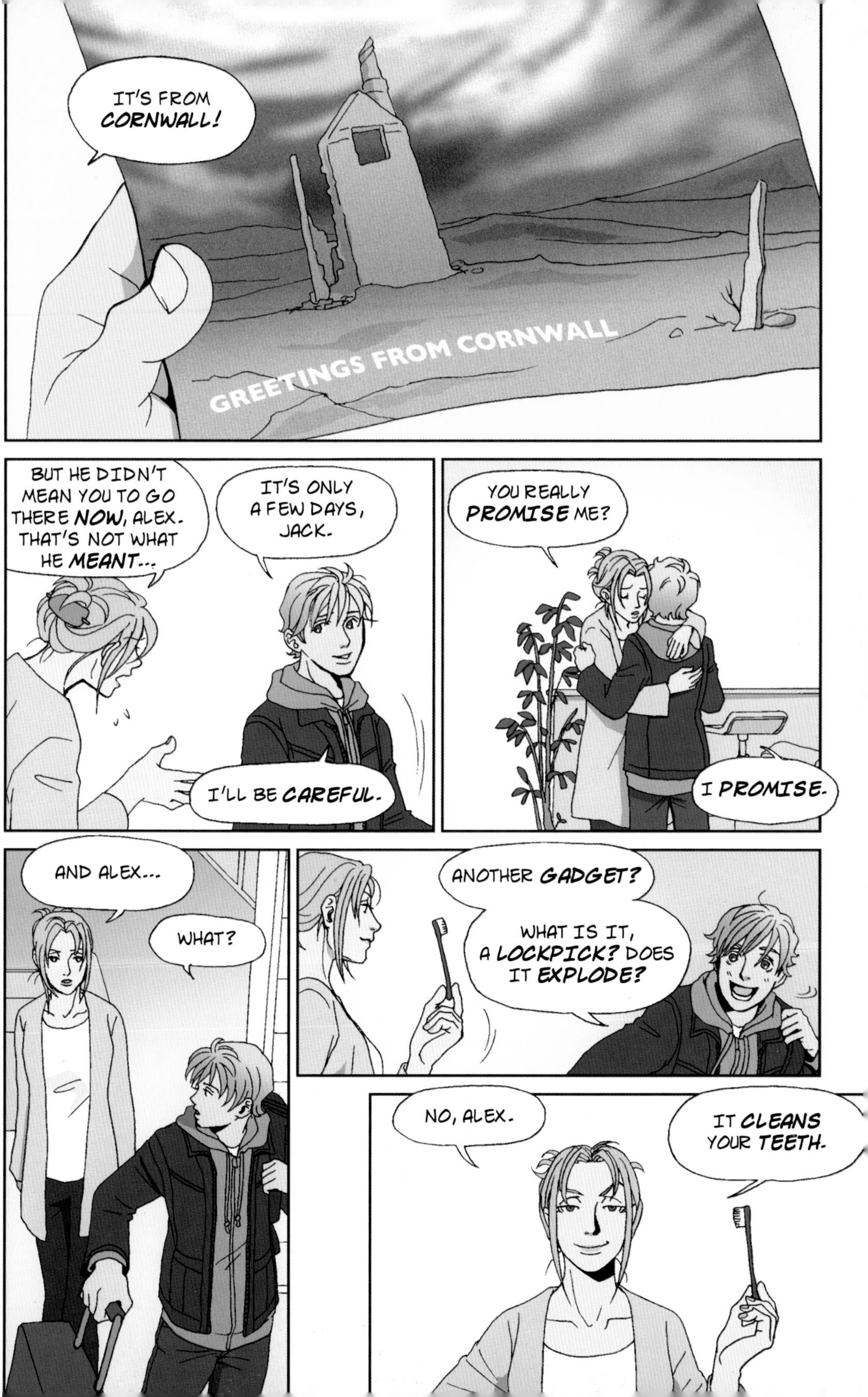
IT'S FROM CORNWALL!
GREETINGS FROM CORNWALL
BUT HE DIDN'T MEAN YOU TO GO THERE NOW, ALEX. THAT'S NOT WHAT HE MEANT...
IT'S ONLY A FEW DAYS, JACK.
I'LL BE CAREFUL.
YOU REALLY PROMISE ME?
I PROMISE.
AND ALEX...
WHAT?
ANOTHER GADGET?
WHAT IS IT, A LOCKPICK? DOES IT EXPLODE?
NO, ALEX.
IT CLEANS YOUR TEETH.

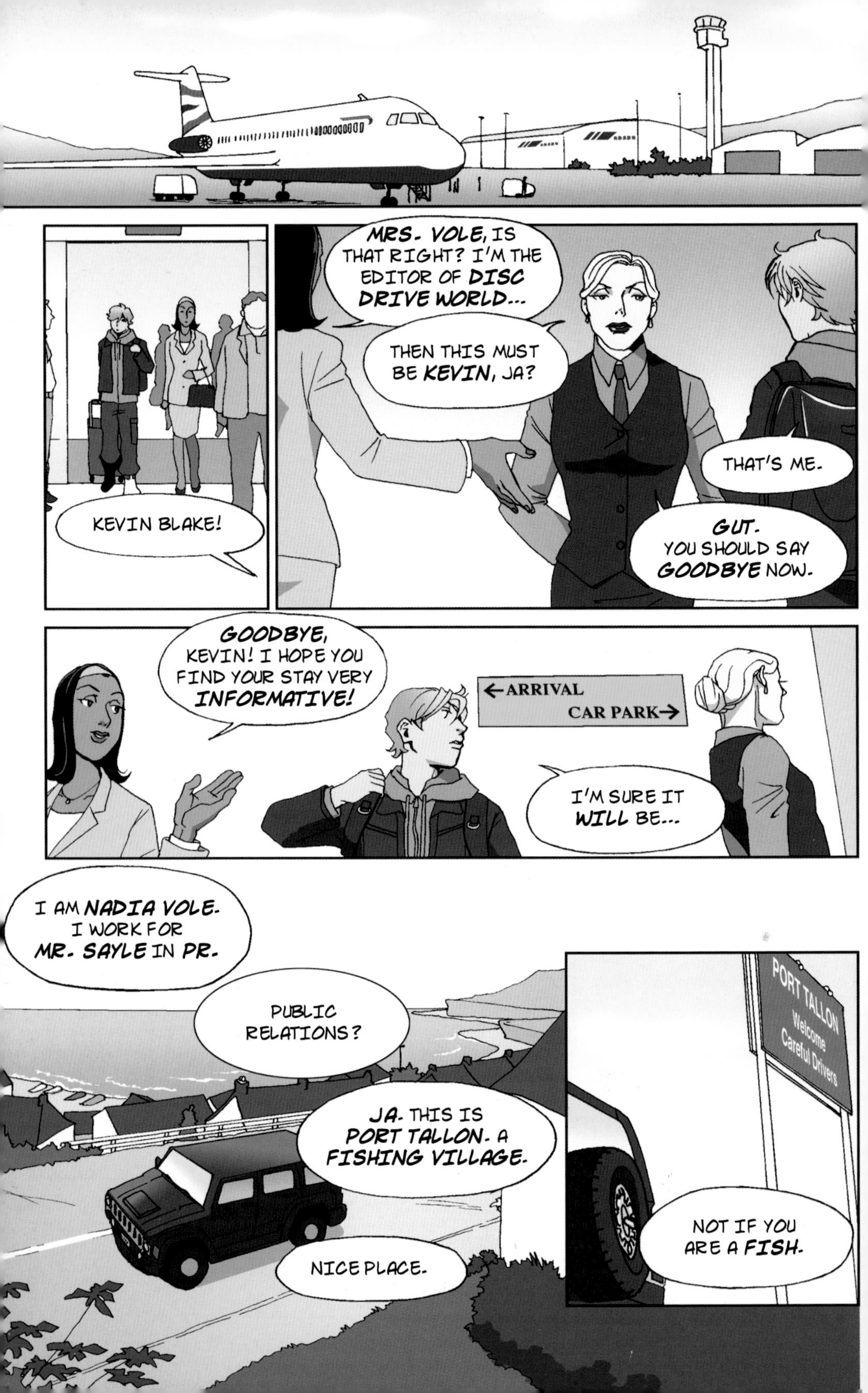
KEVIN BLAKE!
MRS. VOLE, IS THAT RIGHT? I'M THE EDITOR OF DISC DRIVE WORLD...
THEN THIS MUST BE KEVIN, JA?
THAT'S ME.
GUT. YOU SHOULD SAY GOODBYE NOW.
GOODBYE, KEVIN! I HOPE YOU FIND YOUR STAY VERY INFORMATIVE!
←ARRIVAL
CAR PARK→
I'M SURE IT WILL BE...
I AM NADIA VOLE. I WORK FOR MR. SAYLE IN PR.
PUBLIC RELATIONS?
JA. THIS IS PORT TALLON. A FISHING VILLAGE.
NICE PLACE.
PORT TALLON
Welcome
Careful Drivers
NOT IF YOU ARE A FISH.

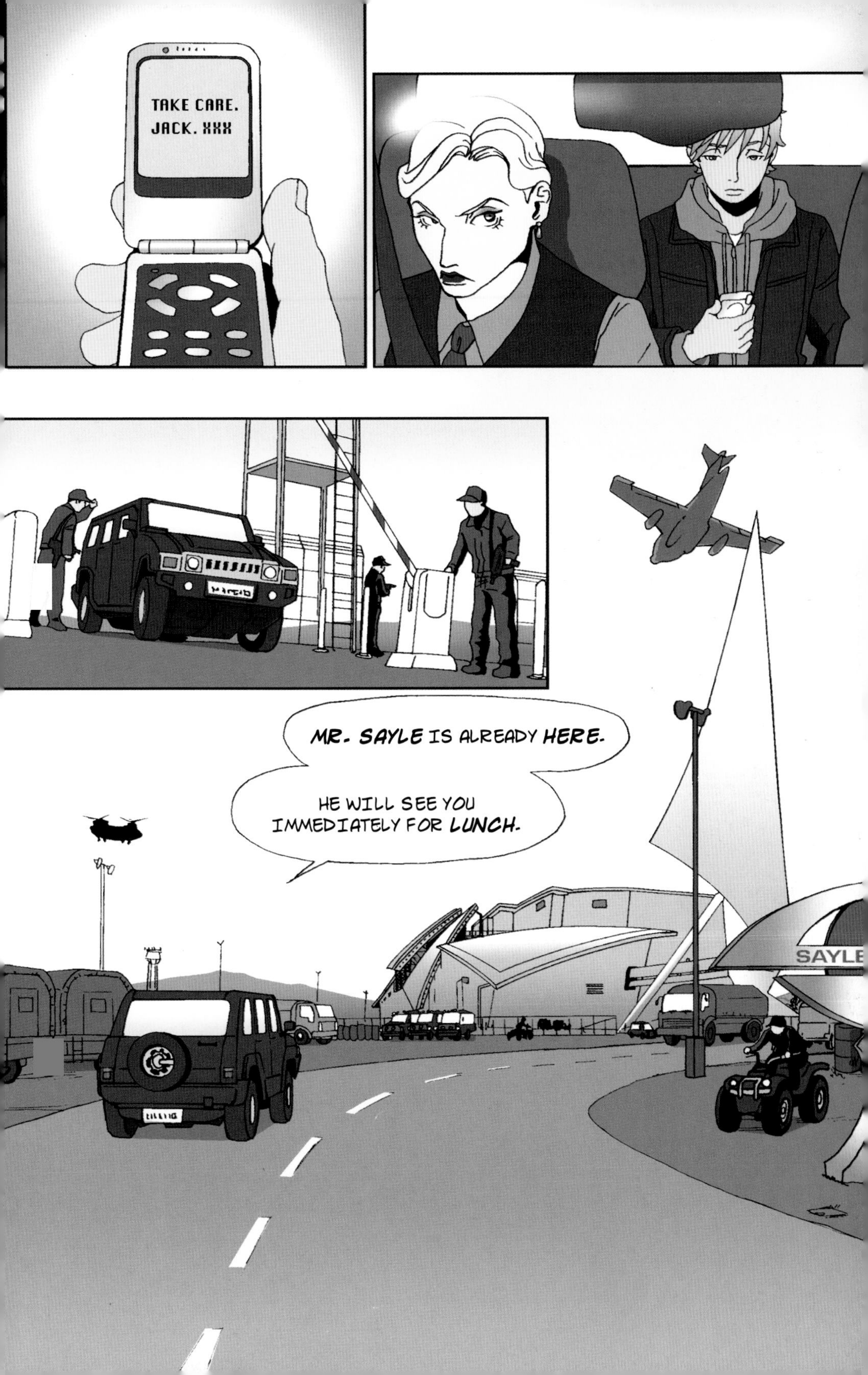
TAKE CARE.
JACK. XXX
SAYLE
MR. SAYLE IS ALREADY HERE.
HE WILL SEE YOU IMMEDIATELY FOR LUNCH.

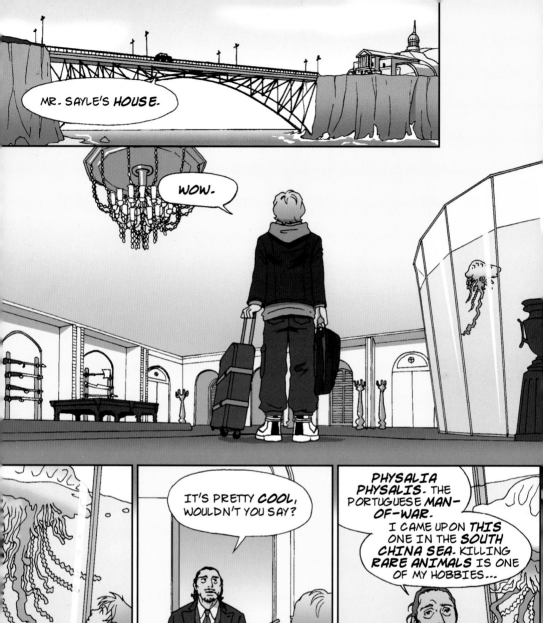

MR. SAYLE'S **HOUSE**.

WOW.

IT'S PRETTY **COOL**, WOULDN'T YOU SAY?

HEY, **KEVIN!** HOW **ARE** YOU?

NOT SURE I'D WANT ONE AS A **PET**...

PHYSALIA PHYSALIS. THE PORTUGUESE **MAN-OF-WAR**. I CAME UPON **THIS** ONE IN THE **SOUTH CHINA SEA**. KILLING **RARE ANIMALS** IS ONE OF MY HOBBIES...

BUT NOT **THIS** ONE. THIS ONE I HAD TO **KEEP**.

YOU SEE, IT REMINDS ME OF **MYSELF**.

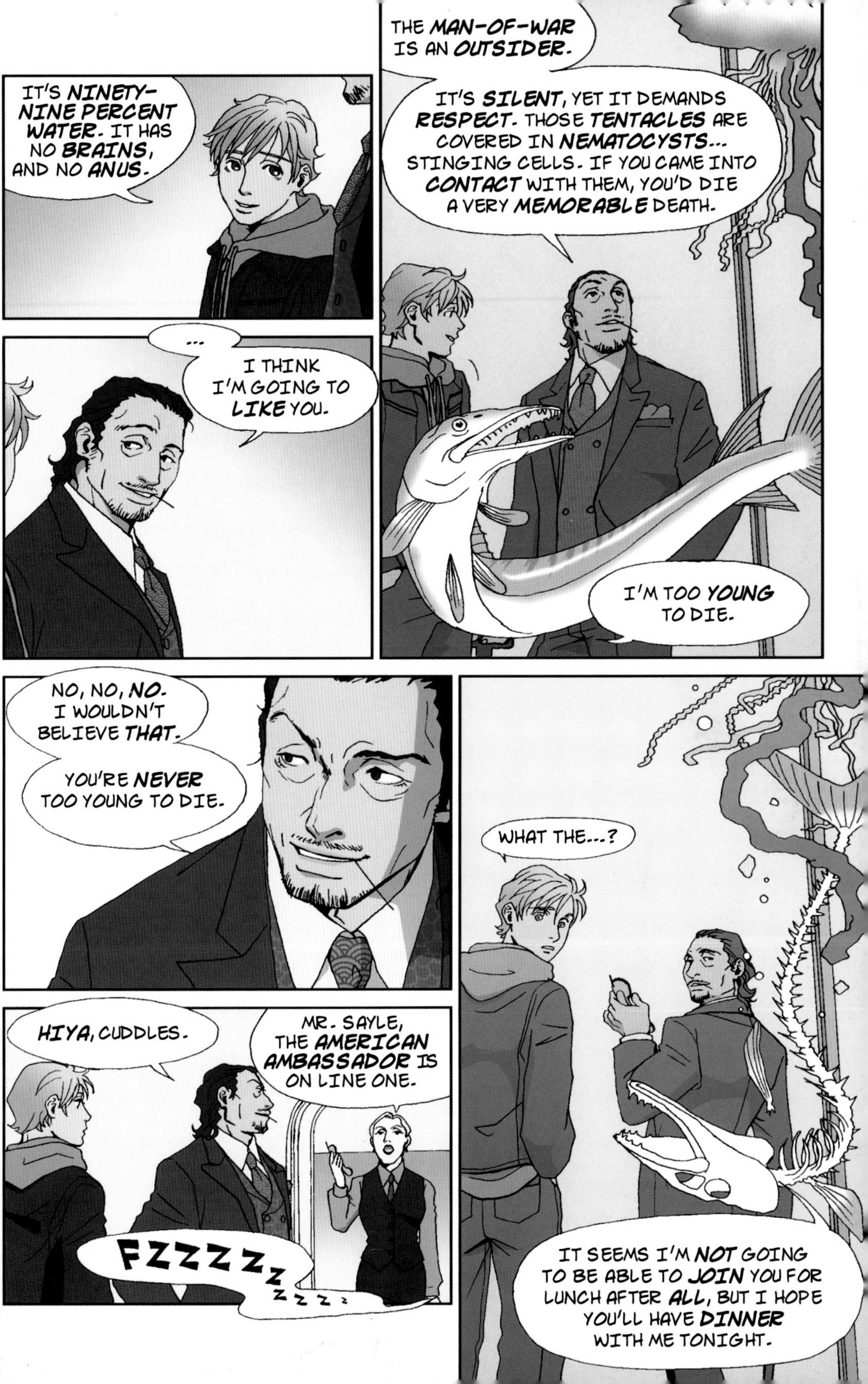
IT'S NINETY-NINE PERCENT WATER. IT HAS NO BRAINS, AND NO ANUS.
THE MAN-OF-WAR IS AN OUTSIDER.
IT'S SILENT, YET IT DEMANDS RESPECT. THOSE TENTACLES ARE COVERED IN NEMATOCYSTS... STINGING CELLS. IF YOU CAME INTO CONTACT WITH THEM, YOU'D DIE A VERY MEMORABLE DEATH.
...
I THINK I'M GOING TO LIKE YOU.
I'M TOO YOUNG TO DIE.
NO, NO, NO. I WOULDN'T BELIEVE THAT.
YOU'RE NEVER TOO YOUNG TO DIE.
HIYA, CUDDLES.
MR. SAYLE, THE AMERICAN AMBASSADOR IS ON LINE ONE.
FZZZZZZZZZ
WHAT THE...?
IT SEEMS I'M NOT GOING TO BE ABLE TO JOIN YOU FOR LUNCH AFTER ALL, BUT I HOPE YOU'LL HAVE DINNER WITH ME TONIGHT.

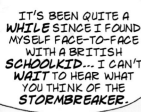 IT'S BEEN QUITE A **WHILE** SINCE I FOUND MYSELF FACE-TO-FACE WITH A BRITISH **SCHOOLKID**... I CAN'T **WAIT** TO HEAR WHAT YOU THINK OF THE **STORMBREAKER**.

THIS IS MY PERSONAL ASSISTANT, **MR. GRIN.**

HE SEEMS TO HAVE **CUT** HIMSELF **SHAVING.**

MR. GRIN USED TO WORK IN A **CIRCUS.** IT WAS A NOVELTY **KNIFE-THROWING** ACT. FOR A **CLIMAX**, HE CAUGHT A **SPINNING KNIFE** BETWEEN HIS **TEETH**...

MURGH.

...UNTIL **ONE** NIGHT, HIS MOTHER **WAVED** TO HIM FROM THE FRONT ROW AND HE MADE A **MISTAKE** WITH HIS **TIMING.**

HE CAN'T **TALK**, BUT HE'LL SHOW YOU TO YOUR **ROOM** AND WE'LL MEET AGAIN **TONIGHT.** OKAY?

HAVE **FUN.**

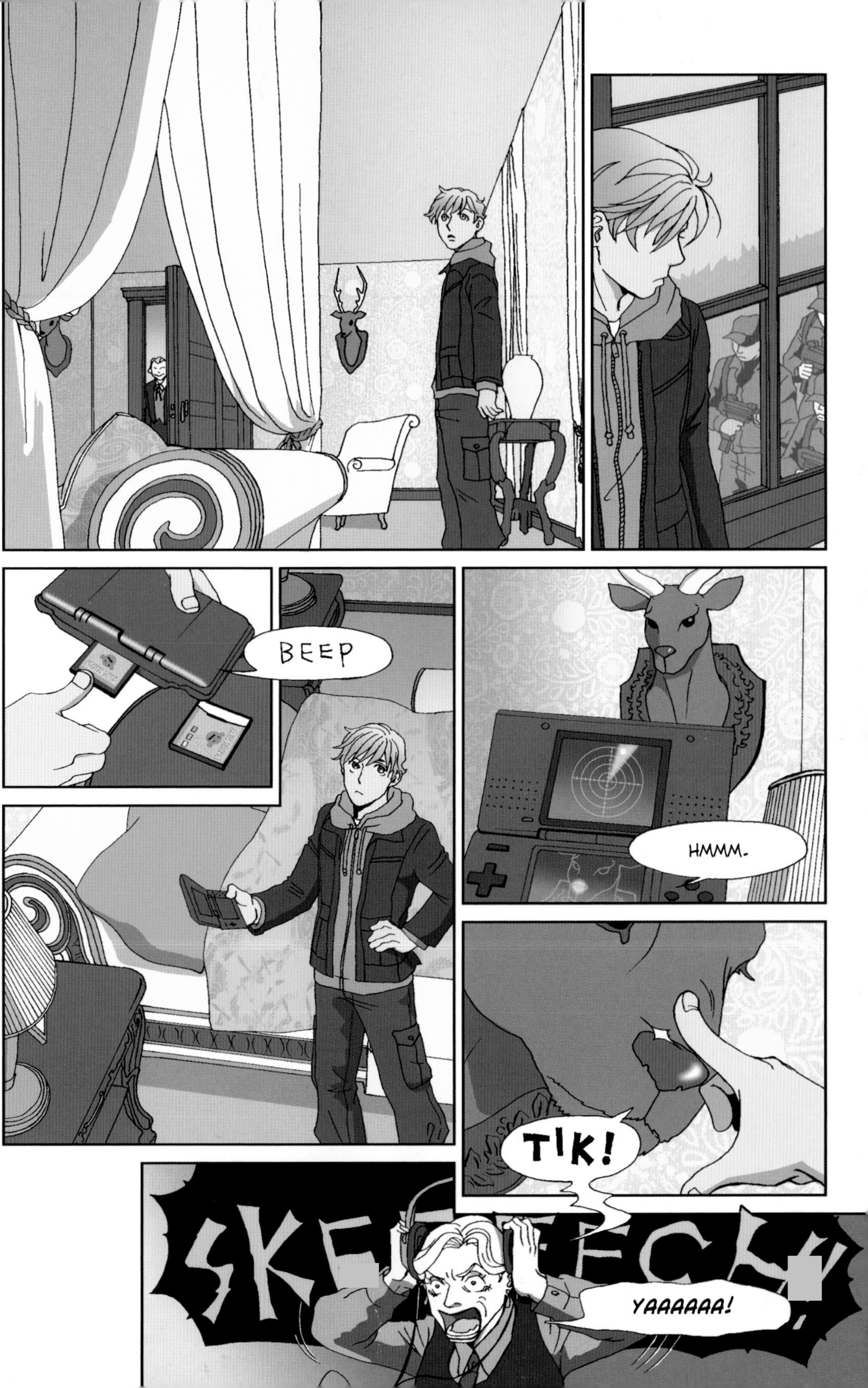
BEEP
HMMM.
TIK!
YAAAAAA!

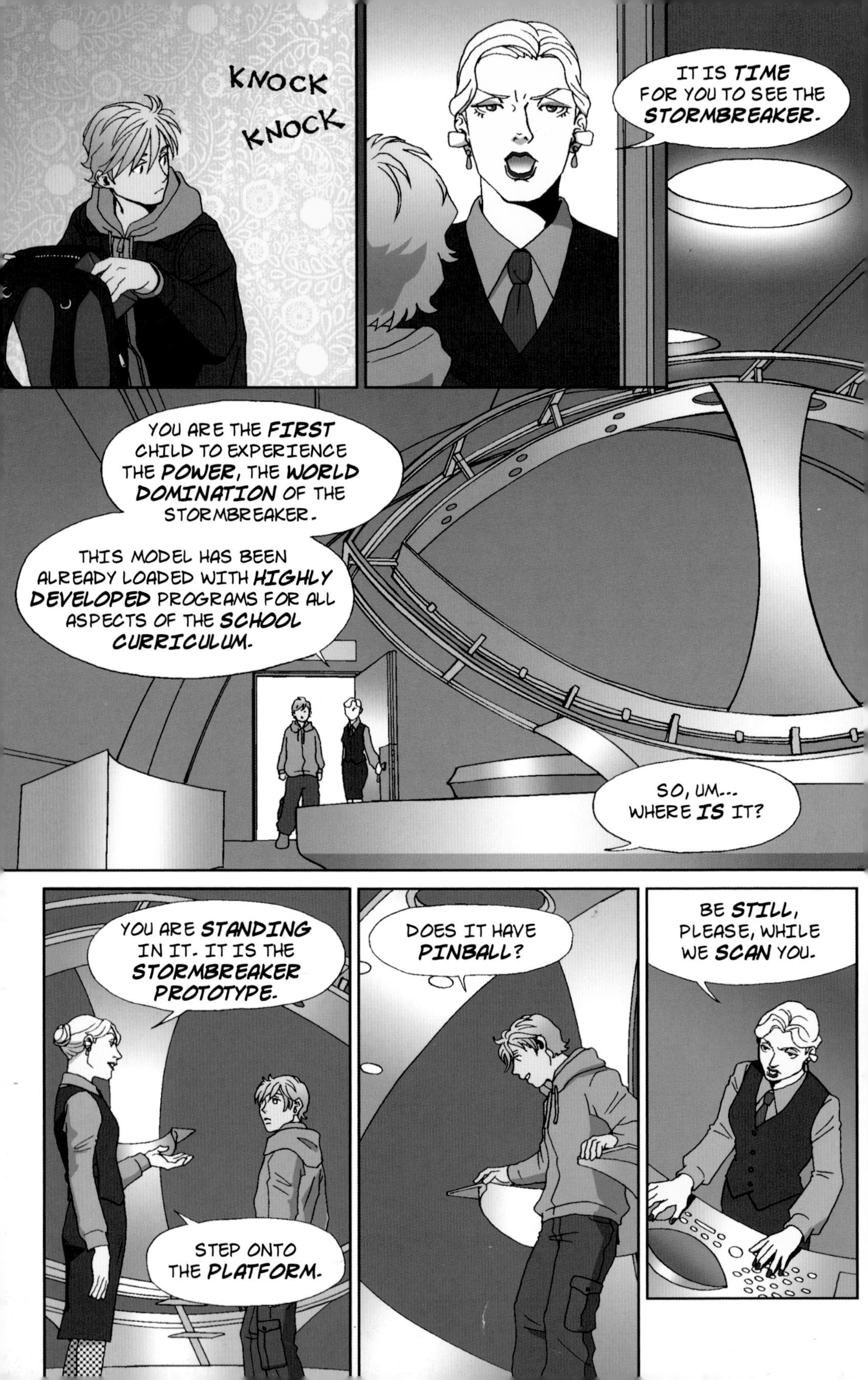
KNOCK
KNOCK
IT IS TIME FOR YOU TO SEE THE STORMBREAKER.
YOU ARE THE FIRST CHILD TO EXPERIENCE THE POWER, THE WORLD DOMINATION OF THE STORMBREAKER.
THIS MODEL HAS BEEN ALREADY LOADED WITH HIGHLY DEVELOPED PROGRAMS FOR ALL ASPECTS OF THE SCHOOL CURRICULUM.
SO, UM... WHERE IS IT?
YOU ARE STANDING IN IT. IT IS THE STORMBREAKER PROTOTYPE.
STEP ONTO THE PLATFORM.
DOES IT HAVE PINBALL?
BE STILL, PLEASE, WHILE WE SCAN YOU.

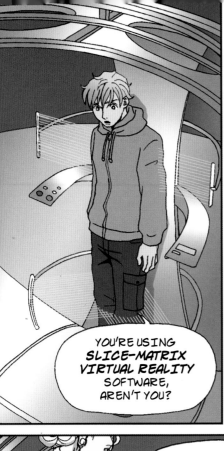

JA! WHO *TAUGHT* YOU ABOUT COMPUTERS, KEVIN?

MY UNCLE.

HE IS A COMPUTER *WHIZ-KING*?

NO, HE WAS A *SECURITY GUARD.* BUT HE *DIED.*

YOU'RE USING *SLICE-MATRIX VIRTUAL REALITY* SOFTWARE, AREN'T YOU?

HOW DID THAT *HAPPEN?*

I DON'T *KNOW.*

BUT *ONE* DAY I'LL FIND *OUT.*

PROGRAMMING COMPLETE

MAYBE.

BUT *NOT* TODAY.

YOU WILL START WITH *SCIENCE.* PRESS *ENTER* TO BEGIN.

SCIENCE, EH? GREAT...

...*NOT.*

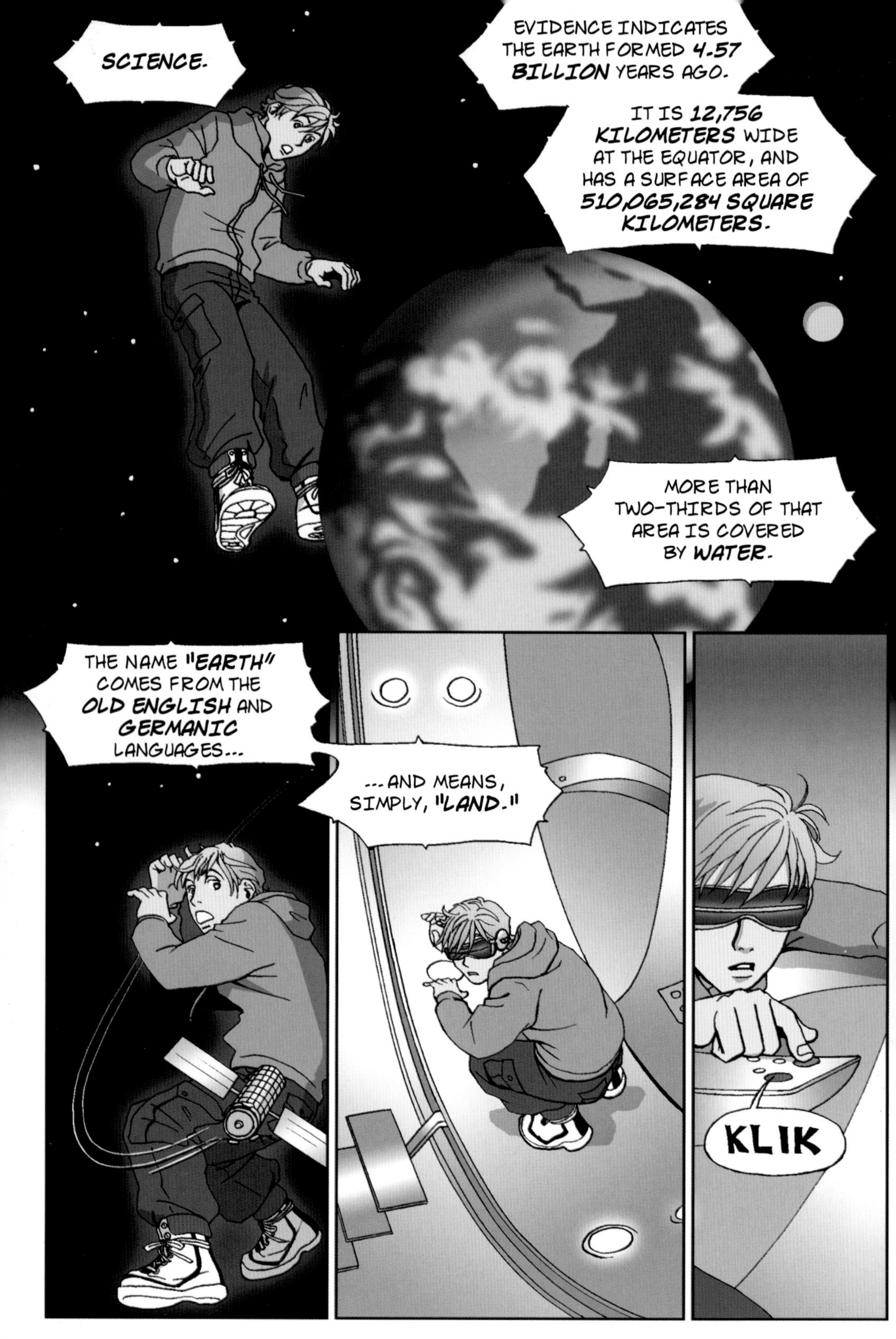
SCIENCE.
EVIDENCE INDICATES THE EARTH FORMED 4.57 BILLION YEARS AGO.
IT IS 12,756 KILOMETERS WIDE AT THE EQUATOR, AND HAS A SURFACE AREA OF 510,065,284 SQUARE KILOMETERS.
MORE THAN TWO-THIRDS OF THAT AREA IS COVERED BY WATER.
THE NAME "EARTH" COMES FROM THE OLD ENGLISH AND GERMANIC LANGUAGES...
...AND MEANS, SIMPLY, "LAND."
KLIK

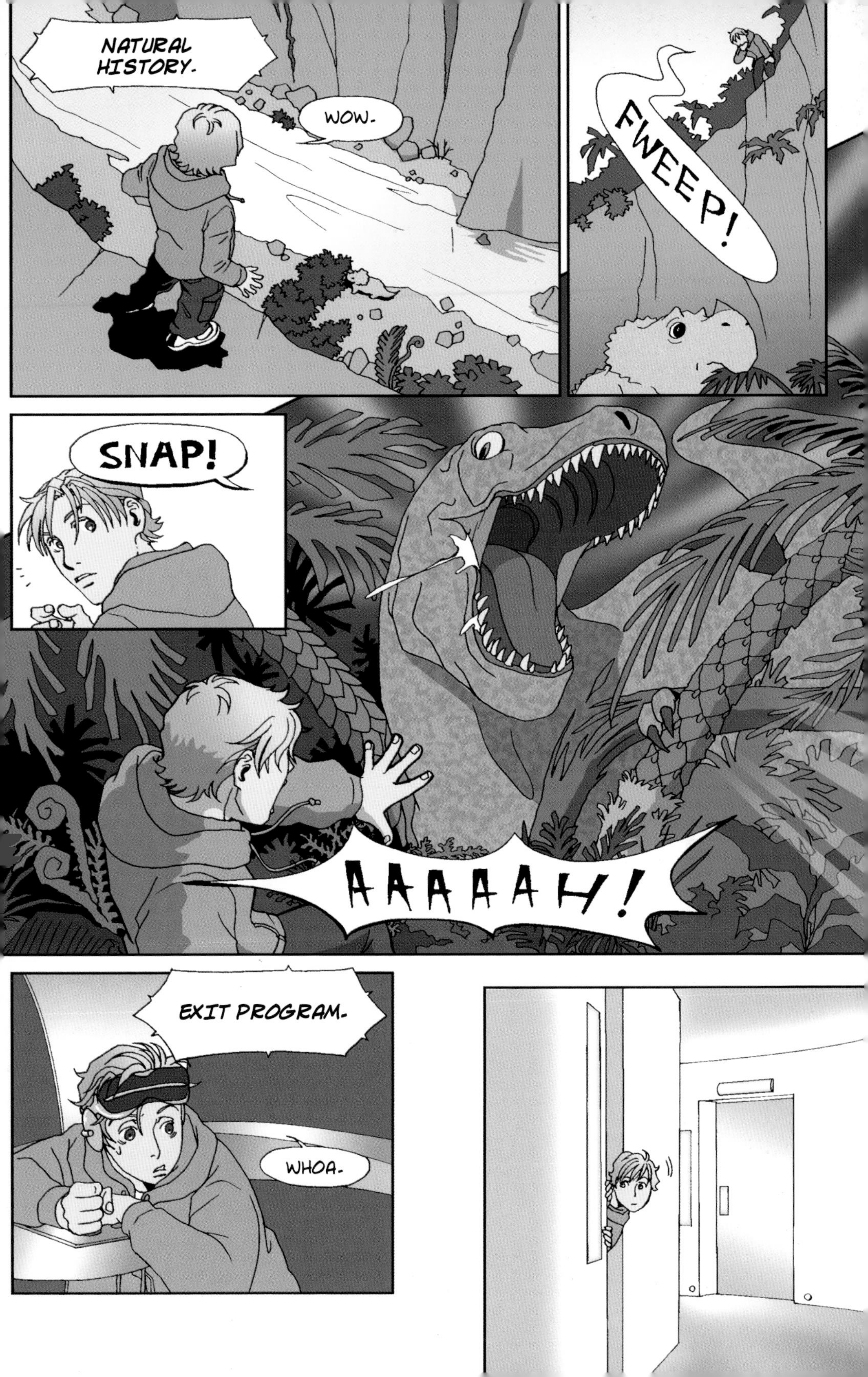
NATURAL HISTORY.
WOW.
FWEEP!
SNAP!
AAAAAH!
EXIT PROGRAM.
WHOA.

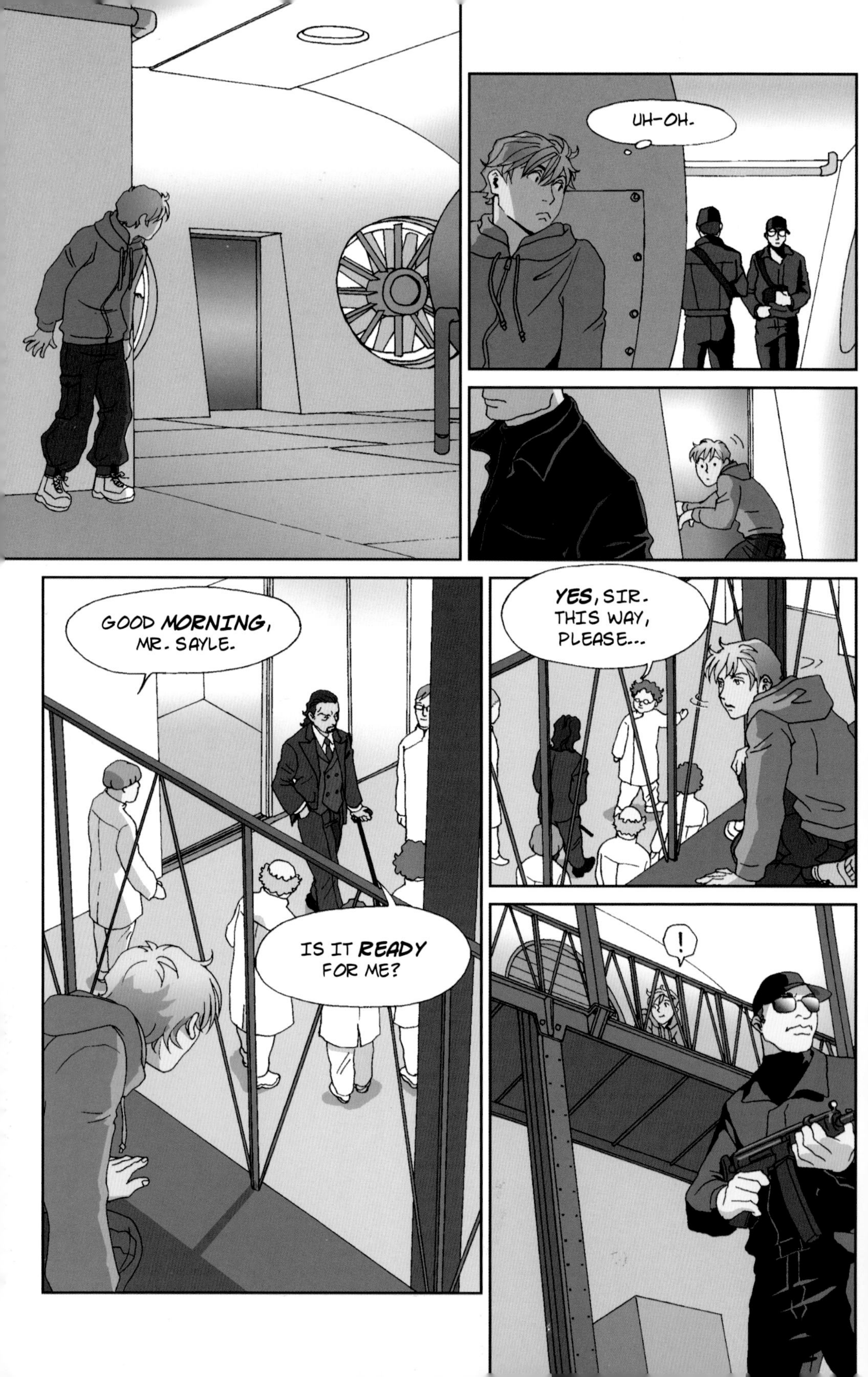
UH-OH.
GOOD MORNING, MR. SAYLE.
IS IT READY FOR ME?
YES, SIR. THIS WAY, PLEASE...
!

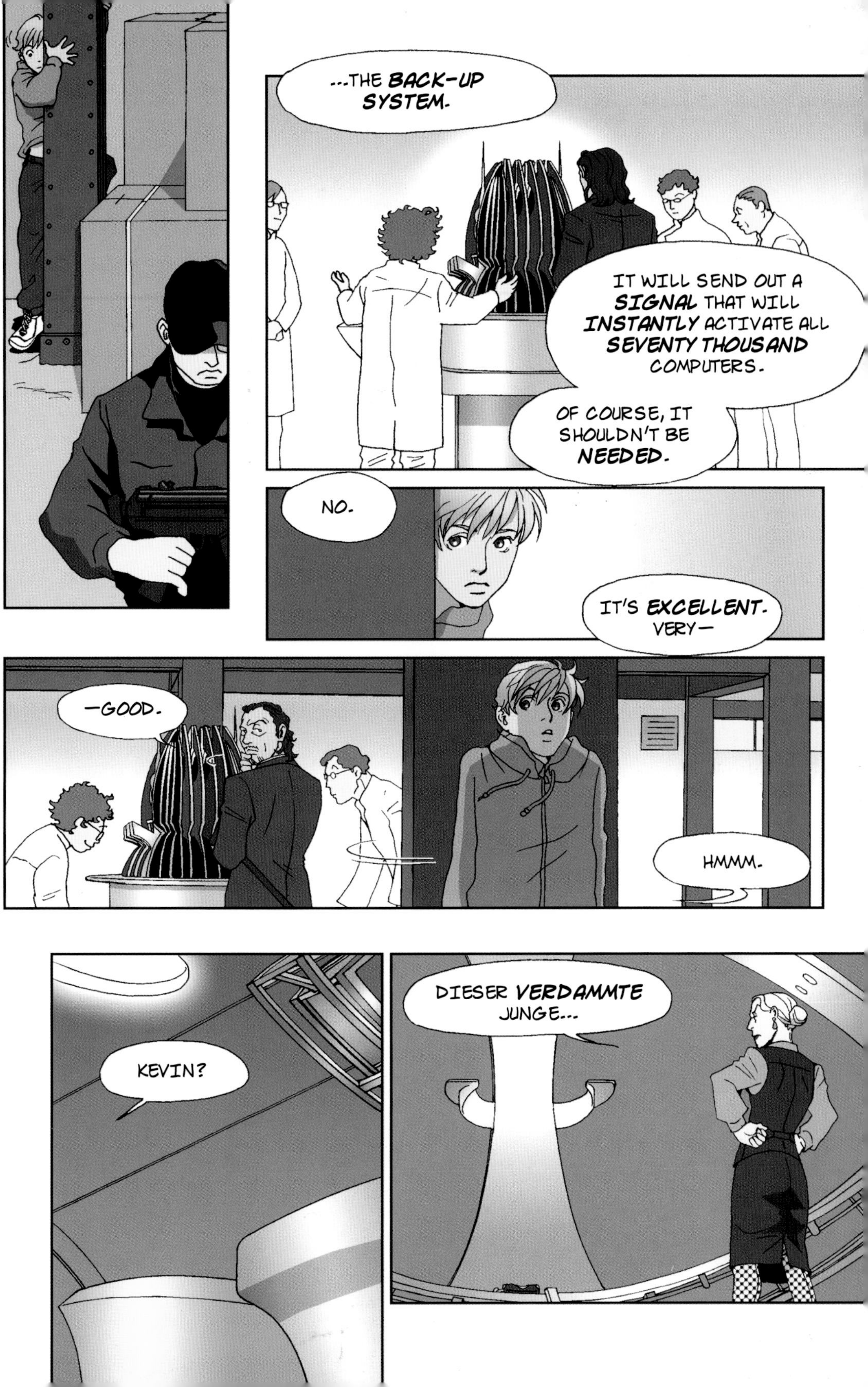
...THE BACK-UP SYSTEM.
IT WILL SEND OUT A SIGNAL THAT WILL INSTANTLY ACTIVATE ALL SEVENTY THOUSAND COMPUTERS.
OF COURSE, IT SHOULDN'T BE NEEDED.
NO.
IT'S EXCELLENT. VERY—
—GOOD.
HMMM.
KEVIN?
DIESER VERDAMMTE JUNGE...

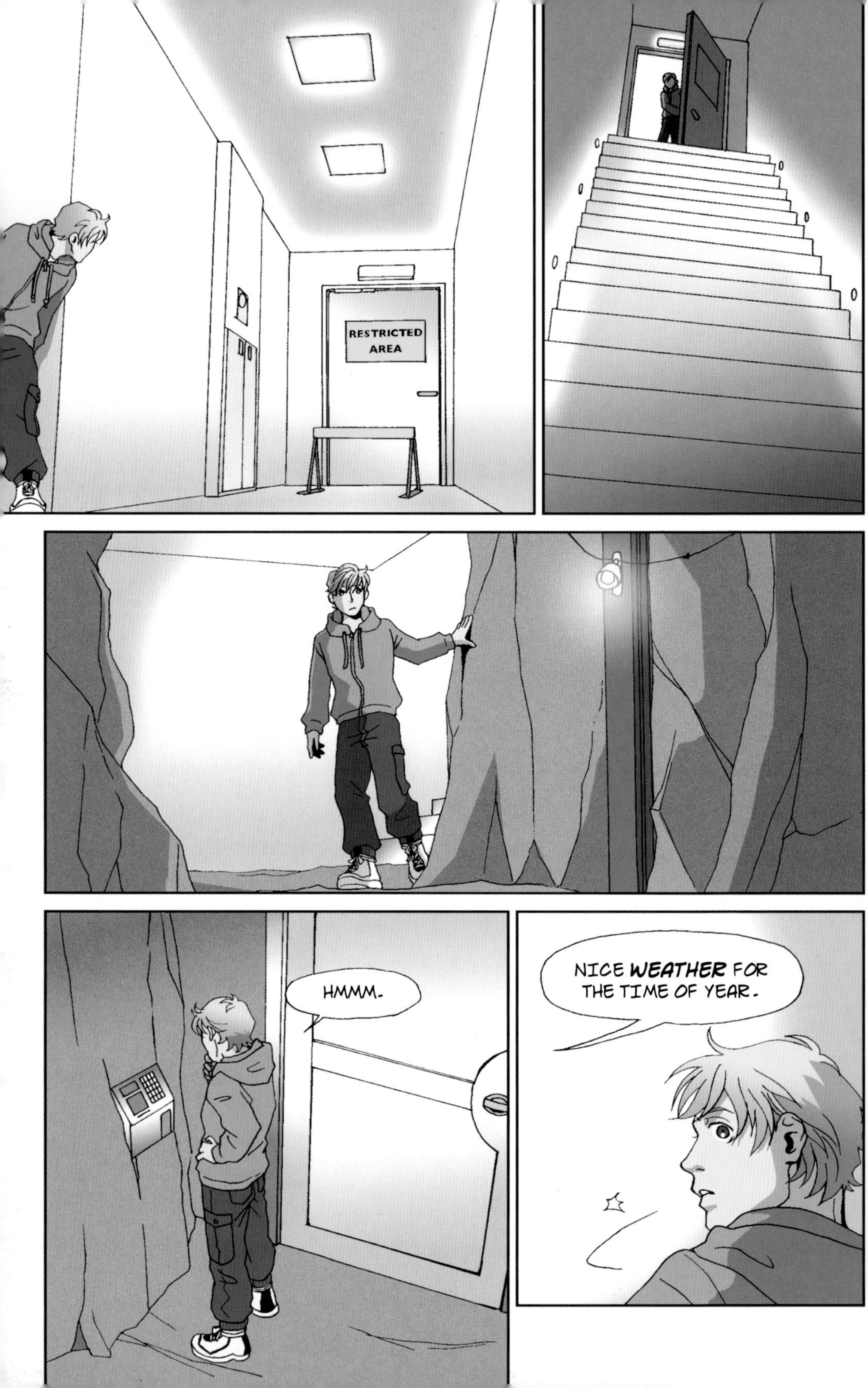
RESTRICTED AREA
HMMM.
NICE WEATHER FOR THE TIME OF YEAR.

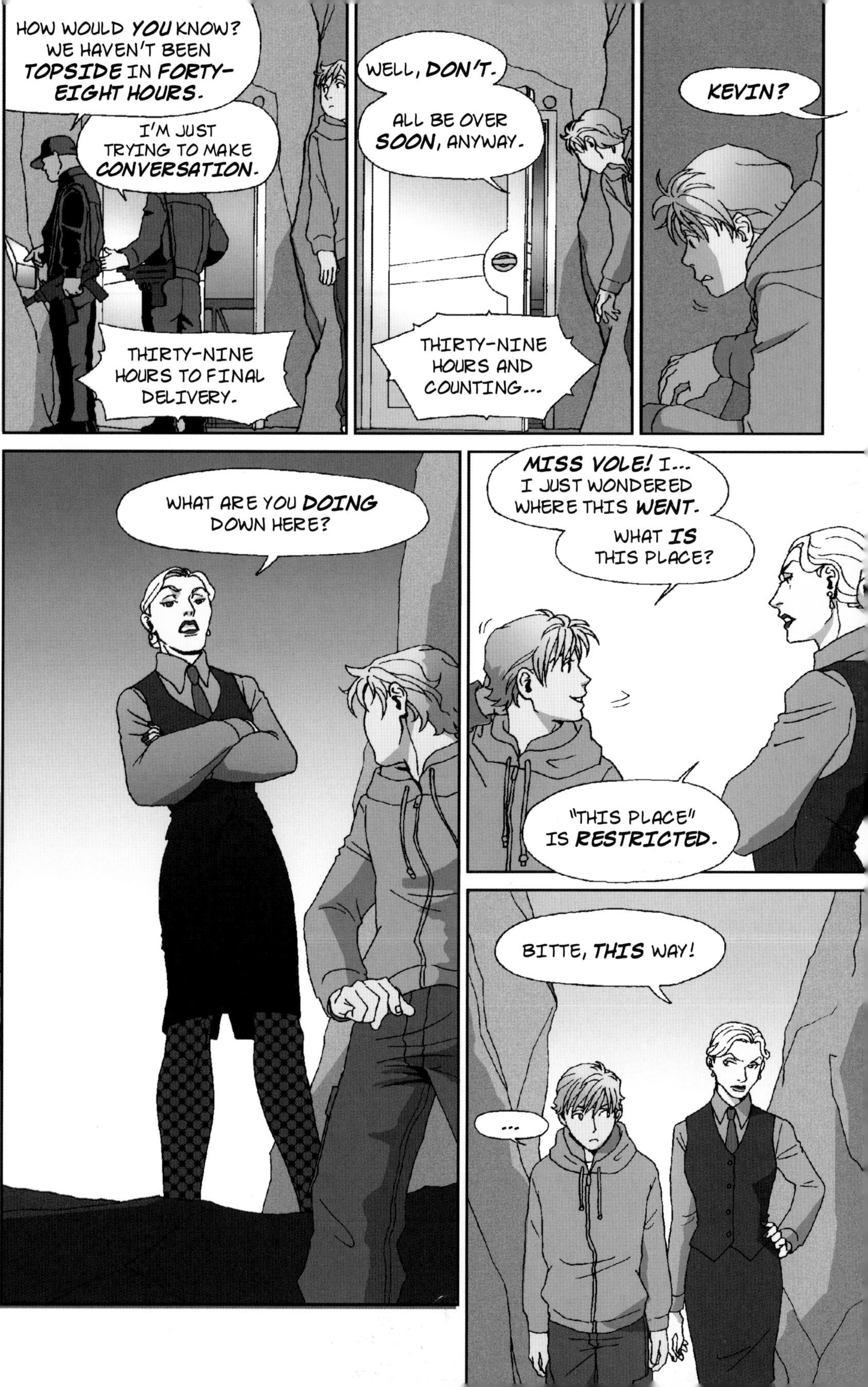
HOW WOULD YOU KNOW? WE HAVEN'T BEEN TOPSIDE IN FORTY-EIGHT HOURS.
I'M JUST TRYING TO MAKE CONVERSATION.
THIRTY-NINE HOURS TO FINAL DELIVERY.
WELL, DON'T.
ALL BE OVER SOON, ANYWAY.
THIRTY-NINE HOURS AND COUNTING...
KEVIN?
WHAT ARE YOU DOING DOWN HERE?
MISS VOLE! I... I JUST WONDERED WHERE THIS WENT.
WHAT IS THIS PLACE?
"THIS PLACE" IS RESTRICTED.
BITTE, THIS WAY!
...

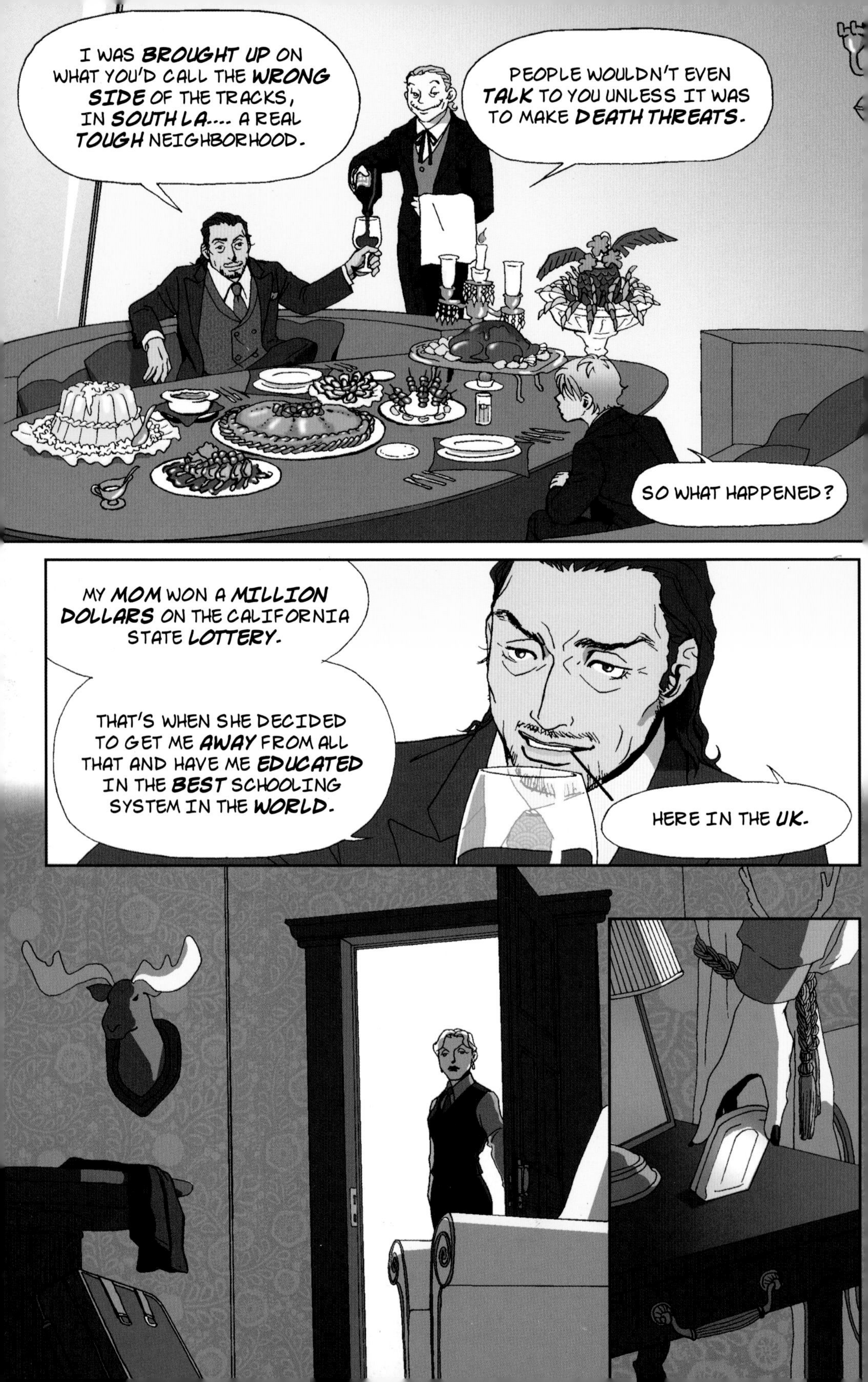
I WAS BROUGHT UP ON WHAT YOU'D CALL THE WRONG SIDE OF THE TRACKS, IN SOUTH LA.... A REAL TOUGH NEIGHBORHOOD.
PEOPLE WOULDN'T EVEN TALK TO YOU UNLESS IT WAS TO MAKE DEATH THREATS.
SO WHAT HAPPENED?
MY MOM WON A MILLION DOLLARS ON THE CALIFORNIA STATE LOTTERY.
THAT'S WHEN SHE DECIDED TO GET ME AWAY FROM ALL THAT AND HAVE ME EDUCATED IN THE BEST SCHOOLING SYSTEM IN THE WORLD.
HERE IN THE UK.

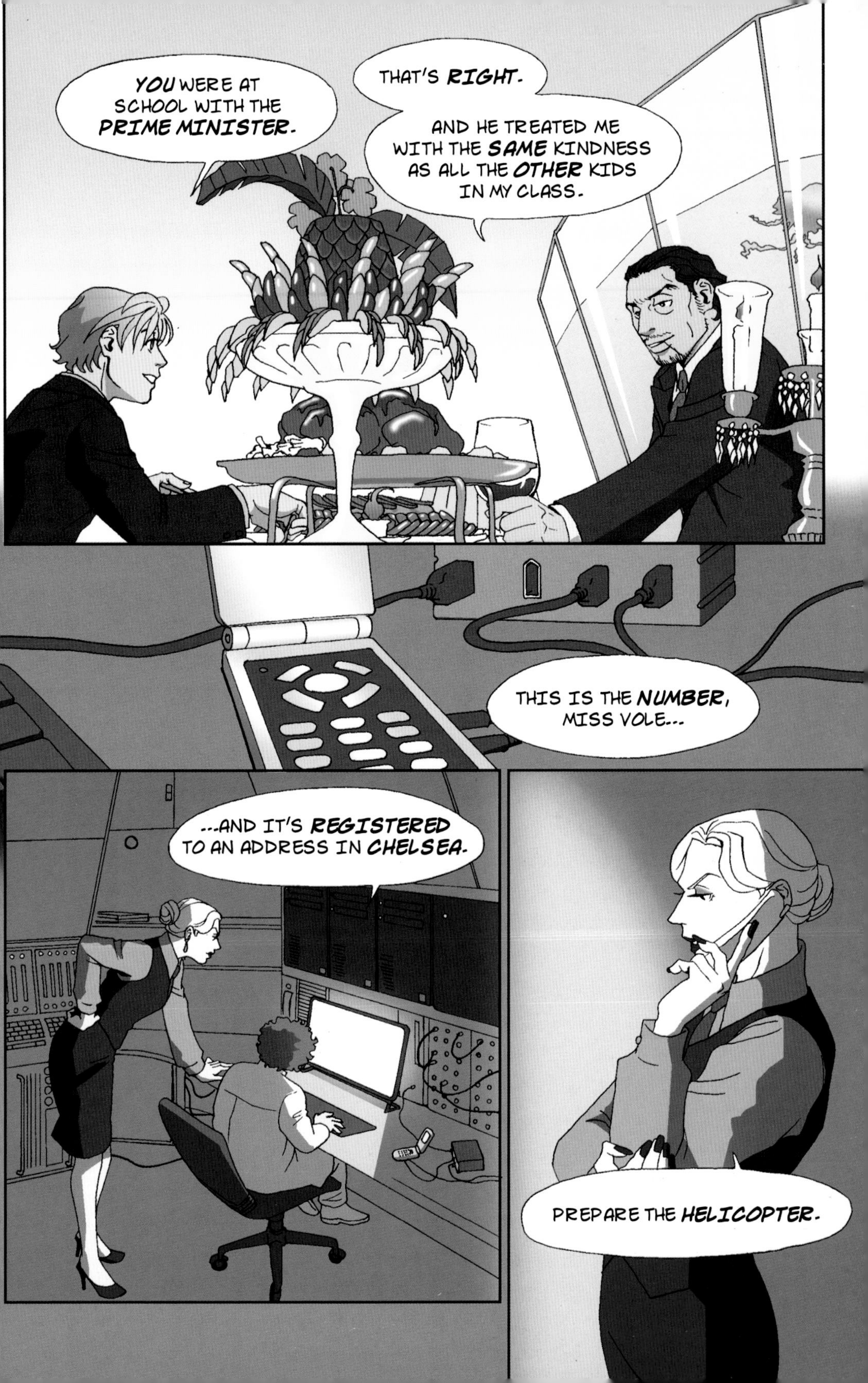
YOU WERE AT SCHOOL WITH THE PRIME MINISTER.
THAT'S RIGHT.
AND HE TREATED ME WITH THE SAME KINDNESS AS ALL THE OTHER KIDS IN MY CLASS.
THIS IS THE NUMBER, MISS VOLE...
...AND IT'S REGISTERED TO AN ADDRESS IN CHELSEA.
PREPARE THE HELICOPTER.

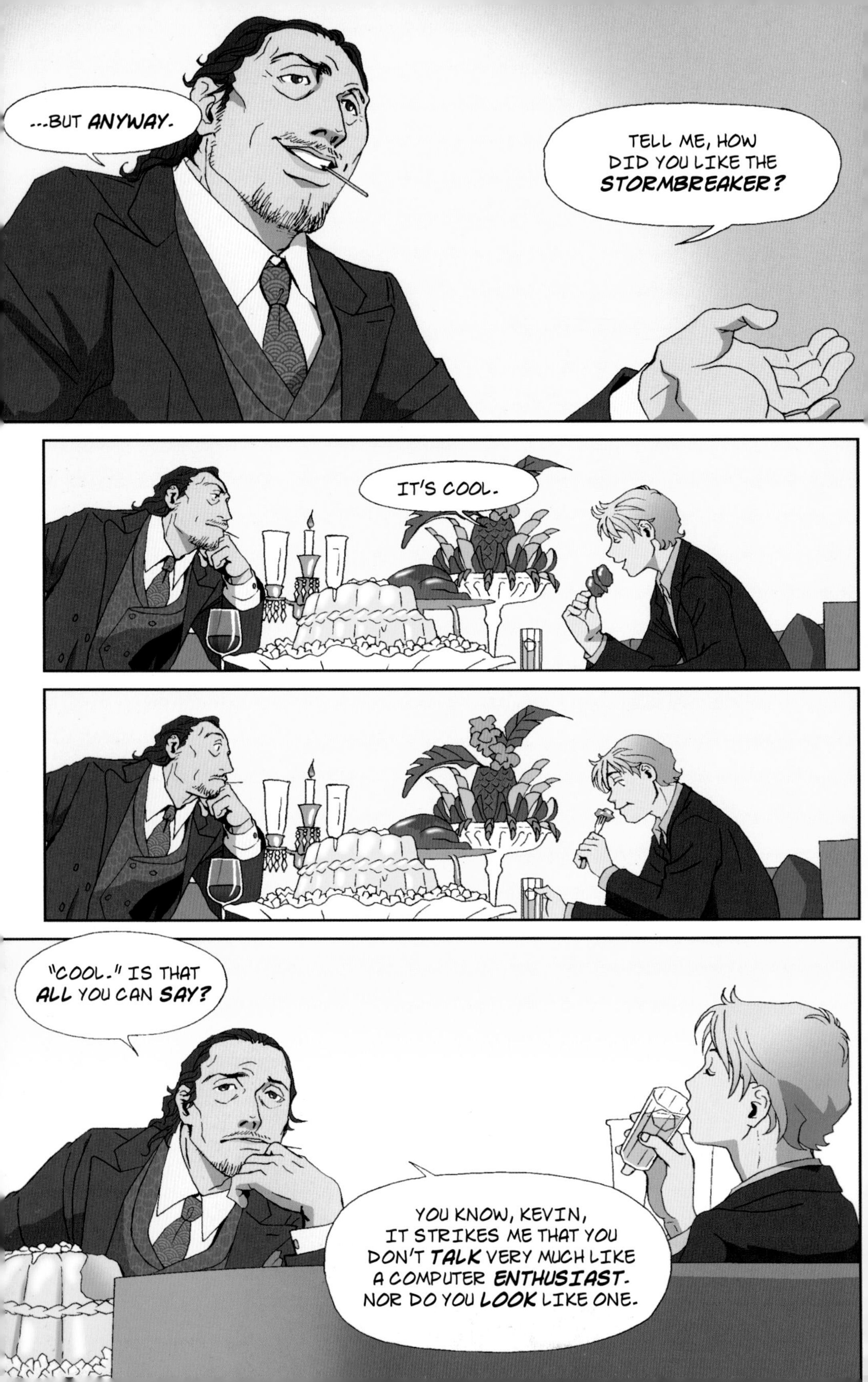
...BUT ANYWAY.
TELL ME, HOW DID YOU LIKE THE STORMBREAKER?
IT'S COOL.
"COOL." IS THAT ALL YOU CAN SAY?
YOU KNOW, KEVIN, IT STRIKES ME THAT YOU DON'T TALK VERY MUCH LIKE A COMPUTER ENTHUSIAST. NOR DO YOU LOOK LIKE ONE.

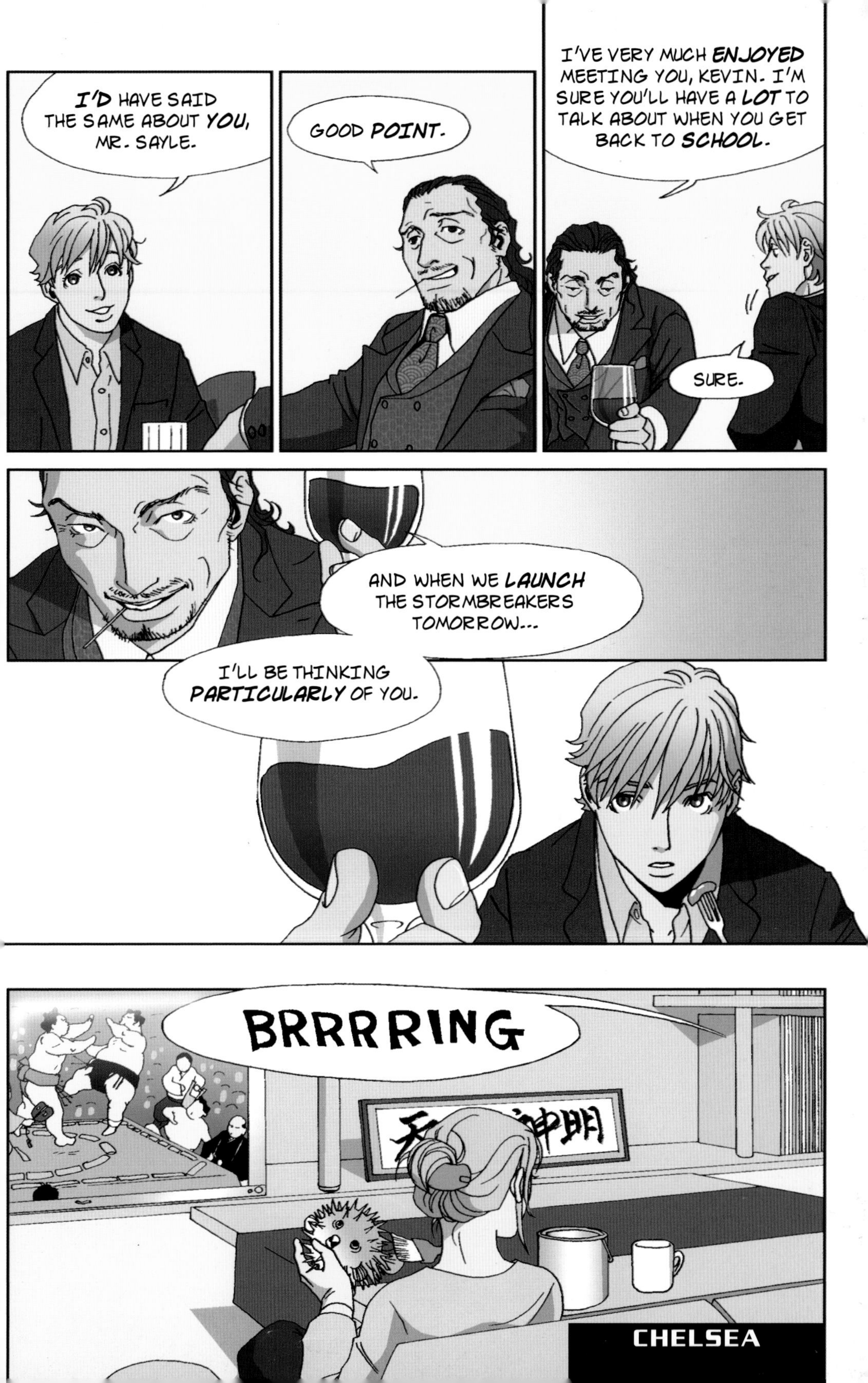
I'D HAVE SAID THE SAME ABOUT YOU, MR. SAYLE.
GOOD POINT.
I'VE VERY MUCH ENJOYED MEETING YOU, KEVIN. I'M SURE YOU'LL HAVE A LOT TO TALK ABOUT WHEN YOU GET BACK TO SCHOOL.
SURE.
AND WHEN WE LAUNCH THE STORMBREAKERS TOMORROW...
I'LL BE THINKING PARTICULARLY OF YOU.
BRRRRING
CHELSEA

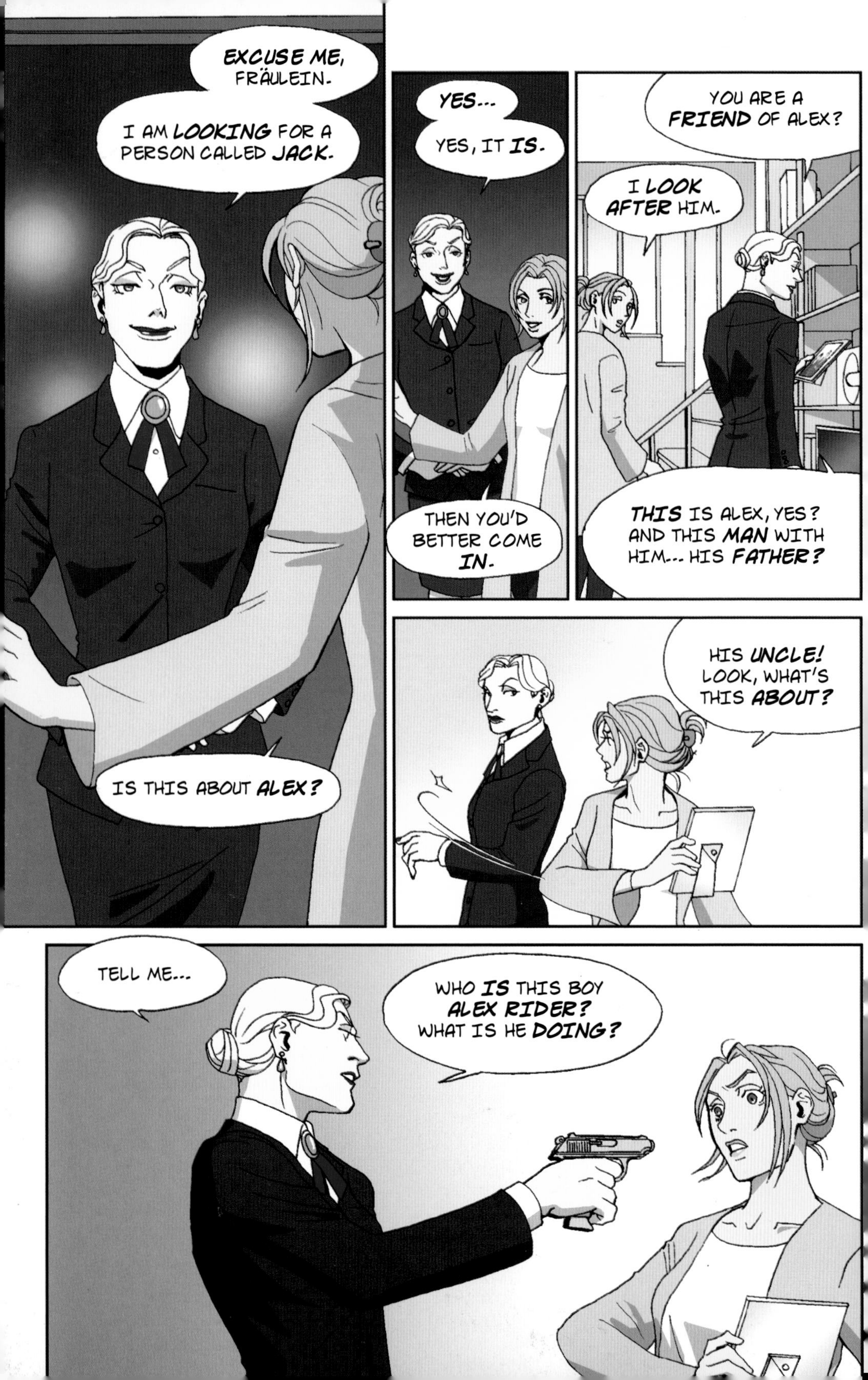
EXCUSE ME, FRÄULEIN.
I AM LOOKING FOR A PERSON CALLED JACK.
IS THIS ABOUT ALEX?
YES...
YES, IT IS.
THEN YOU'D BETTER COME IN.
YOU ARE A FRIEND OF ALEX?
I LOOK AFTER HIM.
THIS IS ALEX, YES? AND THIS MAN WITH HIM... HIS FATHER?
HIS UNCLE! LOOK, WHAT'S THIS ABOUT?
TELL ME...
WHO IS THIS BOY ALEX RIDER? WHAT IS HE DOING?

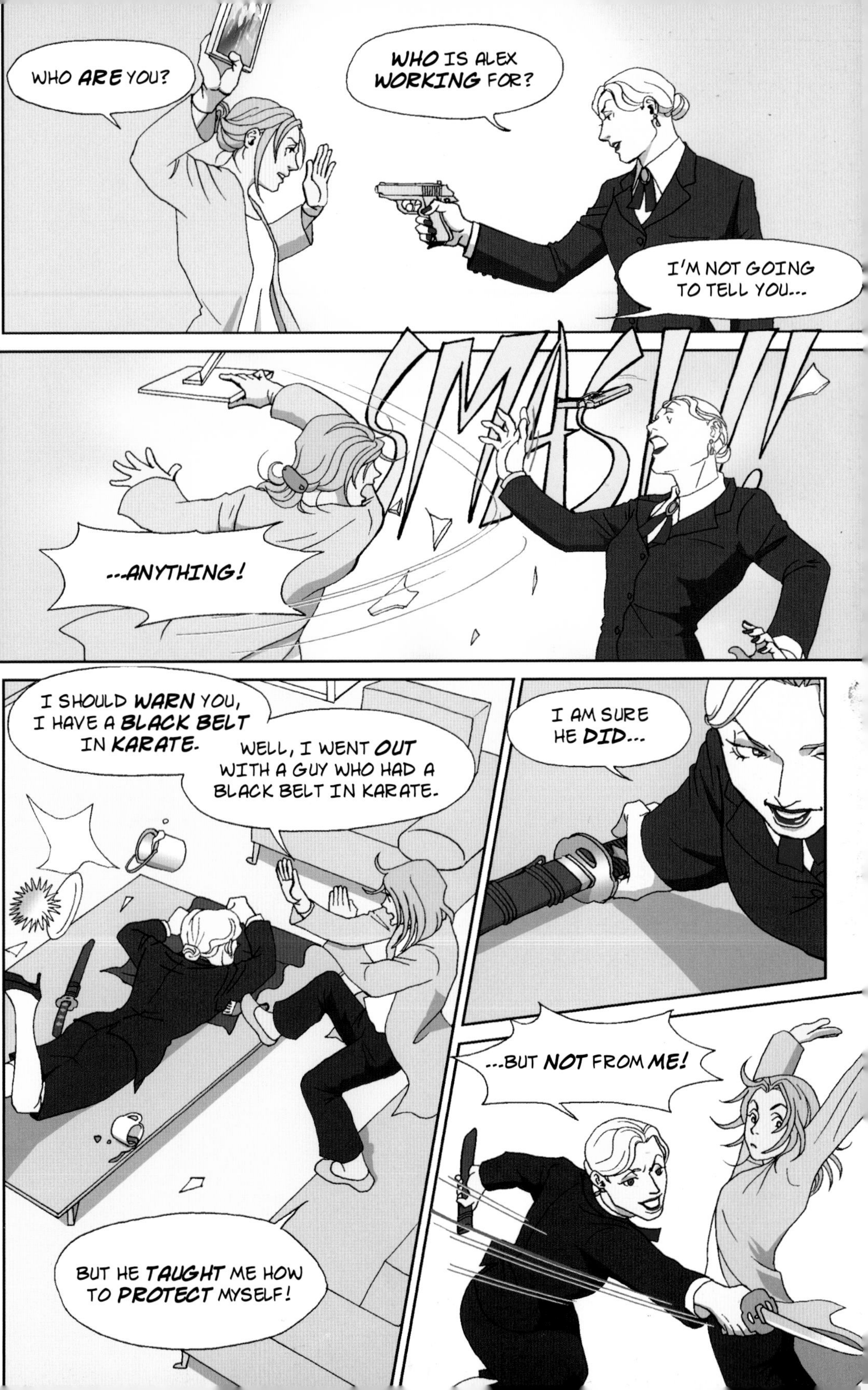
WHO ARE YOU?
WHO IS ALEX WORKING FOR?
I'M NOT GOING TO TELL YOU...
SMASH!!
--ANYTHING!
I SHOULD WARN YOU, I HAVE A BLACK BELT IN KARATE.
WELL, I WENT OUT WITH A GUY WHO HAD A BLACK BELT IN KARATE.
I AM SURE HE DID...
...BUT NOT FROM ME!
BUT HE TAUGHT ME HOW TO PROTECT MYSELF!

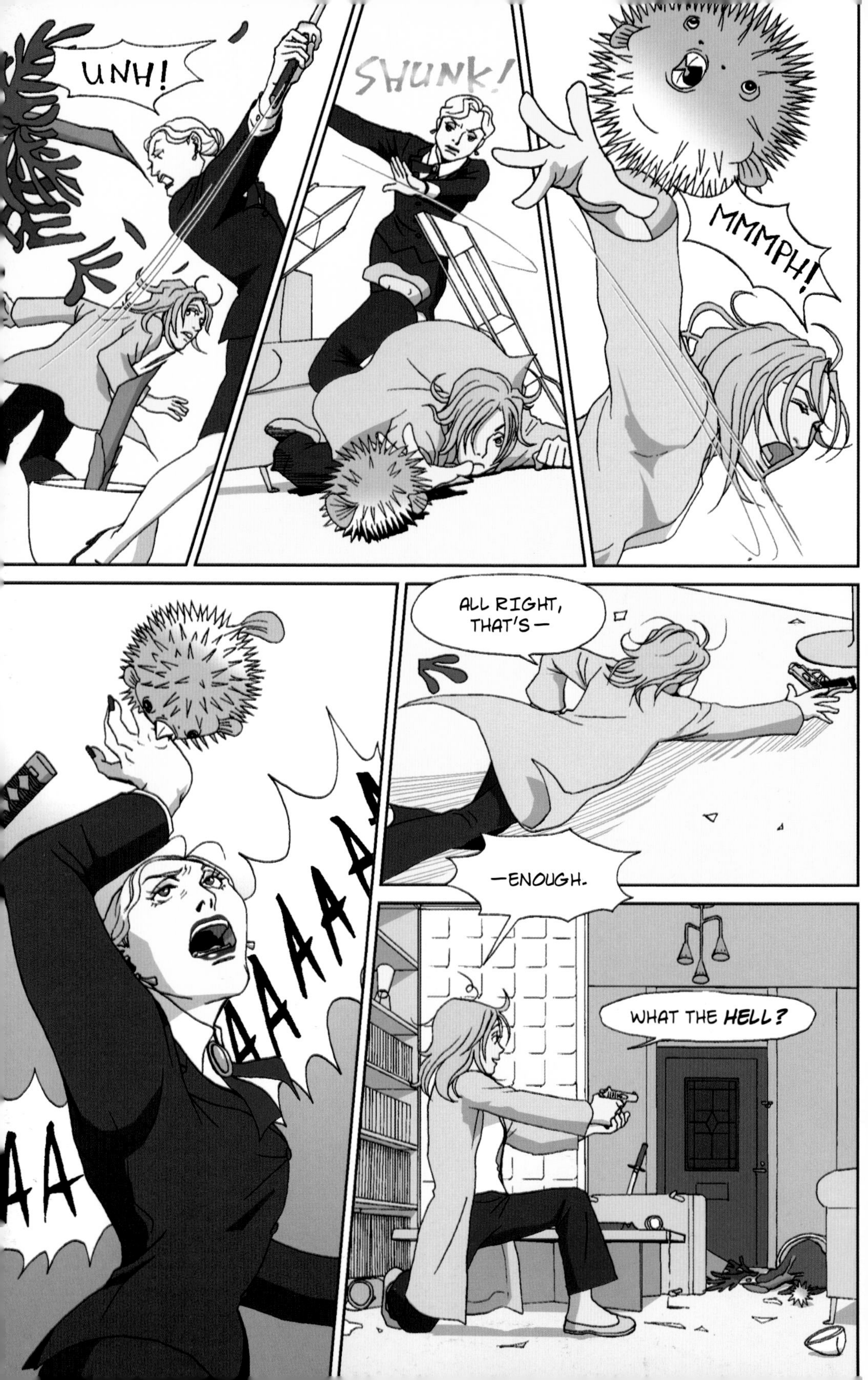
UNH!
SHUNK!
MMMPH!
AAAAAAAA
ALL RIGHT, THAT'S—
—ENOUGH.
WHAT THE **HELL?**

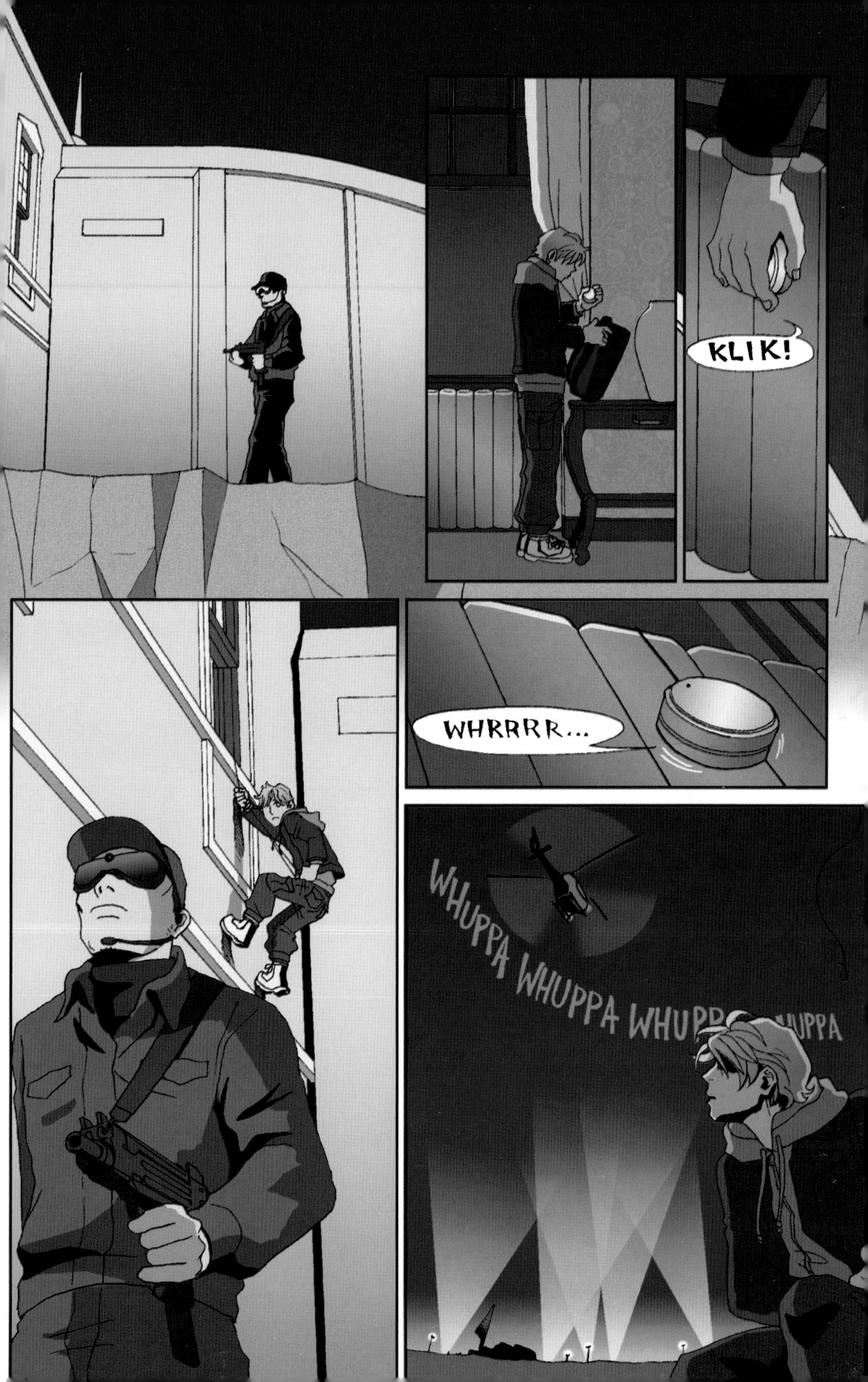
KLIK!
WHRRRR...
WHUPPA WHUPPA WHUPPA WHUPPA

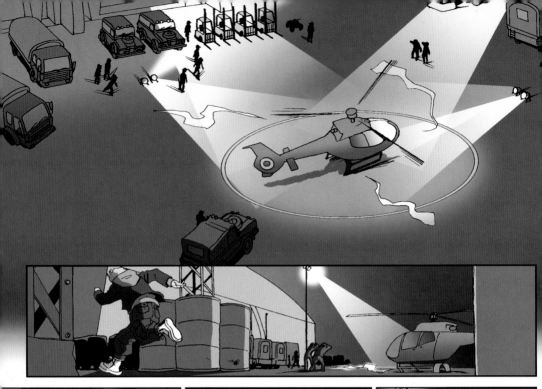

LET US **START**.

MR. GREGOROVICH!

I'M GLAD YOU WERE ABLE TO **JOIN** US TONIGHT.

I DIDN'T **REALIZE** YOU WERE GOING TO COME **PERSONALLY**.

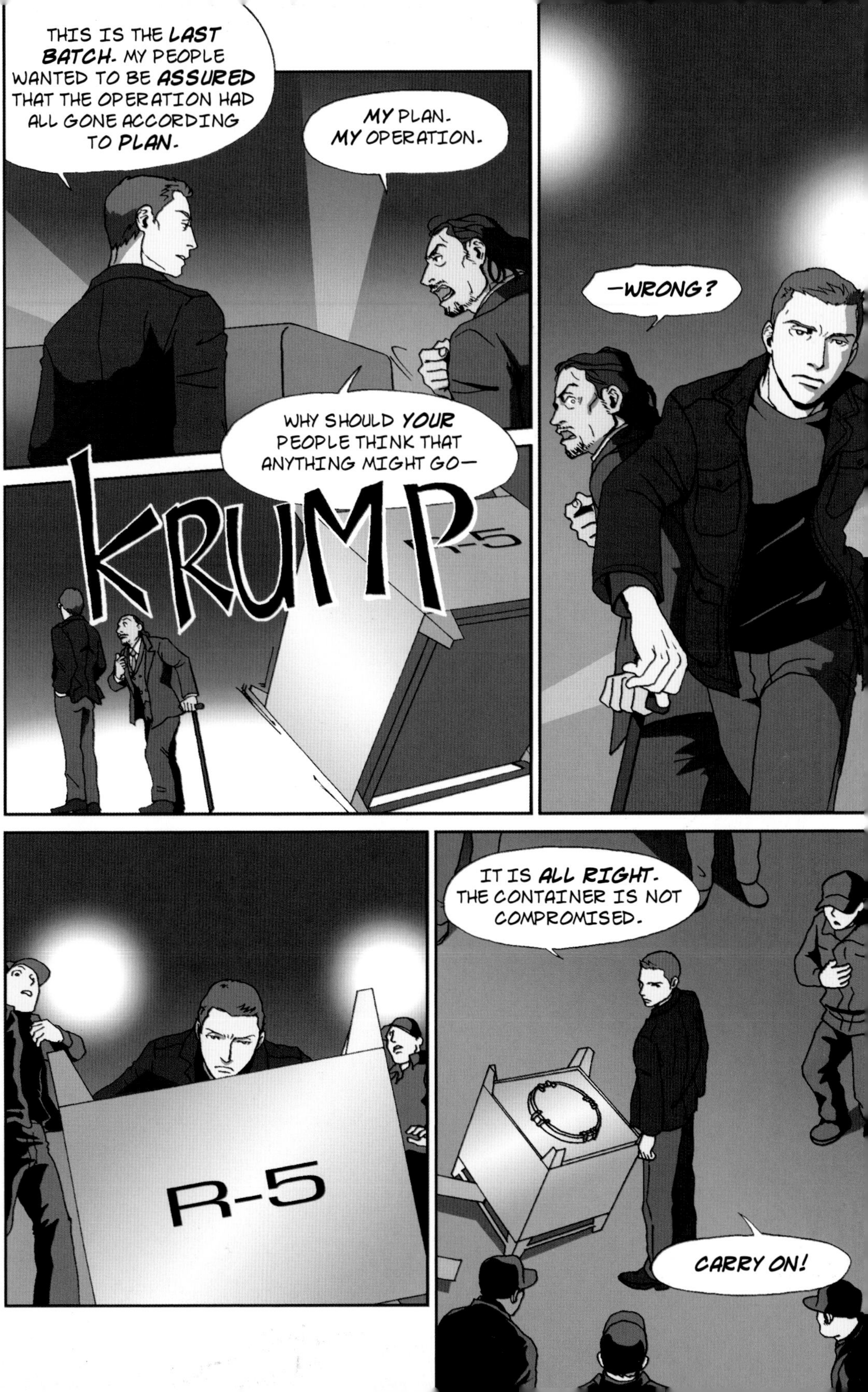
THIS IS THE LAST BATCH. MY PEOPLE WANTED TO BE ASSURED THAT THE OPERATION HAD ALL GONE ACCORDING TO PLAN.
MY PLAN. MY OPERATION.
WHY SHOULD YOUR PEOPLE THINK THAT ANYTHING MIGHT GO—
KRUMP
R-5
—WRONG?
R-5
IT IS ALL RIGHT. THE CONTAINER IS NOT COMPROMISED.
CARRY ON!

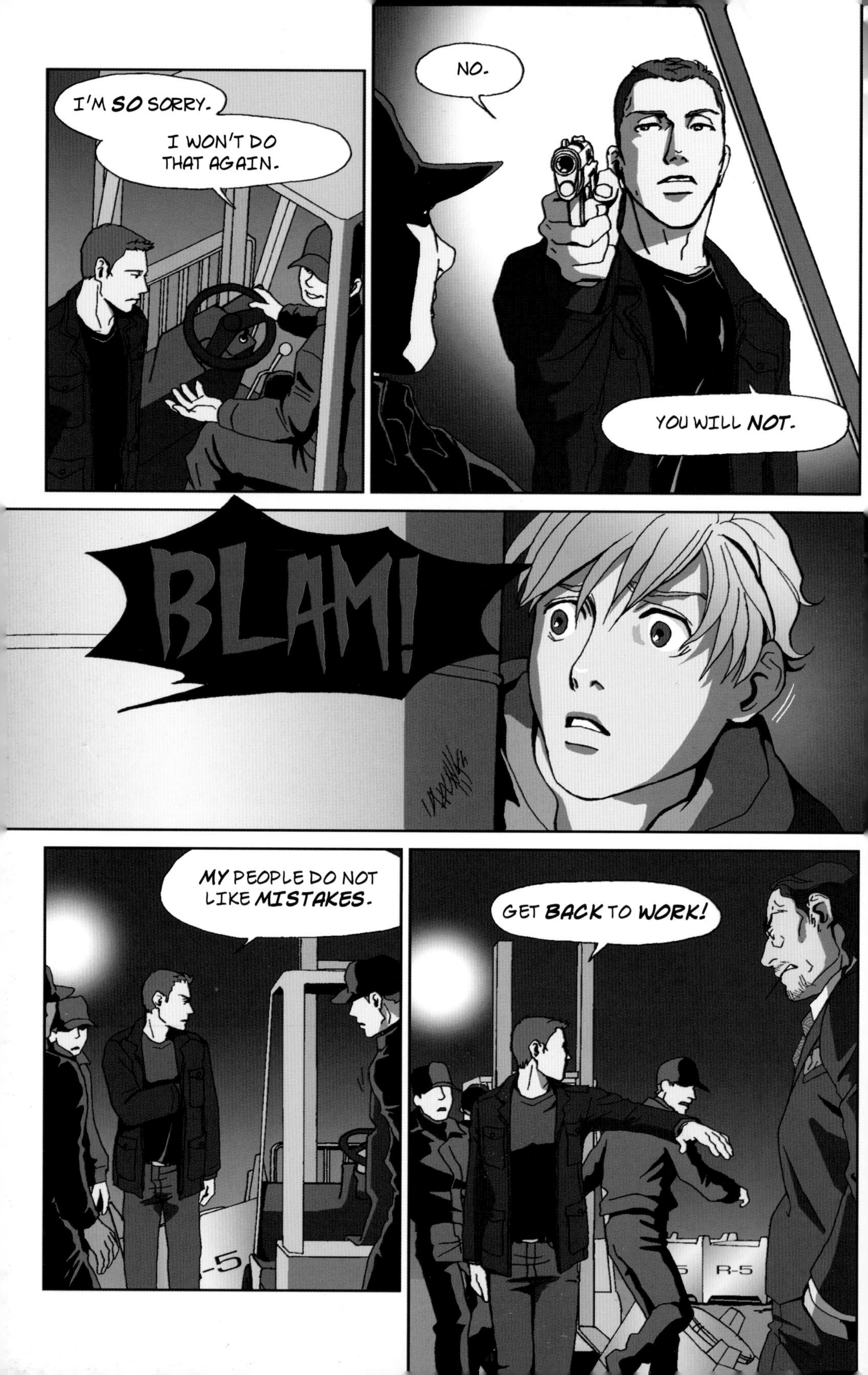

I'M SO SORRY.
I WON'T DO THAT AGAIN.
NO.
YOU WILL NOT.
BLAM!
MY PEOPLE DO NOT LIKE MISTAKES.
GET BACK TO WORK!

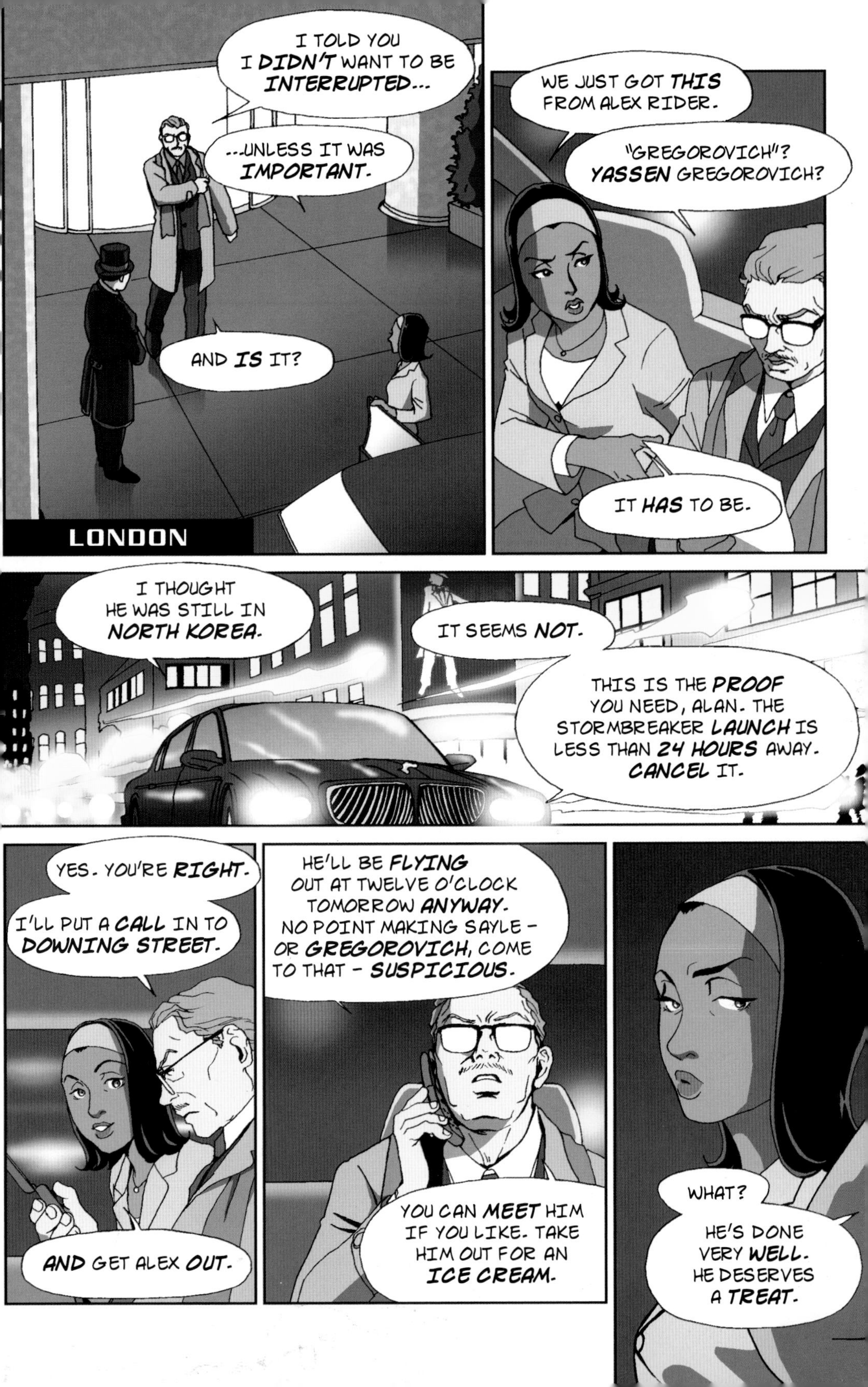

I TOLD YOU I DIDN'T WANT TO BE INTERRUPTED...
...UNLESS IT WAS IMPORTANT.
AND IS IT?
LONDON
WE JUST GOT THIS FROM ALEX RIDER.
"GREGOROVICH"? YASSEN GREGOROVICH?
IT HAS TO BE.
I THOUGHT HE WAS STILL IN NORTH KOREA.
IT SEEMS NOT.
THIS IS THE PROOF YOU NEED, ALAN. THE STORMBREAKER LAUNCH IS LESS THAN 24 HOURS AWAY. CANCEL IT.
YES. YOU'RE RIGHT.
I'LL PUT A CALL IN TO DOWNING STREET.
AND GET ALEX OUT.
HE'LL BE FLYING OUT AT TWELVE O'CLOCK TOMORROW ANYWAY. NO POINT MAKING SAYLE - OR GREGOROVICH, COME TO THAT - SUSPICIOUS.
YOU CAN MEET HIM IF YOU LIKE. TAKE HIM OUT FOR AN ICE CREAM.
WHAT?
HE'S DONE VERY WELL. HE DESERVES A TREAT.

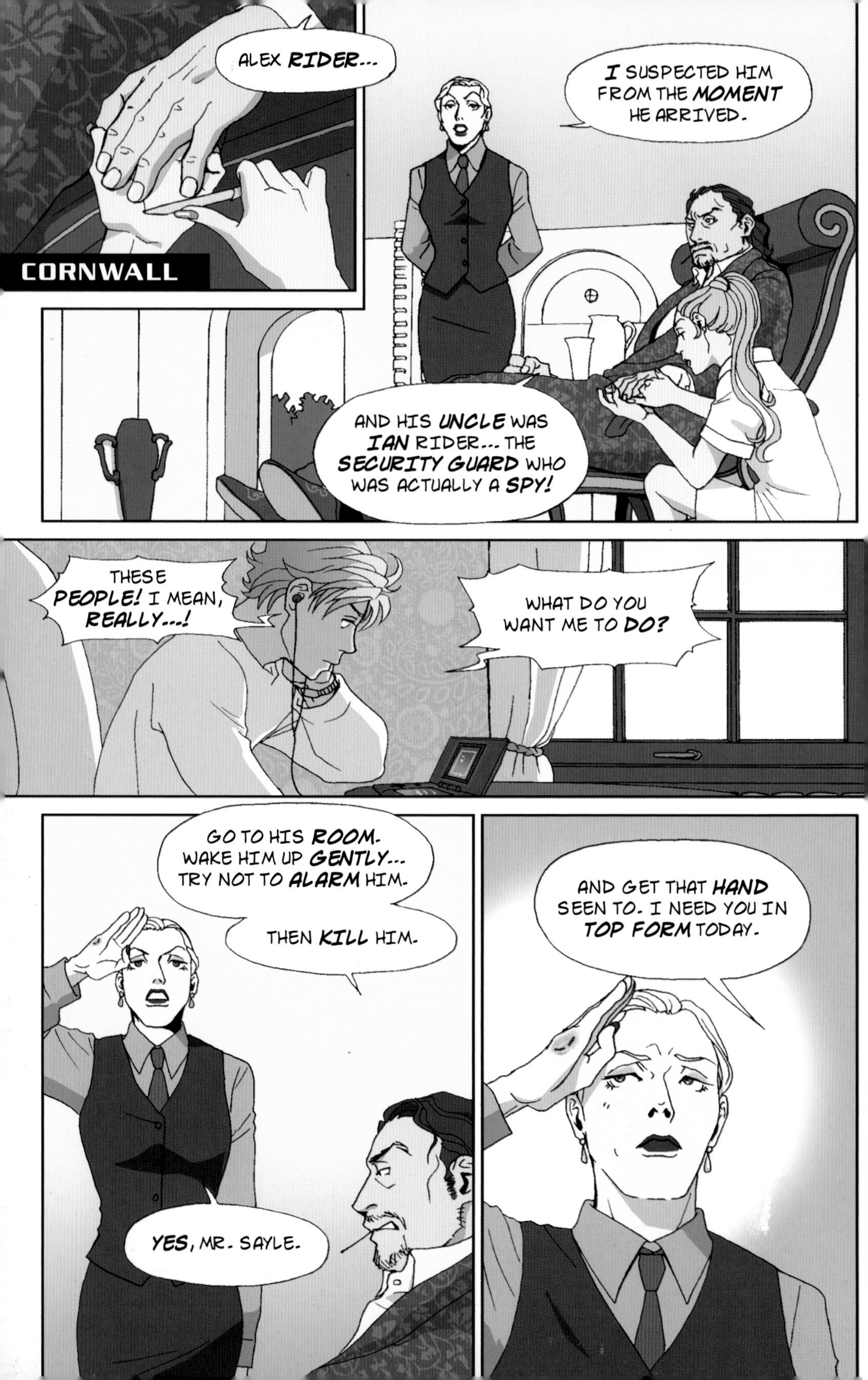
CORNWALL
ALEX RIDER...
I SUSPECTED HIM FROM THE MOMENT HE ARRIVED.
AND HIS UNCLE WAS IAN RIDER... THE SECURITY GUARD WHO WAS ACTUALLY A SPY!
THESE PEOPLE! I MEAN, REALLY...!
WHAT DO YOU WANT ME TO DO?
GO TO HIS ROOM. WAKE HIM UP GENTLY... TRY NOT TO ALARM HIM.
THEN KILL HIM.
YES, MR. SAYLE.
AND GET THAT HAND SEEN TO. I NEED YOU IN TOP FORM TODAY.

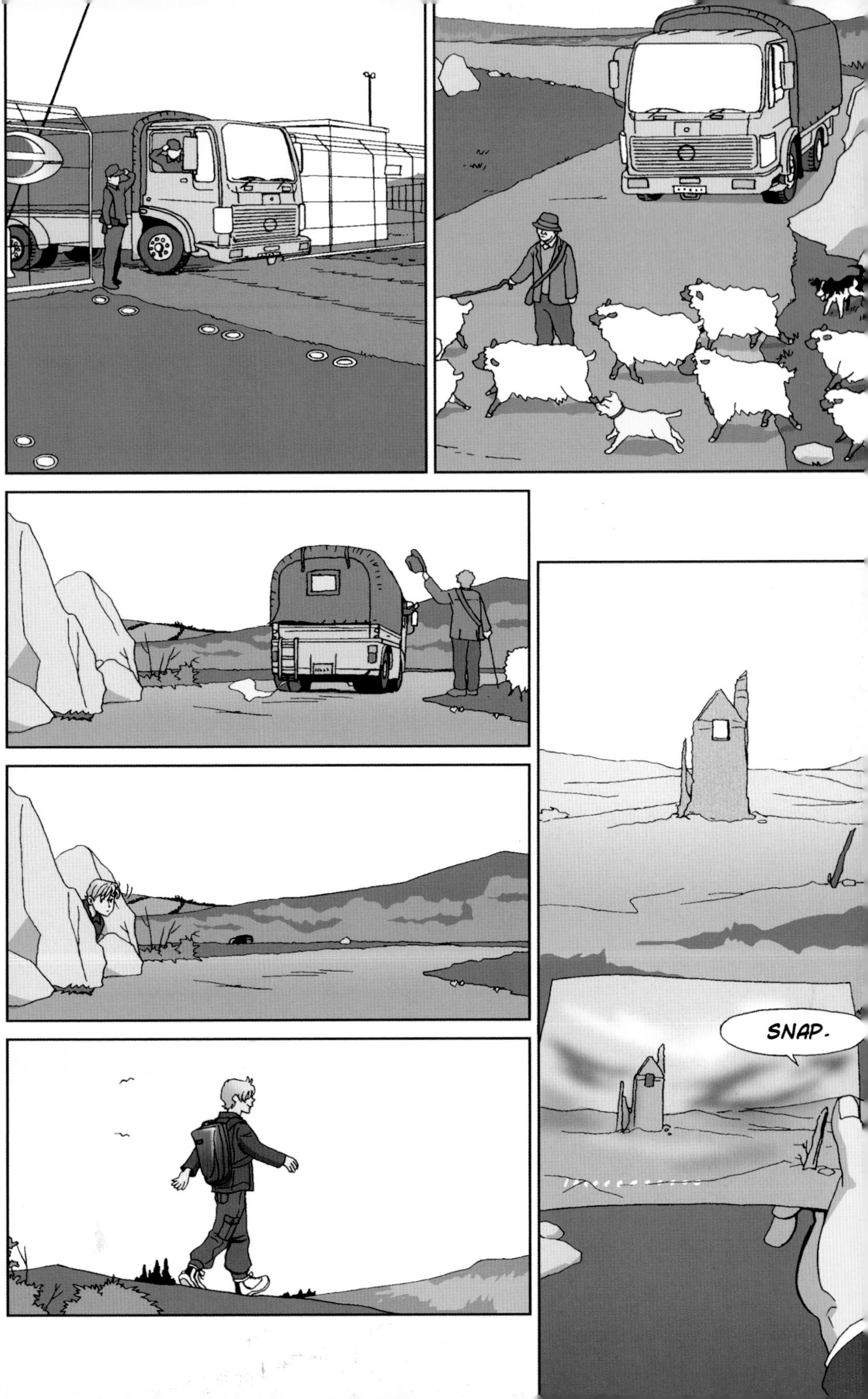
SNAP.

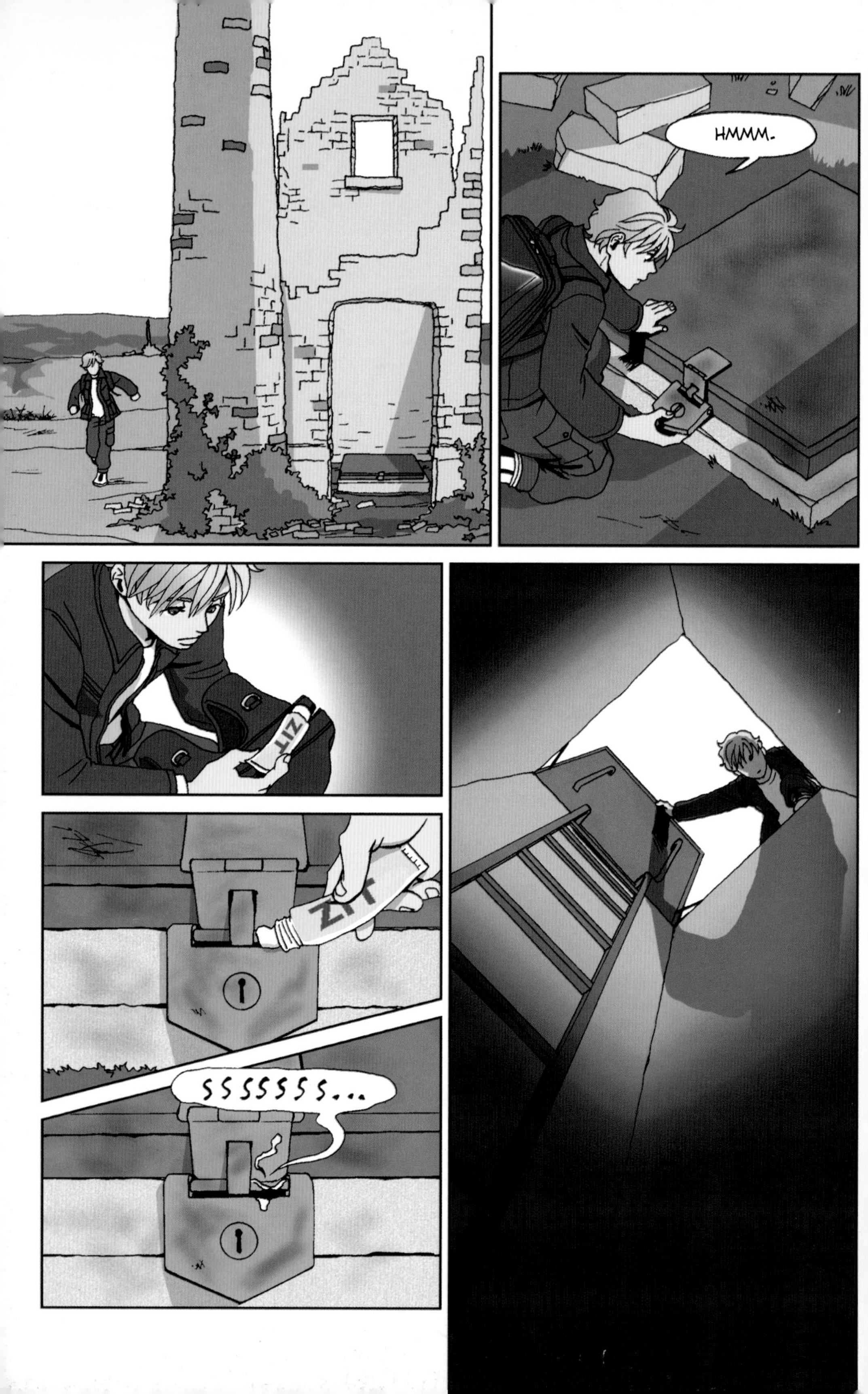
HMMM.
ZIT
ZIT
SSSSSSS...

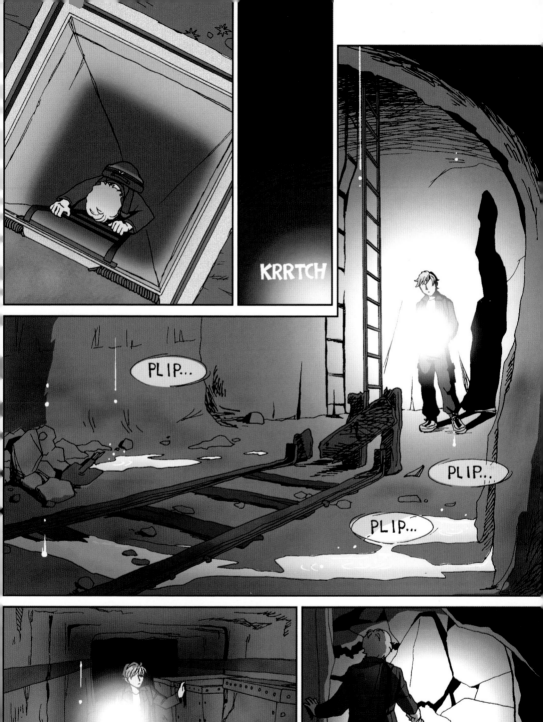

KRRTCH

PLIP...

PLIP...

PLIP...

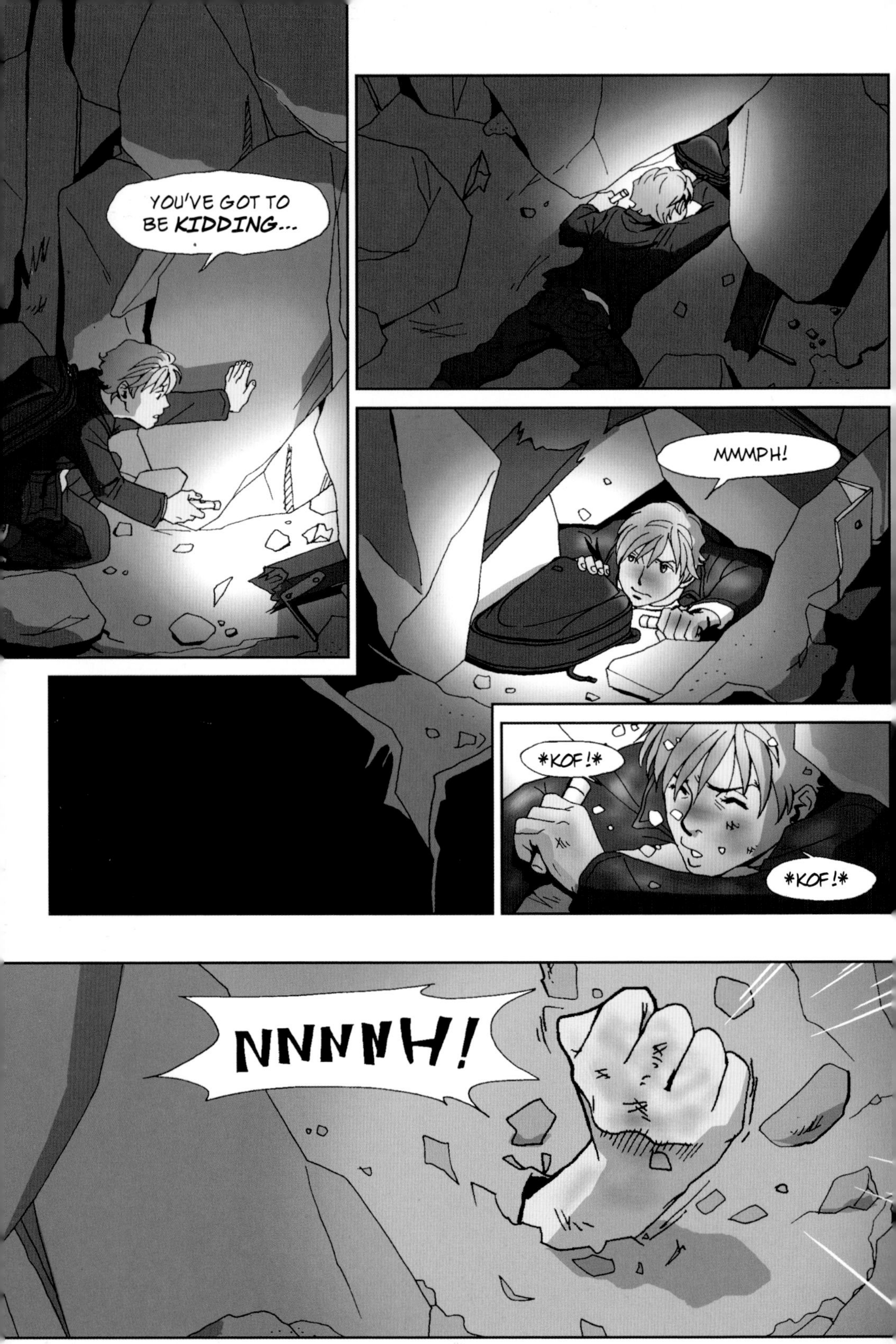

YOU'VE GOT TO BE KIDDING...
MMMPH!
KOF!
KOF!
NNNNH!

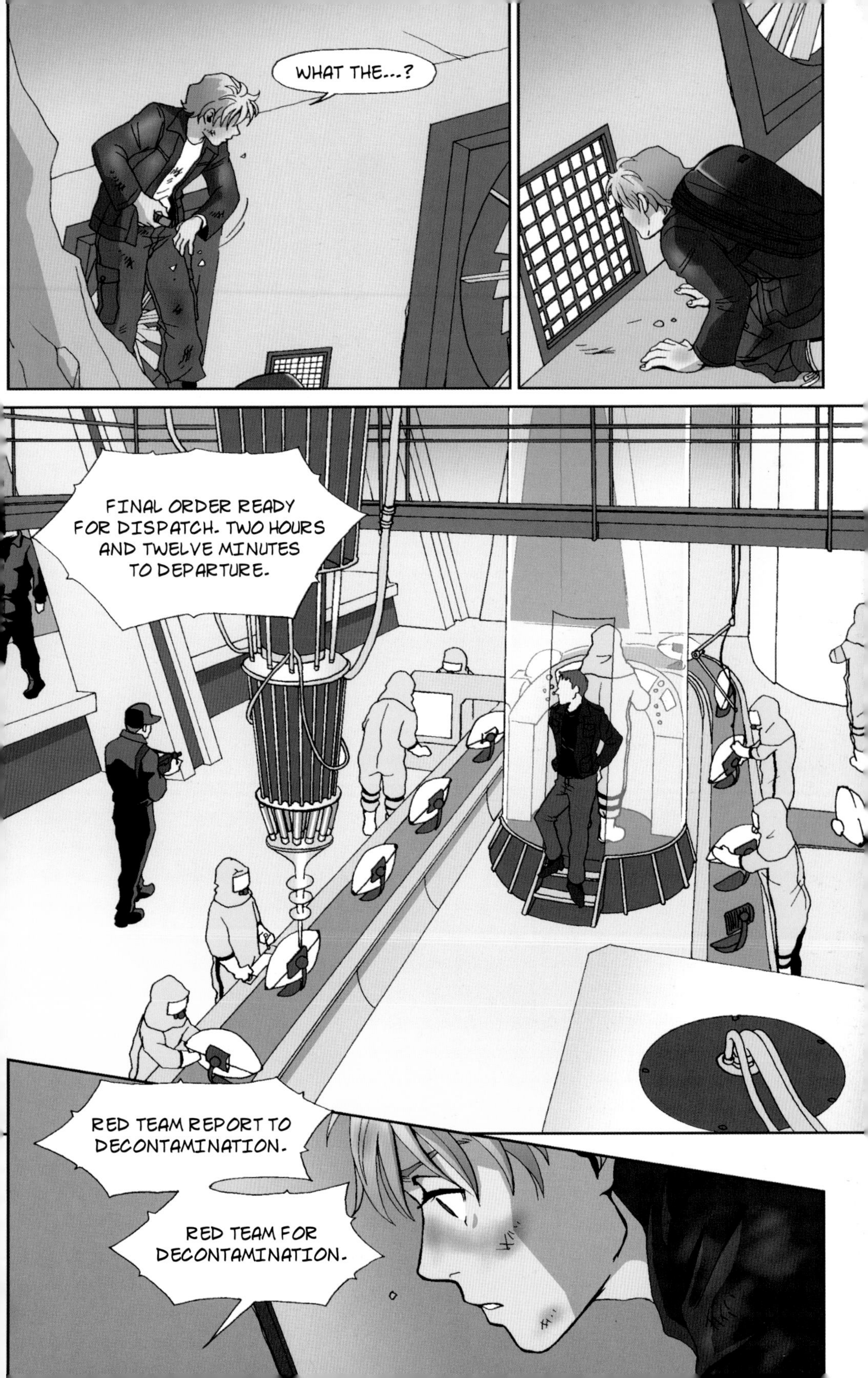
WHAT THE...?
FINAL ORDER READY FOR DISPATCH. TWO HOURS AND TWELVE MINUTES TO DEPARTURE.
RED TEAM REPORT TO DECONTAMINATION.
RED TEAM FOR DECONTAMINATION.

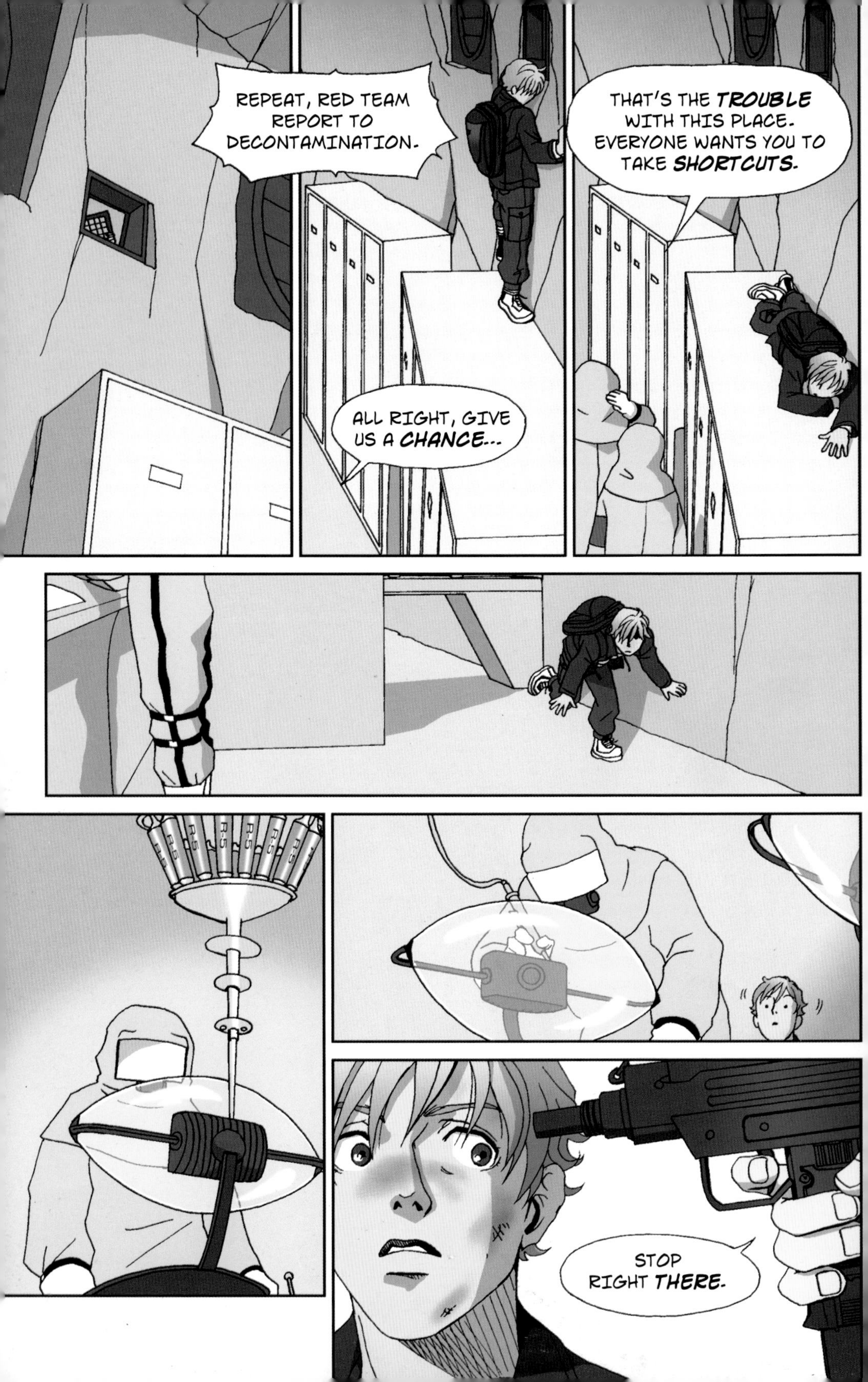
REPEAT, RED TEAM REPORT TO DECONTAMINATION.
ALL RIGHT, GIVE US A *CHANCE*...
THAT'S THE *TROUBLE* WITH THIS PLACE. EVERYONE WANTS YOU TO TAKE *SHORTCUTS*.
R-5
STOP RIGHT *THERE*.

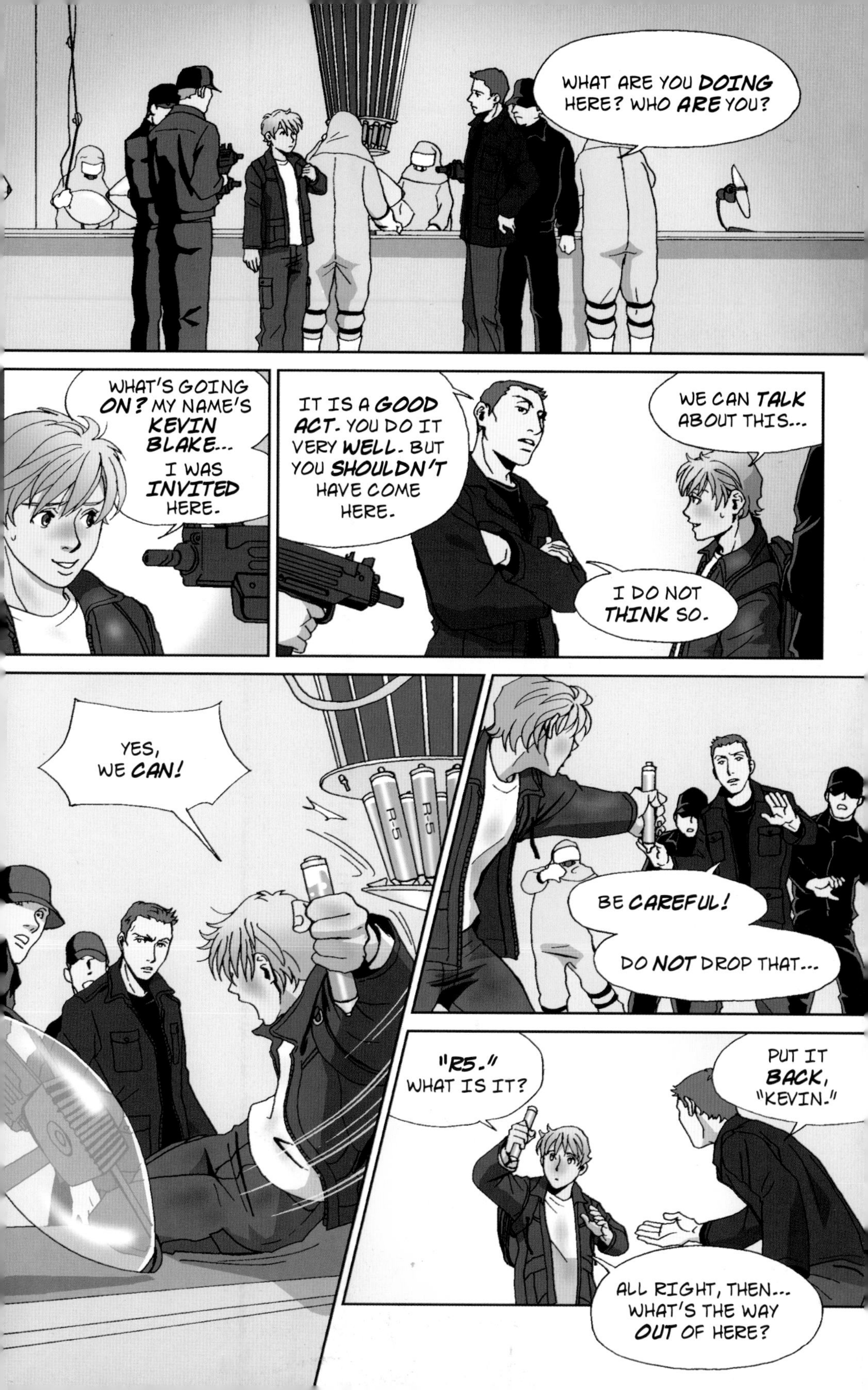
WHAT ARE YOU DOING HERE? WHO ARE YOU?
WHAT'S GOING ON? MY NAME'S KEVIN BLAKE...
I WAS INVITED HERE.
IT IS A GOOD ACT. YOU DO IT VERY WELL. BUT YOU SHOULDN'T HAVE COME HERE.
WE CAN TALK ABOUT THIS...
I DO NOT THINK SO.
YES, WE CAN!
R-5
R-5
BE CAREFUL!
DO NOT DROP THAT...
"R5." WHAT IS IT?
PUT IT BACK, "KEVIN."
ALL RIGHT, THEN... WHAT'S THE WAY OUT OF HERE?

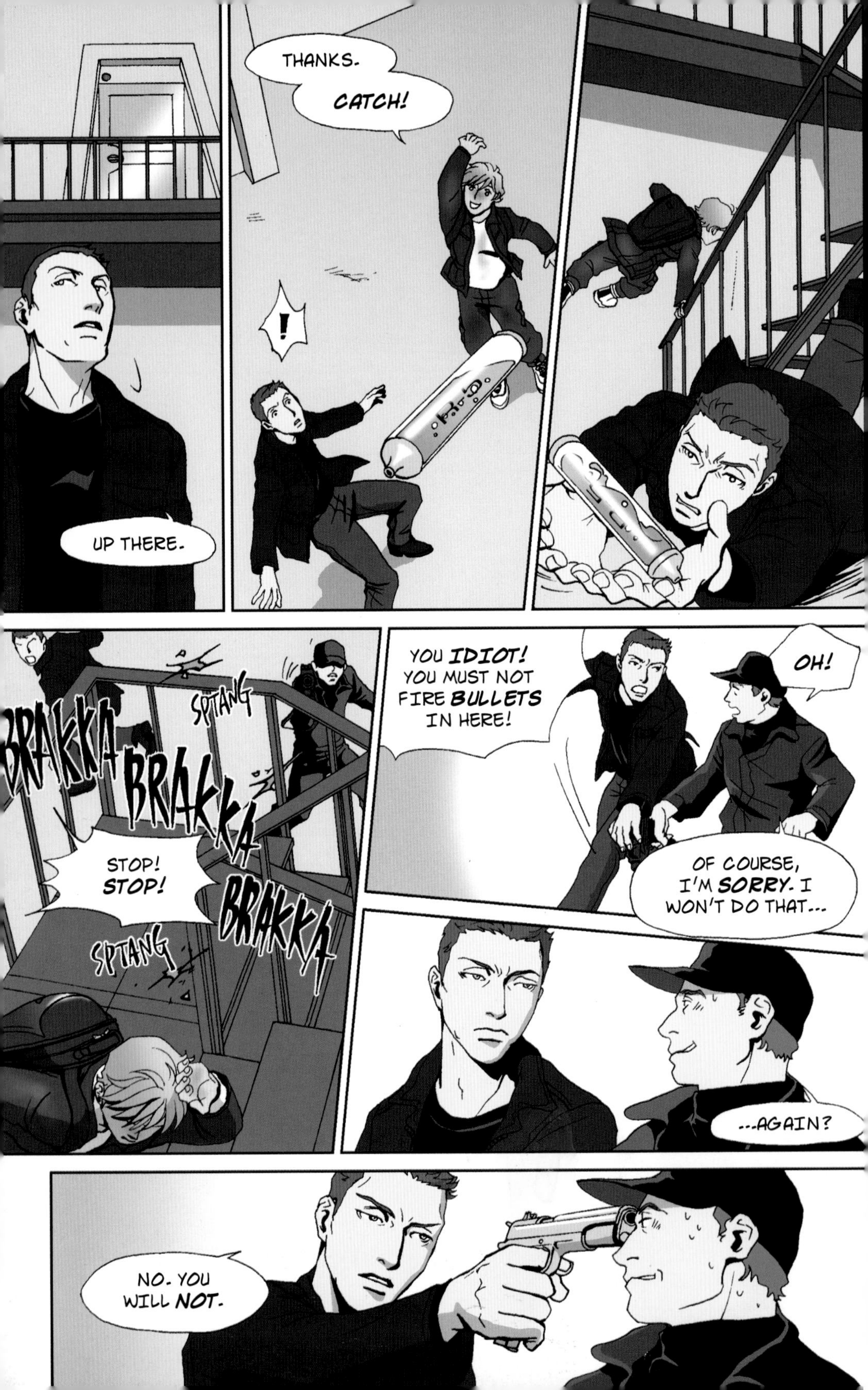
UP THERE.
THANKS.
CATCH!
!
BRAKKA
BRAKKA
SPTANG
STOP! STOP!
BRAKKA
SPTANG
YOU IDIOT! YOU MUST NOT FIRE BULLETS IN HERE!
OH!
OF COURSE, I'M SORRY. I WON'T DO THAT...
...AGAIN?
NO. YOU WILL NOT.

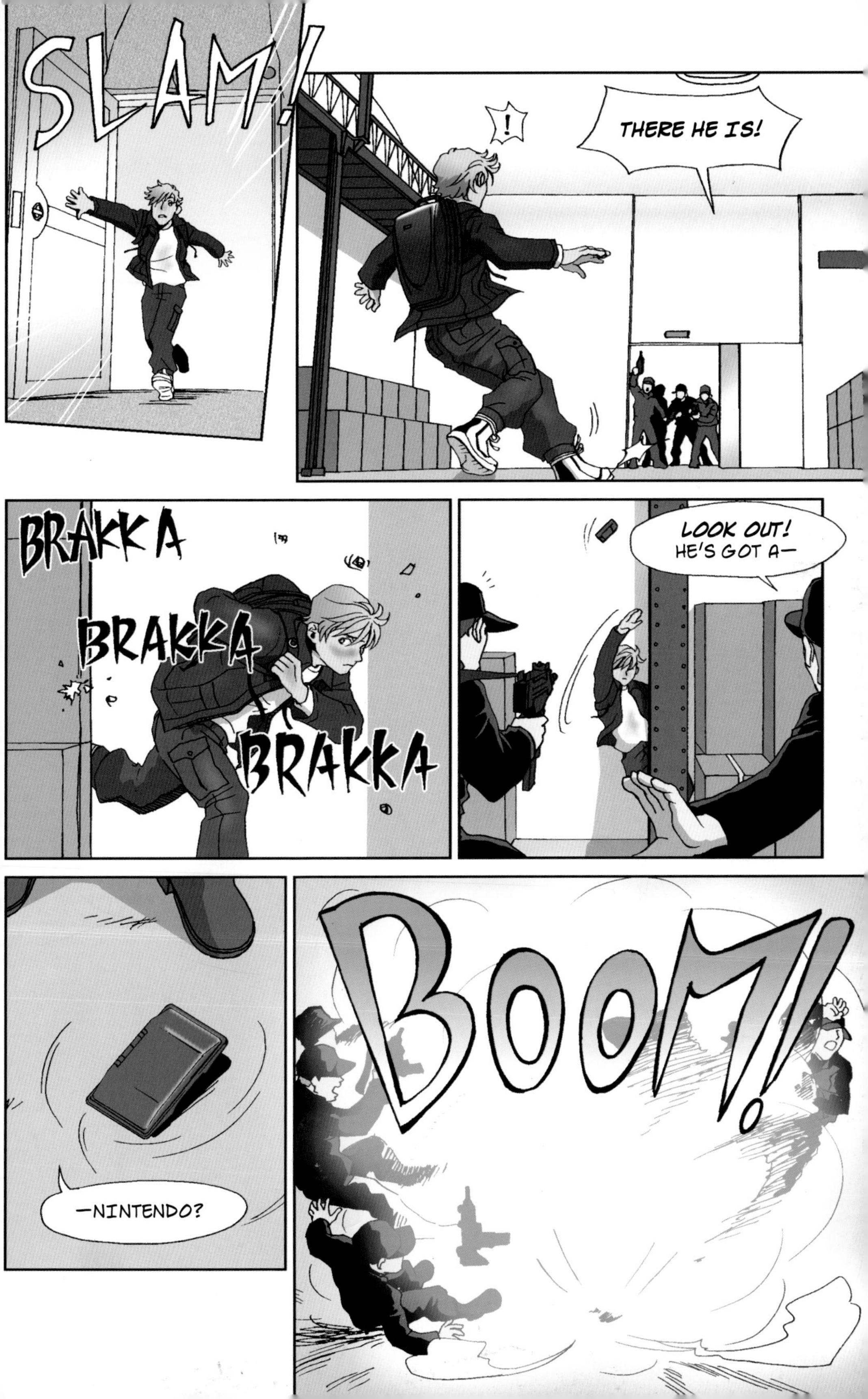
SLAM!
!
THERE HE IS!
BRAKKA
BRAKKA
BRAKKA
LOOK OUT! HE'S GOT A—
—NINTENDO?
BOOM!

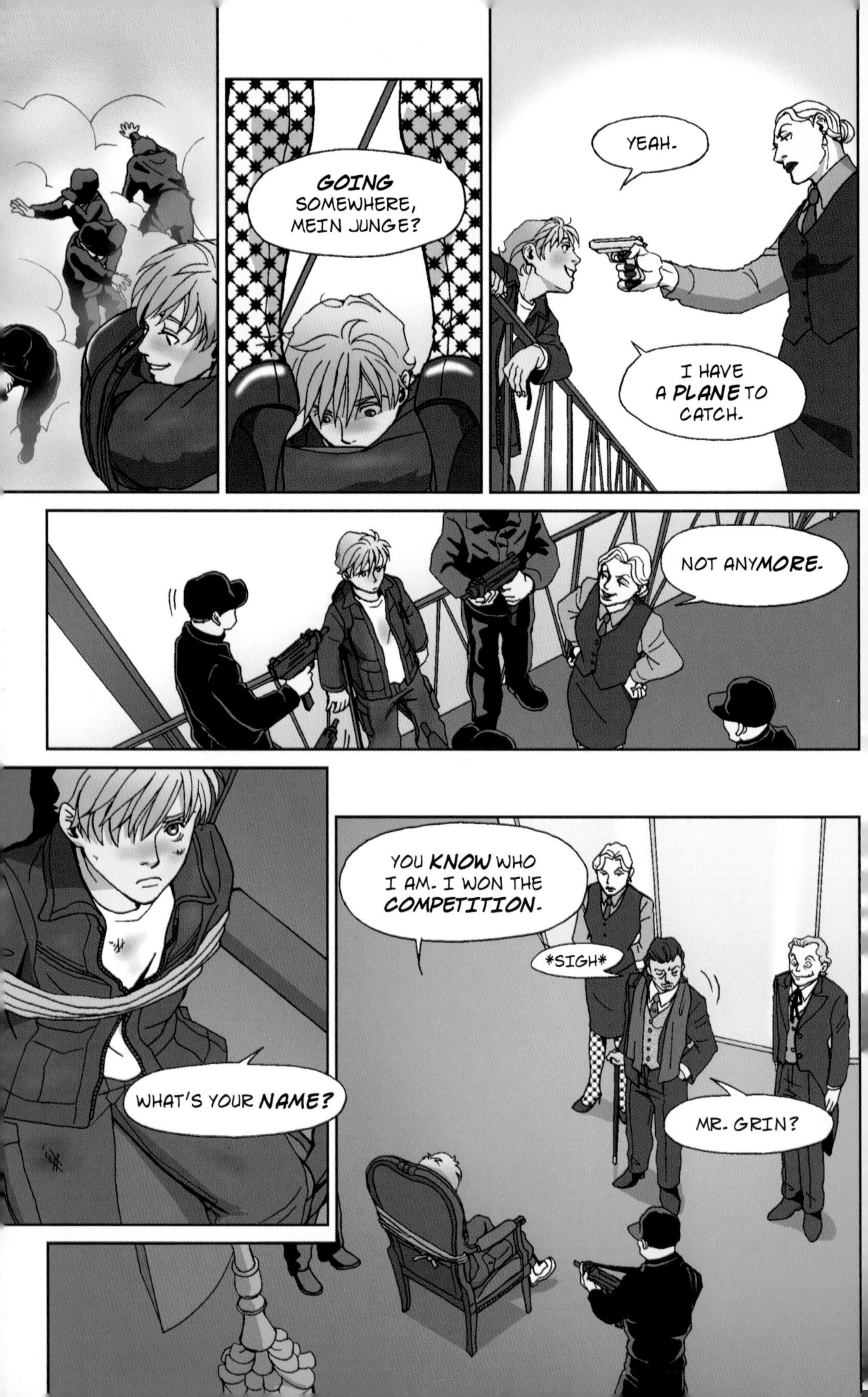
GOING SOMEWHERE, MEIN JUNGE?
YEAH.
I HAVE A PLANE TO CATCH.
NOT ANYMORE.
WHAT'S YOUR NAME?
YOU KNOW WHO I AM. I WON THE COMPETITION.
SIGH
MR. GRIN?

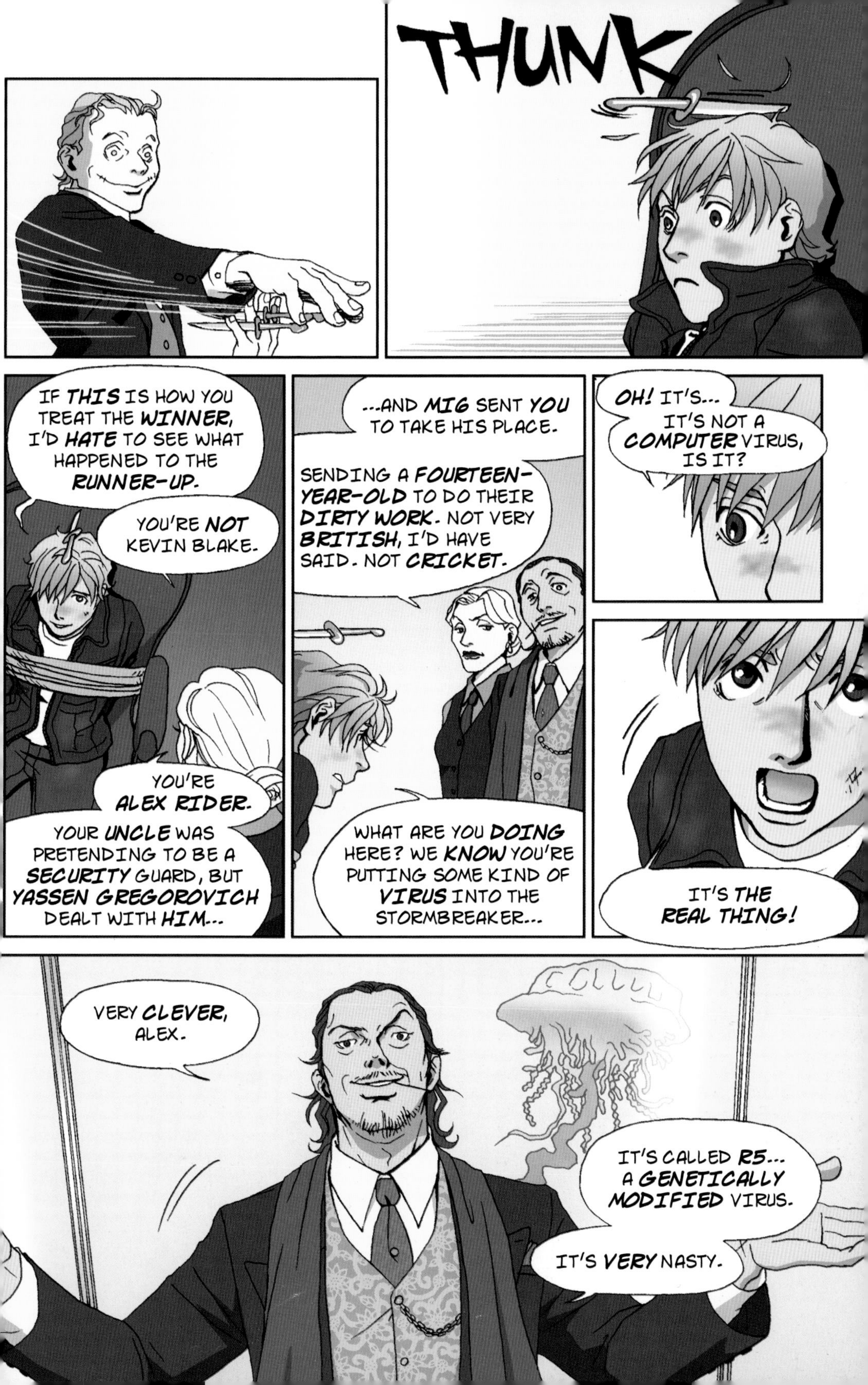
THUNK
IF THIS IS HOW YOU TREAT THE WINNER, I'D HATE TO SEE WHAT HAPPENED TO THE RUNNER-UP.
YOU'RE NOT KEVIN BLAKE.
YOU'RE ALEX RIDER.
YOUR UNCLE WAS PRETENDING TO BE A SECURITY GUARD, BUT YASSEN GREGOROVICH DEALT WITH HIM...
...AND MI6 SENT YOU TO TAKE HIS PLACE.
SENDING A FOURTEEN-YEAR-OLD TO DO THEIR DIRTY WORK. NOT VERY BRITISH, I'D HAVE SAID. NOT CRICKET.
WHAT ARE YOU DOING HERE? WE KNOW YOU'RE PUTTING SOME KIND OF VIRUS INTO THE STORMBREAKER...
OH! IT'S... IT'S NOT A COMPUTER VIRUS, IS IT?
IT'S THE REAL THING!
VERY CLEVER, ALEX.
IT'S CALLED R5... A GENETICALLY MODIFIED VIRUS.
IT'S VERY NASTY.

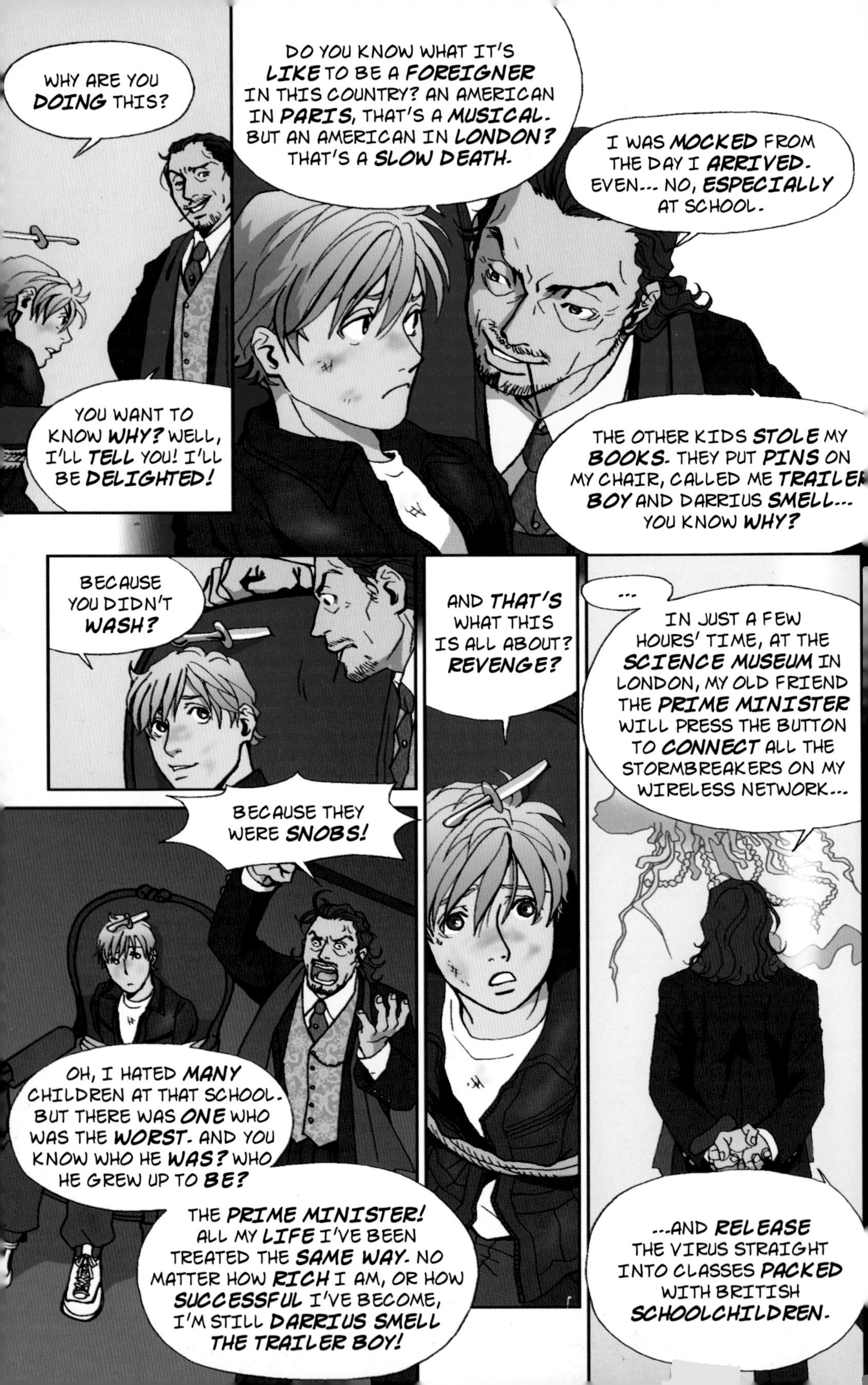
WHY ARE YOU DOING THIS?
DO YOU KNOW WHAT IT'S LIKE TO BE A FOREIGNER IN THIS COUNTRY? AN AMERICAN IN PARIS, THAT'S A MUSICAL. BUT AN AMERICAN IN LONDON? THAT'S A SLOW DEATH.
I WAS MOCKED FROM THE DAY I ARRIVED. EVEN... NO, ESPECIALLY AT SCHOOL.
YOU WANT TO KNOW WHY? WELL, I'LL TELL YOU! I'LL BE DELIGHTED!
THE OTHER KIDS STOLE MY BOOKS. THEY PUT PINS ON MY CHAIR, CALLED ME TRAILER BOY AND DARRIUS SMELL... YOU KNOW WHY?
BECAUSE YOU DIDN'T WASH?
BECAUSE THEY WERE SNOBS!
OH, I HATED MANY CHILDREN AT THAT SCHOOL. BUT THERE WAS ONE WHO WAS THE WORST. AND YOU KNOW WHO HE WAS? WHO HE GREW UP TO BE?
THE PRIME MINISTER! ALL MY LIFE I'VE BEEN TREATED THE SAME WAY. NO MATTER HOW RICH I AM, OR HOW SUCCESSFUL I'VE BECOME, I'M STILL DARRIUS SMELL THE TRAILER BOY!
AND THAT'S WHAT THIS IS ALL ABOUT? REVENGE?
...
IN JUST A FEW HOURS' TIME, AT THE SCIENCE MUSEUM IN LONDON, MY OLD FRIEND THE PRIME MINISTER WILL PRESS THE BUTTON TO CONNECT ALL THE STORMBREAKERS ON MY WIRELESS NETWORK...
...AND RELEASE THE VIRUS STRAIGHT INTO CLASSES PACKED WITH BRITISH SCHOOLCHILDREN.

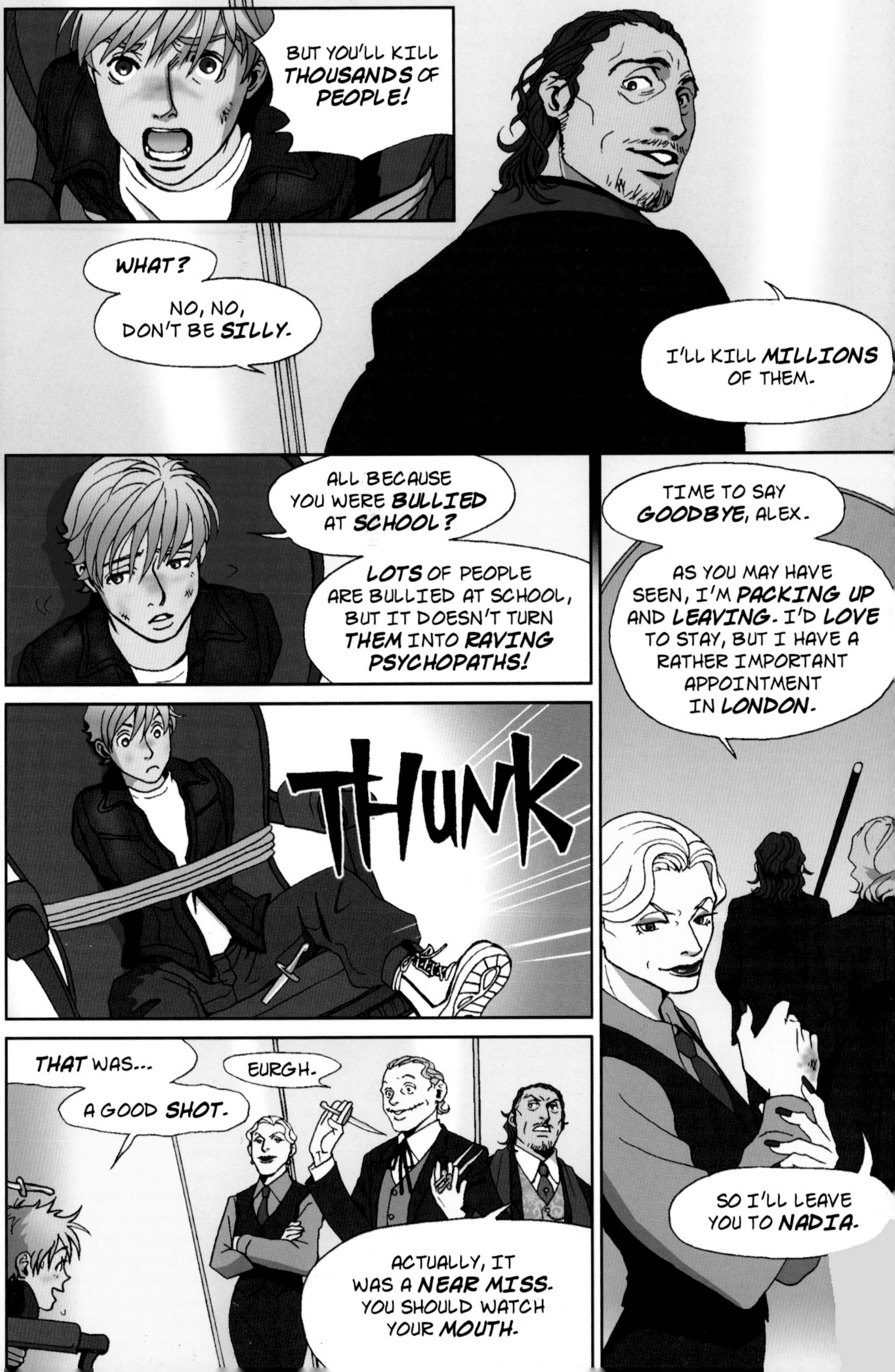

BUT YOU'LL KILL THOUSANDS OF PEOPLE!
WHAT?
NO, NO, DON'T BE SILLY.
I'LL KILL MILLIONS OF THEM.
ALL BECAUSE YOU WERE BULLIED AT SCHOOL?
LOTS OF PEOPLE ARE BULLIED AT SCHOOL, BUT IT DOESN'T TURN THEM INTO RAVING PSYCHOPATHS!
TIME TO SAY GOODBYE, ALEX.
AS YOU MAY HAVE SEEN, I'M PACKING UP AND LEAVING. I'D LOVE TO STAY, BUT I HAVE A RATHER IMPORTANT APPOINTMENT IN LONDON.
THUNK
SO I'LL LEAVE YOU TO NADIA.
THAT WAS...
EURGH.
A GOOD SHOT.
ACTUALLY, IT WAS A NEAR MISS. YOU SHOULD WATCH YOUR MOUTH.

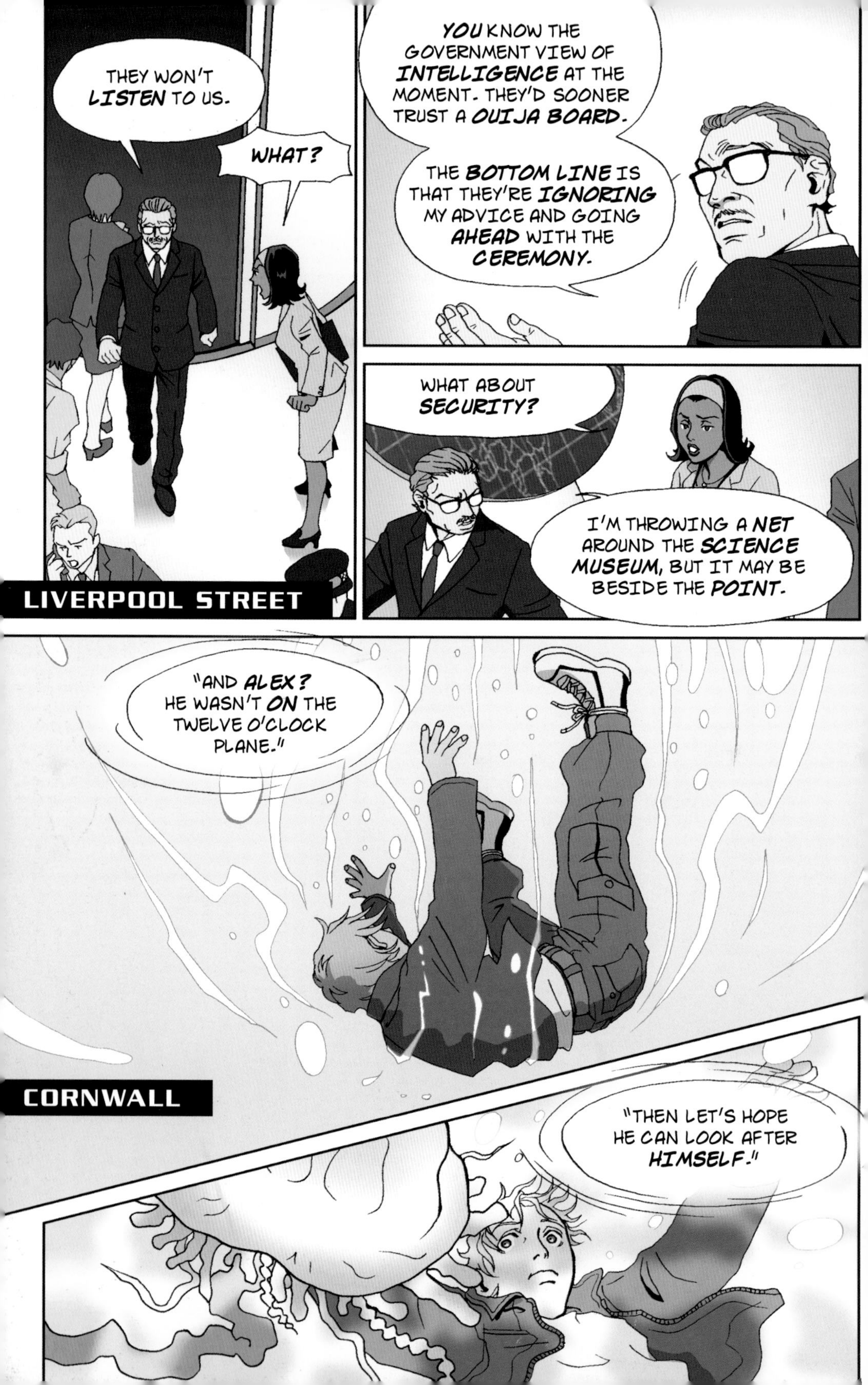

THEY WON'T LISTEN TO US.
WHAT?
LIVERPOOL STREET
YOU KNOW THE GOVERNMENT VIEW OF INTELLIGENCE AT THE MOMENT. THEY'D SOONER TRUST A OUIJA BOARD.
THE BOTTOM LINE IS THAT THEY'RE IGNORING MY ADVICE AND GOING AHEAD WITH THE CEREMONY.
WHAT ABOUT SECURITY?
I'M THROWING A NET AROUND THE SCIENCE MUSEUM, BUT IT MAY BE BESIDE THE POINT.
"AND ALEX? HE WASN'T ON THE TWELVE O'CLOCK PLANE."
CORNWALL
"THEN LET'S HOPE HE CAN LOOK AFTER HIMSELF."

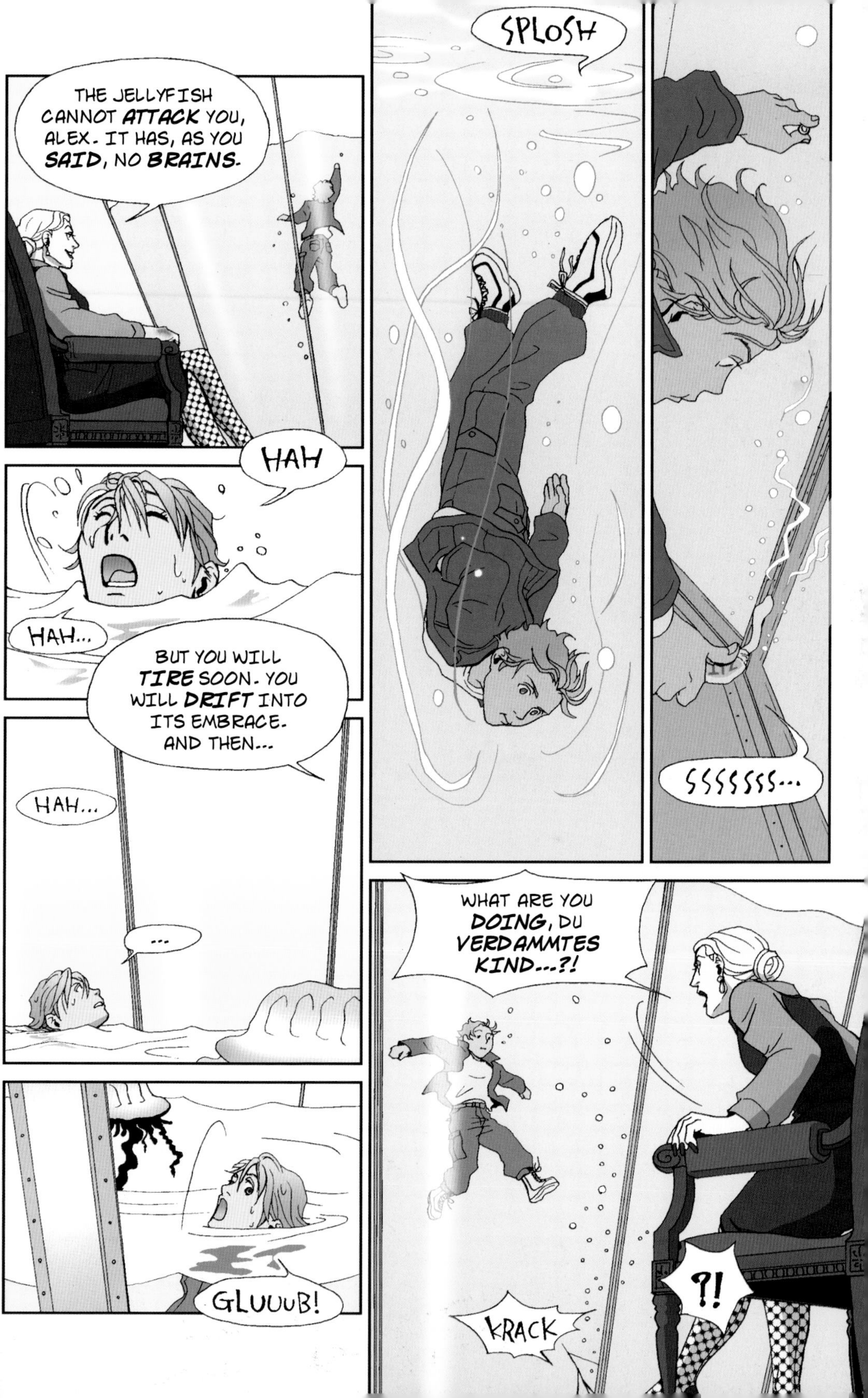

THE JELLYFISH CANNOT ATTACK YOU, ALEX. IT HAS, AS YOU SAID, NO BRAINS.
HAH
HAH...
BUT YOU WILL TIRE SOON. YOU WILL DRIFT INTO ITS EMBRACE. AND THEN...
HAH...
...
GLUUUB!
SPLOSH
SSSSSSS...
WHAT ARE YOU DOING, DU VERDAMMTES KIND...?!
?!
KRACK

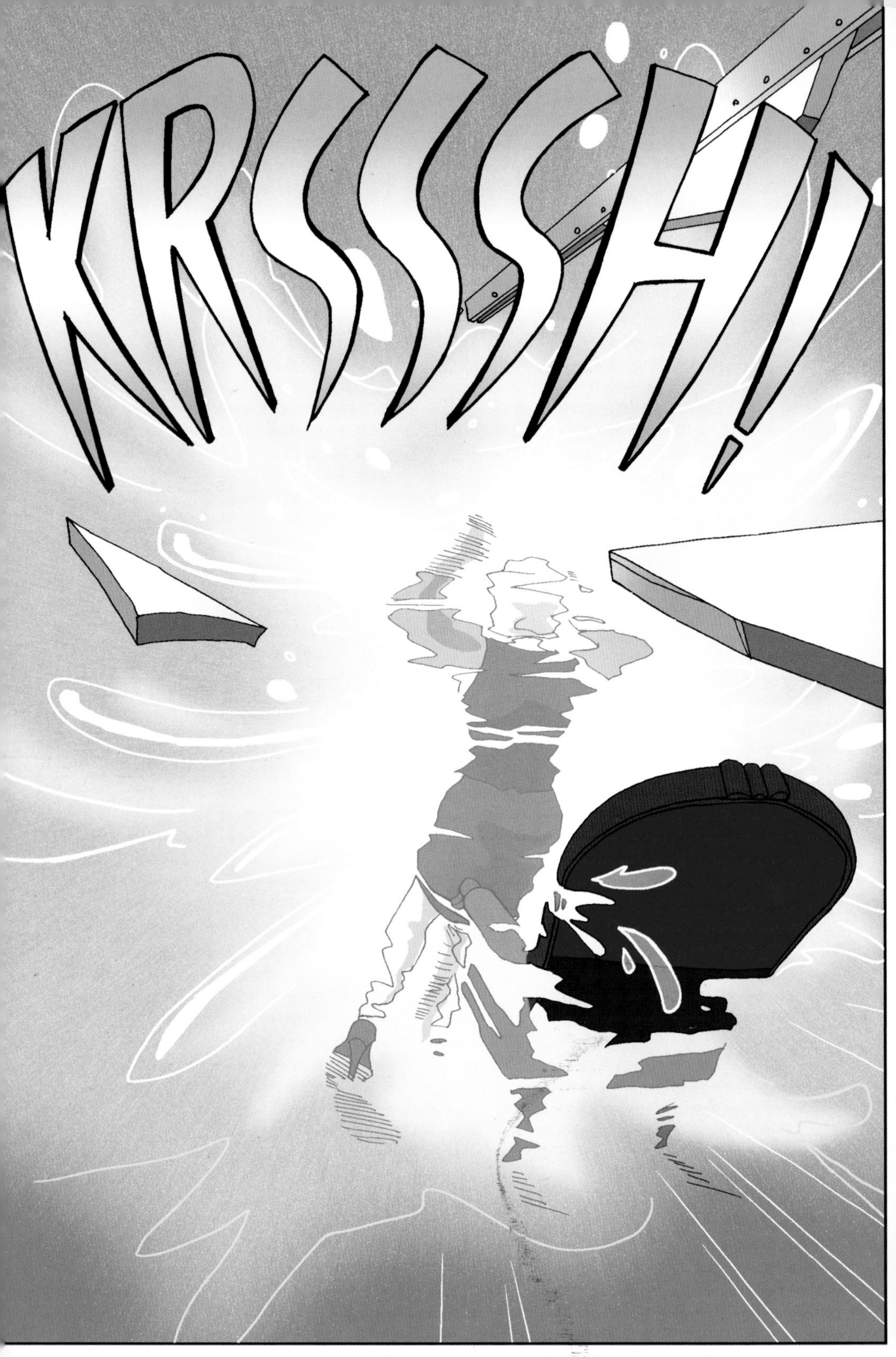
KRSSSSH!

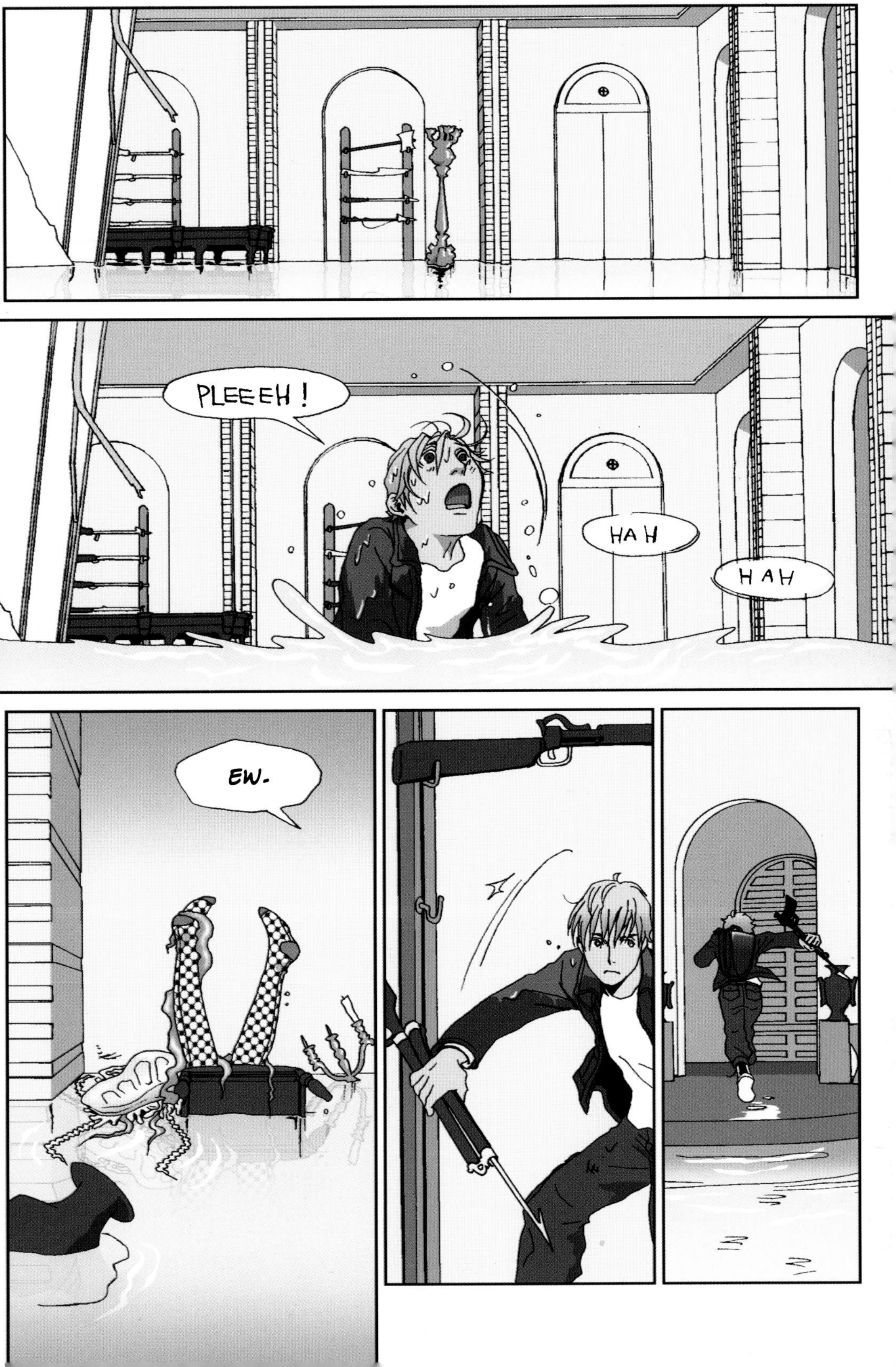
PLEEEH!
HAH
HAH
EW.

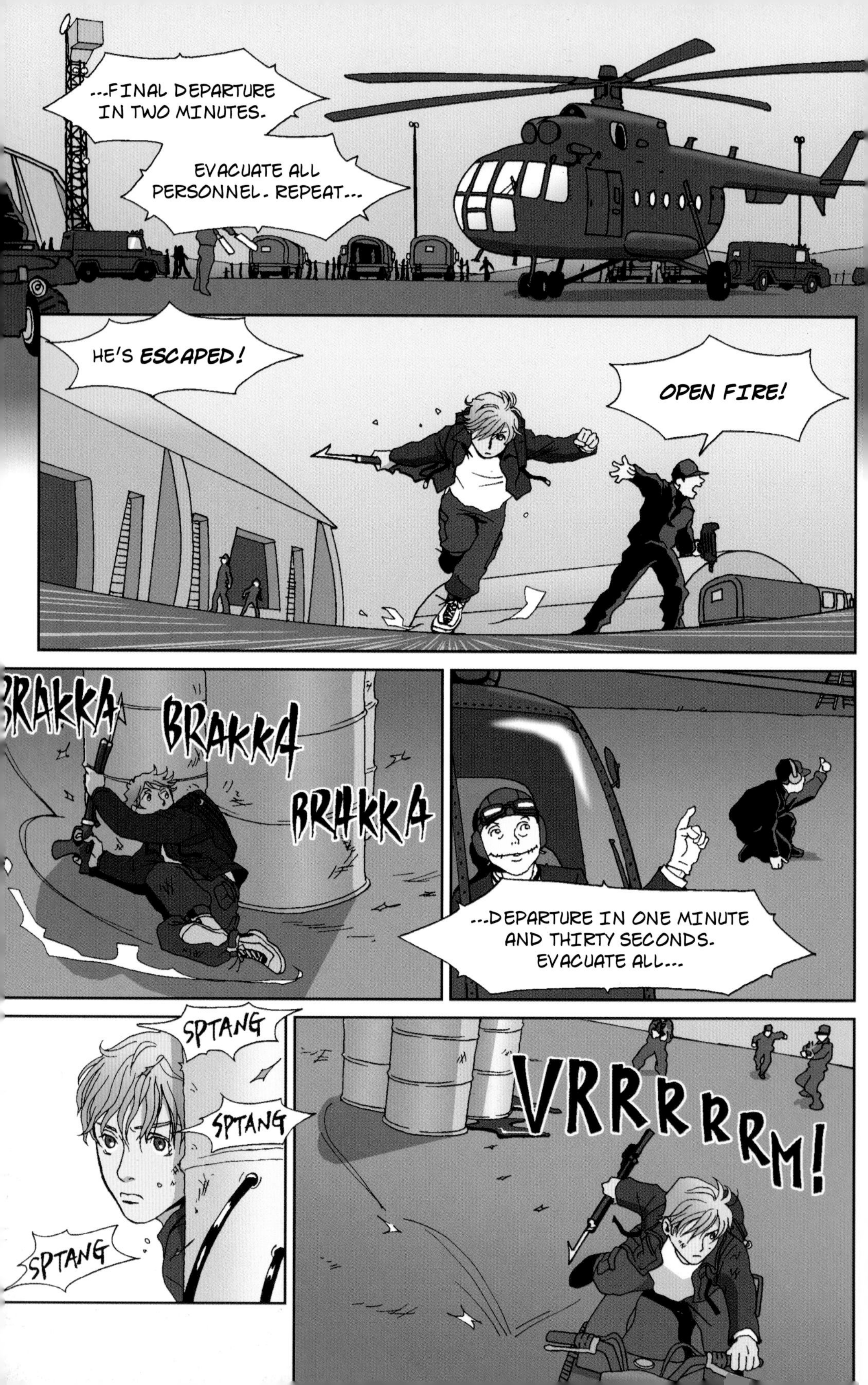
...FINAL DEPARTURE IN TWO MINUTES.
EVACUATE ALL PERSONNEL. REPEAT...
HE'S ESCAPED!
OPEN FIRE!
BRAKKA
BRAKKA
BRAKKA
...DEPARTURE IN ONE MINUTE AND THIRTY SECONDS. EVACUATE ALL...
SPTANG
SPTANG
SPTANG
VRRRRRRM!

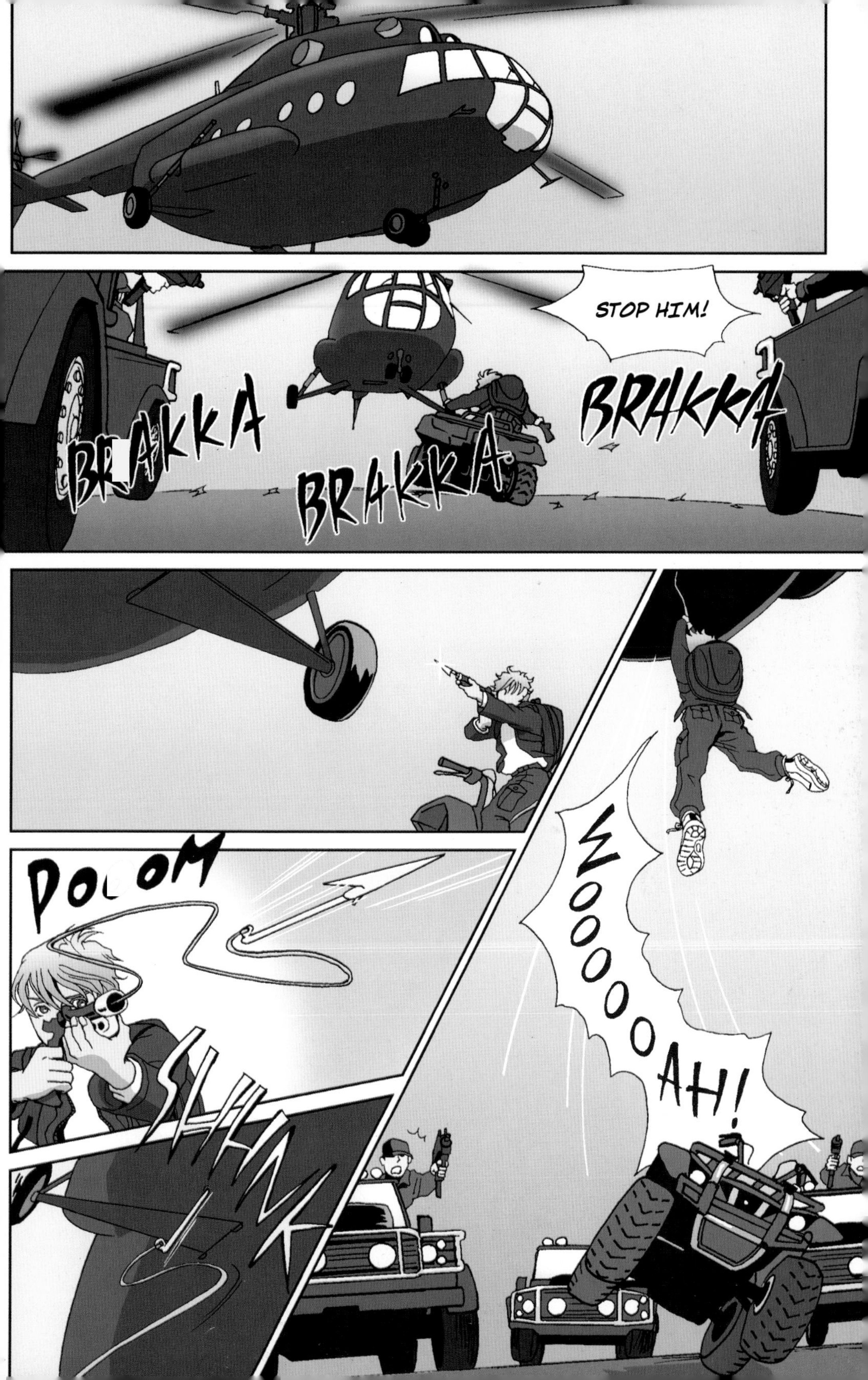
STOP HIM!
BRAKKA
BRAKKA
BRAKKA
DOOOM
SHHNK
WOOOOOAH!

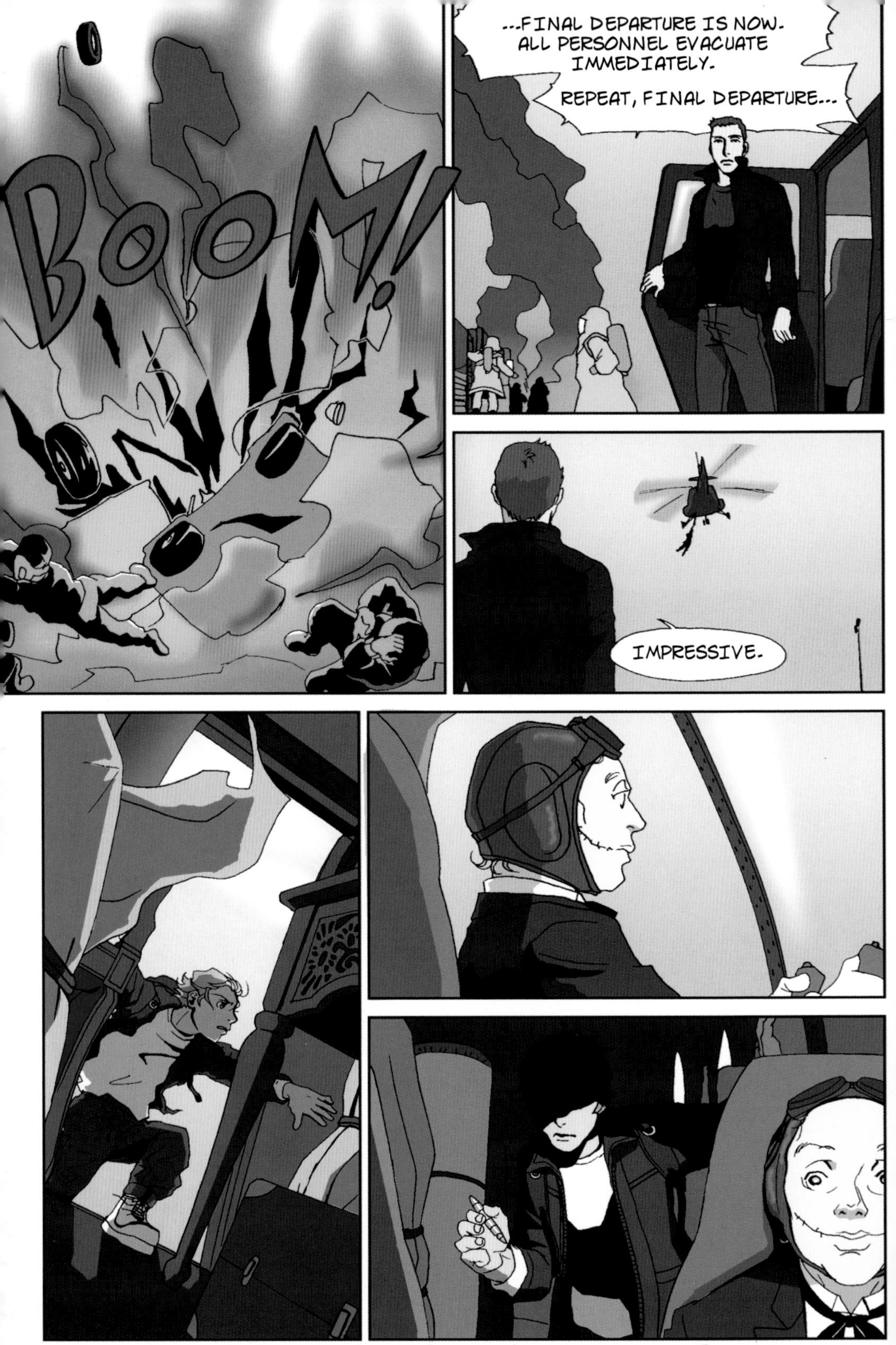
BOOM!
...FINAL DEPARTURE IS NOW. ALL PERSONNEL EVACUATE IMMEDIATELY.
REPEAT, FINAL DEPARTURE...
IMPRESSIVE.

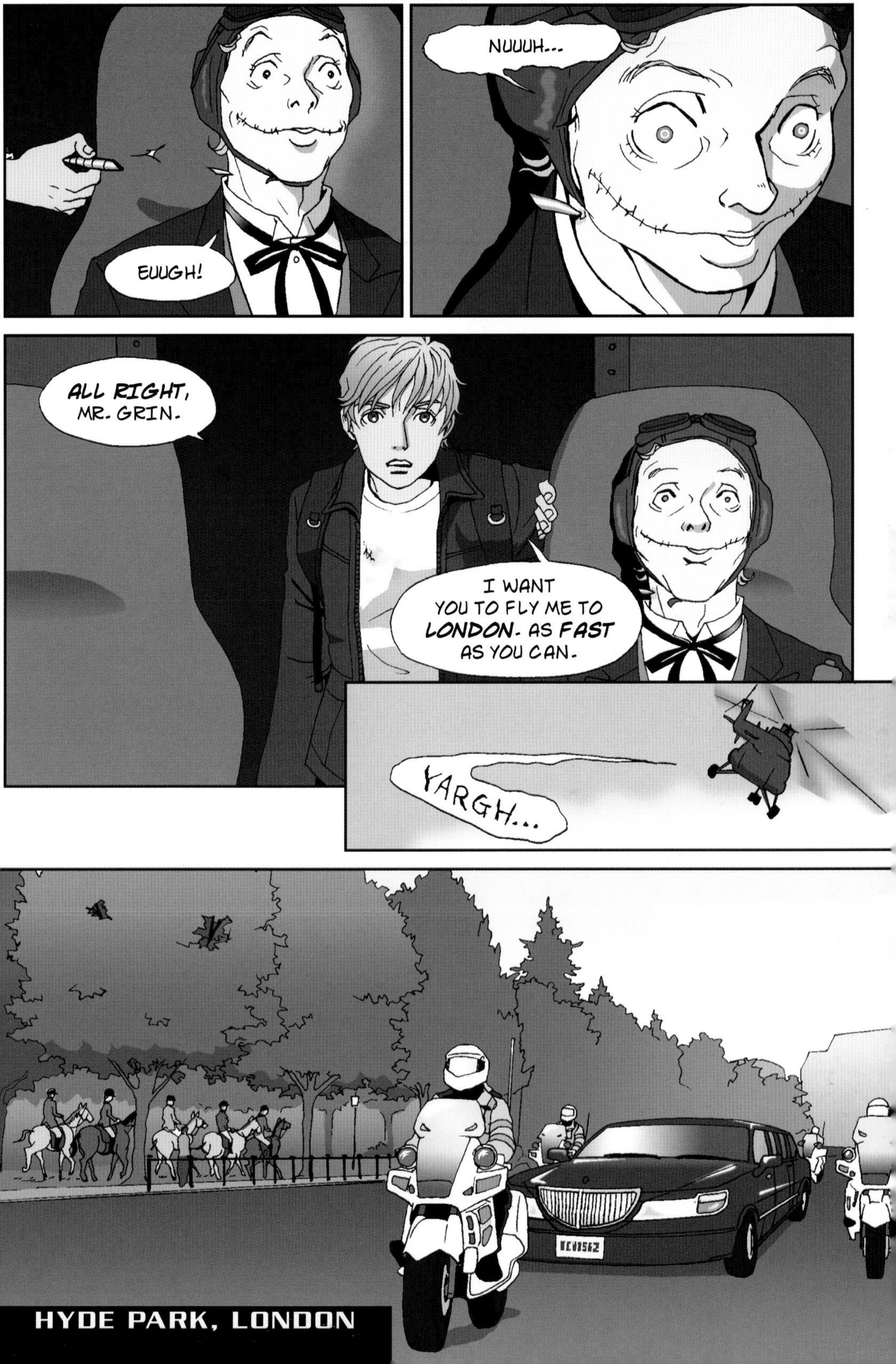
EUUGH!
NUUUH...
ALL RIGHT, MR. GRIN.
I WANT YOU TO FLY ME TO LONDON. AS FAST AS YOU CAN.
YARGH...
HYDE PARK, LONDON

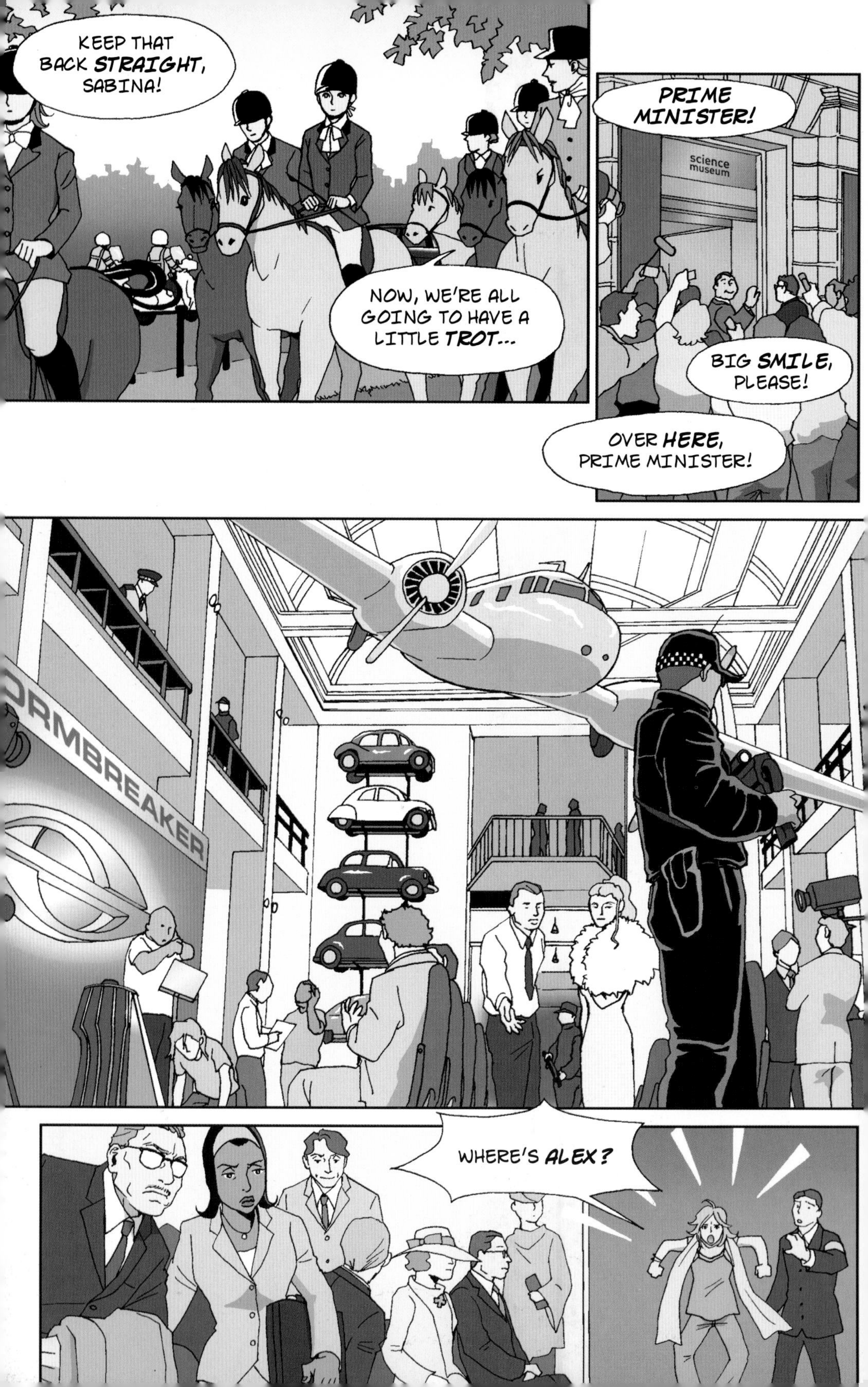
KEEP THAT BACK STRAIGHT, SABINA!
NOW, WE'RE ALL GOING TO HAVE A LITTLE TROT...
PRIME MINISTER!
science museum
BIG SMILE, PLEASE!
OVER HERE, PRIME MINISTER!
RMBREAKER
WHERE'S ALEX?

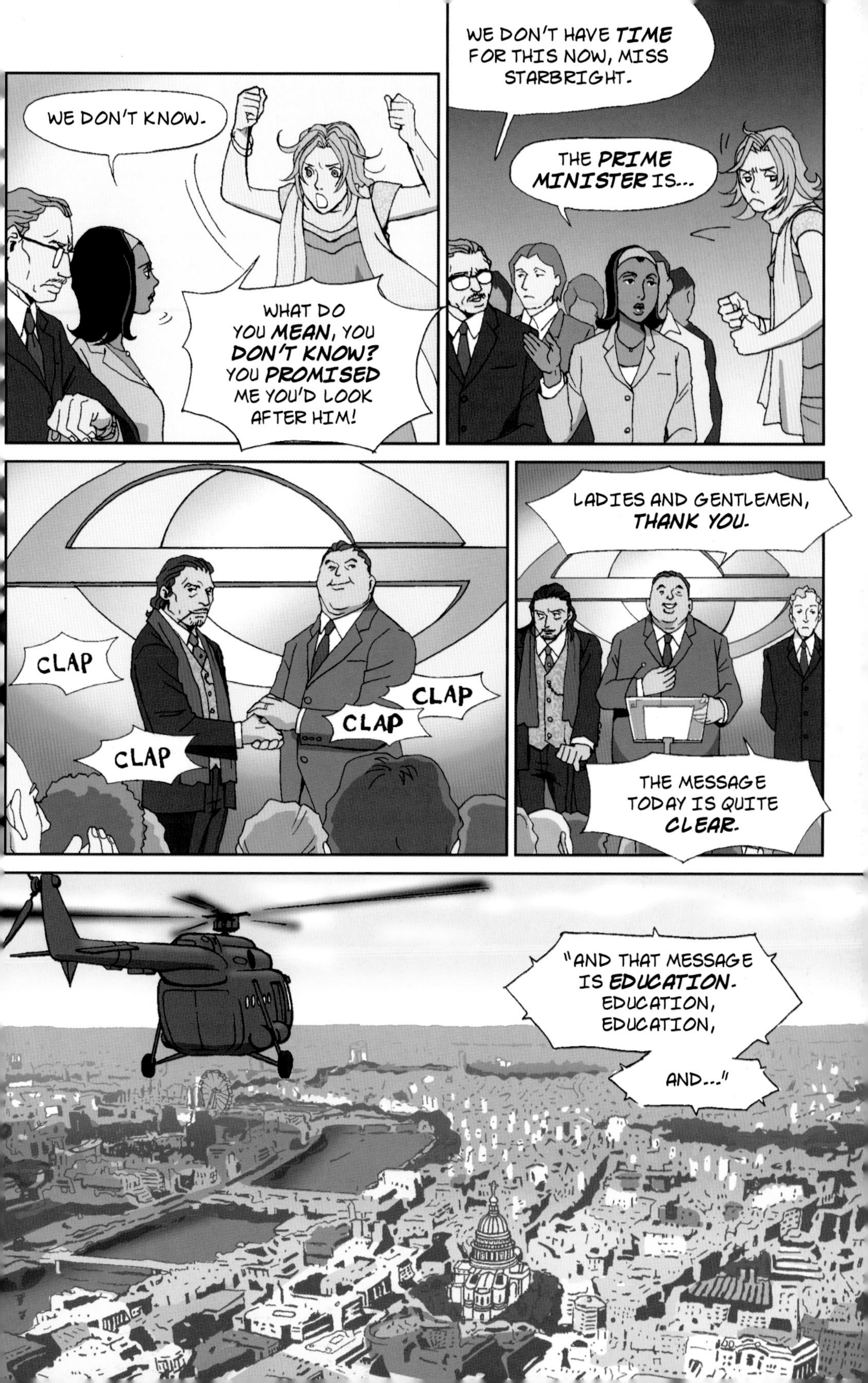
WE DON'T KNOW.
WHAT DO YOU MEAN, YOU DON'T KNOW? YOU PROMISED ME YOU'D LOOK AFTER HIM!
WE DON'T HAVE TIME FOR THIS NOW, MISS STARBRIGHT.
THE PRIME MINISTER IS...
CLAP
CLAP
CLAP
CLAP
LADIES AND GENTLEMEN, THANK YOU.
THE MESSAGE TODAY IS QUITE CLEAR.
"AND THAT MESSAGE IS EDUCATION. EDUCATION, EDUCATION,
AND..."

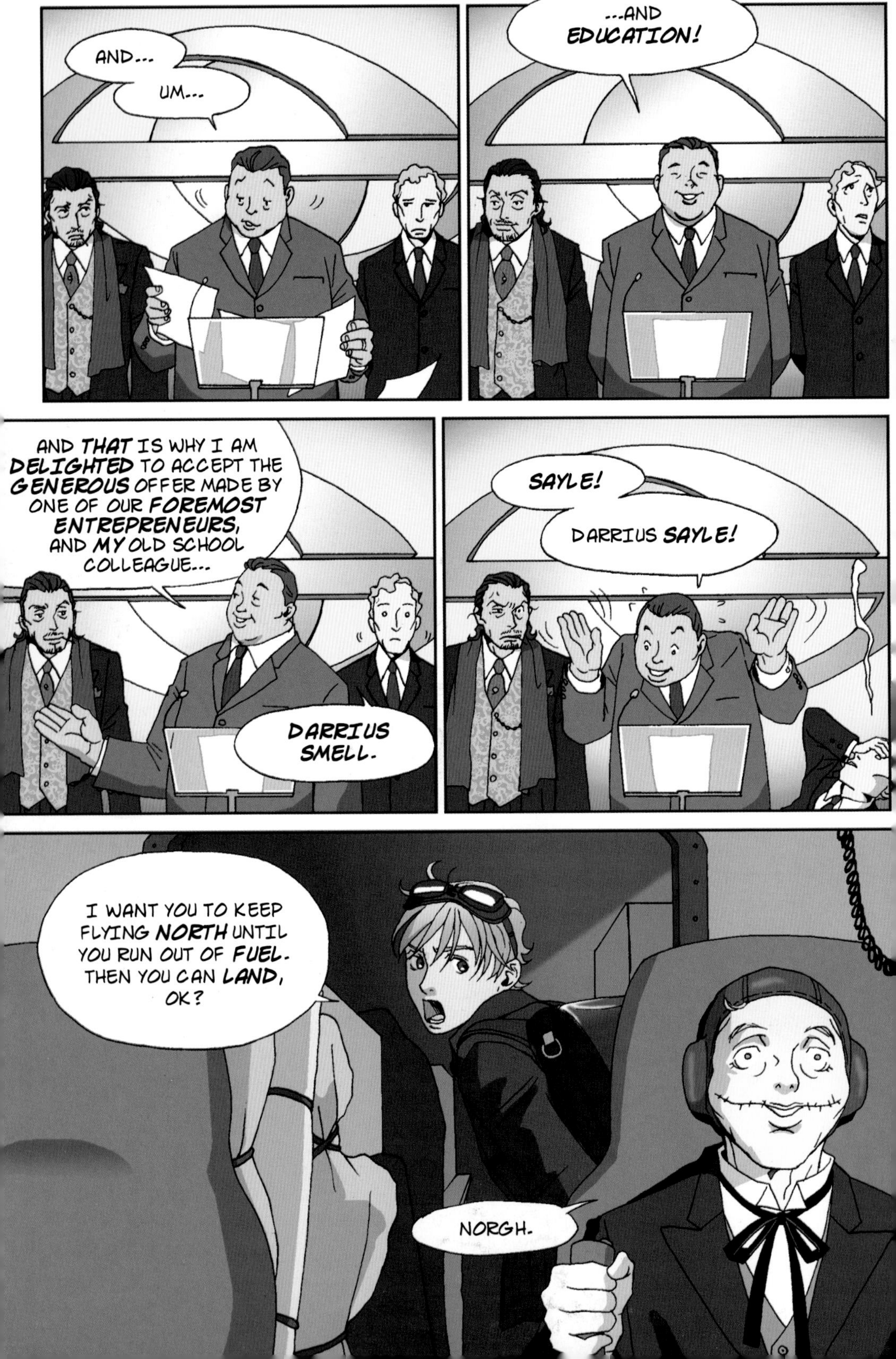
AND...
UM...
...AND EDUCATION!
AND THAT IS WHY I AM DELIGHTED TO ACCEPT THE GENEROUS OFFER MADE BY ONE OF OUR FOREMOST ENTREPRENEURS, AND MY OLD SCHOOL COLLEAGUE...
DARRIUS SMELL.
SAYLE!
DARRIUS SAYLE!
I WANT YOU TO KEEP FLYING NORTH UNTIL YOU RUN OUT OF FUEL. THEN YOU CAN LAND, OK?
NORGH.

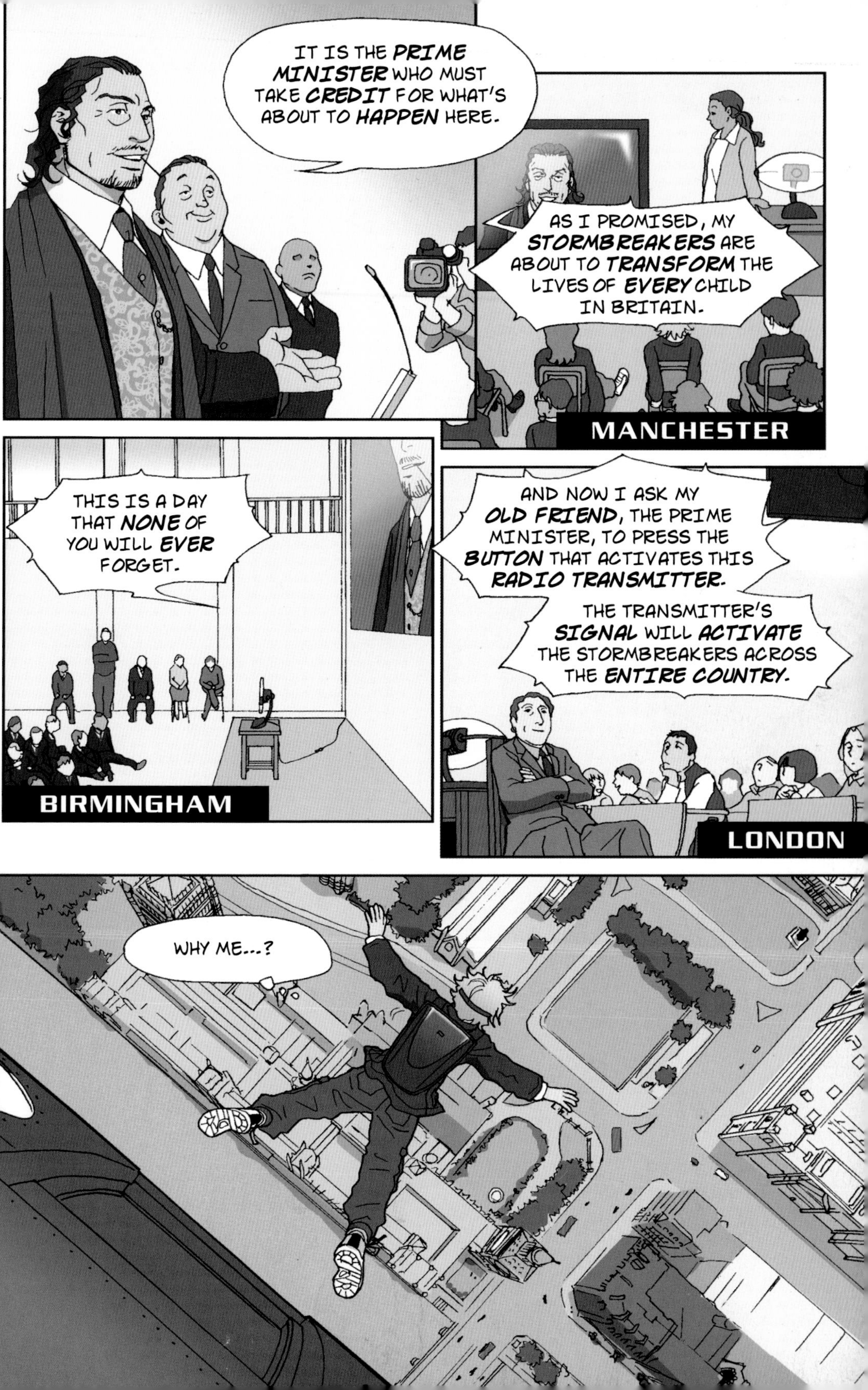
IT IS THE PRIME MINISTER WHO MUST TAKE CREDIT FOR WHAT'S ABOUT TO HAPPEN HERE.
AS I PROMISED, MY STORMBREAKERS ARE ABOUT TO TRANSFORM THE LIVES OF EVERY CHILD IN BRITAIN.
MANCHESTER
THIS IS A DAY THAT NONE OF YOU WILL EVER FORGET.
BIRMINGHAM
AND NOW I ASK MY OLD FRIEND, THE PRIME MINISTER, TO PRESS THE BUTTON THAT ACTIVATES THIS RADIO TRANSMITTER.
THE TRANSMITTER'S SIGNAL WILL ACTIVATE THE STORMBREAKERS ACROSS THE ENTIRE COUNTRY.
LONDON
WHY ME...?

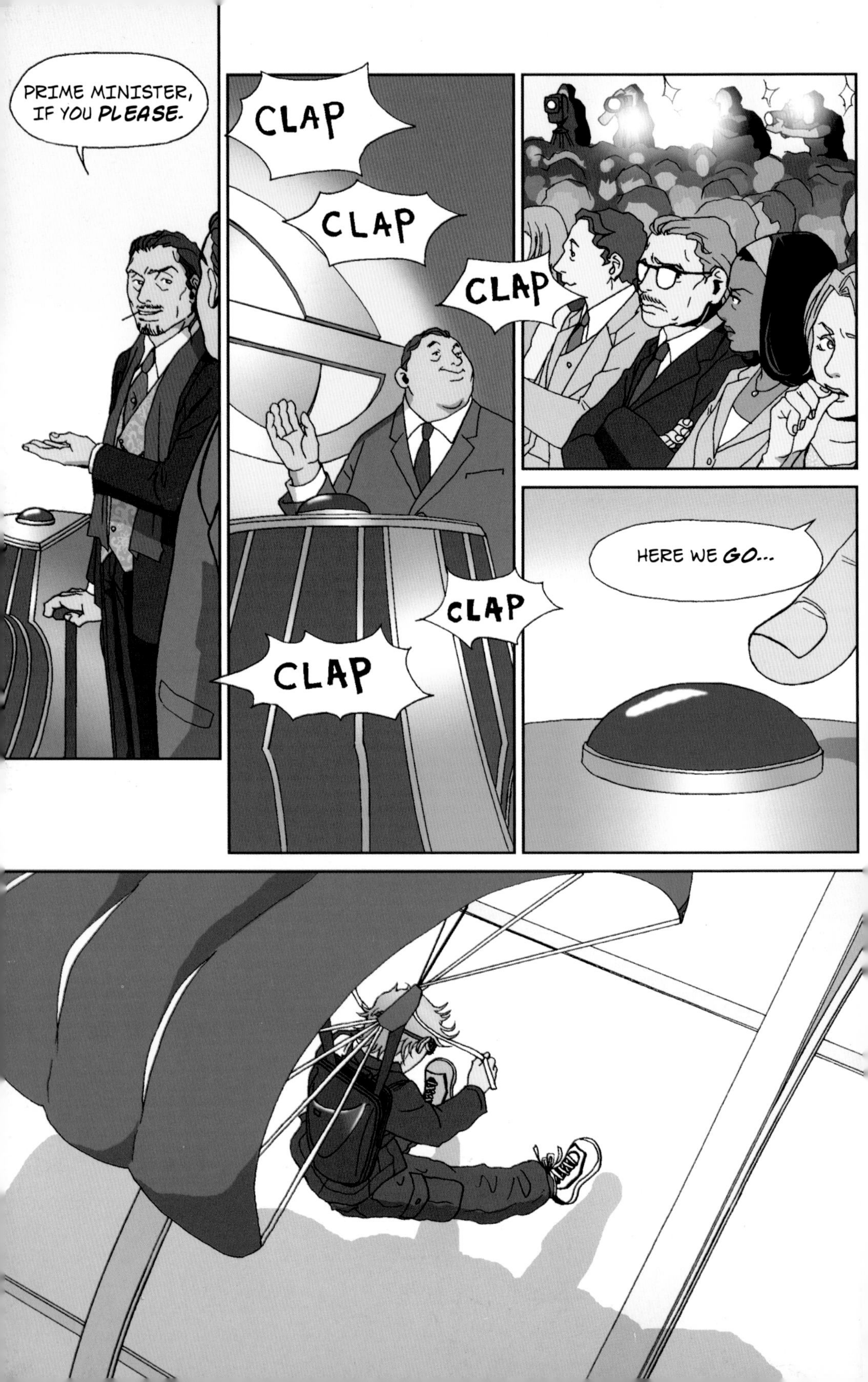
PRIME MINISTER, IF YOU PLEASE.
CLAP
CLAP
CLAP
CLAP
CLAP
HERE WE GO...

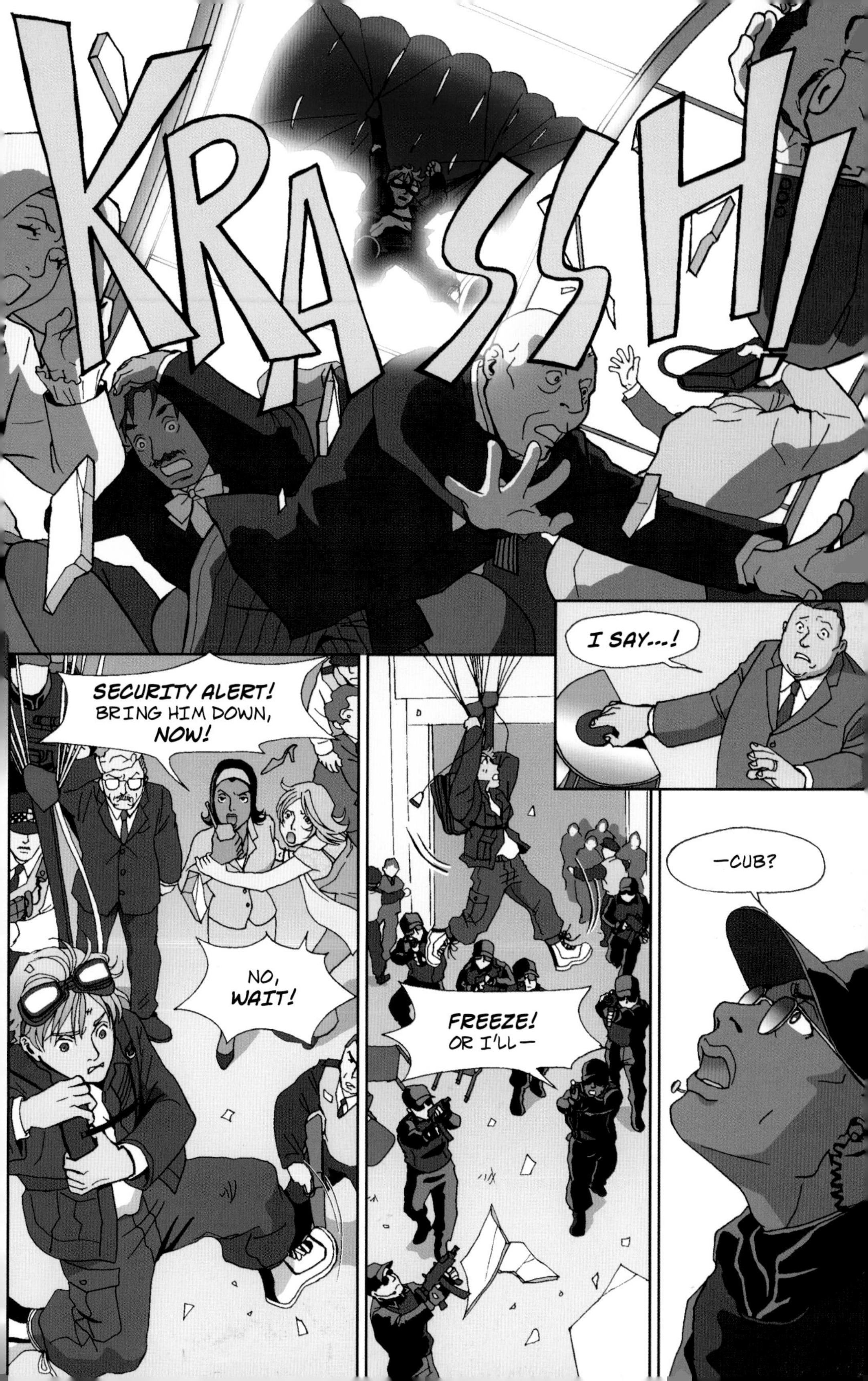
KRASSH!
I SAY...!
SECURITY ALERT!
BRING HIM DOWN,
NOW!
NO,
WAIT!
FREEZE!
OR I'LL—
—CUB?

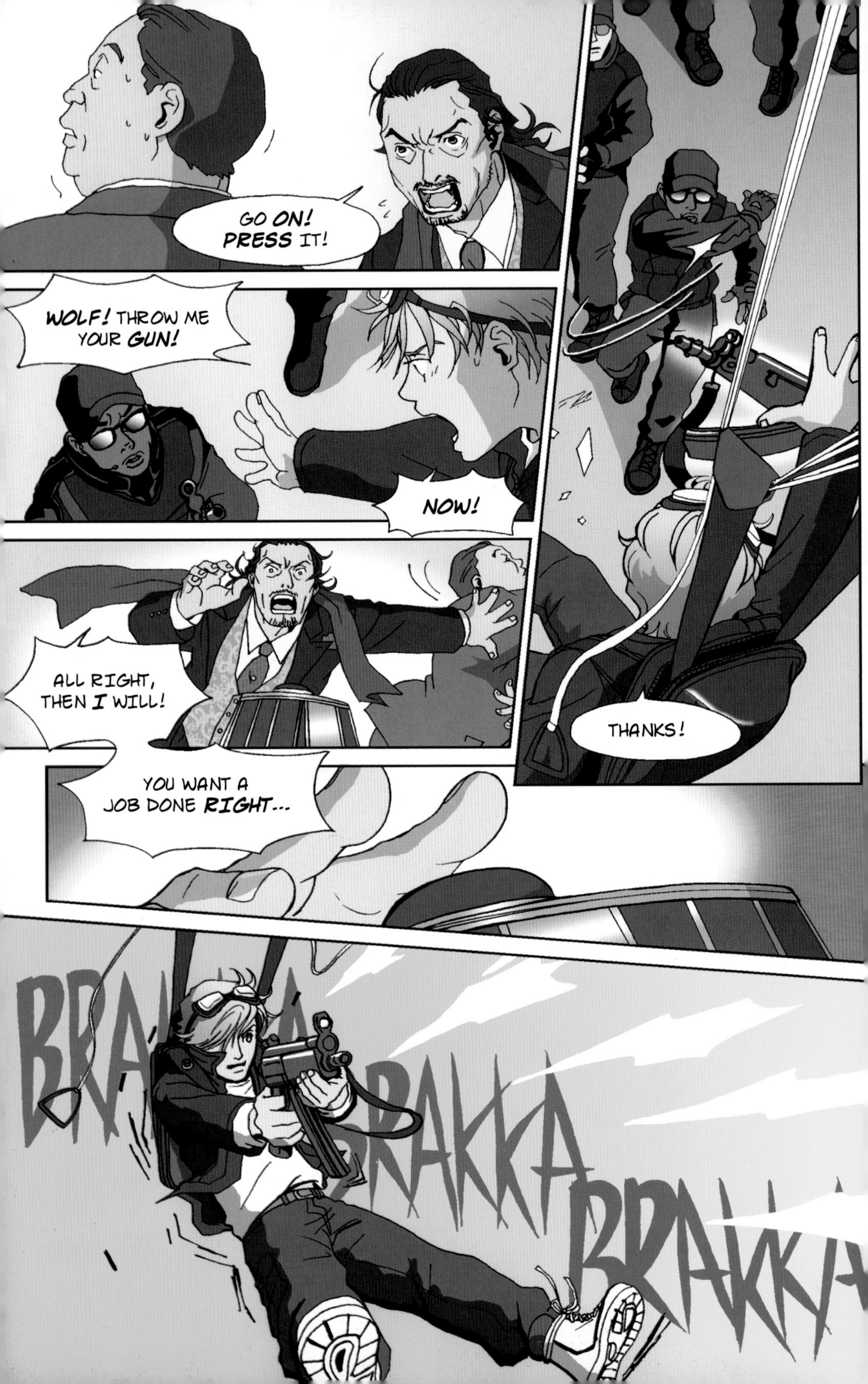
GO ON! PRESS IT!
WOLF! THROW ME YOUR GUN!
NOW!
ALL RIGHT, THEN I WILL!
YOU WANT A JOB DONE RIGHT...
THANKS!
BRAKKA
BRAKKA
BRAKKA

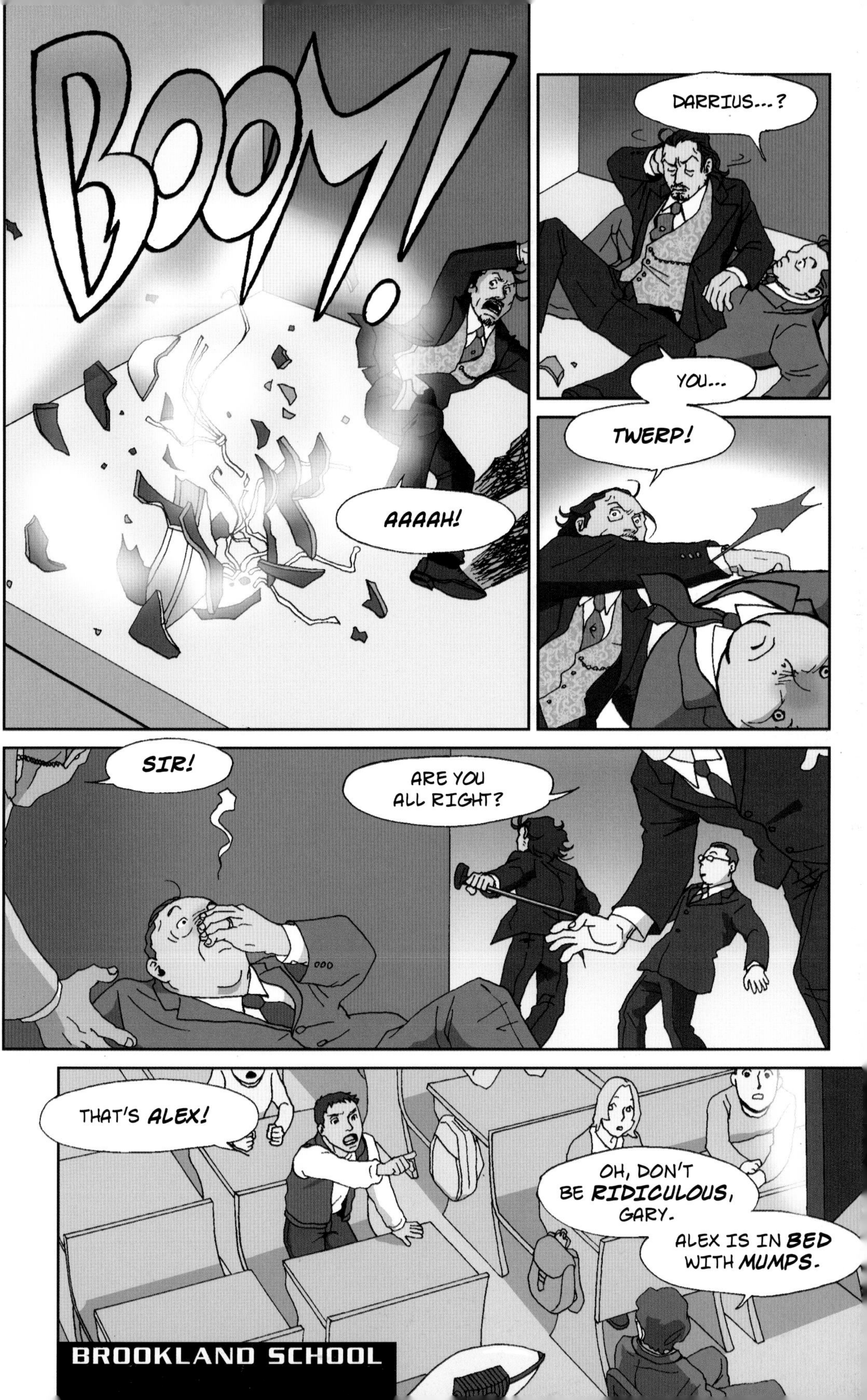
BOOM!
AAAAH!
DARRIUS...?
YOU...
TWERP!
SIR!
ARE YOU ALL RIGHT?
BROOKLAND SCHOOL
THAT'S ALEX!
OH, DON'T BE RIDICULOUS, GARY.
ALEX IS IN BED WITH MUMPS.

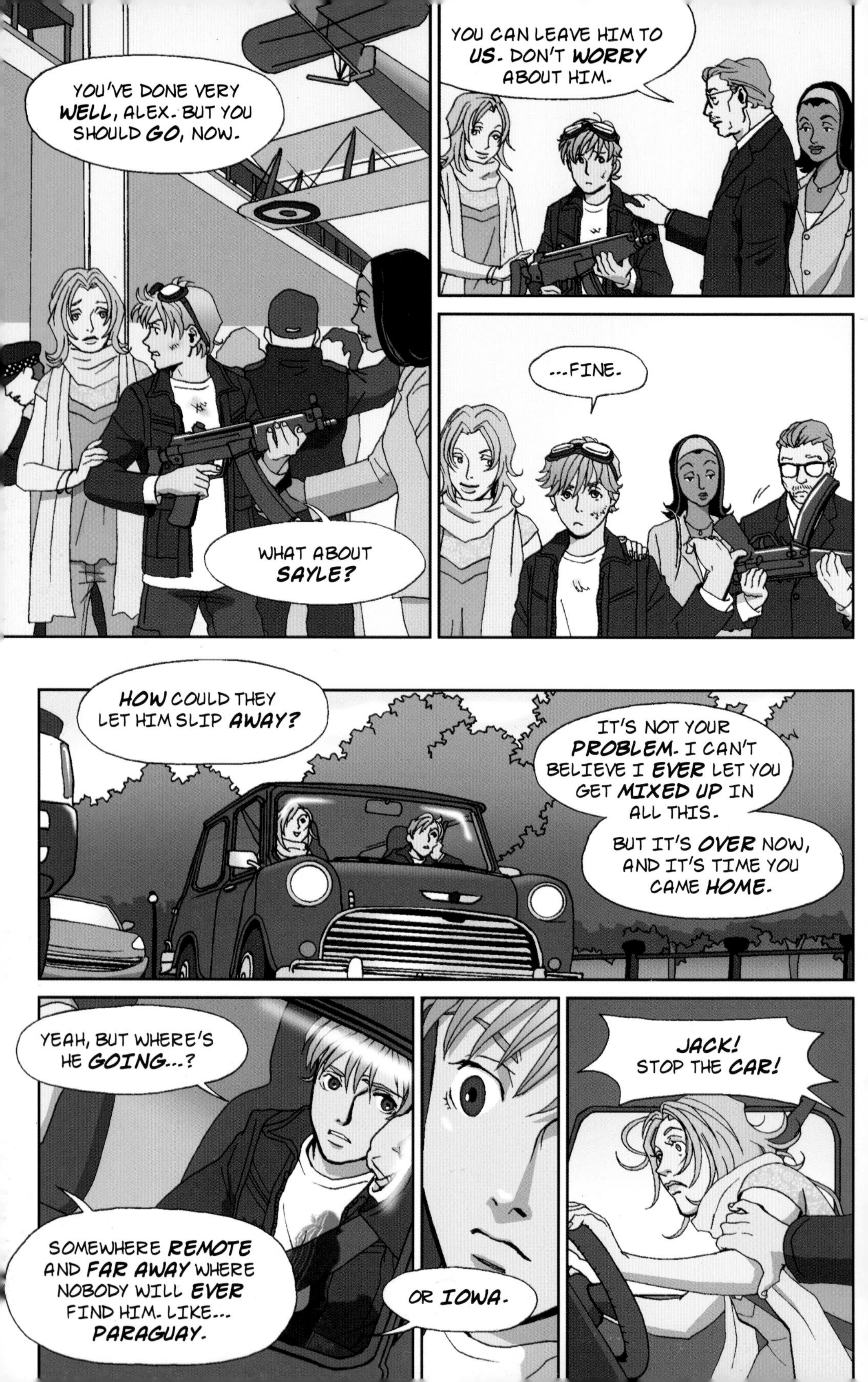
YOU'VE DONE VERY WELL, ALEX. BUT YOU SHOULD GO, NOW.
WHAT ABOUT SAYLE?
YOU CAN LEAVE HIM TO US. DON'T WORRY ABOUT HIM.
...FINE.
HOW COULD THEY LET HIM SLIP AWAY?
IT'S NOT YOUR PROBLEM. I CAN'T BELIEVE I EVER LET YOU GET MIXED UP IN ALL THIS.
BUT IT'S OVER NOW, AND IT'S TIME YOU CAME HOME.
YEAH, BUT WHERE'S HE GOING...?
SOMEWHERE REMOTE AND FAR AWAY WHERE NOBODY WILL EVER FIND HIM. LIKE... PARAGUAY.
OR IOWA.
JACK! STOP THE CAR!

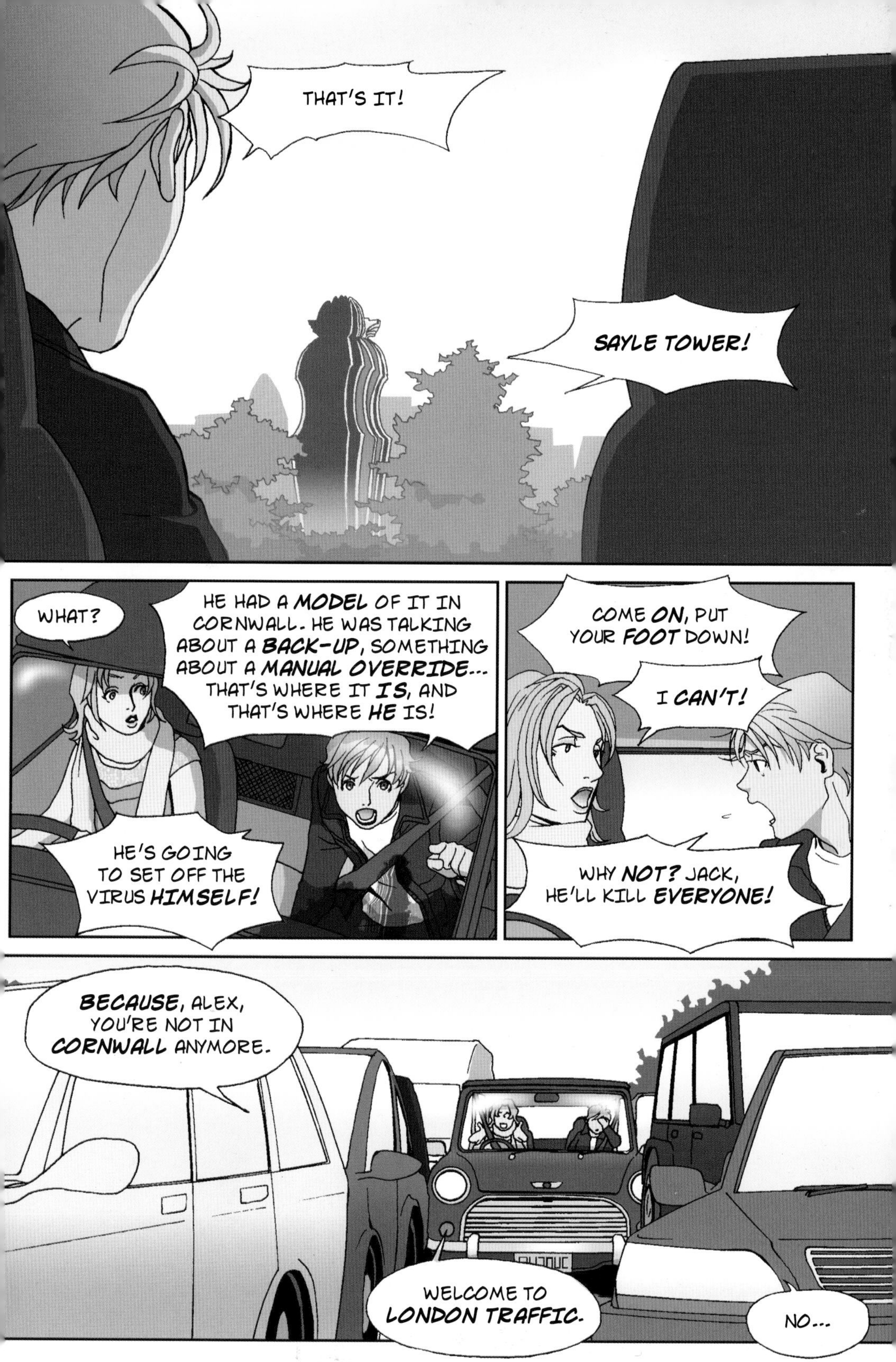

THAT'S IT!
SAYLE TOWER!
WHAT?
HE HAD A MODEL OF IT IN CORNWALL. HE WAS TALKING ABOUT A BACK-UP, SOMETHING ABOUT A MANUAL OVERRIDE... THAT'S WHERE IT IS, AND THAT'S WHERE HE IS!
HE'S GOING TO SET OFF THE VIRUS HIMSELF!
COME ON, PUT YOUR FOOT DOWN!
I CAN'T!
WHY NOT? JACK, HE'LL KILL EVERYONE!
BECAUSE, ALEX, YOU'RE NOT IN CORNWALL ANYMORE.
WELCOME TO LONDON TRAFFIC.
NO...

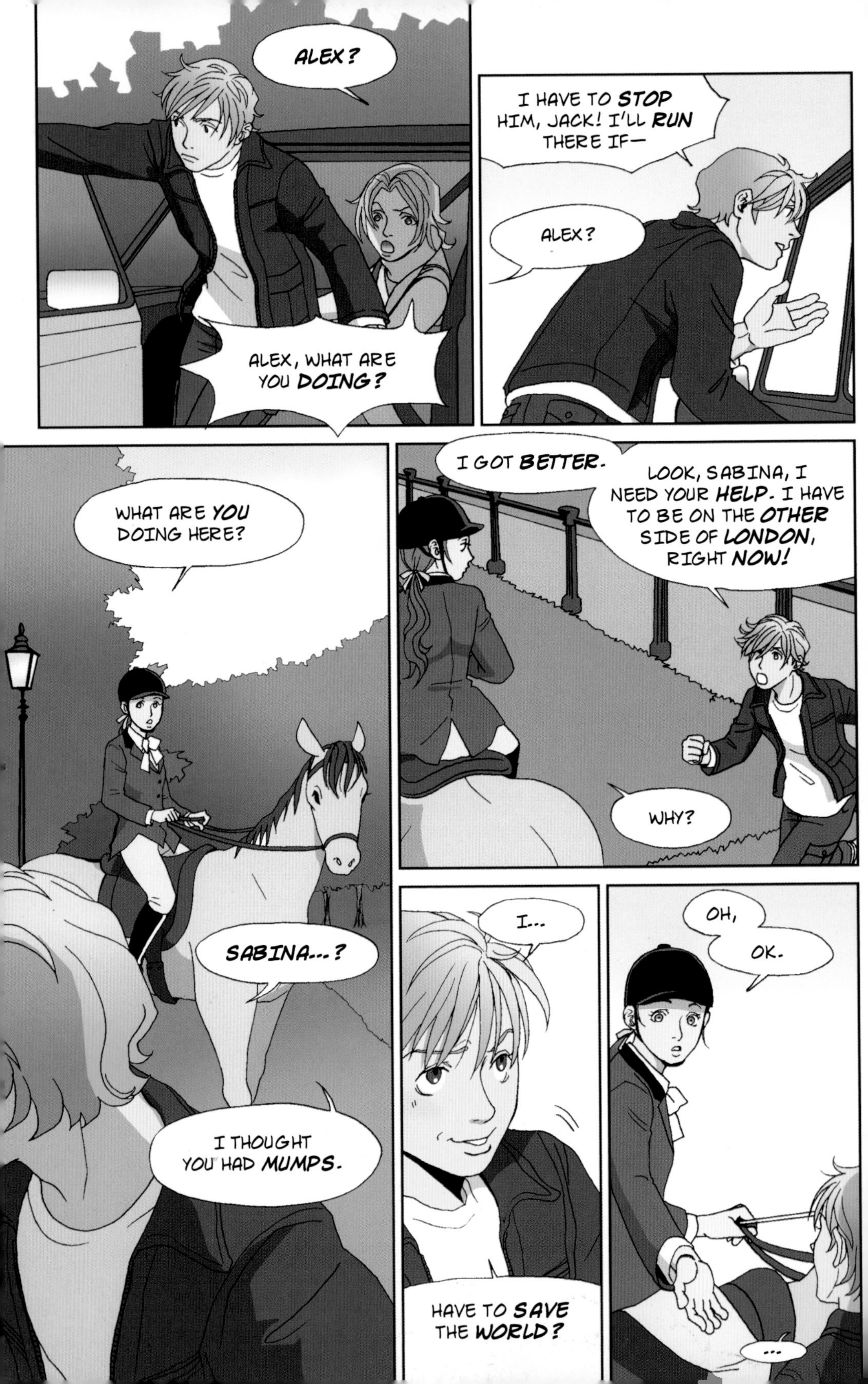

ALEX?
ALEX, WHAT ARE YOU DOING?
I HAVE TO STOP HIM, JACK! I'LL RUN THERE IF—
ALEX?
WHAT ARE YOU DOING HERE?
SABINA...?
I THOUGHT YOU HAD MUMPS.
I GOT BETTER.
LOOK, SABINA, I NEED YOUR HELP. I HAVE TO BE ON THE OTHER SIDE OF LONDON, RIGHT NOW!
WHY?
I...
HAVE TO SAVE THE WORLD?
OH,
OK.
...

THAT'S RIGHT, MRS. JONES!

I DON'T **KNOW** WHAT HER **FIRST NAME** IS! I'M NOT SENDING HER A **BIRTHDAY** CARD, THIS IS **URGENT!** STOP MAKING ME—

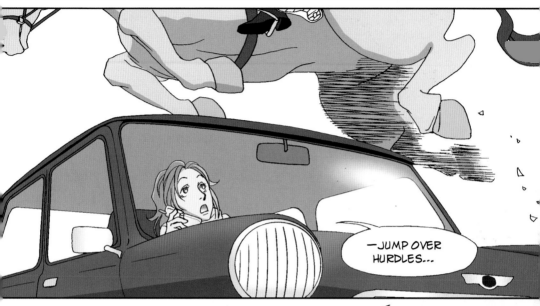

—JUMP OVER HURDLES...

YAAAH!

ALEX...

KEEP GOING!

AAAAH!

WOOOAH!

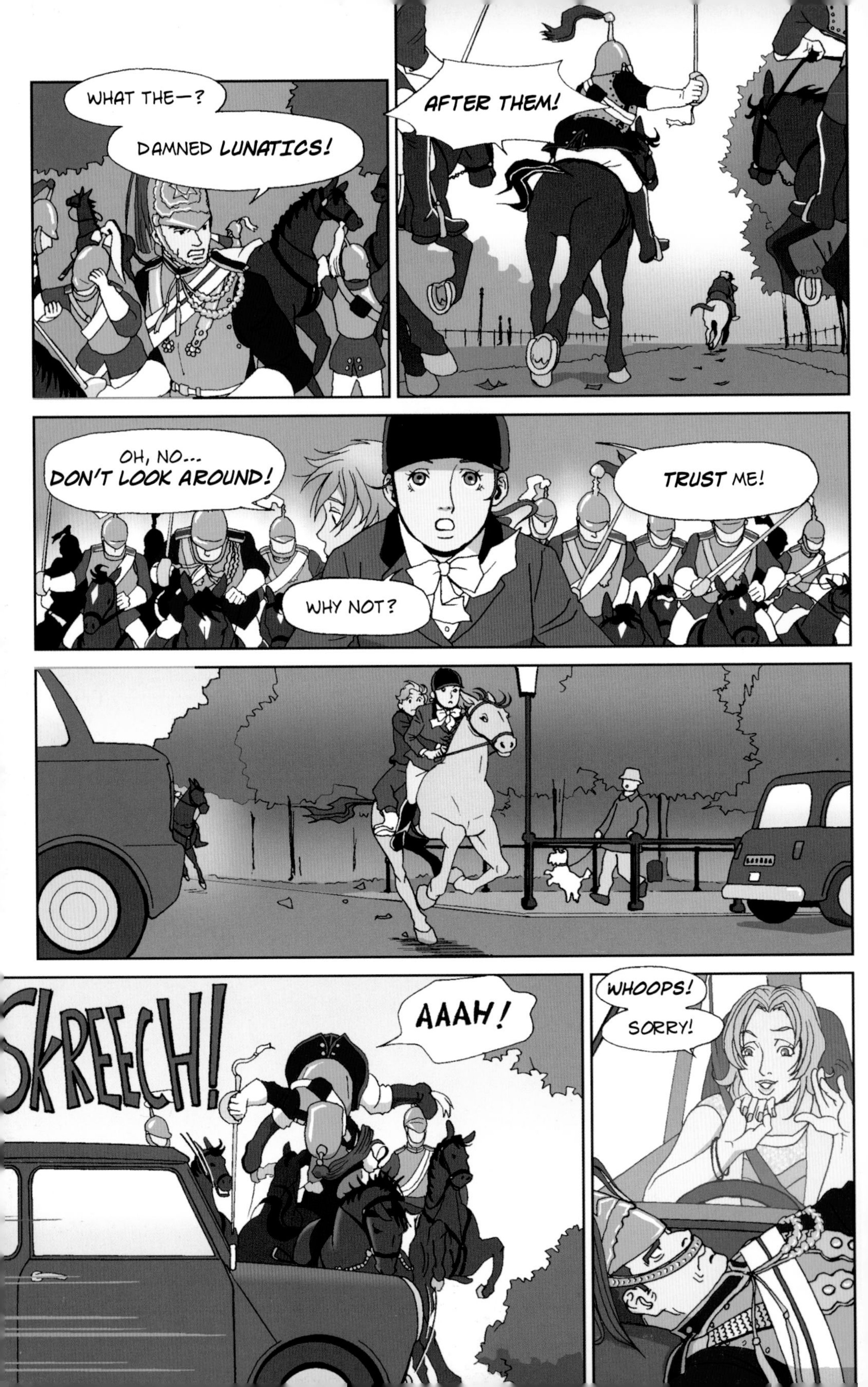
WHAT THE—?
DAMNED LUNATICS!
AFTER THEM!
OH, NO... DON'T LOOK AROUND!
WHY NOT?
TRUST ME!
SKREECH!
AAAH!
WHOOPS!
SORRY!

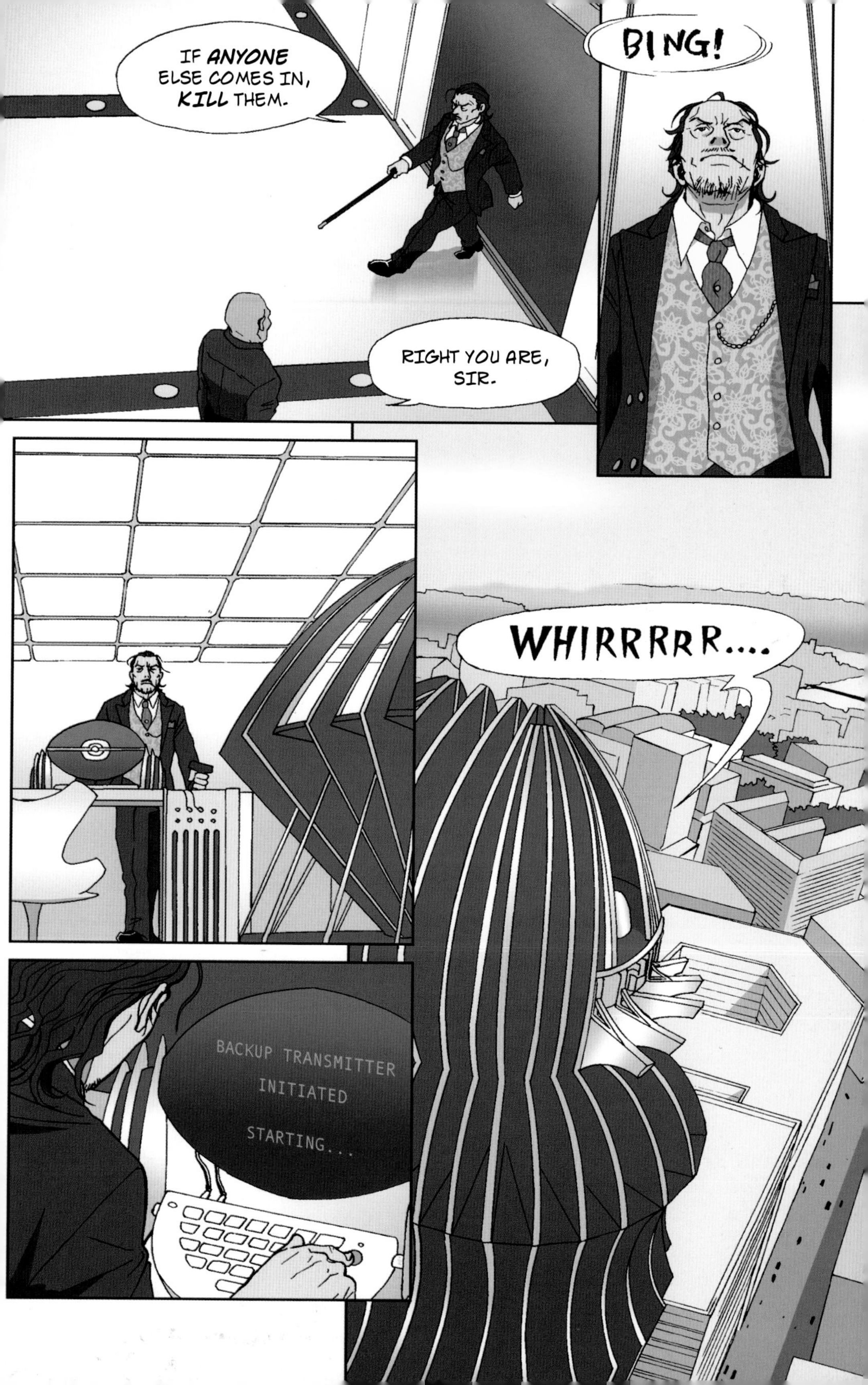
IF ANYONE ELSE COMES IN, KILL THEM.
BING!
RIGHT YOU ARE, SIR.
WHIRRRRR....
BACKUP TRANSMITTER INITIATED
STARTING...

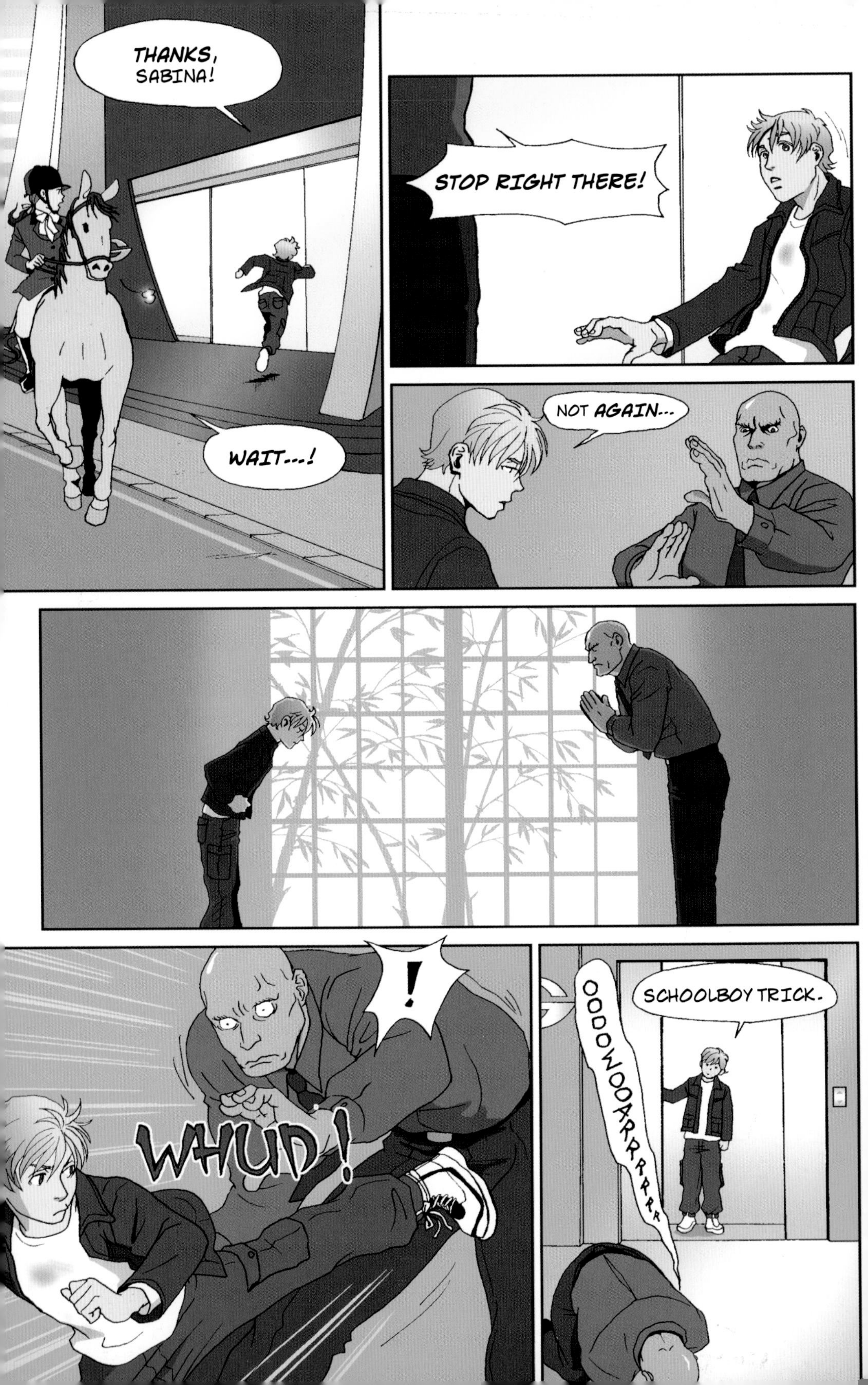
THANKS, SABINA!
WAIT...!
STOP RIGHT THERE!
NOT AGAIN...
!
WHUD!
OOOOWOOARRRRRR
SCHOOLBOY TRICK.

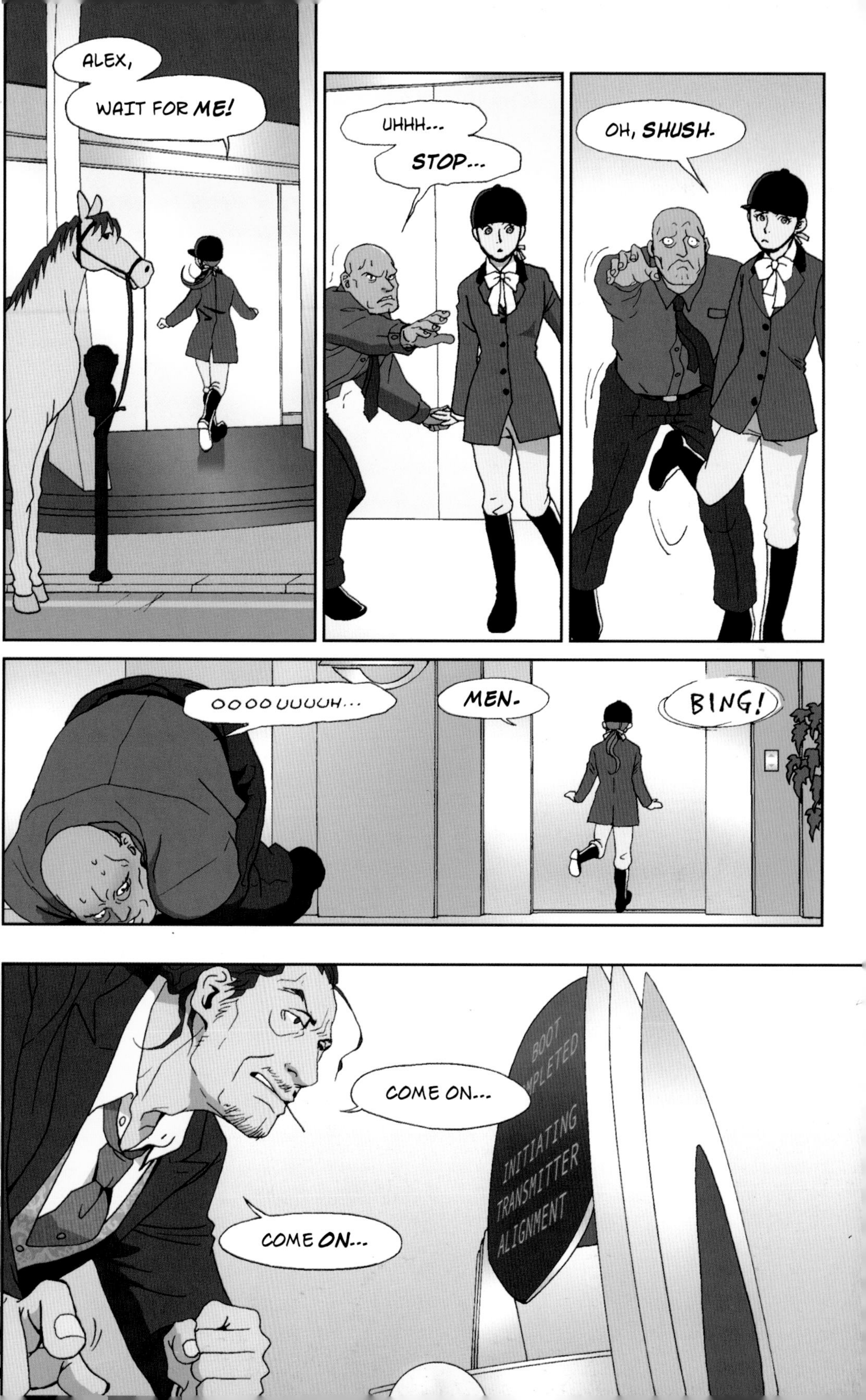
ALEX,
WAIT FOR ME!
UHHH...
STOP...
OH, SHUSH.
OOOOUUUUH...
MEN.
BING!
BOOT COMPLETED
INITIATING TRANSMITTER ALIGNMENT
COME ON...
COME ON...

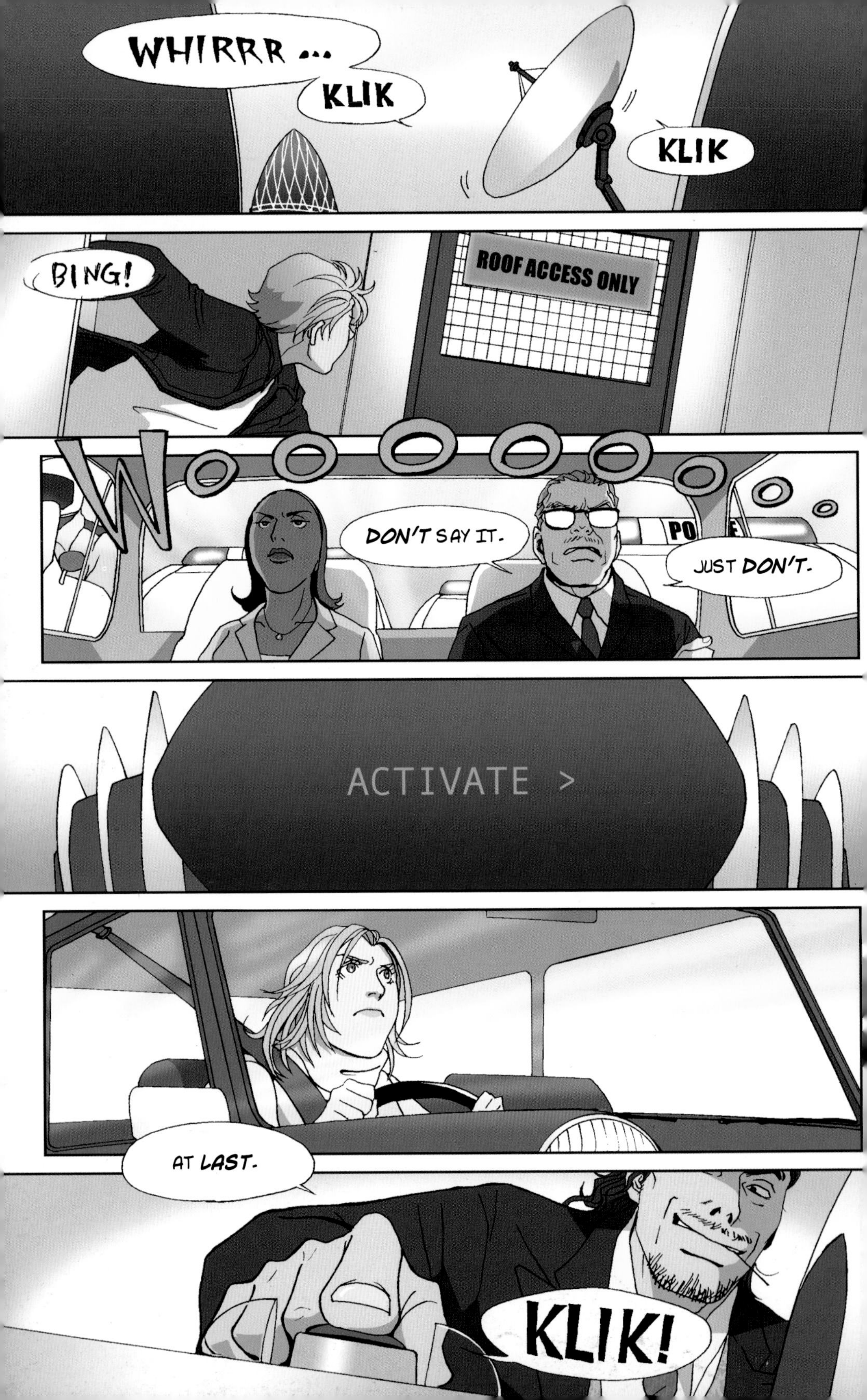
WHIRRR ...
KLIK
KLIK
BING!
ROOF ACCESS ONLY
WOOOOOOOOO
DON'T SAY IT.
JUST DON'T.
ACTIVATE >
AT LAST.
KLIK!

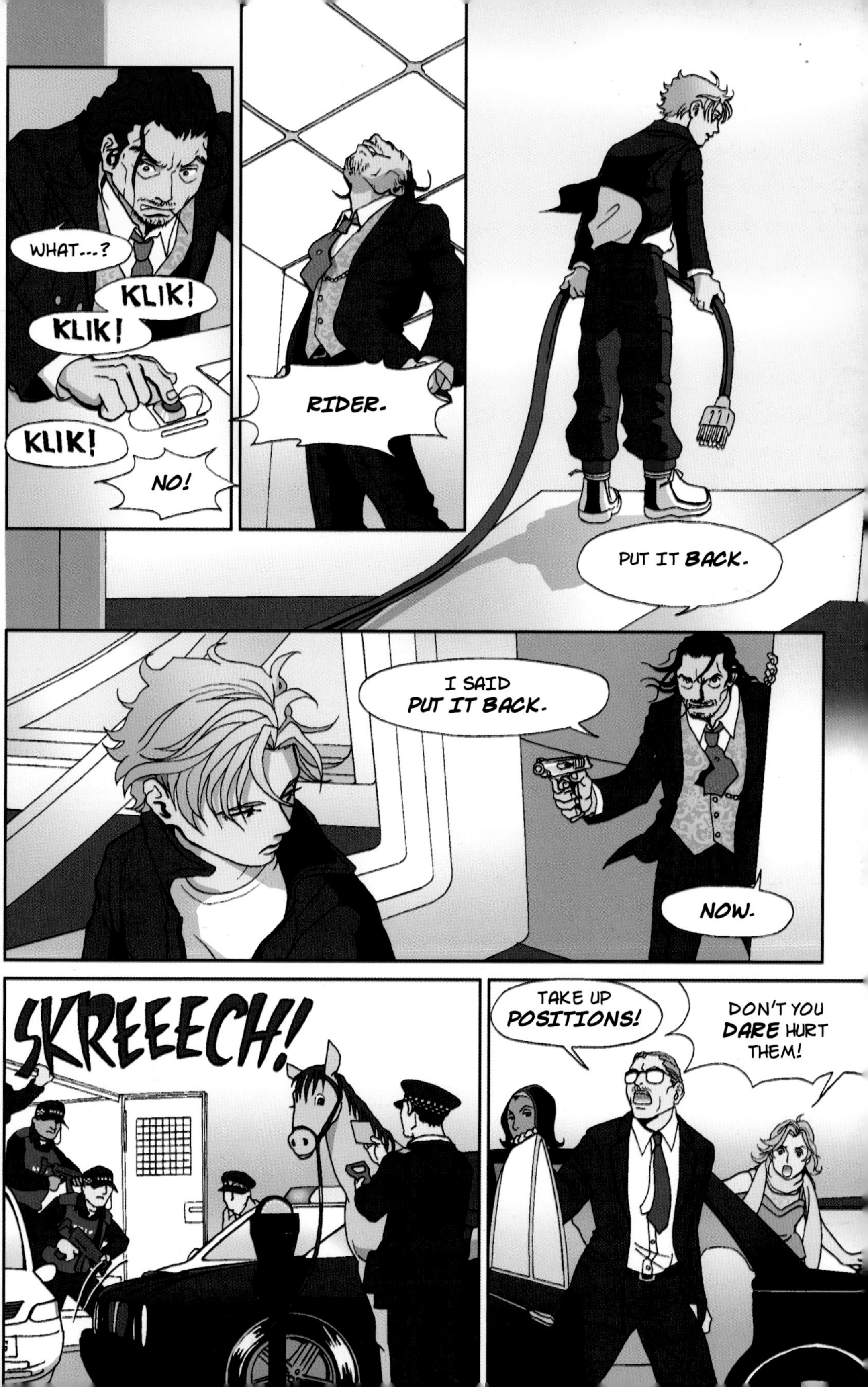
WHAT...?
KLIK!
KLIK!
KLIK!
NO!
RIDER.
PUT IT BACK.
I SAID PUT IT BACK.
NOW.
SKREEECH!
TAKE UP POSITIONS!
DON'T YOU DARE HURT THEM!

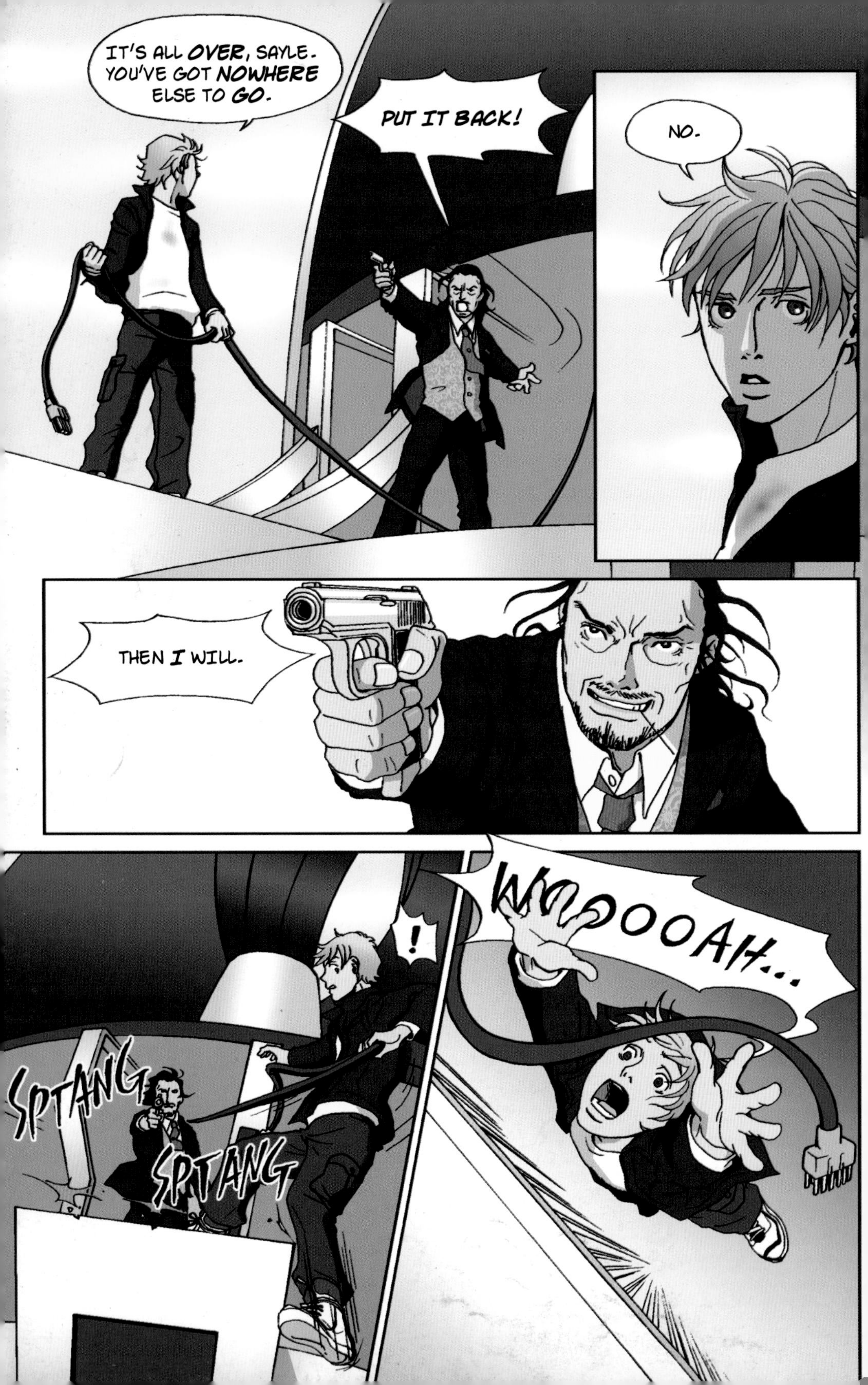
IT'S ALL OVER, SAYLE. YOU'VE GOT NOWHERE ELSE TO GO.
PUT IT BACK!
NO.
THEN I WILL.
!
SPTANG
SPTANG
WHOOOOAH...

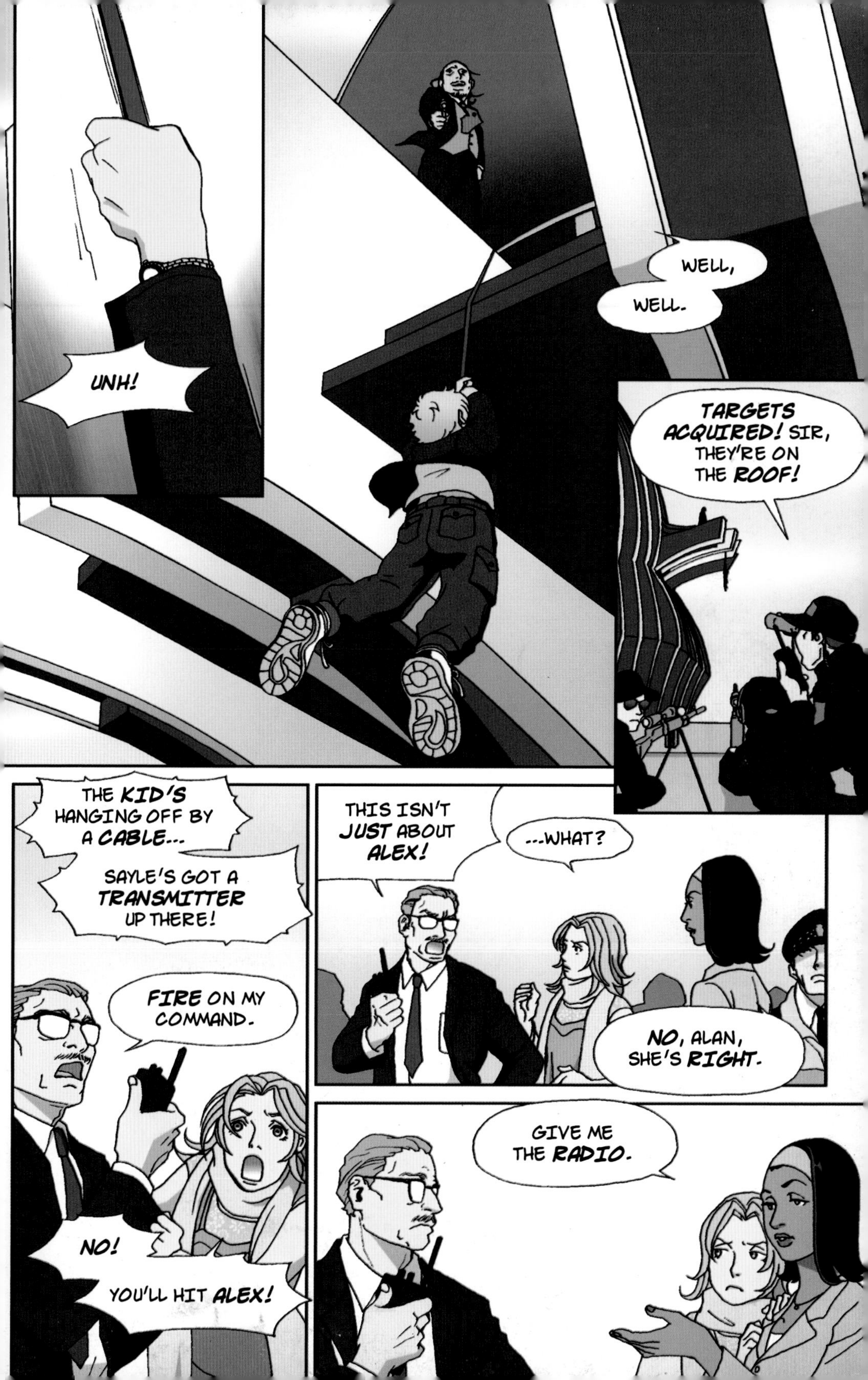
UNH!
WELL,
WELL.
TARGETS ACQUIRED! SIR, THEY'RE ON THE ROOF!
THE KID'S HANGING OFF BY A CABLE...
SAYLE'S GOT A TRANSMITTER UP THERE!
FIRE ON MY COMMAND.
NO!
YOU'LL HIT ALEX!
THIS ISN'T JUST ABOUT ALEX!
...WHAT?
NO, ALAN, SHE'S RIGHT.
GIVE ME THE RADIO.

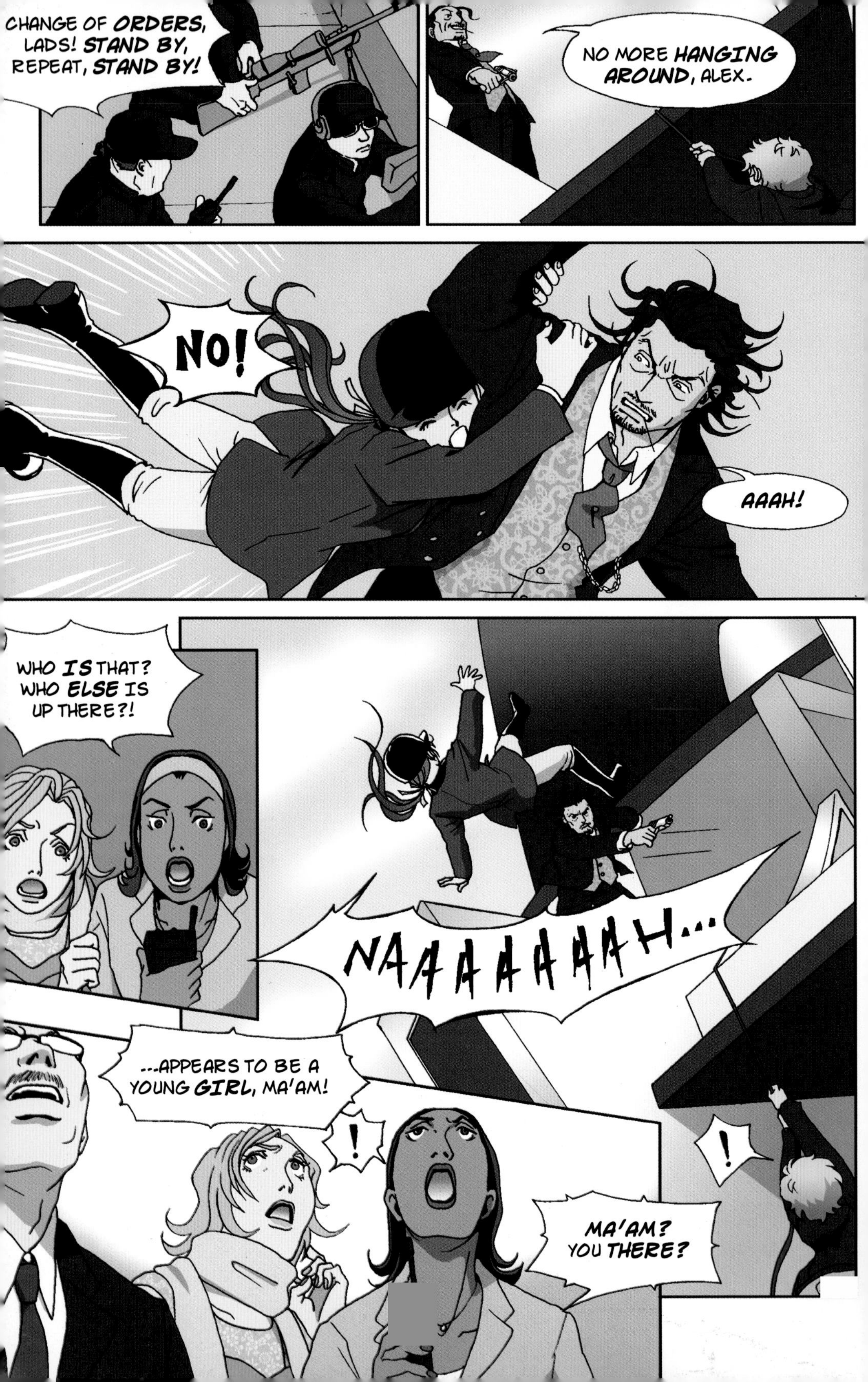
CHANGE OF ORDERS, LADS! STAND BY, REPEAT, STAND BY!
NO MORE HANGING AROUND, ALEX.
NO!
AAAH!
WHO IS THAT? WHO ELSE IS UP THERE?!
NAAAAAAAH...
...APPEARS TO BE A YOUNG GIRL, MA'AM!
!
!
MA'AM? YOU THERE?

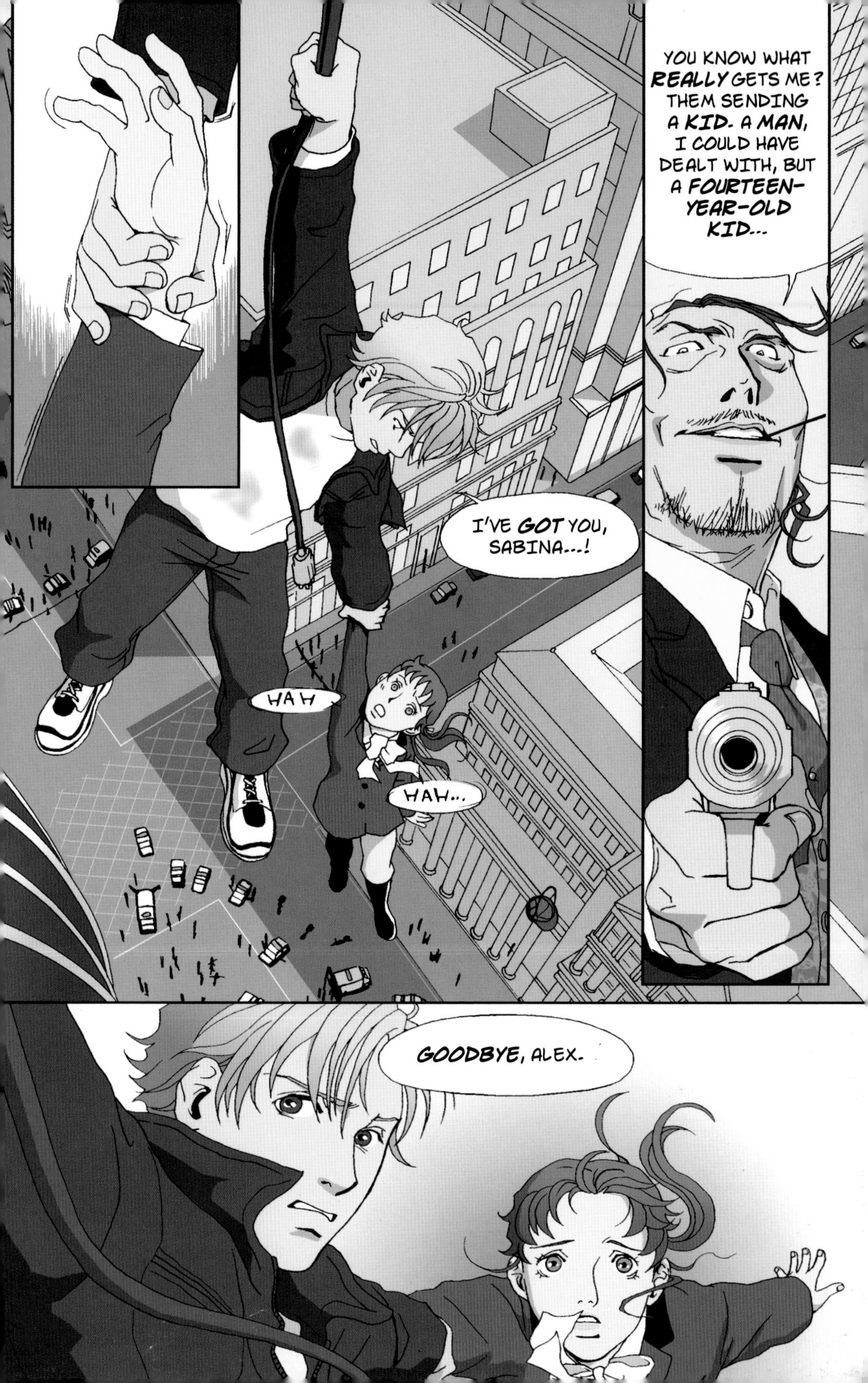
YOU KNOW WHAT REALLY GETS ME? THEM SENDING A KID. A MAN, I COULD HAVE DEALT WITH, BUT A FOURTEEN-YEAR-OLD KID...
I'VE GOT YOU, SABINA...!
HAH
HAH...
GOODBYE, ALEX.

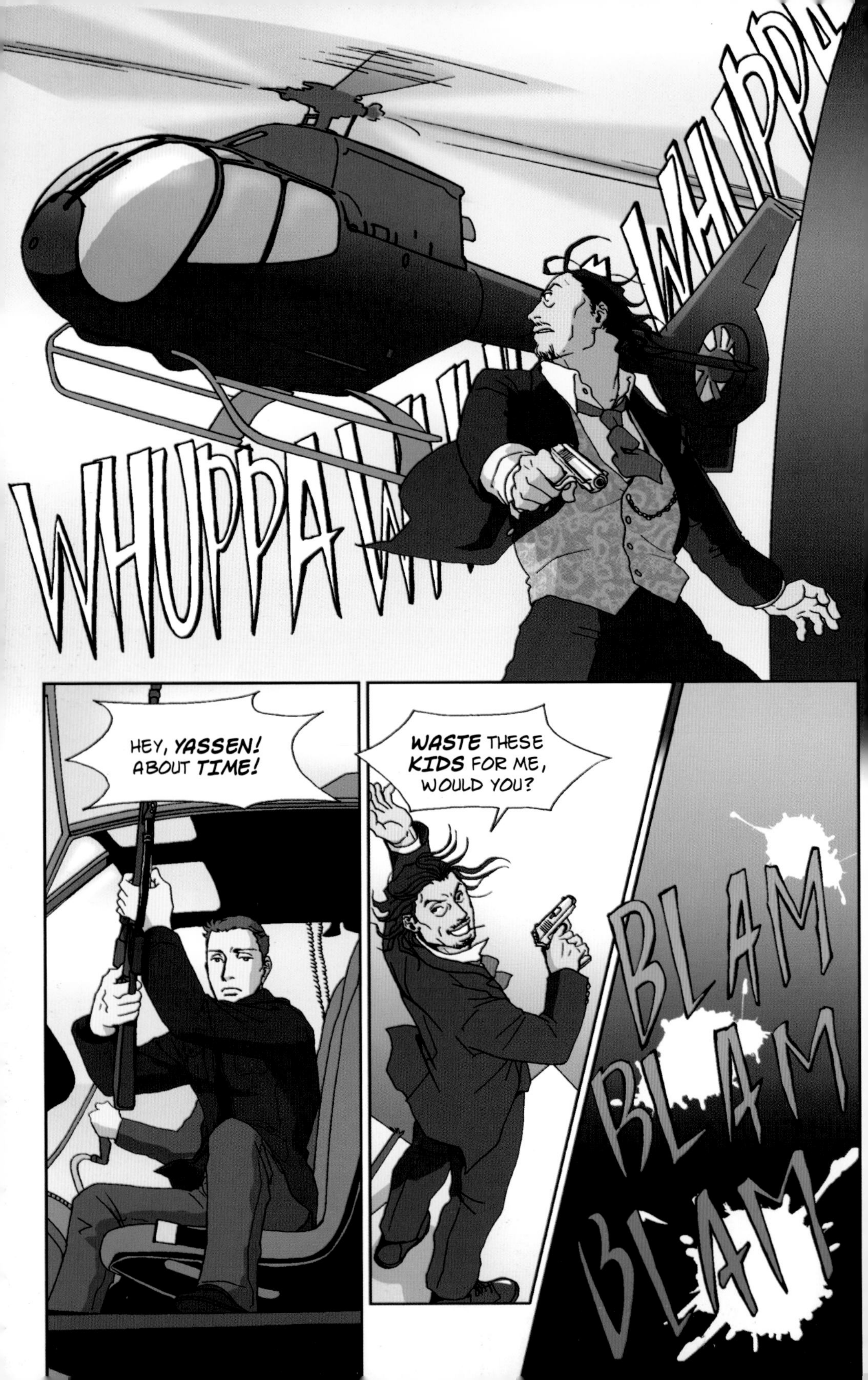
WHUPPA WHUPPA
WHUPPA
HEY, YASSEN! ABOUT TIME!
WASTE THESE KIDS FOR ME, WOULD YOU?
BLAM BLAM BLAM

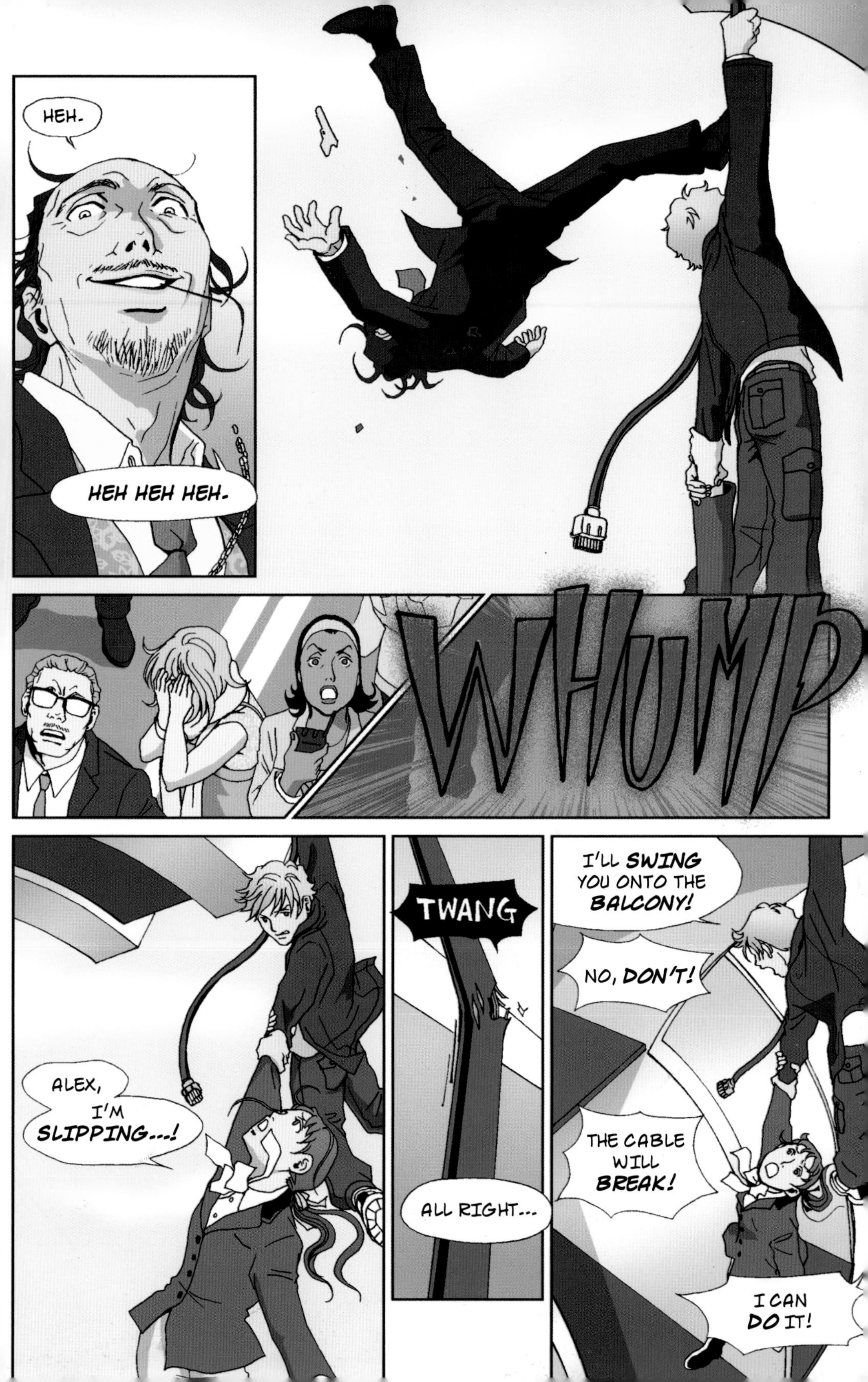
HEH.
HEH HEH HEH.
WHUMP
ALEX, I'M SLIPPING...!
TWANG
ALL RIGHT...
I'LL SWING YOU ONTO THE BALCONY!
NO, DON'T!
THE CABLE WILL BREAK!
I CAN DO IT!

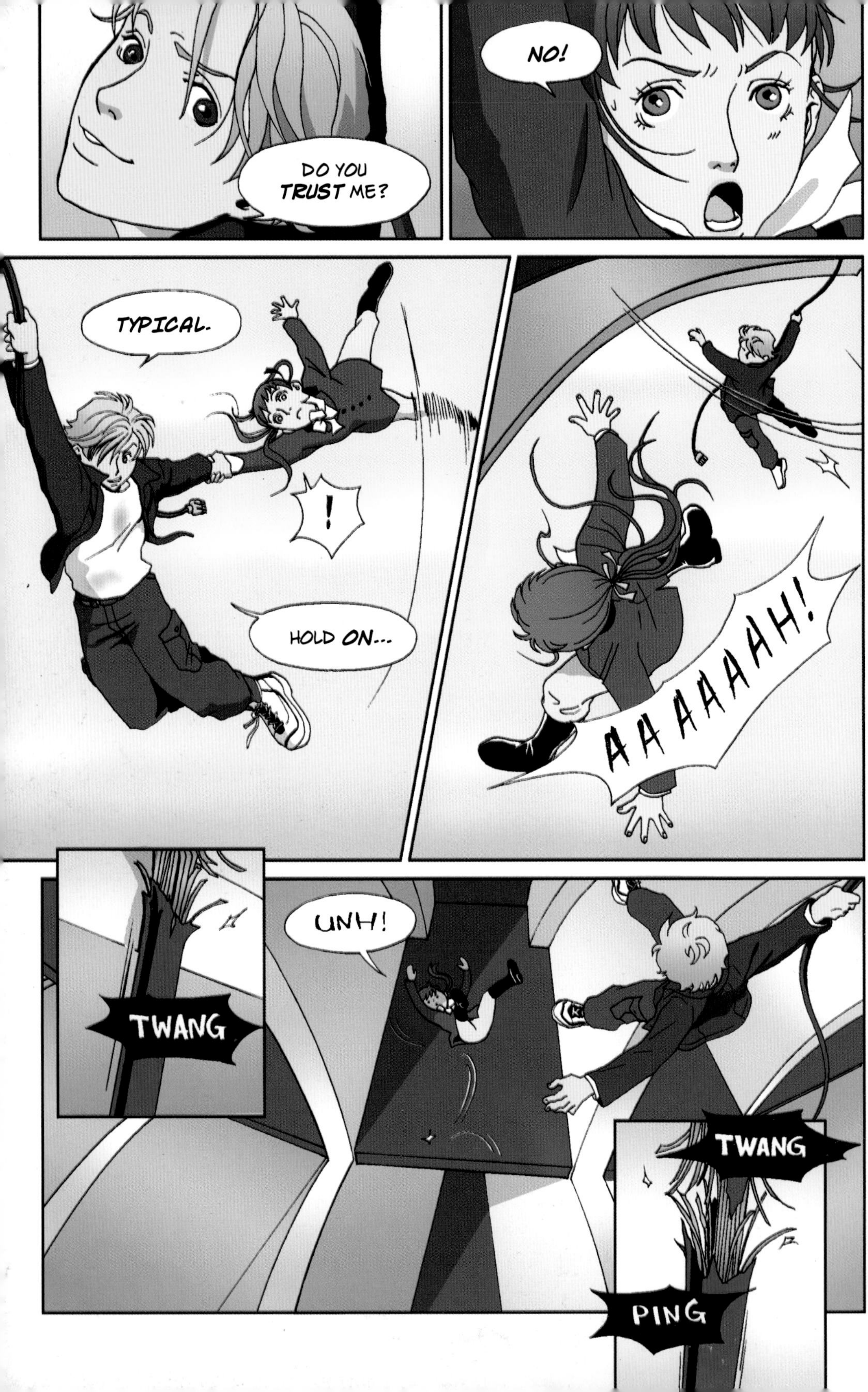
DO YOU TRUST ME?
NO!
TYPICAL.
!
HOLD ON...
AAAAAAH!
TWANG
UNH!
TWANG
PING

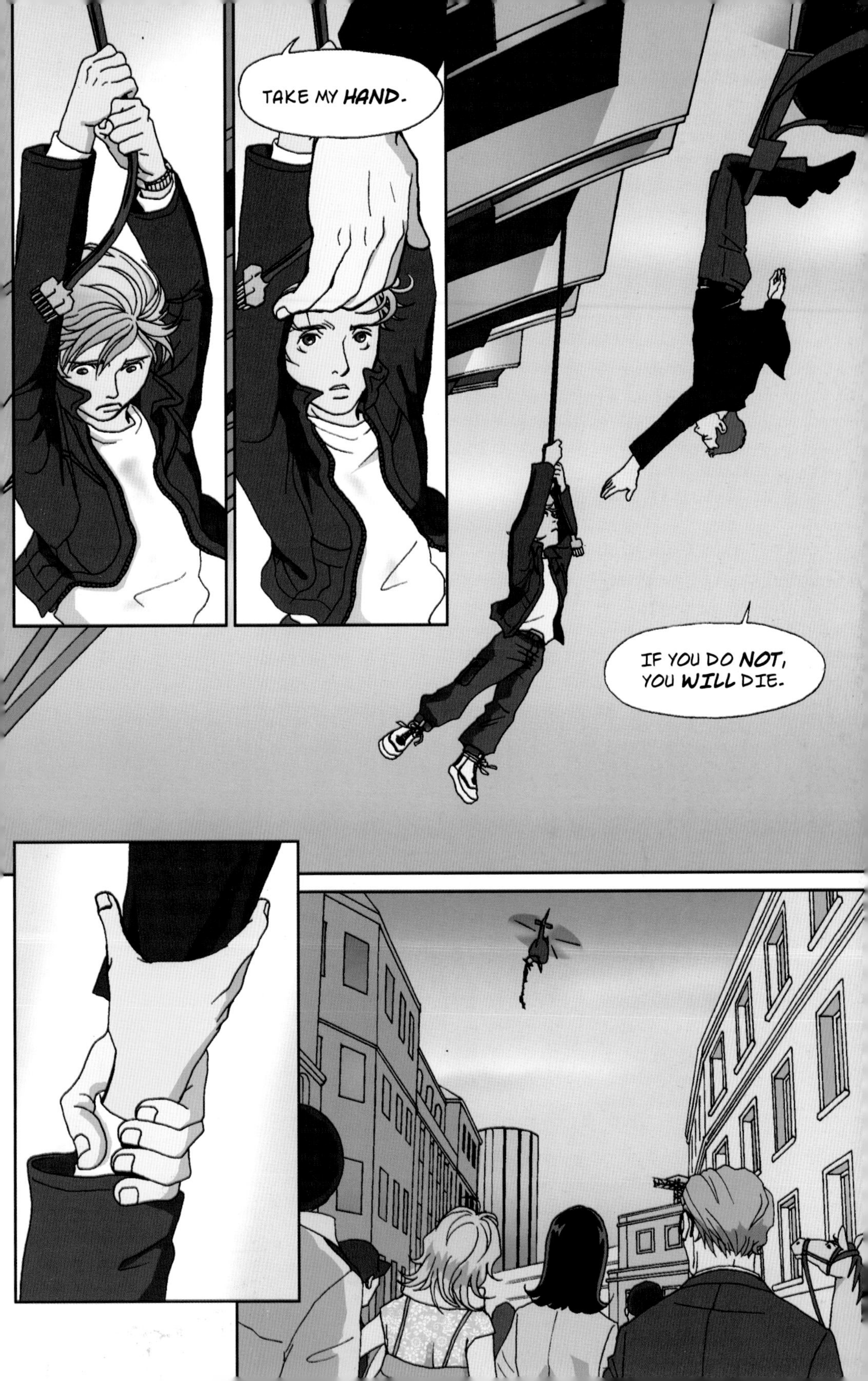
TAKE MY HAND.
IF YOU DO NOT, YOU WILL DIE.

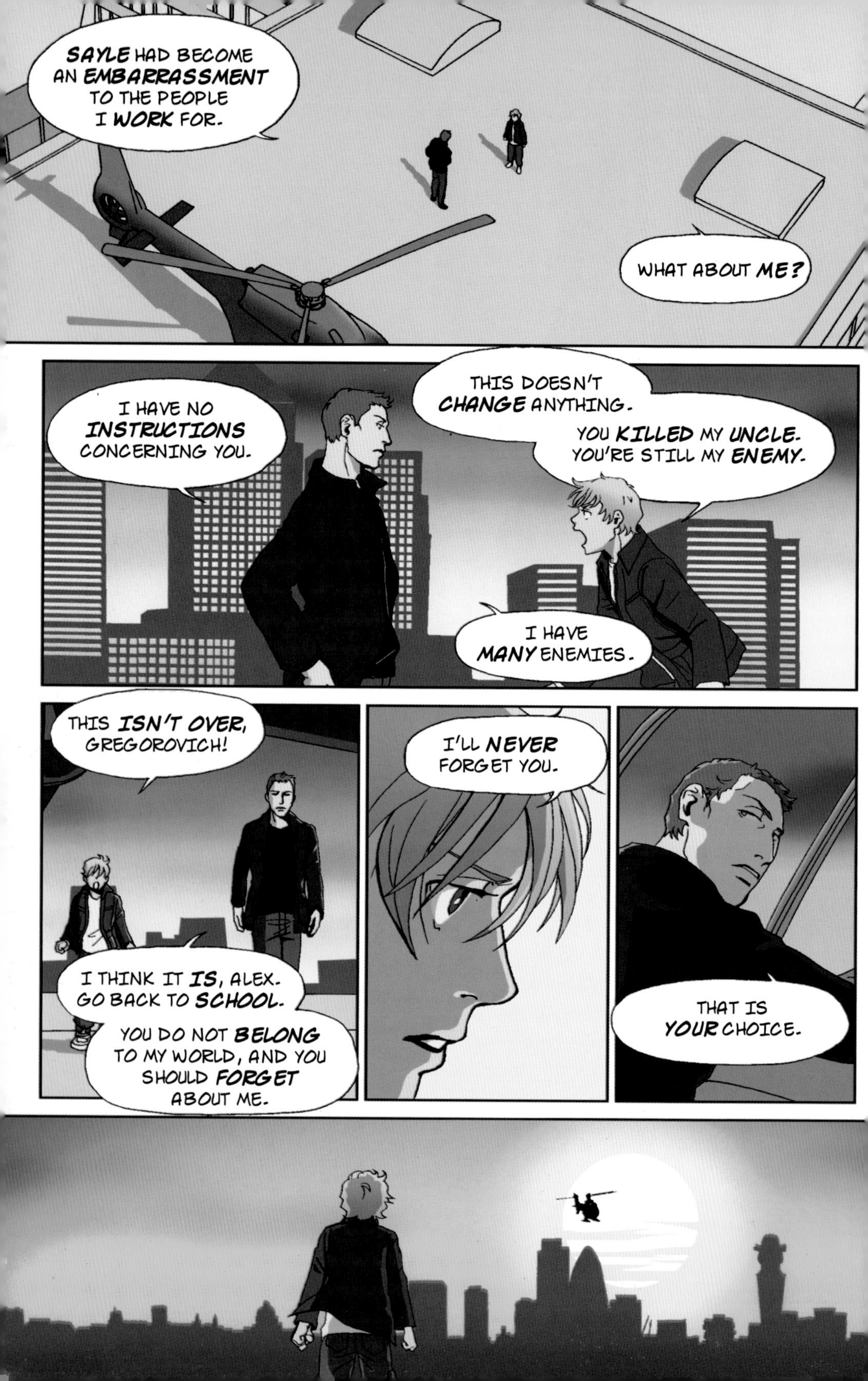
SAYLE HAD BECOME AN EMBARRASSMENT TO THE PEOPLE I WORK FOR.
WHAT ABOUT ME?
I HAVE NO INSTRUCTIONS CONCERNING YOU.
THIS DOESN'T CHANGE ANYTHING.
YOU KILLED MY UNCLE. YOU'RE STILL MY ENEMY.
I HAVE MANY ENEMIES.
THIS ISN'T OVER, GREGOROVICH!
I THINK IT IS, ALEX. GO BACK TO SCHOOL.
YOU DO NOT BELONG TO MY WORLD, AND YOU SHOULD FORGET ABOUT ME.
I'LL NEVER FORGET YOU.
THAT IS YOUR CHOICE.

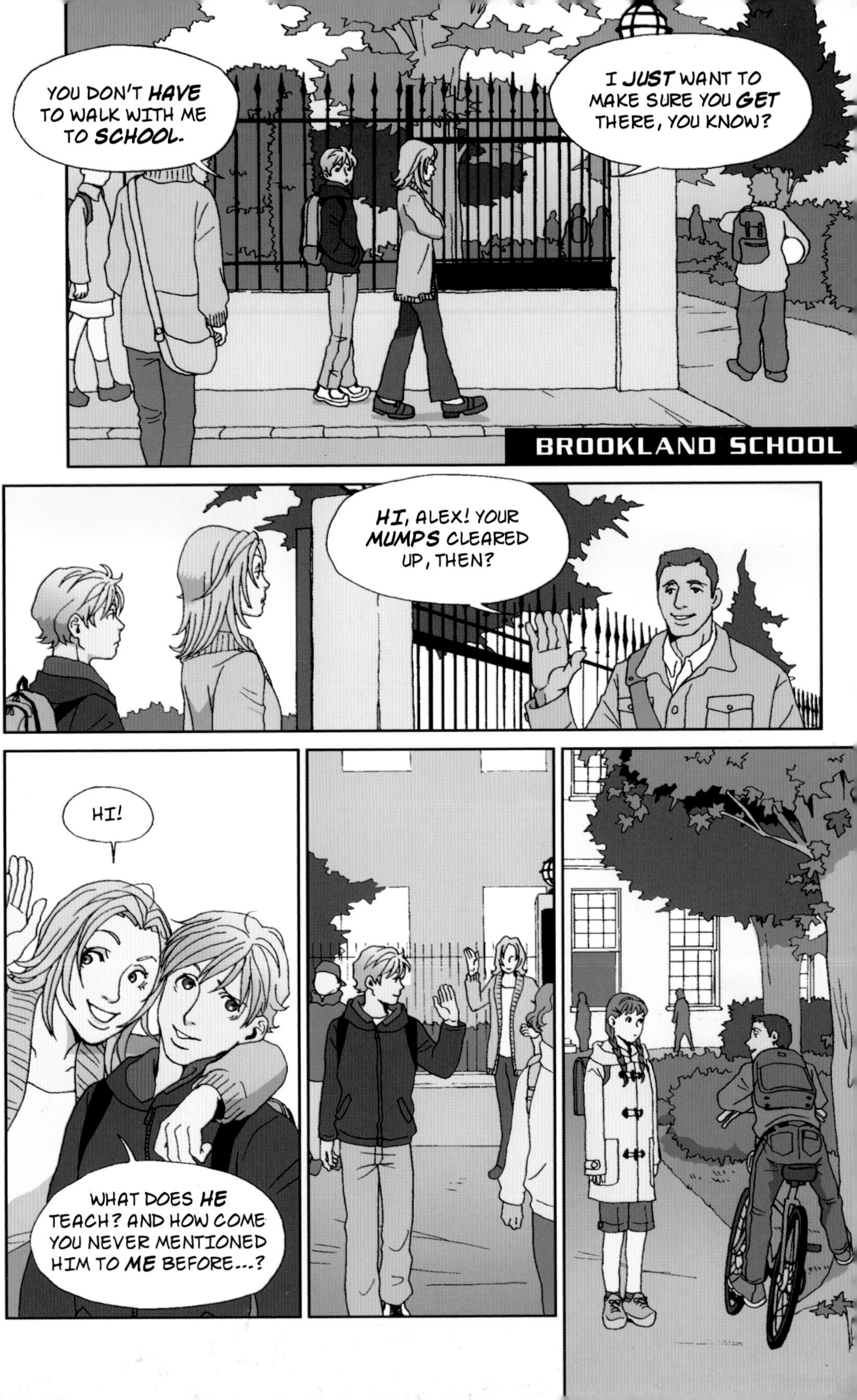

YOU DON'T HAVE TO WALK WITH ME TO SCHOOL.
I JUST WANT TO MAKE SURE YOU GET THERE, YOU KNOW?
BROOKLAND SCHOOL
HI, ALEX! YOUR MUMPS CLEARED UP, THEN?
HI!
WHAT DOES HE TEACH? AND HOW COME YOU NEVER MENTIONED HIM TO ME BEFORE...?

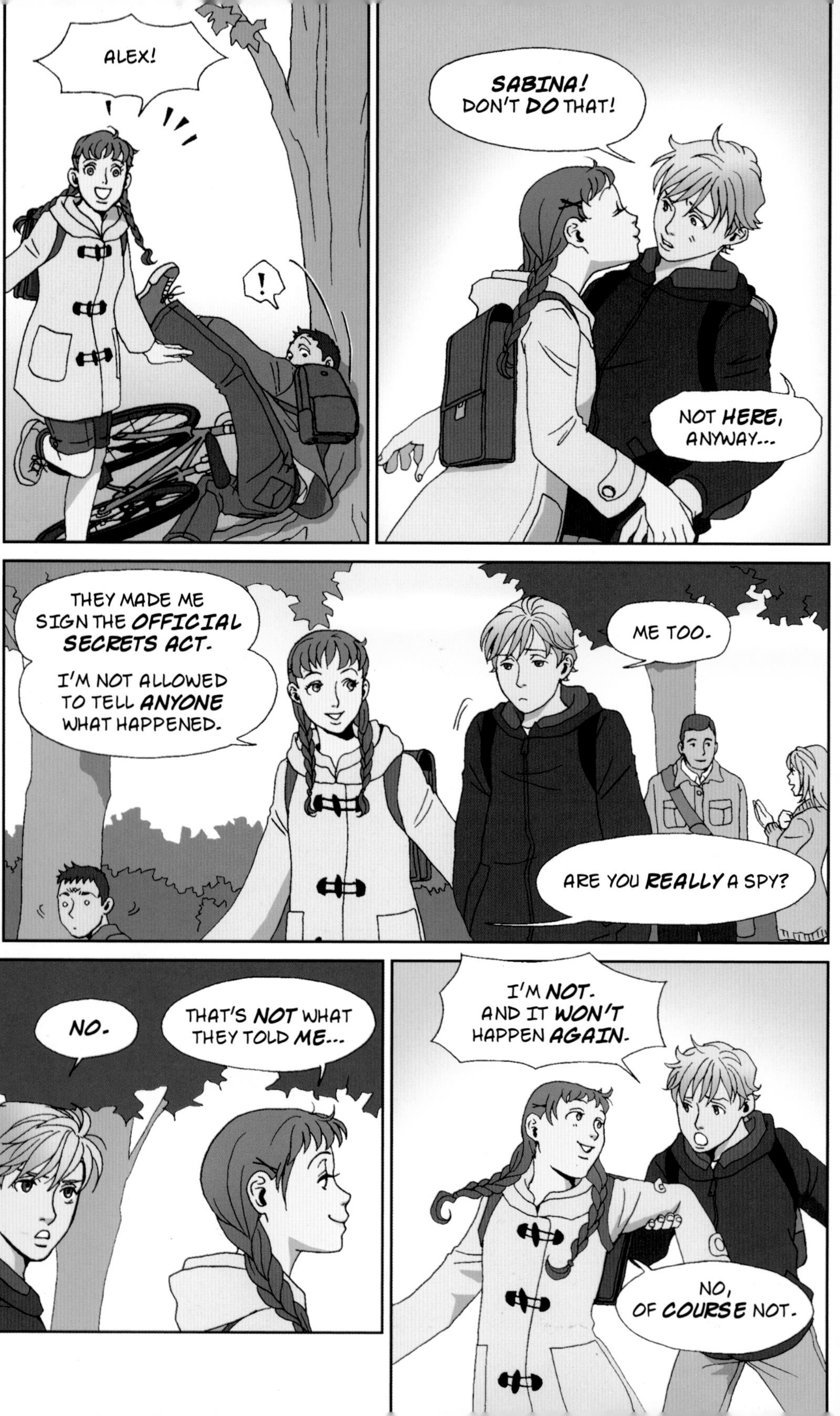
ALEX!
!
SABINA! DON'T DO THAT!
NOT HERE, ANYWAY...
THEY MADE ME SIGN THE OFFICIAL SECRETS ACT.
I'M NOT ALLOWED TO TELL ANYONE WHAT HAPPENED.
ME TOO.
ARE YOU REALLY A SPY?
NO.
THAT'S NOT WHAT THEY TOLD ME...
I'M NOT. AND IT WON'T HAPPEN AGAIN.
NO, OF COURSE NOT.

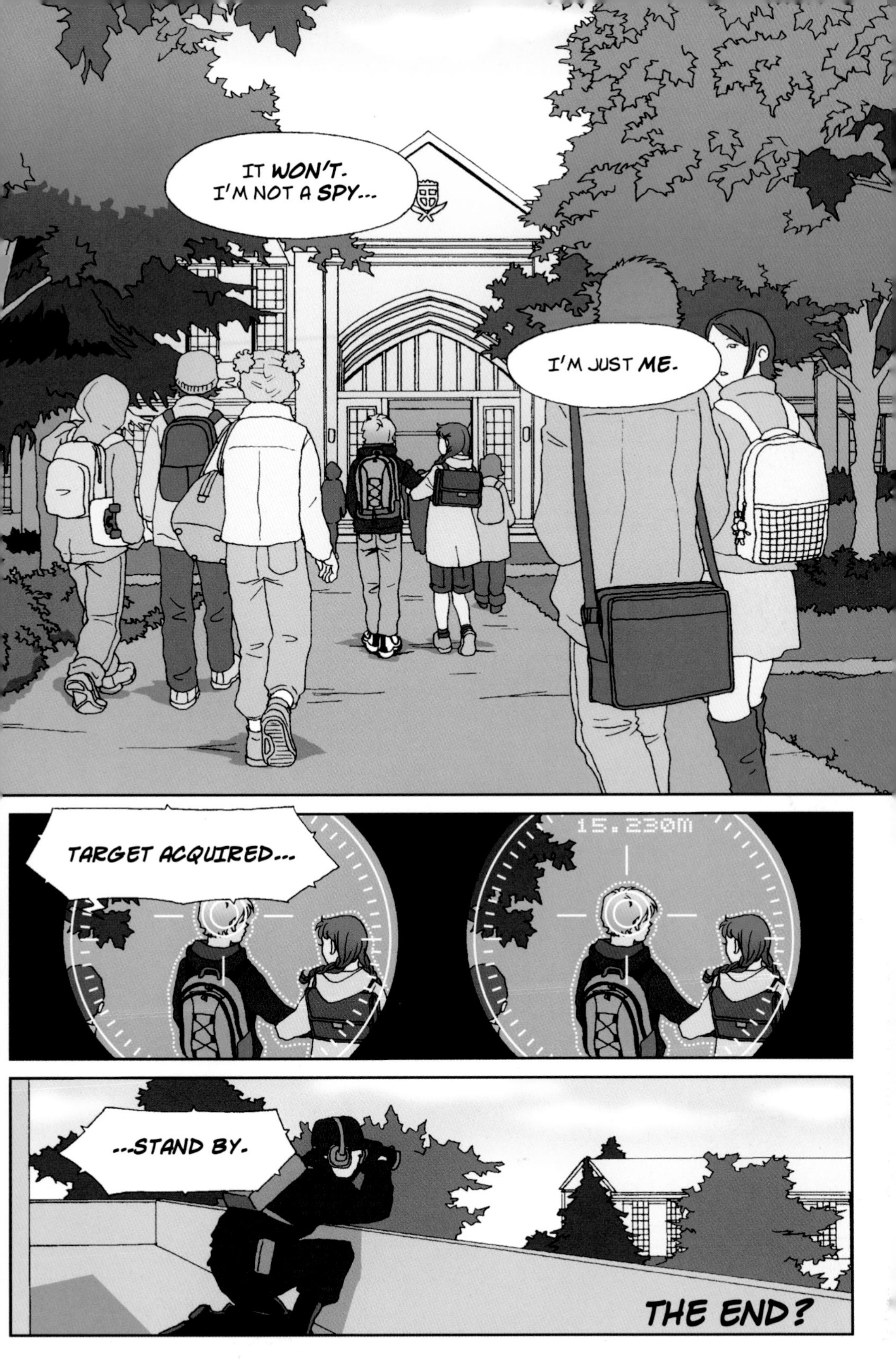
IT WON'T. I'M NOT A SPY...
I'M JUST ME.
TARGET ACQUIRED...
15.230M
...STAND BY.
THE END?

PHILOMEL BOOKS
A division of Penguin Young Readers Group. Published by The Penguin Group.
Penguin Group (USA) Inc., 375 Hudson Street, New York, NY 10014, U.S.A.
Penguin Group (Canada), 90 Eglinton Avenue East, Suite 700, Toronto, Ontario,
Canada M4P 2Y3 (a division of Pearson Penguin Canada Inc.). Penguin Books Ltd,
80 Strand, London WC2R 0RL, England. Penguin Ireland, 25 St. Stephen's Green,
Dublin 2, Ireland (a division of Penguin Books Ltd.) Penguin Group (Australia),
250 Camberwell Road, Camberwell, Victoria 3124, Australia (a division of
Pearson Australia Group Pty Ltd). Penguin Books India Pvt Ltd, 11 Community
Centre, Panchsheel Park, New Delhi - 110 017, India. Penguin Group (NZ),
Cnr Airborne and Rosedale Roads, Albany, Auckland 1310, New Zealand
(a division of Pearson New Zealand Ltd). Penguin Books (South Africa) (Pty)
Ltd, 24 Sturdee Avenue, Rosebank, Johannesburg 2196, South Africa.
Penguin Books Ltd, Registered Offices: 80 Strand, London WC2R 0RL, England.

Text & Illustrations © 2006 Walker Books Ltd.
Based on the original novel Stormbreaker, © 2000 by Anthony Horowitz.

Screenplay © MMVI Samuelsons / IoM Film
Film © MMVI Film & Entertainment VIP Medienfonds 4 GmbH & Co. KG
Style Guide © MMVI ARR Ltd. Graphic Novelisation by Antony Johnston.
Illustrated by Kanako and Yuzuru.
Trademarks 2006 Samuelson Productions Ltd.
Stormbreaker™, Alex Rider™, Boy with torch logo™, AR logo™.
Published by arrangement with Walker Books Limited, London.
87 Vauxhall Walk, London SE11 5HJ.

ISBN: 978-0-399-24633-3

13

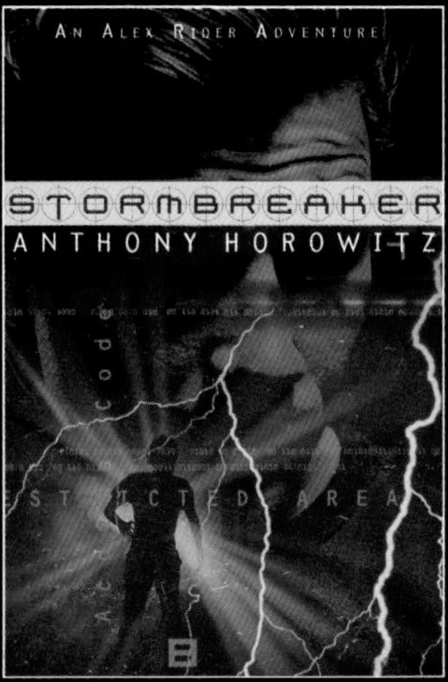
An Alex Rider Adventure
STORMBREAKER
ANTHONY HOROWITZ

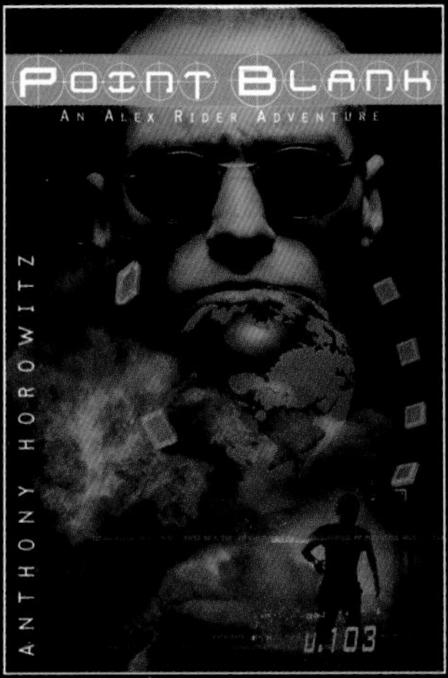
POINT BLANK
An Alex Rider Adventure
ANTHONY HOROWITZ

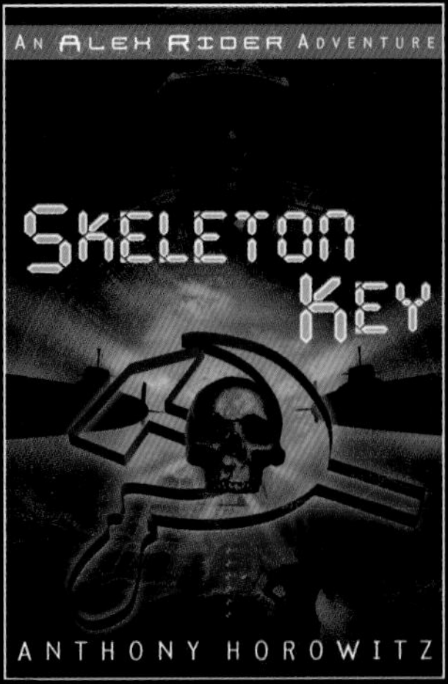
An Alex Rider Adventure
SKELETON KEY
ANTHONY HOROWITZ

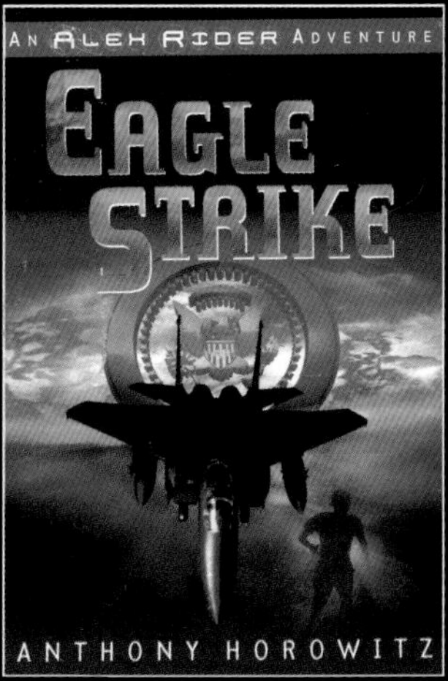
An Alex Rider Adventure
EAGLE STRIKE
ANTHONY HOROWITZ

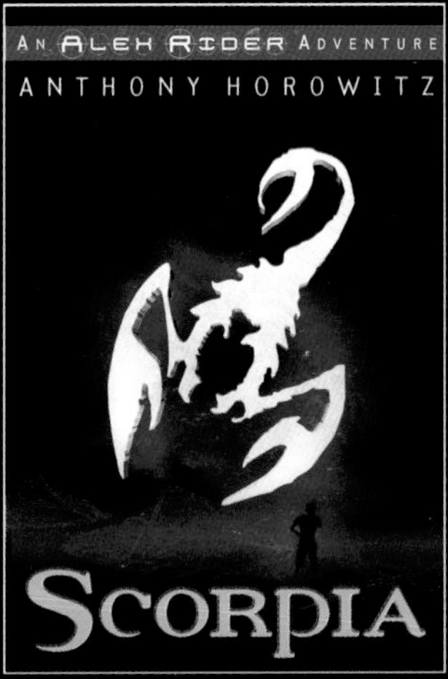
An Alex Rider Adventure
ANTHONY HOROWITZ
SCORPIA

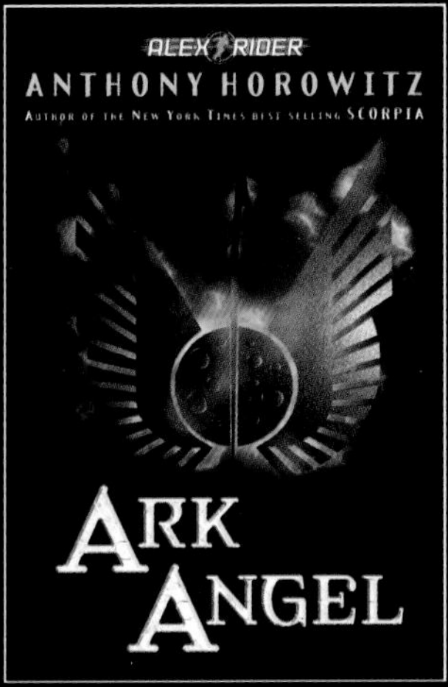
ALEX RIDER
ANTHONY HOROWITZ
Author of the New York Times best selling SCORPIA
ARK ANGEL

ANTHONY HOROWITZ, who scripted the movie blockbuster STORMBREAKER from his own novel, is one of the most popular and prolific children's writers working today. His hugely successful Alex Rider series has won numerous awards and sold over eight million copies worldwide. He has won the Red House Children's Book Award on two occasions, in 2003 for SKELETON KEY and in 2006 for ARK ANGEL. He also writes extensively for TV, with programs including MIDSOMER MURDERS, POIROT and FOYLE'S WAR. He is married to television producer Jill Green and lives in north London with his two sons, Nicholas and Cassian, and their dog, Lucky.

www.anthonyhorowitz.com

ANTONY JOHNSTON, who wrote the script for this book, is the author of nine graphic novels, including THE LONG HAUL, JULIUS, THREE DAYS IN EUROPE and ROSEMARY'S BACKPACK, and the ongoing series WASTELAND. He has also adapted many prose works by Alan Moore into comics form, and is the only other writer to have penned a story for Greg Rucka's award-winning QUEEN & COUNTRY series. Antony lives in northwest England with the three loves of his life; his partner Marcia, his dog Connor, and his iMac.

www.mostlyblack.com

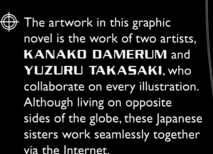

The artwork in this graphic novel is the work of two artists, **KANAKO DAMERUM** and **YUZURU TAKASAKI,** who collaborate on every illustration. Although living on opposite sides of the globe, these Japanese sisters work seamlessly together via the Internet.

Living and working in Tokyo, **YUZURU** produced all the line work for these illustrations using traditional means. The quality of her draftsmanship comes from years of honing her skills in the highly competitive world of manga.

KANAKO lives and works out of her studio in London. She managed and directed the project as well as coloring and rendering the artwork digitally using her wealth of knowledge in graphic design.

www.manga-media.com
www.thorogood.net